the collecte

Tim Winton was born in Perth in 1960. He is the author of two other novels, two volumes of short stories, and three books for children. He lives in a small town on the west coast of Australia with his wife and three children.

ALSO BY TIM WINTON IN PICADOR

Shallows

Cloudstreet

Blood and Water

TIM WINTON

the collected shorter novels of

TIM WINTON

an open swimmer

that eye, the sky

in the winter dark

PICADOR

An Open Swimmer first published 1982 by Allen & Unwin Limited
That Eye, The Sky first published 1986 by McPhee Gribble, a division of
Penguin Books Australia Ltd: first published in Great Britain in this edition
In the Winter Dark first published 1988 by McPhee Gribble: first published in
Great Britain in this edition

This collected edition first published 1995 by Picador
an imprint of Macmillan General Books
Cavaye Place London SW10 9PG
and Basingstoke

Associated companies throughout the world

ISBN 0 330 32555 8

Copyright © Tim Winton 1982, 1986, 1988

The right of Tim Winton to be identified as the
author of this work has been asserted by him in accordance
with the Copyright, Designs and Patents Act 1988.

9 8 7 6 5 4 3 2 1

A CIP catalogue record for this book is available from
the British Library

Typeset by CentraCet Limited, Cambridge
Printed by Cox & Wyman Ltd, Reading, Berkshire

contents

AN OPEN
SWIMMER

This book is for John and Beverley Winton,
two of my best friends.

ACKNOWLEDGEMENTS

I would like to offer my thanks and respect to Michael
Henderson and Denise Fitch for their patience and
assistance in the writing of this book. Thanks for
permission to reprint lines from 'Diving into the Wreck'
by Adrienne Rich are due to W. W. Norton.

I am she: I am he

whose drowned face sleeps with open eyes
whose breasts still bear the stress
whose silver, copper, vermeil cargo lies
obscurely inside barrels
half-wedged and left to rot
we are the half-destroyed instruments
that once held to a course
the water-eaten log
the fouled compass

We are, I am, you are
by cowardice or courage
the one who find our way
back to this scene
carrying a knife, a camera
a book of myths
in which
our names do not appear.

'Diving into the Wreck', Adrienne Rich

prologue

It had been a long fight between Jerra Nilsam and the fish. He pressed the flat end of the oar against its brow. Globes of moisture clustered on its flanks. His father grinned in the stern. The engine was chuckling. Water parted like an incision behind. The fish grunted. His father said it was a turrum. The long fan of tail slapped the gunwale, the gills were pumping, and blood globbed the bottom of the boat.

In the water, the black diamond, the mate, cruised. When he had gaffed the turrum over the side, cuffed on the chin by the tail, the diamond had been there, silver when the sun caught its flanks.

Chuff-chuff, the turrum was grunting. Looking up at him, the eye never blinked. The fish began to thresh, clenching and unclenching. Jerra kept the oar hard over its brow, near the gaff-hole. His palms were bleeding and he wanted to cry. He grinned back at his father.

The diamond curved and straightened, blemishing the surface with its scalpel of a dorsal fin. He wished they had a bigger engine.

Bashing. It was bashing the gunwale. The fish buckled up, almost out of the boat. He fell on it, hugging, feeling the fin spikes in his chest. With a spastic twitch it deflated, mumbling.

'It's dead,' his father said.

He let it go and sat up with glistening scales on his chest and glistenings on his cheeks.

He looked over the side. The diamond had gone.

'Want to open it for the pearl?'

'No.'

'It might have one.'

'I don't want to cut him up, Dad.'

He wished they had a bigger engine and that the fish would be alive again.

PART ONE

the bush

A way to their left, a flight of cockatoos lifted from the gums and swung in a pink cloud over the road and into the bush.

'Petrol?' Sean asked.

'Enough if we find something soon.'

'Bloody tourist maps.'

'Not far. Road's headin' for the coast.' Jerra glanced at Sean, whose pale curls bobbed in the breeze from the open window. He flicked on the beams, lighting up the loose surface ahead.

The road was sloping away, curving, unknotting itself. He saw the thick red tail of gravel dust lifting in the mirror.

'Shaking hell out of the ol' bus,' he said.

'Wonder it's stayed together this long.'

'Be still going long after we're skinned and dried.'

The headlights caught the eyes of animals and held them by the throat, rigid, until they passed in a clattering rush of stones and dust.

A roo floated across, bashing off into the undergrowth.

'Shit, Jerra!' Sean slid back, clutching at his seat belt.

'Had plenty o' room.'

'Should have a roo-bar on this thing. That would've put us in the heap for good.'

'OK if you can afford it.'

Sean shrugged. Jerra hit the horn.

'The roos'll know we're coming now.'

'Great.'

'Be setting up in the dark.'

'Don't talk about it.'

'Remember that time out past Eucla?'

Sean reached over and smacked the horn. Jerra laughed.

'That's for bloody Eucla and the torch batteries.'

Jerra bashed the horn with his elbow.

'That's for the look on your face in the morning.' Already, he smelt crushed insects and the flaky wood under ghost gums. 'The great outdoorsmen!'

Eventually, gravel gave way to sand and banksias and black, fallen marri trunks. The track wound down the rutty slope. The springs groaned as they dropped a wheel into a washout.

'Good for the diff,' said Jerra.

Grass swished along the chassis as Jerra pulled out of the rut. The track cleaned up for a bit, doodling off from side to side, further, deeper. At a flat, clear spot, they came upon an old corrugated shack.

'Ex-residence,' said Sean, noting it. Needlessly, Jerra thought.

Further down, swelling out of the carved-off bank of the track, was a grizzled she-oak with the letters NO pared neatly out of the bark, the O bleeding viscous sap from the white flesh.

The sand was getting whiter and softer, and Jerra pushed through a few soft sections, feeling the VW glide and whip; he flicked the wheel a bit harder than was needed, but it was soft and he didn't know when he might be caught without enough speed.

A clearing. They rattled into the grove, scattering a few rabbits caught in the light. Jerra switched off. There was only the gums and the sea.

Sean dropped a mallee root on to the fire. Jerra rolled the pan. He flipped the stuff on to the plate.

'Here.'

They ate the buttery fried eggs, breathing and talking around the food in their mouths.

'Bit of a turn-up. First time we've ever struck camp without pitchin' on a nest of ants—'

'Or a cocky's driveway—'

'Rifle range—'

'Creekbed—'

'All we need now is to make friends with a possum with the clap—'

'Oh, geez, 'ere he goes!'

They pissed and went to bed. The smell of smoke in his clothes made Jerra feel he had been there for ever.

the distant mutterings of gums

In the daylight, the clearing was another place. Last night it had been as big as a paddock, now there was just enough room to turn the VW.

Poking the ground with their spears, they turned over the leafy crust, revealing a moisture which could survive the heat. The musty damp clung to the soles of their feet.

'Fire's nearly out,' Jerra said, dropping the gear in the shade.

Sean scuffed his feet into the leaves. Jerra went for some wood.

The fire nipped at their knees, spitting. Jerra sat feeling the roughened edges of his hands.

'Sore?'

'Just not used to it. Haven't used 'em for ages. Never liked peelin' leatheries, anyway. Dad always used to do it.'

'Yeah, your dad.'

'S'pose he did most things for me, eh?'

'Yeah.'

'How's your ol' man?' Jerra asked as if he was interested. Probing.

'Into Westam at the moment.'

Catching red emperors, thought Jerra. From the boardroom table.

'Westam?'

'Yeah,' said Sean.

*

Fat congealed, the fire subsided. The late breeze was in when they awoke, sprawling on the thick foam mattress, sucking teeth, farting, hearing the gums bend and unbend.

'Slept in this ol' bus a few times,' said Sean, peering through the sparse hairs on his chest, letting out a long bark.

Jerra gazed at the insect squash-marks on the ceiling, ran his finger through the patina of gravel dust.

'Lots.'

'How many trips?'

'Lost count.'

'Wish you'd stop farting.'

Jerra grinned. It was like lying in the park after school. He could feel the flat leaves of clover under him, see the scabby trunk above bearing all the open-mouthed maggies that chased them to and from school, and he rubbed the little scar on his thumb.

Shadows appeared on the granite spill. Black holes and shafts opened and wavered. Jerra and Sean hopped and stumbled out to the headland. Within an hour there would be no daylight. A breeze tumbled in cool ripples from the sea, and gulls bumped in the currents, up, around behind them as they stepped out to a smooth ledge and began at the tangles:

> *loop,*
> *under,*
> *side,*
> *pull through,*
> *BUGGER!*

. . . bite it off halfway.

'Should've put this bait in water,' Sean said.

'Ooh, ripe.' Jerra flicked his baited hook out. 'A cast at last.'

'Rhymes.'

'Eh?'

Squatting on the warm, grey rock, they felt the air cooling towards twilight. You could feel it, next to the water. A peculiar smell, wet granite. Dark as the distant mutterings of the gums. Against the small flanks of stone came the glugs and laps of the dark water.

The nylon was light on their fingers, rising and falling in the drowsing swell.

'Fish,' murmured Jerra.

'Hmm?'

'Catching an' eating the buggers.'

'Why else would you sit on a rock getting a sore bum?'

Jerra looked into the greenish-black.

'Dunno.'

'Only good when there's something down there interested in getting hooked.'

'Arr.'

'Easier at a fish market.'

'Eating's only half of it. Less.'

'It's something.'

'The waiting. Like this.'

'Bloody frustrating.'

'Like when we were younger and Dad took us. His fault when I didn't get anything.' Jerra remembered the endless mornings anchored on a mirror-calm stretch of water, when Sean was like a real blood-brother to him, when there was nothing but herring on his mind.

'He never missed a bite.'

'Hated him for it. Wish you could fix up the dumb things you do when you're young.' He was unsure what he was really saying. He wondered what Sean was thinking.

'Getting dark.' Sean had packed his gear.

'Let's go.'

'What's that?'

'What?' said Jerra.

'On the beach.'

Jerra stopped walking and peered in the bad light.

'Looks like a dog or something with four legs.'

'Probably a wild one from up the bush.'

It was gone and so was the light.

Dark. They lit the fire. Something mushy was fired in a can, and they sucked tea from tin mugs, spitting tea-leaves into the fire. Bloody tea bags; Jerra knew they were around somewhere, but he gave up and they brewed it in the billy. They went to bed as the dew came settling on their backs.

In the night, Jerra woke to the sounds of movement outside. The food was safe. It was probably the dog they had seen. He slept.

Before dawn, Jerra climbed over Sean and went stiffly out into the half-light and the long crackling wild oats. Dew was ice between his toes, the breeze roughened the skin of his shoulders. He tossed a few sticks on the warm ash, pulled on a shirt, and went down to the beach.

He scuffed along the sheltered meniscus of the shore. In the middle of the bay, waves peeled off in long, smooth folds, crumpling on to the banks, spray wafting from the crests as the swells flexed and collapsed on themselves, rumbling.

There were footprints and scuff-marks in the sand, he noticed. Handprints not footprints. Something had been carved into the sand, but the tide had softened it to a few grooves and channels in the mushy shore.

After breakfast they argued over the swell, avoiding each other's face.

'Come *on*! This is the first surf we've had for ages.'

'Thought you wanted some fish,' said Jerra, dropping the hessian bag.

15

'Fish are always there,' said Sean. 'The swell might be gone tomorrow.'

They stood kicking the dirt with the balls of their feet until Jerra shoved the diving bag under the car in surrender.

'You can go diving if you like.'

'Better stay together.'

Brilliance held the lids against their eyes. Sun beat them into the sand. Gulls slid about as they paddled out and sat in the rolling shimmer, straining their necks, watching for the sets that bumped up on the horizon, the biggest feathering early and a long way outside. That sink and pull in the guts. They fidgeted in that time between seeing the horrie begin to break and deciding where to wait. In the midst of the set, swells back and ahead, there was no horizon, no beach, only the shush of water falling from the crests and the aqua fluting of the hollow troughs.

They felt the breeze and the bite of spray. It seemed a long way to walk back when they could paddle and take off no more.

Halfway back along the beach, a beam protruded from amongst the crackling weed and sand.

'This'd be good on the fire,' said Sean.

'Jarrah, too. Burn like hell.'

'Here,' said Sean, kneeling on the hot sand.

They pulled at the exposed end. Nothing would move it.

'A hell of a long way up the beach to be buried that deep.'

'You know the weather in July this far south.'

'Plenty of wood near camp.'

'Yeah,' said Jerra. 'Not as if we have to excavate fossil fuel.'

Flinging their boards to the ground in the shade of the Veedub, they might never have been wet.

For tea that night, they ate long slabs of sweep and thick abalone steaks prised from the reef, the fire throwing a pale, flesh-coloured circle, a wavering ripple in the black bush.

'Thought what you're going to do?' Sean blinked, his eyes lit red. To Jerra, sometimes, they were like the eyes of a fox drilled in a spotlight.

'Ah, who knows?'

'Have to decide, eventually.'

'How does a bloke decide, these days?'

'I never had much trouble.'

'You were set. All you had to do was get old enough. Yer biggest hassle was buying the blue tie.'

'Hardly.'

Jerra smelt the singed hairs on the back of his hand. He felt that deadness in him when he felt like picking up something heavy, an axe or something, and heaving it into the ocean, just to hear the splash.

'That job with your old man was waiting for you.'

'So is yours.'

'Ah, bullshit.' It really was, he thought. They all feed you bullshit.

'Just a matter of growing up. They were all expecting you to finish at Uni.'

'Who?'

'Your oldies and your grandfather. He put a lot of time into you, you know.'

'Hey, how come you're so respectable all of a sudden?'

'You grow up.'

'When you get a job.'

'Yes.'

'Yes.' When you get a job. Jerra remembered the first day Sean went to work, crisp and aloof. It wan't long afterwards that he left to live in a townhouse in South Perth subsidized by the corporation.

Jerra let the feeling of it pass over him as all those things did now.

'Ah, come on.'

'You'll see.'

'I do now.'

'Everyone goes through it.'

'Through what?'

'You know what I mean.'

'Like getting pubes on yer dick.'

Sean smiled, shaking his head.

'Mine are still there,' said Jerra. 'How's yours?'

'That's piss-weak.'

'Talk about something else, then.'

'Given in to corruption, have I?'

'Ah, I dunno, Sean.'

'You gotta live,' said Sean, tossing a sappy log into the flames.

Jerra turned from the smoke.

Sean slung the tepid tea into the bush. The moon was a pale splash on the bay. He lay still. Sean breathed steadily. Outside, sap hissed in the veins of the green log. Bitter smoke seeped into the van, clouding the windows. The breeze strengthened. Only vaguely could he see the shadows of the bitching trees, contorted in the moonlight.

Just as Jerra was about to sleep, Sean rolled on to his side and said, 'Mum.' He would never have said it, awake.

Jerra could have hit him. He was awake for quite a while after that. It scared the hell out of him, and he couldn't help but wonder how much Sean knew.

An animal coughed in the night, hacking indifferently.

a skeleton with the eyes still in it

There were clouds, and a chill that hung at the base of the trees. Jerra rekindled the fire. Sour ash had sunk into the earth under the dew; sun appeared briefly in a gap in the grey above the hills. A stunted swell struggled through the flecked and flattened surface of the ocean, on to the sand bar, silent, feeble.

'Wonder if there's a spring around here,' Sean asked idly, later in the morning. 'Water's getting low.'

'Nothing on the map,' said Jerra, feeling the ribbed contours on the inside of a shell.

'That means stuff-all, doesn't it? This place isn't even on the map. Only things that are are Perth and Kalgoorlie.'

'Well, there's odds to say we're not at either of those.'

A squabbling flight of gulls blew overhead.

'Bloody seagulls,' said Jerra. 'Just follow you round, waiting for you to drop something.'

'They gotta survive.'

'Bloody scabs.'

Out of the corner of his eye, Jerra saw Sean watching him.

The track was flanked by high rubbery dune scrub. Further into the hills, the trees reduced the wind to a rumour in the tree tops. Tracks of small animals showed riddles in the sand. Birds, tiny blurs, flitted across the track.

'Further than I thought,' said Jerra, oozing sweat.

'We'll end up at one of those dots on the map.' Sean dragged the jerrycan through the sand. 'Gawd knows what the bloody hell we're doin' this for.'

Up ahead, a log in the shade of a rattling wattle.

The log was rough and wobbly. Through the jagged leaves, sunlight mottled their skin. The bay stretched away, a hook, brilliant in the intermittent sun. Inlets and coves melted into the haze. The sea boiled on the cliffs. The Cape loomed like another continent.

They didn't say anything. The sweat and the view let Jerra relax for a moment, and for that moment, it was like it had always been before, with nothing in his head that wouldn't fit.

Jerra thumped his mate. He *was* his mate. The log wobbled. The dry leaves of the wattle shook.

NO, said the tree as they passed. Jerra ignored it cheerily.

Tough grass grew through the fissures in tin and timber, worming up under the boarded windows, and trees had elbowed their way in through the roof, flexing, bending upwards and out, growing inside and almost ready to lift the roof off. Grass penetrated the crust of the truck. Holes in the roof left warm pools on the fermenting upholstery. Jerra saw. It was like the hulks he had seen gaping in the bush where he had wandered after school, watching carefully for snakes and spiders and dirty things. It would have made a good hide-out, with holes to shoot through and bayonet the Japs. A good hide-out, he thought, guiltily. He still looked for hide-outs, despite his age.

'God,' he whispered. 'It looks like a skeleton with eyes still in it.'

'You can hear it rusting.'

All was intact, but disintegrating.

Behind the shed, the water-tank was rusted through at the rim. Jerra thumped it. Little freckles flaked of. Gutters fallen into the undergrowth, the rain had continued to fill, falling through the rusted cover.

Jerra felt the cold greenish tap. A stack of bottles winked green and brown.

'Hey, you reckon we should be knocking it off like this?'

'No one's been here for ages. Who's gonna mind?'

'You mean who's gonna know.'

'Ah, come on, hold the can.'

It filled with a cold, loud rush. Jerra tightened the spout.

'Here, grab an end.'

'Nuh-uh. Not in the contract. I carried it up.'

'Rotten bugger.'

'It's downhill.'

NO, the she-oak was congealing.

'Shall we add an S and a T?'

'Waffor?' asked Jerra, pulling the jerrycan, trying not to notice it.

'SNOT.'

Jerra looked at him and gave him a kick. 'Don't let the employees hear you saying things like that. Give 'em the impression you're the wrong kind of material.'

During lulls in the flames, shadows creased their lips, holes opened where eyes had been. Sean farted and stretched.

'Really quite full.'

'Shows how hungry a bastard can be, when he can eat baked beans and nearly admit to enjoying it.'

'Don't get any better, do they?'

Sean burped a long bark, 'Rrruth.'

'Definitely.'

'My bladder creaketh.'

'Piss.'

'If I must.'

'Must or bust.'

'Back in a sec.'

'Watch the possums. Never know what you might catch.'

'They should be worryin'.'

Things breathed in the fire. Carefully, Jerra watched the dew appearing. It came silent on the rocks, on the softness of grass, on sticks, ropes, beading brown on the blade of the axe, and, unless you watched for it, it came without your knowing. Until you moved. Or ran a hand over something. He chafed his hands together over the fire.

Twigs and leaves moved.

'That was quick.' He turned.

It wasn't Sean.

'Shit!' he cried, almost going into the flames. 'Who the hell—' He saw fire in the beard and eyes.

'Where you from?' the old man asked.

'The city,' Jerra admitted.

'Campin', eh?'

'Where you from?' Jerra asked, tremulously.

'Around.' A vague wave.

'A shack?' He was choking.

'And tank.'

'Oh, Gawd, we ah—'

'Nobody got claim on the clouds. Least not me.'

'Just thought—'

'It's orright.'

Fire twisted. The blood cracked in his ears.

'Well—'

'Would've scared youse off.'

Undergrowth parted.

'Ah, thought I took a wrong—'

'Sean, this is someone from up the hill.'

Sean was stiff.

'Hey look, we didn't take anything. The old joint looked—'

Jerra sat over the fire. It burnt his cheeks.

'Doesn't matter,' said the old man, squatting in the warm. Sean began to say something, but Jerra silenced him with a showing of teeth.

Rims of water glistened in the old man's eyes. His cheeks were red in the firelight.

'Smoke?'

Sean shook his head ungraciously.

'Sorry,' said Jerra. 'Don't smoke.'

'Gawd. Nothin' to be sorry about, son. Bastards 'ave never done me any good. Jus' more pins in the b'loon. Still, they're somethink.'

A doughy wad was rolled across the palms, fingers the colour of scorched twigs. A rolling tongue followed the movement.

'Put the billy on, Sean. We'll have a brew.'

Jerra watched the tobacco rolled into a brittle sliver of paper. There was print on both sides.

'How do you like your tea?' asked Jerra.

'To chew, like real baccy. But as a bev'ridge – dark an' black.'

'Sugar?'

'Nah. Rots yer guts.'

Jerra smiled faintly, picking the black bits out of the powdered milk.

'Thought it was teeth.'

'No problem there.'

Sean lowered the billy into the flames. Drops on the outside turned to steam.

'How long you been here?'

'Maybe twenty years, give or take a war.'

'In the shack all the time?'

'That an' the shed on the beach.'

'On the beach?' said Sean. 'There isn't one on the beach.'

'Gone.'

'Where?' asked Sean.

'Burnt down. A long while back.'

The old man was looking right into the orange twists. He drew out a stick, lit it, watching the flame all the way up to his face and back.

'What sort of paper is that?' asked Jerra.

'Bible.'

'Eh?'

'Ran out of papers. Years ago. Still 'ad a couple of old Gideons we knocked off from a fancy motel. Last one, this. Only just warmin' up on it. You cut 'em up the columns and whack off a few verses.'

It stank. Jerra tried not to grimace.

'Where you up to?' grinned Sean.

The old man chuffed smoke. You could hear him suck on the paper.

'Deuteronomy. Eighteen? Nineteen. Tough goin'. Cities 'n rules. Verse thirteen: *You shall be blameless before your God.* Fourteen: *For these nations* . . . er . . . bugger, I can't remember.' He kneaded the hard of his crusty hands. 'What do you do for a livin', son?'

'I'm a clerk,' said Sean. 'Of sorts.'

'For a company, eh?'

'Yeah, sort of.'

Jerra made a face.

'School before that?'

'Uni, actually.'

'The Uni, eh?' The old man grinned. 'They tell yer anything at the Uni?'

'I majored in history.'

'History. Learn a pack from the past. Yer can too. Ever learn you anythink?'

Sean looked into the fire, lips compressed. Heat ticked in the billy. Wisps weaved through holes in the lid. The old man looked at Jerra.

'I'm out of work.'

'Got a trade?'

'No. But I've worked on the fishing boats back along the coast, last year. Things got a big rough. A tough season. I got laid off.'

'Yeah,' sighed the old man. 'Things'd be rough. Like the boats?'

'It was rough. But OK. I liked the fish.'

Sean, perched on his log, rolled his eyes, scalloping a hole in the dirt with his heel.

'Ah, yeah,' said the old man scuffing his hands together, little greenish flecks of tobacco catching in the hard cracks. He expanded a little. 'Fish. The things a fish'd know, eh?'

'Yep.'

'Know anythink about fish?'

''Bout all he does know,' said Sean.

'Yeah,' said Jerra, ignoring the sarcasm. After all, it was true enough.

'What about one f'every letter of the alphabet?'

'He can do two at least.'

The old man looked at Sean.

'Can he now?'

'Yeah,' said Jerra.

'OK, start with A.'

Jerra looked up at him.

'A . . .'

'Come on.'

'Shit, nothin' starts with A.'

'What about amberjack?' said Sean, smiling.

'Yeah,' said Jerra, embarrassed as hell. 'Abalone?'

'Not a fish,' said Sean.

'Plenty of Bs. What about bastard-of-a-big-barramundi?'

The old man laughed.

They talked names for a while, wandering off the alphabet when cobia came up. Then it was just big fish.

'Nothin' else worth lookin' at, once you've seen a big fish.

25

Thrashin' and jumpin' and thumpin' on the deck, spreading 'is gills like wings.' He watched Jerra nodding. 'Bloody sad business, too, seein' a big fish die. That's somethink else, boy. Ever seen it?'

'No,' he lied. 'I always clubbed 'em before they suffered. Didn't like to see 'em die.'

Hard silver and black, flat against the boards, laced with salty pearls, glistening. The gills lifting ponderously, straining, lifting, falling. A fingertip on the smooth eye. Short, guttural death grunts. Tears of blood tracking the deck. The sleek silver of scales, sinews in the tail wearing to a feeble spasm. Every big one on the deck looked at him the same way as that turrum, dying open eyed when they were ready. Jerra always left them there, stalling, his back to the other deckies.

'Strong lad, you must be.'

Jerra shrugged. The old man pulled on the stinking sea-slug of a smoke.

'Any deep stuff?'

'Not much further than the shelf. We used to pass the whalechasers on their way in. Seagulls stuck to 'em like shit to a blanket.'

With the catch bubbling eyes and gills in the holds, tails flailing, mucous spittle raining, he would wait at the rail as Michaelmas Island came into view, and opening the sea with sneezing jets the porpoises would cut diagonally for the bows, waiting for cast-offs, running back on broad muscular tails, arching back in flourishing sweeps with open mouths, eyes entreating laughingly. Then they would catch up and wait for a whack from Jerra, taking turns at presenting their backs to the flat of the oar.

The morning he was thinking about other things, he hit too hard and the leader squealed. They never came again.

*

'Sometimes we'd take white pointers following the whales being towed in. Big as whales, too. Tearing great hunks of blubber out of the whales.'

'Catchin' them bastards is somethink.'

'Just as they came up on the gaff, I'd have to shoot. A couple of times. To be careful.'

Gaping, writhing in their own spray. Pink sheen. Thud-thud-thud of the tail against the stern. Gulls waiting.

'They're tricky buggers, orright. Mate o' mine, years back, lost a foot to a bronze. An hour out of the water it was. Red took to it with a cleaver.'

'You worked on the boats.'

'Oath. Did the salmon all along the coast. Sharks when it was bad. Small stuff, herring, snapper. We even went to abalone, one or two bad seasons.'

'Who's we?' asked Sean.

'Me an' the wife.' He dragged tea with sucking lips. 'How long you stayin'?'

'Got about three weeks,' said Jerra. Abalone. That's what his lips looked like; wet an' rubbery.

'Can't see anybody wantin' ter stay that long.'

'Pretty good here,' said Sean.

'Lots better places,' said the old man.

'Good coast,' said Jerra.

'Little bus, eh? All set up.'

Jerra nodded.

'Move around a bit yourself?'

'Not for years. Been to Perth. Bad times we drove up and sold straight to the rest'rants. Rabbitin' for a spell. Got away quick, though.'

'Didn't go much on it?'

'Too many big mouths. Bigger'n nor'west blowies.'

'What about smaller places around here? Albany, Ongerup?'

'All the same. Wherever there's a pub an' people to jabber they just go the same.'

'Albany's orright,' said Jerra.

'Yeah?' said the old man. 'What's it like there now?'

'Always seemed the same to me.'

'Probably too young to know it any different.'

'I s'pose so.'

'Bugger of a place, I reckon. Sailors' town. Yanks and Wogs walkin' round with the local girls. Make yer sick.'

Jerra nodded politely. He had friends in Albany once. Most of them had either gone to the city, were in gaol for dope, or had died driving big cars.

Smooth stones clicked. Bitter smoke mingled with the steamy breath of coals. Sean yawned, rubbing salt and smoke from his eyes.

'Fire's out.'

'Better let youse lads get some sleep.'

'Haven't finished your tea,' said Jerra.

'Gone cold, anyway.' He rose stiffly.

Nodding, the old man went slowly up the track, wrinkled khakis merging in the green-black night. Only the single red eye of his cigarette winked. That soon faded too.

sea-junk and amberjack

Mornings. Afternoons. It was pointless counting. How could you count the warbles in the grey, colours in the fires, thuds in the bush, keep record of the morse of cicadas, seeds, sap, stems? Fish bones burnt to a white powder, and scales clung to bark and licks of grass. Feet burred, nails caught, faces rimed with salt and smoke and dirt.

They cruised on the surface, listening to the breath in the snorkels. Jerra clamped on the rubber bit, feeling the goose-flesh creep along his arms, and saw a long slit at the crest of a hump of rocks and weed that crouched on the bottom. Sean dived across at a small goatfish, away from it. Jerra hovered. He kicked and sank into the weediness of the hole, pulling down the rubber. Prongs glinted. A twilight. Down. He cleared his ears, and the space widened as he kicked. Blennies and pomfrets poked their heads from fissures. His lungs pushed against his chest as he settled on the silt. Corroded things lay half buried, twisted formations knotted on each other, furred with algal turf, as if the hole had collected the debris of many storms. He peered along wrinkles and ledges. Morwong shot, with lips of congealed blood, from hole to hole, and specks of light showed through the walls. There were other entrances, fresh currents on the bottom fed from somewhere back in the darkness that went further than he dared to go. His mask distorted: the walls seemed to curve. Breath short, he turned for the bar of light. And froze. Pugnacious jaws opened at him, peg-like teeth phosphorescent behind the blue lips. The pectoral fins quivered, balancing. It was as big as him.

He kicked upwards, hard, pulling at the water, making for the fluorescent bar, then through, into the silver, crashing the surface, gasping the warm air.

Sean surfaced.

'God, I though you'd gone for good!'

Jerra floated on to his back, pushing the mask back.

'Thought you must've drowned or something. Didn't even see you go in.'

Jerra spat the blood that came to the back of his throat.

Dripping gobs of butter, the fillets were sweet and firm. The white flesh broke off in their fingers.

'Lots of fish,' said Jerra. 'Sea-junk.'

'How deep?'

'About thirty.'

'How could you tell?'

'Ears.'

'Risky.'

Jerra did his best to ignore him. He was thinking.

On his back, Jerra drifted in and out. Sean read a hard-covered book. Jerra opened his eyes. His hair felt like unravelled hemp.

'Buggered if I can sleep.'

'Hmm.'

'What you reading?'

'Shit.'

'Catchy title.'

'Hmm.' He flicked a page. 'Seen Ben Gunn since his midnight meeting?'

'Who?'

'The Old Man and the Sea. The wino from up on the hill.'

'Oh, him.' Jerra got up on an arm. 'How do you know he's a wino?'

'Did you see his face? Weathering the years, and more. The more is the piss. He's as mad as a cut snake.'

'Seemed orright to me.'

''Cause he talked about fish.'

'Held a conversation.'

'Flittin' amongst the tombs.'

'Got him sewn up, haven't you?'

'You saw him.'

'You're a bloody cynic.'

'Try it.'

'Must get a prescription.'

Sean went back to the book, smiling as he recognized one of his own lines. Jerra lay back.

'You must admit, though, he did look pretty wild. The shirt held together with nappy pins, the gummy smile.'

'Wonder where his wife is.' So many things were bothering him.

'Probably dreamt it up.'

'He was dinkum.'

'Got you fooled.'

'Least I didn't make an arse of meself.'

'Who says you didn't – amberjack.'

'I would've remembered.'

'He wouldn't know himself, probably.'

'He'd know a lot've things, I reckon.'

'You've been sucked, mate. Again.'

Eventually, they slept.

Into the soft dark before him, a silver gleam. Jerra sank in the blankets of eddying current. On the bottom, a blacker form, inside the skeleton. It sank darker, where he was hesitant. He longed to plunge into the thing, drag it thrashing into the clear, feeling the tough mosaic of scales, the muscle of tail, to brush lightly against the dorsals, to lever open the skull to see the pure white, feel it, hard as a pebble, in his palm. No breath. He clawed up the smooth curving walls for the surface, the clear sheen, feeling the grey coarseness against his cheek and neck, dry, chafing. In the smoke and gasps of kookaburras, his hands smelt of fish.

'Sean?'

'Yeah.' He rolled over.

'You remember the kinghie my old man caught on the jetty?'

'That was years ago.'

'I was eight.'

'What about it?'

'Remember the pearls?'

'Oh, you're not on that, again.'

'It happened.'

'You were eight years old; you imagine all sorts of bloody things, especially you. Gawd, between you an' your grandfather and . . .'

'It happened.'

'An' so there's these things inside a fish's head. It's all fishermen's bloody superstition.'

'Yeah.'

'Geez, Jerra. Next thing you'll tell me is that you know God and Father Christmas.'

'I've seen 'em.'

'Who, God and Father Christmas?'

'No, the pearls.'

'Arr.'

As an eight-year-old he remembered the noises the kingfish made as the air bladder deflated and the gush that came when his father opened it up and pulled out the roe, then opened the head and took one of the jewels from the base of the spine.

'Why don't you take them both, Dad? One for you an' one for me.'

'Leave one for the fish, eh?'

He did not understand, but his dad knew. They put the pearl on the jetty next to the fishing bag, and took the fish down on to the lower landing to wash the guts out and throw the head away.

When they returned, the pearl had gone, slipped between the rough sleepers and disappeared into the dredged green.

all the men . . .

Mornings were cooler. Jerra walked along the beach, up and back in the arc, crossing and re-crossing tracks and prints, crab, bird, mud-skipper, man. His own tracks, hardened and smoothed, looked as though they might hold water if it rained. He spat into a baked footprint and the gob disappeared, even the little stain gone in a moment.

There was often new debris along the high-water mark; globs of plastic, splinters of soft pine, bottles, a petrel without legs (this disturbed him greatly), lengths of nylon rope, sea slugs, abalone shells like pale, open hands, all tangled in the thin stain of weed which relined the brow of the beach. And lines in the sand half obliterated by the tide that could have been sand crabs, but there were hand marks, too.

Gulls would follow, hovering.

At a gilt dawn he found a seal under a wreath of birds. The eyes had gone. Flesh had perished and ruptured, peeling, burst upholstery. A green slit, the hollow belly opened to the sky. It was big, old. Some of the weedy whiskers still showed. Gulls snapped, and the stench, too, forced him back. Jerra could not take his eyes from the slit of belly. He wondered how long his mind could remain numb. He pretended that he was not pretending.

Sitting by the glowing mound spilling through the circle of rocks, Sean glanced up as he got back into camp.

'How's the swell?'

'Piss-poor.'

'Anything new?'

'A seal. Dead on the beach.'

'Goin' fishin'?'

'Yeah, some squid left.'

It was apathetic conversation, even for them.

Flakes of pollard dried on their hands. Lines bobbed on fingers. The squid dried in the sun, curling at the edges.

'Thought they'd bite this morning,' Jerra murmured.

Sean suggested seal meat, remembering Jerra's mention of the dead seal, but Jerra vetoed it quickly, stubbornly. If they were that desperate, he said, then he could dive and have a feed in ten minutes. It sounded arrogant, even to him, but it was true enough. He wasn't using the carcass of anything washed up to catch a fish.

Then Jerra had a hard bite that slashed the line down and across, wrenching his arm. A silver flash like a mirror.

'Skippy!'

He pulled hard, hand over hand, the beaded line coiling at his feet. The skippy came out, slapping and smacking the water. He held it against his leg, threaded the hook out, saw the trickle from the corner of its mouth, and tossed it into the bag.

'More of those, my son.'

It kicked in the bag.

'Bit of fight for a small fish,' said Jerra, wiping the papery scales onto his jeans.

'That's 'cause they swim sideways coming up.'

'Smart fish, skippy.'

'Trevally.'

'Not this side of the border.' Jerra cast again. He spread some pollard on to the water. 'What are you, a Sydney poonce?'

'Ho!' Sean dragged line. The fish slashed, skipped, shied, and was lifted on to the rock. 'Howzat, mate? Nearly a pound!'

Jerra meant to reply, but his line cut again. Down and across, then away, shivering. His hands burnt.

'He's turning, he's turning.'

It was bigger still, cold and sleek. The flanks were so fine, almost without scales. Sean laughed, slapping his side.

'They're bitin', mate!'

'That's the last of the squid,' said Jerra, threading it.

'Arr. Just when they were biting.'

'Oh well, there's enough for a feed.'

'What about seal meat?'

Back on to seal meat.

'Bugger off. You don't know what it's got in it. Been pecked over enough, anyway.'

Sun glared hot from the water. Sean sighed.

'What about the skippy? Why don't we cut a strip off one of those?'

He sliced the head off the biggest. It writhed in his hands. Blood ran on the rocks. He slit the belly and dug out the guts.

'What's this?'

Jerra leant over his shoulder.

'That? Worms.'

'Worms?'

'All through. Look.'

Sean threw it on the rock.

'You'd better try the others,' said Jerra.

'Ah, it couldn't be in all three.'

Jerra watched from the corner of his eye. The line shivered in the breeze. A gull screamed.

'All of them! Every bloody one!' Sean stabbed with the chipped blade. 'Oh, what a fucken waste.' He hurled the shabby things out on to the water.

They picked their way back through the rocks, pollard and scales clinging to their palms. Birds bickered on the water.

Sean strode ahead, muttering and looking up towards camp. Carrying the fishing bag, Jerra glanced down to the other end of the beach where he saw the tiny figure of the dog again. It got up on two legs and walked into the dunes.

Later in the day, after a depressing tinned lunch – pork and beans and a Big Sister self-saucing pud (cold) – Jerra went walking – for wood, he said to Sean who looked at him with curiosity – and he found himself heading back up the hill on the rutted track.

The grey ruts had smoothed in the afternoon winds. A rabbit scuttled across the track. The breeze blew his hair forward into his face. His hands smelt of fish. His jeans were crusty with pollard, sauce, blood, and scales.

Nothing was different. Only the crumbling footprints and drag marks from the jerrycan. Twenty-eights tittered in the movement of the trees.

Up at the shack, he stood for a while observing the silence until he found the courage to call out without unnerving himself.

'Hullo! You there?'

He tapped the door.

'Anyone there?'

He picked his way round the side, past the webs and rust of the tank, through the grass, flecked with hard old scales, past the brown and green bottles, until he was at the door again. Through cracks and knots in the shutters he could see a dim desolation, a fur of dust on the floor, broken glass in the corner, webbed, fluffed with dirt. Nothing lived here, he knew it.

As he trudged down the track, something thumped in the bush. A roo or perhaps a rabbit.

NO, said the tree in scars and clots. He agreed, whatever it meant. NO sounded fair enough. Until you thought a bit.

He sat on the crest of a dune overlooking the crescent of the beach, the sun pummelling his back, and wondered about fishing. He wondered about the waiting his father said was so good. Dad's still waiting, he thought sadly. Geez, what'm I waiting for? To grow up?

He told himself to bugger off and started a poem, the sun on his back.

'All the men . . .' he said aloud, and nothing else came. 'All the men . . .' Stupid talking out loud, anyway. He gave up.

His grandfather was stuffed in the head thinking he would ever write poems. Jerra tried to remember the lines he had learnt but all he could remember was the deep mirror of water by the brewery and his little feet looking up at themselves.

Then he remembered Gran bringing cups of tea, all afternoon, tending Granpa's foot, hearing him whine, calling her out to the back yard.

Remembered his own feet looking up at themselves as he hung over the retaining wall by the brewery, trying to learn C. J. Dennis, and catch tailor on the scummy night tide of the Swan River.

He had forgotten the wood. He would get some tomorrow.

Sleep came slow. Sean breathed a metric rhythm. Dying fire flickered on the windows. Surf rumbled, coming, going. A cricket began, then faltered, started, stopped again. Jerra rolled on to his side.

N . . .	O . . .
no	*oranges*
not	*old*
needy	*orientals*
nok	*off*
neighbour's	*oxen*
Nag	*O'Sarkey*
nourishing	*octopus*

> NOel   NOel
> now   oracles

NO, said the scar-faced tree, in his blackness of sleep.

Hovering. This wasn't waiting. He hesitated, plunged into its diamond side. It tore the spear from him. He went for the opening. It fled, jammed halfway, flexing, writhing, tearing. The water clouded. No breath, and the entrance was obscured.

Sean stirred, talking again.

The beach breathed deep.

fish and women and bollocks

Bleached white as the sand, the beam wouldn't be moved. Whiskers of weed had caught in its coarsened grain. Bare white sticks, spindly crooked things, were all he could gather. Wind slopped the swell on to the shore. Sand was dredged up, swirled grey in the foam, almost settled, and was churned again as the shore ran with seething white.

Jerra sat on the beam, seeing the wind whip the bay. There was no real wood around. Not that he expected much. He gazed towards the granite tumble at the other end of the beach. In all his solitary walking, the bleary dawns when he felt cold inside and had to walk and convince himself that Sean knew nothing of his secret – he wouldn't be just cool and bitchy, he thought, he would be maniacal, tear him to ribbons – he had never ventured further than those blunt-faced boulders. He set off towards them, skirting the burst carcass of the seal that frightened him so much, triggering off all the memories. Close up, the rocks lost their darkness and smoothness and were blotched with little varices and pock marks, dissected by veins of algae, ribbed with salt. He climbed, walked carefully around the bigger boulders, and hopped to and from smaller ones. Nearer the surge, their surface was shiny and black, slick with turf, and in cracks and crevices running white with foam, beams, planks, and twisted white branches were wedged tight, old, old wood swollen and stuck hard in the rock.

Stumbling down the other side, he saw a crazily constructed

dwelling – a humpy of sorts – beyond the crisp high-water mark of a small cove beach. Dense brush, ferns, high timber and magpies crowded in on the little shack, hinting at a freshwater source, a spring, perhaps. The white hook of beach ran to more piled granite on a sheer fault-wall, toppling into the water. Gulls flitted across the cove, settling in the trees. Jerra whistled.

'Didn't expect to see you.'

Jerra spun. The old man.

'Frighten yer?'

'Yeah,' Jerra breathed. 'Again.'

'Lookin' for wood?'

'Right.'

'None 'ere. 'Cept for the hut. You can't 'ave that.' The old man wound his way down to the sand and sat at the base of a boulder, out of the wind. Jerra sat.

'Find anything?'

'Nah.'

'Haven't been up this end before?'

'Thought I'd come and have a look.'

'Caught any fish?' The old man didn't look up from rolling. The paper darkened as it slid along his tongue.

'A few skippy. Sweep, leatheries.'

'Fair enough.'

'The skippy had worms.'

He lit the end and Jerra watched it smoulder. It stank. The old man rubbed his scaly arms. Jerra carved in the sand.

'You said you lived in the shack up from us. Were you bullshitting?'

'Hmm.'

Jerra thought this over for a moment, waiting for the old man to explain, then, realizing the old man had nothing to add, turned his attention to the humpy.

'Where'd you get the wood for the hut?'

'Driftwood, mainly. Found the tin on the other beach.'

'Must've taken ages.'

'I got plenty o' time.'

The ply walls shivered slightly in the wind, leaning in on themselves.

'Boat ply, isn't it?'

'Yeah.'

Smoke burnt Jerra's face, wafting over, a thin edge in his nostrils. Boat ply.

'Pretty rough, living out here alone.'

'Alone, yeah.'

'You like it, I s'pose?'

'Have to.'

'Lonely as hell.'

The smoke was shoved into the sand. A wisp seeped out, disappeared. The old man's belly strained against the safety-pins. When you looked closely at the sand, it was not really white, but a motley of gold and black. After a time, the black became dominant. Jerra blinked.

'See many people out here?'

'All that come.'

'Many come?'

'Enough.'

'When was the last?'

'Couldn't be sure.'

'Anyone been here before?'

'Not here. Not this beach. You're the first.'

'Always a first time.'

'Everything's been done. At least once.'

Both sat, eyes on the sand.

'You don't get on with him, do you?' The old man stated with authority.

'Yeah, sure I do.'

'Doesn't look like it.'

'How would you know?' He glanced quickly at the eyes behind the clotted beard.

'I met 'im. You remember, after a while.'

Jerra got to his feet, annoyed.

'Hey, who owns this land? The Crown?' Jerra was getting edgy about all this; he had enough on his mind already.

The old man smiled, taking out his stinging mixture to roll.

'It's mine. To the high-water mark.'

'We're trespassers, then, eh?' Jerra lifted his chin. 'Didn't see any signs.'

The smile was bent.

'Well, didn't you now?' He rolled without looking. 'What's a sign? People shoot holes in it, knock it down.'

Jerra rubbed his thighs in agitation.

'They see you don't want 'em around, so they think they'll have a look. Wouldn't blink at the place, otherwise. Not lookin' for anything in particular.'

'Well—' He thought of that damned tree, puzzled.

'Still, what people can't have is what they want most.'

'What the hell are you smoking?' Jerra asked in exasperation to change the flow of talk.

'Stinks?'

'Not baccy, is it?' It was impossible.

'Me mixture. Tea leaves, seaweed, all sorts.'

'Stinks.' Jerra laughed. He sat again. 'Smells like the bollocks of Ben Cropp.'

'Ben Boyd, more like it.'

Then suddenly the old man was singing.

> *Well the south seas're fickle*
> *In the winters of June,*
> *An' the wind from the Pole sings the*
> *Riggin' a tune,*
> *When the sperm and the humpback*
> *Come northwards they say,*
> *When we found them in shallows*
> *Down at Two Peoples Bay, Two Peoples Bay.*

Jerra smiled, nervous.

'An old whaling song,' said the old man, sucking on his smoke. 'My ol' man taught me that. We 'ad whaling in the family, right back to Two Peoples Bay.'

'At Two Peoples?'

'That's where it started round here. Used to whale here when the bay whalers spread in the 1830s. Ten or fifteen blokes dropped on the beach with a keg of rum, a boiler, a boat, and a gun. Used to row out to the whales that came in to sun and harpoon 'em, then wrestle one for a mornin' an' tow it back in. If they wasn't all towed out to sea. Next land south is the Pole. Bugger of a life, that. If the whales didn't get 'em, the Abos did, or they shot each other.'

'Now they use harpoon guns and spotter-planes and fast little chasers.'

'Not the same.'

'Yeah, I sup—'

The old man rattled off into the song again, mucus bubbling in his throat as he growled the swinging lines.

> Well we anchored her in and off old Coffin Island
> A nor'-wester blowin' the best of a gale,
> An' the beach was as white
> As a sweet vargin smilin' –
> The air around smellin', smellin' of whale.
> – Smellin' of whale.

The old man smacked a hand on his thigh as he sang the chorus.

> Out in the longboats, then sailors,
> Put your backs to the oar,
> Mind a big bull don't
> Come up an' nail us,

Or we will be sailin' no more.
– We will be sailin' no more.

'Good song,' said Jerra when the old man didn't continue.

'Me an' the wife used to sing it.'

'Where's she?'

'On the other beach.'

'Eh?'

'She died. Burnt in the shed on the beach.'

'Shit. That's rough.'

'We used to argue a lot. She lived in the shed on the beach after a while.'

Jerra tasted it at the back of his throat.

'Some things you can't do anything about.' The old man fidgeted.

'Yeah, things go that way.'

'Yer just get the feeling of it all comin' down around you. Like sinking. Drowning.'

'Yes.' Yes! he thought.

'Like I said. What people want most. Always wanted to be a real man with the bollocks of Ben Boyd. Anyone's. I had to settle for the boat. That was the only time we were together, on the boat. It was orright then, with the boat. We wiped its bum like a kid. Still it was just a boat and not a kid. When she sank that there was nothin' left to hold her. So she thought, my lovely Annie. Gave her the pearl out of a kinghie's head, once. Beautiful. An' why do they throw it away an' want what you can't give 'em, eh? Eh?'

Then it was true. The pearl was true. He had heard nothing else. And he'd let it go, that time as a child in the boat, not letting it be cut up. A turrum should have one, his father said, but Jerra said no, seeing the eye staring again and the stricken mate diving at the moment of death.

'Why do they?'

'Not sure I follow you.' Jerra was thinking of fish; the old man was talking women and bollocks.

The old man got to his feet, disgusted.

Jewel. The name wouldn't go away. He couldn't always catch the face any more. There were so many of them. A new face with each mood, each collapse, each mistake. But he wouldn't forget. Not if he could.

The seal had really irked him. He admitted it now, lying awake. Sean slept. Jerra was grateful. He doesn't look like her at all, he thought bitterly.

After a time, Jerra slept also. It was a trammelled sleep crowded with fish and women and bollocks.

little pieces came away every time he touched

S un warmed their shiny black skins as they basked on the rocks. A clutter of gear surrounded them, glistening, the salt appearing as they dried, and below their feet, the glossy kelp rose and fell with the surge. They talked idly, drawling, deliciously drunk from sun and exertion. Jerra had been thinking about their growing apart. He knew it wasn't just the money and the intimidation. Deliberately, he turned the conversation towards women. It was a wilful thing. He wanted to prove himself right again. He mentioned Mandy Middleton.

'You remember Mandy. Course,' he said, eyes shut tight against the white of sun. Come on, you prick, he thought, tell me you don't.

'No. I don't.' Sean unzipped his wet suit.

'You and Mandy were pretty close, weren't you?' he insisted.

'We got into a habit,' Sean sighed, irritated.

'She was a nice one, though. Gave you a good run.'

Sean snorted. 'A good run.'

'Always thought you'd get married, you know.'

Sean buzzed the zip up again, then down.

'You were, weren't you?'

'No.'

'Never did figure out why she left town in such a hurry. Always thought it would be you who pissed off.'

'Thanks.'

'You had your job to think about, though.'

'Yeah.'

'She must've met someone bloody good.'

'Hmm?'

'She was off quick. Didn't seem any reason. Heard she was in Geraldton.'

'Who said?'

'Someone down the beach front. Ages ago. Phil. Said she was on her own.'

'Dumped, I s'pose.'

'In a nice motel.'

'That's good,' he said dully.

'Dunno how she can afford it.'

'Probably works. Some of us do.'

'Hope she comes down again, some time. She was good fun.'

'I don't think she'll come back.'

'No. Maybe not.' Bastards. Same as your old man. Just get rid of 'em to save embarrassment.'

A crab tumbled across the rocks below. It skittered into a crack above the waterline. Jerra lay back, satisfied that he had confirmed it again. He smiled, perversely, bitterly. He almost enjoyed the hurt of knowing it was all over between them; it was only a matter of time. And, a second later, he wished it could be still the same as the old days. He cursed himself. It was all bloody stupid. God, we're all bloody stupid, he thought.

'Where'd you go yesterday?' asked Sean, rubbing the hairs on his chest.

'Up the beach.'

'See anything?'

'Driftwood.'

'Didn't bring it back.'

'Wedged into the rocks.'

'Lot of use in the rocks.'

'Got some mallee roots up the track this morning.' Always me getting the wood, he mused bitterly.

A leg reached from the dark, scorched red and orange. The claw flexed and retreated into darkness.

'Coming in again?' Jerra asked, feeling the hard teeth of the zip on his chest.

'I'll stay in the sun.'

Jerra clipped the weights on. His feet slipped into the flippers. One yellow, the other blue. Like thongs. Never a pair. Different brands, even.

'Why do you reckon I've got odd flippers?'

'You can't pick a pair.'

'They're a pair.'

'Not even the same size. No wonder you get fish. Curious to see what sort of dickhead they're up against.'

'Arr. Jealous.' He thumped Sean matily, and slid down to the water.

The crab skidded across the rock into darkness. The water was cool.

Leaning under, he slid down shallow and followed the bottom, the curving fall, as long as he could bear it, then surfaced, clearing his snorkel, and wandered along the surface. He pushed out past the big, incongruous hump towards the limits of the reef, wrinkled with trenches, channels, open pores of holes with weed sawing back and forth on itself, wallowing on the crags that sheltered schools of tiny pomfrets and bullseyes clouding silver and yellow in potholes. Green wrasse cruised the bottom for food.

Jerra watched from above, gliding, with a wrasse circling idly in the cover of his shadow. He ducked and slid down behind the fish, took out his knife, and prised an abalone from the bottom. It sucked on his palm. He dropped it. The wrasse watched. He floated up. It circled the exposed meat. After a few moments, it nudged the shell and left.

In a long, steep trench, Jerra saw a clutch of queen snapper feeding near the bottom. He descended from behind, feeling the rubber bite into his thumb. The fish clung. Just as he chose a target, the leader turned side on. The others balked, spreading blue, and Jerra lunged, catching the leader behind the gills. They struggled all the way to the surface, trailing a mist of blood. It was as big and blue as his left flipper, the yellow lines radiating from its eyes like wrinkles. He thrust it, threshing, into the bag, tore it from the barbs, and dived.

The others had grouped further along the trench, about six of them, wary and slow. They fanned quickly, seeing the black shadow descending. Jerra chased one of the bigger fish to a pothole, weeded over and dark. He waited, his guts tight. The blue head appeared. Prongs pierced the forehead and gills. It was dead before Jerra had it on the surface.

The bag and his legs were heavy. He struck for the rocks. As he slopped the bags on to the rocks, the first fish twitched.

'A couple of blues,' he said, nasally, the mask pinning his upper lip.

Sean looked up.

'Bit of quality for a change, eh?' He slipped them out, fingers in the gills, and laid them on the rock. 'Nice size, too. A few pound. Let's go back and have an early tea.'

'Nah,' said Jerra, spitting a pink gob on to the water. 'I'm going back for another look. Check 'em for worms first.'

He shivered. Always colder the second time. Worse the third. His white nails glowed against the blue of his fingertips. Tiny bubbles gathered on his knuckles. Shafts of light webbed the water. It was like swimming under a net. He tightened the weights.

He found the holes again, in the odd-shaped hump in the reef.

It opened darkly, awash with trailing strands of black. He kicked down, tightening, and followed the clean silver of steel. His spear scraped the rock, leaving a welt. Sweep and morwong cluttered the shaft and fanned like red and black feathers as he approached. A crusted circle of barnacles lay in the silt. Ledges opened black on all sides, as he rolled to see them all, wondering why they were so even and well formed, so precisely hewn by the sea. It was unnerving, this orderly cave.

—A porcelain globe faced him, solid as the head around it, encasing it. Scales fanning from the heavy gills, flat terraces fading into the distance of tail and cave. It watched him, monstrous, motionless, current drifting cold from behind. Jerra's palm met the soft bottom. The hard edge of something pressed into his thigh as he settled, aiming. The rubber of the handspear cut. He waited. Longer. The fish turned and bared its side, jowls twitching. Jerra aimed for the softness and the spine behind the gills. It was gone into the dark.

He turned to surface. Rust chafed his leg. He pulled at the curious formation. It peeled from the barnacled bed of its own imprint and he held it against his side, uncovering rotten wood as he found a hand hold, aghast as well as almost black from exertion. Timber gave way beneath his heels as he rammed up.

Sean was gone. Jerra slid up on to the flat rock. The fish were still in the bag, floating in a rock pool. He chased an orange crab from the pool. A corner had been chewed out of the bag, but the fish were untouched.

'That's right, leave me to clean the bloody fish.'

Knots of guts fell on to the rock. The gulls hung, cackling. He washed the clean, firm, curving fillets, and kicked the offal into the pool that was scummed at one edge with a skin of larvae. Flies walked on the water's skin.

'Get it while you can, crab, you crazy ol' bastard.'

Jerra threw his gear into the big sack with Sean's, put the rusty circle in, and tossed the lot over his shoulder. It was coarse on his back.

'Some cave. Reckon we're both crazy.'

The crab clattered.

*

The old man eyed Jerra, pools quivering in his eyes.

'Whatcher got there?'

'Ringbolt. Isn't it?'

'Could be.'

Birds were fidgeting in the ashy sand.

'It's a ringbolt for sure.'

'Hard to tell.' Keeping distance. 'There's no bolt left, nothin' to attach it to anything.'

'Worn away. Yours, isn't it?'

'Could be.'

'It is. I know.'

'You don't.'

'Don't you want it?' Jerra offered. The old man retreated.

'What for?'

'Dunno. Thought you might like to keep it.'

'You keep it.'

'You should.'

'I said I don't want the bloody thing!' The old man snatched it from him and held it over his head, as if to fling it into the water. He dropped it at Jerra's feet and walked away.

It was a crusty, eaten thing in Jerra's hand as he climbed back. It left stains on his hands. Little pieces came away every time he touched.

The day after, Jerra went back to the clinker-built fossil in the reef and found that there were crays nestling in its hoary beams which he had previously overlooked, and he brought one of them – the biggest, like an armoured car – back to camp where Sean had spent the day reading *The Rise and Fall of the Third Reich*. Sean, he had to admit, was impressed.

'Two pounds if it's an ounce.'

'Metric now, mate,' he said, happy for a moment.

'Same in metres.' Sean laughed. 'How long since we had one o' these?'

'Dongara.'

'When you speared that ray.'

'We all have our moments.'

Jerra propped the bucket in the flames, chuckling at the memory of Sean being towed along the bottom by the startled foot-mat of a ray.

'Were there any more?'

'A few.'

'Should have got them.'

'Yeah.'

The water stirred, clusters of bubbles at the edges. Sticks and flames bone-cracked. It boiled.

'Put 'em in.' Jerra got up.

'Where you going?'

'The annexe. Gonna tidy up.' The rattle of limbs thrashing. Flesh. Boiling. He closed the flap.

A verse almost came to him in his half-sleep. He held his breath while it fumbled around inside him . . . *all dressed in clobber white . . . An' as their snowy forms go steppin' by . . .* Something, something. It escaped him.

Pickets, tickets, wickets. Crickets: the clicking tongues of a drumful of crabs, each their own clock, ticking. The smell of crayfish twitched in the blankets. He opened his eyes.

'Funny we never saw any of those crays before,' said Sean with his chin on the pillow. He had been shaving. Orange and yellow firelight flickered on the window.

'They were hidden away.'

'Odd colour.'

'They're called golddiggers. A southern cray.'

'Strange so close in.'

Jerra had a few ideas why they were so close in. Like the boat being loaded with a catch when it went down.

'How come you're not diving?' he asked Sean.

'Oh, it gets a bit silly after a while. Swimming in circles.'

'Thought you liked it. You were crazy on it, once.'

'Oh, it's the same stuff.'

'You always see something different. It's never the same.'

'Who wants to swim in circles the rest of their life?'

The moon was a pale fillet. Jerra saw it in the hairs on his arm. Sean's eyes were pink, blinking.

'Ever thought about diving to the bottom more often? In the caves. Always different. Another world.'

'Taking it a bit seriously, aren't you?'

'What do you take seriously any more?'

'There's other things in the world.'

'Yeah?'

'Fish! It's not the only bloody thing there is.'

'Oh yeah?'

'For you, maybe, and your father, and the crazy ol' bastard up the hill, but not me.'

'We don't appreciate the *better* things, I know.'

'Arr.' Sean laughed.

'None of which you could think of for the shares in yer head an' the shit in yer heart. What are you now?'

'Talking like a loony!'

'Everyone's a fucken *loony*. A loony. Someone that doesn't suck the crap is a loony. You learned orright. You got taught well, mate.'

'So? You learnt fish. Ah, yes.'

'An' you ate 'em. You lived it. It was the only family you had, mate – ours! Where was yours! Flittin' around EU-rope havin' a good time!'

'Fish! Fish! Shit!'

'Didn't hear you complain. Ever.'

'Yer too obsessed to hear.'

'That what you told yer old lady? Never gave her a bloody moment. Oh, yeah, she was a bloody first-class loony.'

Sean laughed hard. 'And a bloody idiot, Jerra. Like you.'

Jerra shifted back, pulling even breaths. Then he knew that Sean didn't know about him and her. That would have been the moment of a lifetime, an opportunity Sean would not have missed if he had known and been waiting.

'You talk in your sleep, you know.'

'So what.'

'Oh—'

'Come on.'

'You called for your mother.' He waited one second. '"Mum", you said.'

'Get fucked, Jerra,' said Sean quietly. 'Just get fucked.'

Jerra pulled the blanket up. It was hot and the blanket itched where he sweated. His face itched with triumph and shame.

'Sean doesn't love his mum.'

'Yes, he does.'

'Has he ever said it?'

'Nah, boys don't say it.'

'I've heard you say it.'

'Well, I'm a bit strange, 'cause I hang around with you.'

'Yes, I'll bet,' said Auntie Jewel, sipping her lemonade that smelled funny, looking out over the quay.

In his dream the half-stern shuddered with all the fish in the ocean, living in the skeleton that had grown a skin again. He swam off the edge, looking for the cutting edge of the bow. It was blue for ever; he blacked without reaching bottom.

Walking, next morning.

A glimpse only, but he was sure. The tree grew an arm which disappeared suddenly. A crackle of leaves, the outline at the crest of the dune. Enough to give you the creeps. The ragged shirt was unmistakable.

All morning Jerra walked the same arc of beach, guiltily picking over the weed, uncovering tiny new things, textures, smells. He felt the corrugated skin of a shell, different shades of white and black in the sand, the minuscule air holes left in the wet sand by the sand crabs that came out and ruttled around in the dark with their run-stop-run-stop movements, and disappeared in the day, buried in the wet sand of the shore.

He tried his poem again. He'd call it 'NO', just to satisfy the tree.

> NO
> *All the men . . .*

All the stuffed men? 'Stuffed' was no good; not poetical enough. 'Pushed'? 'Cut'? He thought of whaling and fishing for a moment, and the old man's song that he couldn't really remember. Bollocks. Bollocks to the rowlocks. That's how he felt: balls to the wall. He tried the poem again.

> NO
> *All the severed men.*

As Jerra turned again to walk back, the old man tumbled down the dune at the end of the beach. Jerra could hear the rattly breath.

'Son! Son! Aren't you gonna come back home an' see yer mum? She'll be pleased, orright. Geez, you've grown. "Born of . . . fire," eh.'

'What?'

He really stank this time. His hands were filthy, covered in heavy black flies.

'She'll take me back, she'll forgive me, no one will laugh, she'll love—'

Jerra stood back. The old man was peering into his face, but the eyes weren't there. Focused elsewhere. He stomped, moving around and back, slapping his thighs.

'You orright?'

'They'llcomesoonif yerdon't comeandseeer she'llbe surprised we'llbe alltogetherbutwegottahurry!' The eyes were gone. There were pieces of bark in his beard.

'Who's coming?' Jerra laughed. 'Must be a gala thing every time somebody turns up.'

'Nnono! Yerdoanunnerstan! Sheelbringitallback, floatitagain!'

'Who? Float it? Who?'

'Quick, quick.'

Jerra kicked at the shells and the little air holes. The old man was hobbling up the dune after somebody else. Jerra had his own problems.

'Alistair Maclean?' Sean asked, smiling drily.

'So?'

'Shit.'

'Thought you'd like him.'

'Alistair Mac-bloody-clean?'

'Makes millions.'

In a tree this time. Sleeping in a tree, wedged in the fork beneath the umbrella of twigs and leaves. He decided not to go close. The old sod might fall, he thought.

'I just can't understand it.'

They argued about Alistair Maclean again.

'Arr, not again.'

'Same plots shuffled differently each time.'

'. . .'

'Same faces.'

Jerra drew joining triangles in the dust on the roof. A diamond. Grains settled on the blanket.

'Nothing changes. It doesn't get any better – or worse.'

'Just talked yourself up yer own arsehole.'

'Bullshit. How?'

'What's history? You read *that*, and stay awake a lot of the time. Don't talk to me about repetition!'

Sean fell back on the pillow. Jerra switched the yellow light out. Probably was crap, he thought, but you had to say something. Anyway, he'd seen repetition, *and* the bastards had gotten away with it, like father like son.

. . . A tart I knoo a 'undred years ago . . .

He knew that line.

Next day, he dived in the bowels of the wreck.

He came up with a writhing cray in each hand, heavy tails punching water. Near the surface he let them go. They spidered down, straight for the slit, disappearing into the black, feelers last. It was too much like grave-robbing.

Late in the afternoon, he went in search of the old man; he needed to talk, and probably to listen. The humpy was empty, showing no sign of being slept in for a while. The coals were old. Jerra saw the magazine pictures – *National Geographic* – stuck on the walls, yellow, ragged things with touched up teeth and gums.

The bunk had blankets. A tin full of whale oil stood on a

box in the corner, and bent hooks, knots, and twists of nylon and gut hung from nails in the beams which held back the ply walls, which, in turn, were clawed by weeds from the outside and grizzled with the skeletons of mussels and barnacular flakes like so many scales. A sliver of mirror stood against the windowsill, half obscuring a brown curlicue of lace; it cast a blade of light on to the Perspex window. The window, distorted only slightly, was caked with fat and fingerprints.

Out on the little beach, gulls huddled white in the sand. Jerra sat on the mouldy bunk and picked up the empty spine of a Bible, the cover of which was soft and green with mildew, with the blue vein of a marker still intact. Inside, catching on the seam of the binding, were a few tiny slips of paper, fragments cut crookedly which Jerra smoothed with a thumb.

> – innocent blood –
> – the guilt of –
> – in your land –
> – careful –
> – cities of refuge –

Jerra turned them over. Only half-words on the back. He closed the empty spine, thoughtful, and put it back on the floor. What floor there was to the place was deckboards, he knew. A shattered, watermarked compass, big as a head, stood on a crate by the bed. The fireplace was a cairn of limestone poking through the roof where splinters of light pierced the warped, black tin.

He waited. The old man did not come.

'I came over yesterday,' said Jerra, unbending the wire.

'I know.'

'Where were you?'

'Around. What's that?'

'Wire. I found it on the beach. Thought you might want it.'

'What for?'

'The loose tin.'

'Yeah.'

'It'll leak, this winter.'

'Yeah. I'll caulk it up, somehow.'

Jerra tossed it next to the old man. It coiled again, how he found it.

'Why didn't you want your ringbolt?'

'How would you like livin' with a corpse?'

'Eh?'

'Look, son, you know what I've done. They'll come out an' get me sooner or later. You can't do somethin' like that an' expect to get away with it.'

'Your wife?'

'Confessed a million bloody times, but no one's ever heard it. Heard nothin'. The screams, the boards crumblin' and the roof groanin' . . . but I'm not gonna just let 'em take me. Orready done me time, I 'ave. I got burnt, too, you know. Standin' there all night. Pouring diesel on. Just white an' black when the sun come up, again. Smell of diesel, clothes . . . can't give 'em what they want most . . . they ruin what yer have . . . that boat was our marriage. Only thing bindin' us. Then you ruin what's left once yer alone with yer conscience. So. I've said it.' He laughed and bit the heel of his thumb.

Jerra would have spat.

'Well, I'm not going to tell anyone. I promise.'

'Arr.'

'Bloody beans,' muttered Sean. He tore the label off and put the can in the flames.

'Eatin' like the poorer classes, eh?' Jerra said pointlessly.

'Like eating rabbit shit.'

A crash in the bush.

'Close,' said Sean.

'Should've brought the .22.'

'Even beans are better than roo.'

Jerra poked the can with a stick. The fire was feeble.

'I'm thinking of leaving soon.'

'What? There's a week left.'

'Yeah. Well I thought we might move on.'

Sean was shaking his head, red eyes laughing.

'In the morning.'

'Shit, why not tonight?'

'Plenty of other places.'

'The old man of course. Geez. I don't *believe* it.'

'You know how ol' blokes like that are.'

'Yeah. But do you?'

The fire smouldered, smoke easing from between the teeth of coals. Sean dragged the black can from the ashes.

'Doesn't look like it's gonna get any hotter without wood,' he said, rolling it in the damp leaves at his feet.

'If you want some wood, there's plenty o' bush,' Jerra said. 'If yer not sure, the dead stuff usually burns best. You'll probably find it lying on the ground.'

Sean slapped beans on to the buckled plates.

'Here, smart-arse. Mind the bones.'

Sean was calling, asleep in the VW. Jerra couldn't stand it. He felt like going in there and throttling him. He sat by the circle of blackened rocks, scraping the soot away with a stick. The limestone showed dull white, bone, beneath. Dew settled on the back of his neck. No wind. Not a leaf moved.

He left the fire. It was too late to bother about more wood. He stumbled down to the beach in the moonlight. The white flickered through the trees. The sand was loud. Footsteps crunched, the broken teeth of shells. Walking near the still shore, he saw the buried beam, longer and whiter in the moonlight.

Difficult on the rocks. Shadows made it impossible to judge blackness as solid rock or air, and he fell a few times, opening an elbow and a shin. Feeling his way over the surfaces with his palms, he came upon the gulls, crowded, sleeping in a hollow. He avoided them, climbing closer to the water, slipping on the damp felt of algae.

Orange and red, the fire lit a circle in front of the humpy, rippling shadows across the sand, lighting the eyes of the old man, squatting, staring in.

He was cutting with little scissors, a pair of women's nail scissors.

. . . neighbours' landmark, which the men . . . of old have set. Fifteen: *A single . . . wit . . . ness shall not prevail against—*

Rolling, rolling the stuff between his fingers.

. . . or see this great fire any more, lest I die . . .

Jerra jumped from the last rock.

. . . And the rest shall hear, and fear, and shall never again commit any such evil among . . .

The old man, without a shirt, stood up and backed away.

'No, not me. Go away. I had to!'

Jerra stopped.

'No, hang on, it's me.'

The old man hobbled into the darkness of the humpy.

'Not all my fault. Don't, no burning. Please!'

'Hey, it's only me. It's orright,' called Jerra, going over to the hut.

'She sank it on purpose, you know. She ever tell you that? Did you ever . . . were you ever with her? Eh? Must've been the only one left in town, then. Was it yours? What she had in her? Not mine, oh no. Couldn't've. Not that she'd know. *A single witness . . .* go away.'

'I am,' said Jerra, annoyed. 'Tomorrow.'

'No. Go now. I loved, that's somethin'.'

'Yeah.'

'Been waiting, you know. Hard to find, eh? Have to get me twice if yer countin'. *Two!*'

'I could meet you up at the shack, tomorrow.'

A confused muttering from the darkness. Short laughs. Something scraped on the floor. A piece of wood fell in the sand next to Jerra.

'I've 'eard yers talkin' about me in me dreams . . . *send* n' *fetch him* . . . an' *fetch* . . . can't drag me down there to burn. Arr, yer bastards!'

Climbing the rocks, Jerra could hear the hollering, a flat echo off the rocks.

The VW hawked, then started with the old clatter, and the exhaust blew dust and scales from the grass behind. Sean slopped some water on the windscreen and got in, slamming the door. It fell open again. He cursed, slammed it again.

Jerra turned in the clearing. He gazed a moment at the windblown beach and the cairn of blackened stones.

Rain had hardened the sand. It was darker and packed in the ruts.

'Anti-bloody-climax,' murmured Sean, against the window.

'Veedub's mine. We all have our moments of power.' He slid into the bends, frightening birds into the air, and the shack came into view. Jerra pulled over.

'The last farewell,' Sean sneered, glancing at Jerra's grazed elbow.

Jerra went over to the hut and hit the wall. He thought the old man might have come up to say goodbye.

'You there?' Bubbling of the VW. 'It's me.'

'Might've slipped to the other side. You know, psychically.'

'Pass some paper.' Holding the paper against the window. 'Ah. Hadn't thought—'

'Hmm?'

'His name. Can hardly write anything if I don't know his name.'

'Jekyll?'

'For shit's sake!'

'Seen it all before. Movie, perhaps.'

'Bugger it,' said Jerra, climbing in and slamming the door. He yanked the handbrake. 'Let's just go; that'll be enough.'

He gave it a little. And missed second with a crunch.

PART TWO

what you'd want most

Sudden cold days of autumn. Jerra felt the dull hardness of the bedroom walls as he overlooked the prim tablecloth of the garden next door, its zig-zagged edges, hem-stitched borders with bougainvillaea and little drooping mauve things that clung tight; seeing the same things that had excited him in those early years when it was like living in a tree-house looming above the silky oaks, being higher, even, than the jacaranda clouds that were now an old, hard purple, and thick enough, it seemed, to walk on. The two storey house in Nedlands had been an abrupt change, he remembered dimly, from the weatherboard place at North Beach. Night times, when he couldn't sleep, Jerra would lie listening to the tide coming in at Cottesloe; it was six miles away, his father said, but he could hear it, anyway. Now all he heard was the traffic on Stirling Highway and the long breath of the downstairs air conditioner.

Sunlight was a neat square on the shag. There were books and photographs on the shelves, dents in the wall from bats and balls, and, above his pillow, a small footprint that wouldn't come off.

Under the silky oak the downy leaves were the same, crackling beneath his feet, wet in the coarse chill of the mornings. Early, the man next door tortured the mower into life and chased it around until lunchtime, shouting when the soft cores of dog turds bit into his shins.

*

Jerra was watering the nature strip, which didn't need it.

'Son.' His father nodded, hands in the pockets of his loose grey trousers.

''Lo, Dad.' The water was numbing his fingers.

His father sniffed, staring at the kangaroo-paw.

'Been thinking much?'

'About what?'

'What you're gonna do with yourself. Long time since you had work.'

'Yeah, I know.'

'Thought you might've stuck at the boats longer. I thought you liked fish.'

'I do.'

'Better still, you liked catching the buggers. Not often you'd be disappointed on the boats. Caught a pile. Or you said so in your letters.'

'It's not the same.' He was spraying the pickets of the fence, long lashes on the rough boards, for the sake of the kangaroo-paw. 'It's the skill. Learnt that, if nothin' else. Like you used to say, the touches on the line, or like divin' for 'em on their own terms, not hauling them in by the ton with a winch. That's like . . . mining, or something.'

He heard the quiet breathing over the spray of the hose. A dog cleared its throat.

'Yeah. Not the same. But you can't expect—'

'Sure, nothing's all roses. But it's just not right. Nothing seems to be right.'

'When I was your age—'

'Dad—'

'Orright, just listen. Younger than you, I was, and your grandmother came home one day, pulled me in by the ear, and said—'

' "Yer an apprentice boiler maker", I know.'

'And that was it.'

'Easy.'

'No choice.'

'And no big decision.'

'It's never just one decision. But I went.'

'But time—'

'Seven years.'

'Then what?'

'I shot through.'

'Convincing me of the wrong side, Dad.'

'But you got a choice.'

Jerra stamped his feet.

'I ended up doin' a million things.'

'Ever happy?'

'Sometimes. There's always something else.'

'Then, there was. This is now. It's different.'

'Maybe.'

'Be easier if I had something to inherit.' Jerra grinned. 'Then I could just take over when you went dribbly.'

'Sean?'

'Yeah. No problems, eh?'

'No choice, either.'

'Choice is nothin' when there's zero to choose from. A shop with one product. That's choice?'

His father kicked the grass.

'Take it away, and that's what you'd want most.'

'Well, what made you settle down?'

'Dunno,' said his father. 'Got tired, I s'pose.'

'Not satisfaction?'

'Maybe that's one o' the things you stop worryin' about.'

'Where does that leave *me*, then?'

'Maybe you'll find something. I thought you might finish Uni, like young Sean, and get qualifications.'

'And end up like him? A degree to be a clerk for his old man. In a shirt business? Working out the pay and the collar measurements. What a life?'

'He could've got a job elsewhere.'

'Dad, BAs aren't worth a piss in the river these days.'

His father turned off the hose. It went limp and Jerra threw it down. The pickets shone.

'I don't care what you do, as long as you find something you can be satisfied with.'

'Take me till I die.'

'I thought that once.'

Jerra looked at the greying man, the loose skin around his neck, the pitted palms he remembered gloved in pollard.

'Not the same,' he said, certain.

'I'm not so sure.'

City streets were cold in the mornings where Jerra wandered, squinting into shopfronts, sitting with the hung-over drunks and the picking birds in Forrest Place, walking mornings without recall, looking dully into the brown froth of the river, over the shoulders of bent old men who fumbled with empty hooks, muttering. They spat on the water, the gobs floating out in the viscous current, like jellyfish. He might have spoken to them, but they just looked over their shoulders, as if to accuse him of scaring the fish away. He could have told them that there were none left, only their jellyfish. They muttered, and cracked their knuckles.

Jerra met eyes he knew, letting them blink by, clacking up the footpaths amidst the stink of rotting flowers, fluorescent windows of scaled, headless fish, the chatter of money in tills, on bars, in pockets, gutters.

Faces in the street had that grin. That tight sucking back of the lips. He was grinning, aching. His father was grinning, hand tight on the throttle. And the turrum was dying. In murmurs. But he had worked hard for it. He ached. Wasn't that enough?

He caught the grass-green bus home. Next door, the man was scraping up the turds with a shovel. A disgrace, it was, and he didn't even own a dog! Jerra grinned, ran his hand along the sucked-in cheek of the dented VW, and went inside, his clothes reeking of cashews from Coles, the newsprint and cement.

'Books,' his mother murmured, smoothing the wrinkles of his bed. 'Always used to have your beak in a book. Ever since I can remember. *Robinson Crusoe*, *The Swiss Family Robinson*, that little skinny book you read at school . . . here, *The Old Man and the Sea*. A writer, you said, that's what, Mum. And you'n Auntie Jewel would sit out there in the afternoons, planning your career. Scribbling those little poems. Didn't know who was worse, you or Jewel. Those funny little love things she used to write. She was a dear.'

> *Petals fall like scales on to my hand . . .*

Jerra half smiled, feeling the wall.

'You used to read everything, once. News, pamphlets, magazines. Even the *Digest*.'

'Yes.' He smiled truly. 'Even the *Digest*.'

'Why is it you don't read any more, Jem? The hardbacks, all the old writers. What about Laurie . . . Laurie, no Lowry, the drunken bum.' She found *Lunar Caustic* on his shelf and worried it out. 'That's him.'

'Dunno, Mum.' Jerra didn't look. The books turned him cold. 'It just wasn't real. You kid yerself, sometimes.'

'You used to say it was more real than anything.' She shrugged, pulling at her cardigan. She gazed at the curling photos, dusty on the wall, and pointed. 'Where was that again, love?'

'Near Esperance. I forget.'

'Lovely.'

'Yeah. It was.'

'Who took the picture?'

'Sean. Sean did. He had the camera.'

He glanced out on to the street.

'Haven't seen our Sean for a while.'

Sprinklers rattled.

'Have you seen him since the trip?'

'No,' he lied.

Coming back from the river, he had gone into a bar. Lunch time, and it was crowded with smoke and the smells of powdered bodies swirling in the crush. Office girls laughed. A race-caller jabbered. He bought a beer and found a red table with vinyl seats. As he nudged the bitter foam, Sean came in, hesitated, then recovered and sat down.

'G'day, mate,' he said cheerily.

'Hullo, Sean.'

'How's things?' He flicked back his tie. The name tag looked impressive and a bit pathetic.

'Orright.' Jerra pushed a soggy coaster.

'Got a job, yet?'

'Nah.' He smiled. 'How's the shirts?'

'Well as can be expected, I s'pose. Which reminds me, I'm due back.' He stood, leaving a handmark on the hot red of the Laminex. 'Listen, I'll drop by soon and we'll go out somewhere on a weekend, orright?'

'Yeah, sure,' Jerra said into his beer.

Then only the smoke and the races. And the beer was awful.

'. . . can always remember it. Auntie Jewel would never have forgiven me for sending him there. Such a rough mob at that school.'

'Eh?'

'Auntie Jewel.'

'Talk about being sent.'

'Well, Sean's dad thought it was for the best.'

'His best. Runs in the blood.'

Through sand.

'Everything's all right between you and Sean, isn't it, Jem? Nothing happened while you were away?'

'Nothing.'

'Hmm?'

'Ah, it's OK, I suppose. We just . . .'

'What?' She picked a piece of fluff from his jumper.

'Oh, I dunno. It's not the same, any more.'

'Oh, Jerra, what happened?'

'*Nothing*. Hard to explain.'

She ran a palm along the shelves.

'All those years. Since you were babies.'

'Yeah, I know.'

She sucked her top lip.

'Wasn't it a good trip? You did come home early.'

'Oh, it gets to the point where it's a big of a drag. Seems you spend all your time sitting round keepin' the fire going.'

'I'd better get tea on.'

He lay back on the bed.

'Don't think it's all me. You don't know him any more, Mum. I don't either.' Or maybe I do, he thought. Only too well.

'Jerra.'

'All those years, his old man prancing around, droppin' her in hospital every time they slipped up. Having *him* here, like an adopted son, or something. Sean doesn't give a turd. You raised somebody who doesn't wanna remember. We're dirt!'

'I'm going downstairs for the tea.'

'Downstairs! I wish you'd sell this place, if it was ever bought. We don't belong here.'

'You speak for yourself. Your father and I do.'

"Cause you were weak? Or was it more complicated than that? It stinks. Maybe we are a bit dirty? It makes yer feel grubby.'

'What rubbish you talk!' His mother blinked. 'All this lying around has softened your head. Come down and peel the potatoes.'

'There's things you haven't told me, isn't there?'

'Jerra, of course not!'

'Is it about this house?'

'Don't even know what you're talking about.'

'No, neither do I.'

'That's not a bad poem,' he said.

'A bit soppy?'

'Only a bit. The sand bit's good.'

He mouthed the words, and she stretched in the sun.

'The sand bit, yes,' Auntie Jewel whispered.

The day he came home from the beach, after the police and the ferrety reporters.

'Sean, she's dead.'

'Yeah.' Sean closed the door of his bedroom in Jerra's face.

Falling against the wall, sick with it, Jerra cried out.

'You called for your mother.'

'Get fucked, Jerra. Just get fucked.'

'You're a bastard! Sean! You don't bloody care!'

Laughing. Behind the door. Jerra wanted to see his face.

'So she's dead.'

My love seeps like water through sand . . .

Buried alive.

Papers and cans rolled along the tacky bitumen. Seagulls scrabbled over a pizza, picking at the vomity stuff, pulling it out of each other's beaks. Goatee-ed surfers were sitting on the bonnets of their vans. Boards piled up on racks, bright, glossy. A paunchy man with a metal detector combed the sand, stooping, straining it through his fingers.

There was a hole punched in the bin next to Jerra. Around the rusty puncture was scratched:

$a_r s e^h O l_e$

Salt crusted the cyclone wire of the fences. People were leaning, talking, brushing the bleached hair from their eyes.

'I s'pose they told you about last night,' said the old lady on the bench next to him. She was chewing, chewing. There was nothing in her mouth, not even her teeth. She chewed a bit more.

'No.' Jerra put his feet up on the fence in front. He watched the swell breaking through the diamond pattern of the wire.

'Young people. Don't know what to do with themselves.'

He knew she was including him. He had the hair.

'Yeah.'

'That young boy. In the telephone box.'

'What did he do?' He felt he had to ask.

'Went crazy. Kept sayin' things. That they'd done to him. That no one would help him. Kept yellin' out, "Listen, – listenlistenlisten—"'

'Then what?'

'Blew his own head off. In the telephone box, over there.'

75

'God—'

'If someone don't put 'em away, they do it themselves.' She chewed.

Jerra kicked the bin. It toppled over, spilling its slop. The birds came.

Graffiti. Etched into the red paint. A few people watched from the pinball joint. Jerra opened the door. The clockface of the dial, the chipped receiver, dangling like a tendon. DIAL THE WORLD DIRECT with cigarette-burn punctuation. There were different graffiti on the glass and the ceiling. A chip of sky showed.

Jerra walked past the shopfronts, aching. On a picket fence, somebody had sprayed:

LIFE IS A SHIT SANDWICH
the more bread you get
THE EASIER IT IS TO TAKE

And he wondered if the bloke had seen it. Maybe he'd written it. Sean would've had something smart to say, poor bugger that he was.

Silence nicked and sliced by the sound of cutlery. Dessert on the table before anyone spoke. Jelly shivered as elbows shifted.

'Over at the Home today,' said his father, smacking the flat red of jelly with the back of his spoon.

'Hmm?'

'I said, I was over at the Home today.'

'Yeah?'

His mother glared, flushing.

'Granpa doesn't look too good.'

'And I should go over and say the last goodbyes, eh?'

'Wouldn't hurt you.'

'Come on, Dad. How many times now? He pretends he's

scaling the last wall every time he wants to be the centre of interest. Ol' wombat.'

His mother clapped the plates together, scraped the fat from cold chops, and threw scraps on to a sheet of newspaper.

'No way to speak about your grandfather.'

'Arr—'

'No one goes over to see him much any more,' said his father, pressing an imprint into the jelly.

'He drove them away.'

Newsprint was crumpled into a flat parcel. Dark stains appeared. It went into the kitchen tidy.

'Oh, Jerra,' said his mother, 'you just don't make sense any more. Your grandfather, now. Never complained when *you* were the favourite grandson. All the stories. About the war. Helped you write your poems.'

'Yeah, Mum.'

'Hardly spoken to him for years.'

'Since Gran died.'

'What's that got to do with it?'

A chair shuddered. His father left the table.

'I'll be going over tomorrow with your mother,' he said as he went upstairs.

'Now look what you've done.'

'I didn't do anything.'

'Story of your life, my boy,' she muttered, squeezing detergent.

'And others',' he said.

'Who do you love?'

'Nobody.'

Granma sipped.

'Course you do.'

'Boys don't.'

'Granpa did.'

'That was the olden days.'

'You love me, your ol' Granma?'

'Yes.'

'See? You're fibbing.'

Jerra squirmed at having it drawn out of him.

'What about Mum?'

'When she's not sad.'

'Dad?'

'When we go fishing. He's grumpy sometimes.'

'Who else?'

'No one.'

'Sure?'

'Auntie Jewel.'

'Oh?'

'Her pomes.'

'What about Grandad's?'

'Just blokes, blokes, blokes. They talk stupid an' never do anythink. *Got the pip wiv yearnin'*—'

Granma placed her cup roundly on the saucer. Dragonflies hovered over the hydrangeas.

His father's head beat slow time on the steering-wheel. Sunlight lulled Jerra almost back to sleep.

They caught their reflections in the glass doors, and inside smelled of things Jerra remembered: postponement, the brittle smell of rotten wood, the smell of blackened lemons. Doors were open and thin heads protruded from stiff sheets, noses and cheeks twitching.

46-B. The B was coming off. Sunk in the bed, the hairless old man watched them come. His eyelashes were gone and the eyes were those of a reptile or a bird. His father's would be the same. Hands, the colour of ash, clawed the sheets.

Jerra followed in and leant on the bedside cabinet. It creaked.

'Hullo, Dad,' said his father. 'How's things?'

The mouth contracted.

'Hullo, Grandad,' said Jerra, trying to keep the lips from his own teeth.

It was cold in the little room. On the cabinet stood a cactus in a Vegemite jar. He squeezed, carefully, the firm flesh. He glanced at his mother, who smiled, lips dry and pale. A stocking was slipping, he could see. She smiled again.

'How's *he* been?' the old man rattled.

'Jerra?' his father asked. 'Oh, he's fine, aren't you, Jez?'

'Yeah.'

'Job . . .'

'What was that, Dad?' asked his mother.

'A job. Has he—?'

'He's workin' on it,' said his father, looking sideways.

'Get him something to do, Tom.'

Thin membranes fluttered.

'I can't do it for 'im, Dad. Boy's gotta find something for himself. He's had work. Fishing. I told you about that. Might even go back one day, eh son?'

'Don't let 'im sit around. Doesn't do us any good.' The old man tightened his grip on the sheets. 'You gotta do something, Jerra.'

Jerra nodded, managing not to look away.

'Jump in.'

His mother clasped the knuckles on the sheet.

'He's doing his best, Dad,' she whispered.

'Jobs are hard to get,' said his father. 'I don't want him settlin' for anything. Like me.'

She glanced.

'I never did much,' said the old man. 'You get old 'fore you get around to doing anything.'

Jerra almost smiled, leaning on the cabinet, but the cactus caught him.

'Didn't do anything *wrong*. Not a bad man . . . sometimes

79

you almost think you can see . . . the light on the surface . . . too far away . . . Oh, why do they give me the pills?'

Tears. A nurse came.

'Come on, Mr Nilsam. Cheer up, shall we?' She folded him neatly into the pillows. 'I think it's time for your medication. And a rest, eh? A nice rest?'

She was still at it as they went up the corridor.

the cut

The funeral, a few weeks later, was the third Jerra had been to; it was almost as hurried as Jewel's, though there was no embarrassment, only resignation and dull skies. His father was tired. Jerra noticed his patient handling of the relatives, the jolly handshakes, the meaningful sorrow-filled glances. At the cemetery Jerra's mind strayed from the burnished RSL badges and Glo-mesh handbags to Jewel's funeral where he had stepped in time with the other men, the coffin not quite resting on his shoulder, his arms aching to keep his corner up, and he saw in front of him the reddening neck of his father, red, he thought then, because his father was older than the others and was feeling the strain, but it was the same unmentioned colour that had come into his face the first day in the big house in Nedlands, and the day, a week later, that Sean moved in. Jerra often saw his father with that complexion in his younger days, standing at the window overlooking the jacarandas, hands fisted in his pockets. No, he thought, watching the serpentine movement of the Glo-mesh skin in front of him, Dad wasn't angry then, but something stuck in his guts. He knows a few things, my poor old man.

The will was read two days later.

After the relatives had left, and the lamingtons gone, Jerra's mother came up to his room with an old wooden box. Her face was dark, cut deep under the eyes. She was out of breath from the climb. Freckles of dust had settled on her forearm; her hair was limp and dull.

'There are these,' she said. 'You were to get them all, but most of them are lost.'

'What are they?' Jerra got up.

She set the gritty box down on the bed, took out the tiny, dark key and laid it on top.

'His diaries. Your father might like to look at them, later, too.'

'Finally got it sorted out, eh?'

'Hmm. Vultures, they are. Never see them otherwise, still, there wasn't much to argue over. That upset them.'

'Anybody have anything to bitch about?'

'No more than usual. Mabel had a migraine, Jean was disappointed.'

'No more than usual.'

'Uncle Jim was there. Brought a gigantic wreath for the family.

'The Power, eh? Where'd he fly in from?'

'Don't know. Nice of him, anyhow.'

'Oh, a nice man, is ol' Jimbo. He's not even family; what was he doing involved with that?'

'Bit hard, aren't you? He's done us well. He was probably just there to see we all got a fair deal. His solicitors are the executors.'

'He's a snake.' Like his wriggling son, Sean. No, he thought. He's a fox – with rabies. They both are.

She blew the tiny balls of dust from the hairs on her arm.

'Better get on with me work.' She opened the door. 'And be nice to your dad, Jem. It's all been a bit hard on him.'

He opened the box. Inside, smelling of age and storage, were three parcels in dark, frayed envelopes. He opened them all, carefully fingering the paper. Two were bound ledger books, like thick, hard exercise books, and the third was a small note-pad, gritty and soiled.

He glanced at the florid figures, the brownish ink. One of the larger books, ending in 1949, had been torn in half. He was revolted by the smell of the paper. He put them back in their envelopes, and the envelopes in the box.

Jerra met his father on the way down to the toilet. They nodded, his father haggard from the shift.

'Comin' down to the shack? My holidays start next week.'

'Orright. Yeah, that'd be good.'

'Have to take your chariot. Your mother's going to Mabel's.'

'Sure. Needs the run.'

'Don't leave the packing to the last minute.'

'I'll start now.'

Rain roared like a breaking wave, hammering on the tin. Jerra crossed the lino, his feet bare. He packed the bait into the freezer. A strange smell, whitebait and newsprint. He pulled the greatcoat tighter around.

His father came in, shivering.

'Have to bail the bloody boat out before we put it in the water.'

'Heavy, orright.'

A backwash of thunder. Rain spraying.

The tilly flickered on the table. Rain was still pummelling the darkness. Jerra watched his father twist and knot, holding swivels in his teeth, looping, splicing.

'Why back and over?'

'When the fish hits here, see, it flips the hook this way. Always a chance of weakening.'

83

Jerra held out the garlands of hooks, gangs of barbs glinting in the lamplight.

'Vicious-looking—'

'Vicious eaters.' He showed the marks on his fingers. 'Tailor. Slice up the fish bigger than 'emselves.'

'Funny how the vicious ones have better meat.'

'Eat better.'

Smooth skin of the river parted behind, an incision folding back to the banks. The engine chuckled just how he remembered it from his boyhood. The river coiled out to the estuary channel. The estuary was a broad tear-drop, meeting the ocean at its narrowest point.

Jerra sat in the bow, trailing a hand over the smooth flesh of water. Old pickets stood out on either side of the channel. Across the estuary, at the deep cut to the ocean, Jerra stood and rattled the chain over. Rope burred on the gunwale, vanishing in the green. It found bottom, slackened, and floated taut in the tide.

'Here,' his father said, 'I'll lash it.'

'I—'

'Here.' The old hands, shiny with their hardness, twisted the rope into a good knot.

From the estuary channel another motor.

'That bloke with the pelican still lives here, eh,' said Jerra, glancing up.

The hooked neck of the pelican showed plain against the grey smudge of boat and water.

Tailor scudded near the surface. His father brought one over the side. It whipped in the bottom of the boat. A moment later he had another.

'Wassamatter? Forget to bait up?'

'Do you yet.' Jerra grinned.

'Wup!'

The surface broke and his father was dragging. A whiting rippled out of the water, gills fluttering.

The bird croaked. It shoved up from the clinker-built dory, pushing it askew as it lifted, circled high, then came low over the water, following its own shadow. Between the shoulders of the breakwater, it skimmed out towards the sea. The fisherman passed them in the cut, rolling in the swell as he went into open water. His hat was over his eyes, and he stood straight in the stern, clasping the tiller.

Whitebait skipped together. It was like a handful of gravel-stones hitting the water. Jerra nudged the whiting with a toe. The pale yellow pectorals fluttered.

'Nice-looking fish.'

'Yeah,' said his father, bent over the gunwale, rubbing the skin under his throat.

'Wish Mum would come, sometimes.'

'She's got other things.'

'Not any more. I'm not a baby any more, and Sean's pissed off to his poncy townhouse in South Perth.'

'Yeah.' His father bent over, a hook-shape, looking into the water.

The lead sky could support itself no longer. Rain broke the water like a million whitebait. Jerra and his father pulled their greatcoats tight, lifting collars.

'Should try for a kinghie on the tide,' his father said.

'No need.'

'Good on the clean tide.'

'Oh, these littluns'll do.' Jerra looked into the grey-green. The thought of a kinghie excited him. But frightened as well. What if he proved himself deluded?

As they were paring out the guts, dropping it over the side, scaling and washing the herring and tailor and whiting in the stinging cold water, the fisherman came back through the cut, lolling in the swell, with the pelican perched in the bow on the nets, fish grummeling down its throat. His father nodded. The fisherman may have nodded back; it was hard to tell with his hat so big and low.

'Saves on an echo-sounder,' said Jerra.

Fillets lay flat on the table. His father was trimming pieces, nipping off tails. Rain fell still. A tiny crab clattered across the lino.

'Moving around in the rain,' said Jerra.

'Little buggers.'

'Still no wind.'

'Good tomorrow.'

'If we catch the tide.'

'What about some fish?'

Jerra steered out to the estuary channel and his father took over.

'Lots of shallow banks,' he said. 'Can't be too careful.'

The channel was too murky to tell. Jerra moved up to the bow, a little peeved. Birds milled on the flats, strutting the thin strips of beach, lifting their wings.

'What about trying towards the flats?'

'The cut will be better.'

'Might be crabs at the flats.'

They headed for the cut.

In the first hour, Jerra took two big tailor on the flick-rod. Then nothing. Water surged thickly in the cut; the granite boulders of the breakwater were dull in the brief moments of sun.

'Jim owns the house in Perth, doesn't he, Dad?' It seemed a logical enough conclusion: the sudden move from the North Beach house in Jerra's last year of primary school. Mail for Jim. Jim at the funeral. All the uncomfortable talk. Sean's mocking glances.

'A favour. We did him one when Sean needed a home.'
Jerra couldn't say anything more.
Another motor. It was raining. They couldn't see.

His father slept on the bunk. As he slept, Jerra brought out the
box. He laid the diaries on the table.

August 3rd, '36
Warmer today. Job shaping up well. Ellen helping
organize the deliveries. She has a good head for figures.
Apples are up. Mr Chambers says they'll fluctuate.
He's probably right. Young Jeannie is well. Five in
October. Alf and Horrie got seven dozen tailor in the
river last night. Brought some over.
    6 Eggs.

The handwriting improved and deteriorated with each
entry. Days were often missed. It resumed, usually in poor
writing, and got better with successive entries.

May 6th '37
Ellen no better. Big confusion over the money. I don't
know where it goes to. They'll have me out by the end
of the week. Mabel is staying home from school to
look after Ellen. She worries that Ellen will not get
well. The Rugby is playing up.
    4 Eggs.

May 12th '37
Have been helping old Henderson with the hens since
the weekend. It will do for a quid until I find something
else. Nothing interests me, but there is the kids. The
trams just get worse. Haven't seen them so erratic since
the bad times. Almost went for a job selling clocks in a

shop, yesterday. The sound would send me barmy.
Reminds me of the noise prawns make in the trough on
the way home. Took Ellen down to the river with the
kids last night. Thought it might take her mind off the
worry. Will have to sell the old Rugby, though I will
regret it.
    2 Eggs.

Great gaps of months appeared in the rest of the entries, the
last being in December 1939.

December 5th '39
Joined AIF today. Have asked for Catering Corps,
though I do not know whether or not I will get it.
Sounds like a good wicket. Could not find boots to fit
properly and had to settle for a size too big. Went to
church yesterday. Will go again at Christmas if we
don't travel.
    8 Eggs.

The rest of that diary was empty yellow pages. Jerra tossed
it aside and picked up the notebook. Pages were stained and
gritty with dust. Many pages were folded back and torn. There
was a brown stain on the cover. It could have been ink or boot
polish. Most of the erratic entries, starting from 1940, contained
troop movements, rumours, and descriptions of mates. Jerra
flicked through '41.

December 1st '42
Greece has given me a bad stomach. Cooking the mush
that we do makes it worse. Am writing this because
Ernie Morris had a spare pad, and there is nothing else
to do. Ernie says it's hard cooking when you don't
know salt from dust. I don't know if I care much.
There doesn't seem to be much hope for us.

A few old photos of men drinking in a café, pinned to the page, blurry shots of buildings and women.

April 15th, '42
Writing this from hospital (that's what they call the damn place). Was hit in the foot by shrapnel during the bombardment a few days ago. They say I might be shipped out. What luck! Still, it hurts a lot. I will see young Tommy for the first time. Ellen will be glad.

The last volume, though incomplete, was better preserved, neater. The little crab scuttled under the table.

October 5th, '46
The foot has been acting up, lately. Ellen up all last night, trying to help. Work at the markets is no good. Never thought I would see the day when I would hate the smell of fish.

Saw some kids near the Causeway, paddling in the water (yesterday). It reminded me, for some reason, of a kid I saw in Athens, before I copped my lot. I was sitting with a couple of mates at a café, drinking the vino. A little boy sat on the edge of a fountain. His legs were too short to reach the water, and I could see that he badly wanted to get them wet. He looked at a loss, for a while, then, quite suddenly, he jumped in feet first. I went over to see if he was all right, and there he was, neck deep in the pool. I offered to fish him out, but he smiled and shook his head. Strange, those foreign kids. I would have given anything to get my boots off, big clods that they were, and get my feet wet, too.

Funny, seeing the little Wog jumping in. I'd bet a fiver he took a gamble on how deep it was. Maybe it was deeper than he expected, it was a bit . . .

The spine of the book had worn, or, as it looked, had been torn in half, and with it went the rest of the sentence. Jerra slipped it back into its envelope and closed the box. Nothing of any interest there. A drink of water was what he needed. It was the dust.

For tea they ate some tailor and whiting fillets, fried in butter. Rain fell on the roof. His father looked across in the light of the Tilly-lamp.

'I've got another one,' he said.

'Another what?'

'Diary.'

'Oh?'

'One of the later ones. When he used to live here, after Gran. Best bit is — never forget it — "So-and-so-date: Tom married May. Met her family. Queer mob. 4 Eggs." '

'So this shack's all you've got?'

'And what's in the Nedlands house. We own a lot of the furniture and things.'

'Not much, is it?'

'Oh, I can do this up. For when we retire. No, it's not much.'

He brought a small cloth-bound book from a cupboard.

'He threw the others out,' he said, putting it on the table. 'Do the dishes, will yer? I'm knackered. Think I'll pat the mat.'

The writing was neat and compressed. Almost every day had an entry. Jerra read one of the last.

August 5th, 1968
Young Jeremy good. Tom and May left last night.
Fished for bream down near the Brewery. Caught two
apiece. Taught him a bit of C. J. Dennis. He can
remember the first verse. Will write his own if he gets
past the first verse. He's got a soul that boy. And he
thinks no one knows.

Jerra sat back in the chair. His chest. He must have swallowed a bone. He closed the book.

'Spring song,' he muttered. ' "A Spring Song":'

> *The world 'as got me snouted jist a treat;*
> *Crool Forchin's dirty left 'as smote me soul;*
> *An' all them joys o' life I 'eld so sweet*
> *Is up the pole.*
> *Fer, as the poit sez, me 'eart 'as got*
> *The pip wiv yearnin' fer – I dunno wot.*

Why doesn't anyone tell me anything, he asked himself. Why do they just let you go on and then give you a letter or something or write it down in a poem instead of telling you?

He went to bed, comfortable in the pretence that he didn't know.

'We're late for the sea tide,' said his father in the bow.

'Didn't hurt to sleep in.'

The boat cut the brownish river. The pickets in the channel were rotting stumps of teeth. In the cut, the water was still, the anchor rope slack as the boat turned on itself. Sun burnt through the film of cloud, lighting up the water. It hurt their eyes. Plip! Whitebait being chased, they both knew. Jerra clicked his tongue. His father nodded, not lifting his lids.

The bird croaked. The long boat slid over the shallow banks, the Hat punting with an oar, watching the bird's shadow on the water. It wafted around in a loose curve, without moving a feather, beak flat against the sky.

Jerra saw swirling spectrums of whale oil in the water, purple and yellow, even when the sun was sucked back into the clouds. He heard the slop of the net on the water.

The line tightened, singing, Jerra had a fish, struggling off at an angle, going deep. He swung it up out of the water and into the boat. It beat itself against the boards. Then another, and another. His father shifted. The Hat was poling the boat away from the net. Corks jostled on the surface.

'Must've seen something in those shallows,' said his father.

'Him or the bird?'

Jerra smiled. His father glanced across. Inside the perimeter of shimmying corks, the water was coming to the boil. A tail slapped the water. The Hat beat the water with an oar.

The bird-shadow flickered across. Jerra pulled in another tailor, the oar beating and slapping as he baited up. The pelican croaked playfully. He hoped it wouldn't scare the fish off. He saw it settle just outside the perimeter of the net. Fish boiled the water. The pelican was becoming excited.

It rained, heavy.

'Not going too good?' he smiled.

He looked up. It was hard to see. He saw feathers and the oar coming down on the water driving the fish into the net. Feathers ruffling, excited. Something tearing? Jerra couldn't make out the sound. Beak skyward; pink webs of feet. The bird was inside the net, churning about in the living mass. Churning. Then, the oar not hitting water. Blemishes appeared on the water outside the net from a volume of escaping fish. It was caught up in the net; a bumper catch fleeing. Shouts. Rain fell harder. Frightened croaks. Where? The rain was blinding. The bag-throat appeared again, quivering. For a moment he saw nothing again and looked away. He looked again to see the bird-rag on the surface and flagellant rain and the spreading feathers.

All around their boat, fish were jumping, flattening themselves on the water. Jerra pulled in another as the anchor chain cleared the water.

Out of the brown river the tide was oozing into the estuary towards the sea. Brown pickets. Jerra sat in the bow, wishing they had a bigger motor.

hooks

Town was gritty with the dry powder of leaves rasping along the footpaths. Windows offered, reflected, but he was reluctant to look. Horns and tinny music. From the railway bridge he watched the trains slither and jolt, their roofs dusty below. Often he wondered how far down they were. Since a child, he had wanted to drop something, a peppermint or a stone, on to the carriages as they passed. He wondered whether anyone had jumped. They had from other places. And made the papers.

Across the railway, he wandered through the sleazier streets, past dead neon, the tight restaurants, clubs, bars. A man opened the door of a wine bar, pinning it back with his broom. Bearded and weary, he nodded as Jerra passed, but got no response.

He completed the circle; crossed at the western bridge.

'Granpa's teachin' me C. J. Dennis.'

'Oh? Is he?'

'Yep.'

'Gone off love poems?'

'Oh, no,' he said, pulling at a sock. 'Love's orright.'

'Orright, eh?'

'That's how people get married.'

She smiled, long legs shining in the sun.

'Yes.'

'I'd marry you, Auntie Jewel. You're orright.'

'Don't worry, Jem, I'd take you up. You're the only man for me. You and your old man are OK. Your mum's got a good deal.'

'Yeah, she's orright, too.'

He went home.

In his room, he sat with his head against the marked wall. What a bunch of cripples, he thought. To resort to writing diaries and letters ... and bloody books; he looked up at hopeless, drunken Malcolm Lowry whose spine still protruded from the tightly packed shelf.

He sniffed his hands. They smelt of buses and handrails and dust, not fish; they didn't even smell of *him*.

He sighed and got on his knees beside the bed and pulled the bottom drawer from the desk. Feeling in the space behind it, he worried out a long manila envelope. He put it on his bed and was about to open it when he remembered the door and got up and locked it.

He shuffled through the letters, reading excerpts.

Dearest Jerra,

Thank you for your lovely visit. It must be quite a shock to you. You didn't show it, of course. You never have. It's nice to think of yourself as a tough little biscuit. Your poems are better. Quite sexy, some of them. I didn't know you were so advanced. I'm sorry about saying what I did. I'm not used to the smell of fish, that's all. I expect you'll be all hurt now and wear a screechingly clean collared shirt, have red-raw hands and shoes and all, next time you come. You'd better not! I'd feel awful. And I wouldn't recognize you, anyway!

Send me some more poems when school becomes a
torture.
> Much love,
> Jewel

A letter from Rome. There was a trip after the first
'breakdown'.

> ... will be home in May to see you all and show you
> what an immaculate conception is all about. Do you
> know whether businessmen are supposed to have more
> prostate trouble than other middle-aged men? Look it
> up in your Biol. for me, will you? There must be some
> excuse for it.
> People here are entertaining in this city. Really, my
> boy ...

Then, something from hospital marked August '76. Not the
mental hospital; a private hospital by the river.

> ... Your poems, my lovely man, are well meant, but
> lacking in truth. *I know* what it means to have my
> insides torn, and it's not like those words. Replace
> 'collapse' with 'mutilate'. ...

> ... *Means?* why the preoccupation? Irrelevant.
> Sounding like your father when young. Means are
> painful delays, ask my doctors. Ask the saints. Don't
> fuss so ... Let's not have ideals, let's surrender to the
> men of *Ends*. Hence the joke at business luncheons
> about getting your end up. *They* are ends in
> themselves. END HEADS. Eh? ...

After the quick move to Heathcote:

95

. . . Repetition is a good device. Good God, it's a real enough pattern! He would have been a crazy beautiful baby Latin. Sean, my loving son, would be mostly unmoved. He has decided that he is of illegitimate origin which explains your confusion. He has been convinced, of course. A beautiful foreign bastard brother shouldn't bother him, then. Curious the minds of boys that are men and men that are boys. Why are they never people, though?

Jerra read a few sentences from the months that haunted him. Was he mad then? Madder than her. He sighed and read.

. . . It's beautiful when it happens. O, of course. Of. Course. Do not be afraid, my Jeramiah. I think you always wanted . . . yes. This is indestructible! *We* are!

At the bottom of the page were two stanzas plagiarized from Sylvia Plath's 'Lady Lazarus' (he only discovered its true origin in a tutorial at Uni). It froze him still.

> *The second time I meant*
> *To last it out and not come back at all*
> *I rocked shut*
> *As a seashell.*
> *They had to call and call.*
> *And pick the worms off me like sticky pearls.*

And there was one thin envelope, puce, with cambric pigmented texture, that he would not open. It was postmarked February 1977, when Jerra was away on the boats, trying to forget and grow up and *do* and please and forget. It was something he neither needed now, nor wanted to refresh his memory with. He promised to let go. His problems and everyone else's. Maybe Sean was right.

'You gotta live,' he told himself lamely.

Jerry went out – back into town – wandering.

Smoke twisted on itself, rising and falling in the dimness. In one corner, near the open gutless Wurlitzer, a table was free. Jerra bought a burgundy and sat, glancing at the initials carved into the piano. A guitarist was hunching into a long, slow blues, his head above the clouds of smoke.

> *Lord it's a mean ol' world*
> *When you livin' o' ba yoursel';*
> *If ya caint get the one that you lovin',*
> *Then you gotta put up wi' somebuddy*
> *else.*

The wine was warm; he'd never drunk it before and it hardly wet his throat as it went down, each bitter swallow. The blues moaned to a tortured finish, and Jerra clapped, alone, self-consciously. The guitarist nodded, and mumbled about Walter Jacobs as he tuned, squinting at the ivory tuning keys.

A chair burped on the boards.

'Anyone sitting here?' She had long hair, a glass of port and a leather shoulder bag.

'No,' he mumbled. 'Siddown.'

Hair and bag swung down into the seat across the table; the sort of chair they pop out a hundred at a time, with that rugged, individual look. The slide whined on the strings. Elmore James.

Wennawekupinnermornin abelieveadus'mablooz!

Next to him, the freckled hand beat time on the pine table. Port jiggled, a rosy quiver in the shapely little glass. There was a fingerprint near the rim, quite clear. The guitarist stuttered, calling his baby back home. She smiled lightly, rolling a cigarette, and Jerra drained the bitterness from his glass as the guy believed his time weren't long and sent 'is babe a tel'gram.

And they both clapped at the finish, Jerra feeling less foolish. It was a good old song.

'This is a smooth little joint,' she said while the guitarist was tuning again.

He smiled, looking around at the beards and batik.

There were lines under her eyes, and dusty freckles on her forehead and cheeks that made it difficult to guess her age. She might have been older or younger than him. Older, he thought, noting the weariness and the way she held the glass with her thumb poking over the edge, like shearers he had seen in those cruddy little pubs out east.

Another blues. It swayed on itself, building and falling, chunka-chunka-whine-wizz, glass slicking up and down the fretboard.

'Muddy Waters,' she said into his ear, as if he didn't know. Still, he thought, it was nice. He smiled and nodded, lured under by the swirling rhythm. The wine was swilling around inside him as he stomped his foot. Again, they clapped, together and alone. There was a break. Jerra bought a port, holding the little eye-dropper glass awkwardly, and sat back, not minding the smoke so much. She smiled and sipped.

. . . Do you understand these letters? You show no sign
of understanding me, sometimes . . .

'Well,' she asked, pulling back a swirl of hair with short little fingers. 'What do you think of him?'

Jerra licked the edge of the glass. The port was warm and sweet; it reminded him of neat Ribena.

'He's not bad, actually. Plays better than he sings.'

'You want a smoke?' She had small hands.

'Don't smoke, thanks.'

'Good idea,' she said, as they all said, blowing a stream from the side of her mouth.

She talked about smoking and health in general; she was a vegetarian, concerned about the toxins in meat and the garbage people devour following the mindless instructions of television advertising. Jerra agreed, listening uncritically, curious about jasmine tea, Rajneesh and Poona, but paying more attention to the fine powder of freckles on her skin.

'Do veggies eat fish?' he asked.

'They do now.'

'You mean they didn't once?'

'But it's OK now.'

'It's in this year, then, is it?' he said, making an attempt at dry sophistication.

. . . I didn't know you were quite so advanced . . .

She hit him on the shoulder with the back of her hand. It wasn't an unpleasant sensation.

'What's so special about fish?' she asked, looking about.

'Dunno,' he admitted. 'I just can't imagine anyone not eating fish.'

'Some people don't like it, you know,' she said patronizingly.

'That's 'cause they can't be stuffed picking out the bones.' He laughed, self-conscious; it seemed a bit of a hopeless comment. 'No, I s'pose they don't like it, some people.'

'Really coming up with some gems, aren't we?' She cuffed him across the shoulder again, brushing against his old corduroy jacket. He felt like grabbing her hand and feeling the little fingers, freckled prawns, wriggling in his palm.

'You ever done any?' he asked suddenly.

'What?'

'Fishing.'

'Yes. As a girl. A few years ago, yes.' She laughed. 'Of course I couldn't guess that you do a bit yourself.'

'Yeah,' he said enthusiastically. 'Ever since I could sit up and hold a line.'

There was a pause during which Judy appeared restless. Jerra fidgeted.

'Did you like it?' he asked at length. 'When you went, I mean. Fishing.'

'Yes. Yeah. Sure.' She looked at him, mildly curious.

'Why?'

'Pardon?'

'Why did you like it? What was the best thing?'

'The best thing?' She plucked at her skirt which flowed in dark ripples to her ankles. She squinted, mouthing, and Jerra watched, almost annoyed by the way she took her time. 'Well, I always fished from a boat – a big one – with my father and brothers. Canal Rocks, Hamelin Bay, places like that, catching skippy and herring with handlines. All those tangles.'

'Skippy, yeah.' He would have liked to hold one shivering in his hand, now. Not in a boat.

'I think the best thing was when you pull them over the side into the bottom of the boat, and then take the hook out.'

'The hook?'

'I was taught to hold the fish against my leg. Like this, see? My old man was pretty good at it. When he was younger. Like this,' she said, pinning the small leather bag to the side of her thigh. 'Hold the fish with your right hand, and unthread the hook with your left.'

'Well?' He didn't know whether she was telling him how to do it, or if she was merely reciting something.

She held the bag flat against the gathered skirt.

'Power. The moment you take the hook out and hold that fish in your hand, you have a lot of power.'

Jerra smiled.

'At that moment, you decide the future of that fish, whether to put it in the bag, or throw it back. Life or death. Like . . . political masturbation.'

Jerra laughed, blowing all the air out, holding his legs, like when he'd taken an elbow in the guts playing back-pocket for the school. Then he was sorry. Sean used to say it, anyway. Some of their port had spilled with his rocking.

'Well, what's wrong with that?'

'Nothing. Really.'

'Well?' She could have been hurt. Or pretending, that little freckled forehead crinkling.

'Something wrong with that theory.'

She plopped the bag on the table, careful of the stain.

'The power bit, or the idea of masturbation?'

'The power bit, I think.' He had to smile. He watched her finish her port, tipping it in little sips with her fingers around the edge of the glass and her thumb up.

'Sorry about laughing.'

'OK. Not all that serious.'

'It was a bit off.'

She set the glass down carefully on the table.

'Well, you did ask me.'

'I did that, orright.'

'Anyway, I have to go,' she said, easing the bag on to her shoulder.

'Coming here tomorrow?'

'Don't know,' she murmured, sliding her glass around the table.

'We could talk some more. About fishing. And I could think some more about your theory.'

'Oh yeah.'

The freckles disappeared when she stood up. They were so small.

. . . Do not be afraid my Jeramiah

*

Jerra's hands were numb on the wheel as he pulled into the rutty dirt patch. He switched off, looking at the STAFF ONLY sign with the footprint in the middle. There were tears of dew on the frosty blisters of paint. The engine was cooling with that clicking that people made when they slept on their backs. He slammed the sucked-in door of the VW extra hard; it was getting a bit tough to close. A car started somewhere, a grinding whirr of starter motor, a brief fart, and silence. It started the second time, wheezing, the choke out six feet. Sixty feet, he thought.

He pulled his coat off as he went in through the back door that connected with Al's house. The dunny was between the shop and the back door, probably a security measure; he wondered if they had the septic on, or if they ever emptied it, though he never dared find out. A generation of thick turds packed into one confined space, behind that peeling door. Even the paintwork felt it. It was a relief to escape into the stench of sweets and cold meat pies.

Al met him at the Coke fridge, rubbing his hands on the apron that was stiff with filth. His hands were blue.

'Two mornings, an' not late, eh? I don' belief it.'

'Said I would be on time, didn't I?'

Al didn't look much like an Italian. It was the moustache, Jerra decided; he didn't have the moustache. And he was probably taller than five one. He could have been forty, he might have been fifty.

'Pies in the oven,' Al said at his blue hands.

Jerra separated the frozen pies and piled them on to the tray. Could have dropped one and broken a toe.

Then there were the sausage rolls, the pasties, and then the frozen red frankfurters he dropped like pink fingers into the big scummy pot. Rosa came in as he was piling up the mountains of potato chips in their loud orange packets.

''Ello, Jerra,' she said, finding something in her teeth as she crossed to the till. 'Big test today.' She laughed. 'Sat'dee makes yer or breaks yer.'

'Can't wait.'

Al was watching, cleaning his hairy ear with the rubber end of a pencil.

Rosa was fat, a distended, turgid hot-dog about to burst its red skin. Her hands often strayed over the open boxes, smelling of the hard sweetness of lollies. Jerra pretended not to notice.

At nine Al went out the back to read the paper on his stinking dunny. Jerra heard the noises that disgusted him.

Rosa began at him again. She thumped him on the shoulder, and he could feel her mouth stinging his cheek.

'Two years of Uni,' she said laughing, 'for this?'

'Yep.'

'Dad took me outta school when I was thirteen.'

'Why?'

'Said it would be better leaving to work for him, than go on with school and end up on the dole.'

'Hmph.'

'Maybe he was right, I dunno,' she said, sucking something red, round and sweet. Her dress seemed to belong to someone else. Like the bags they put the fruit in, fruit always soft and a bit bruised.

'Reckon I shoulda gone on, you know.'

'Yeah?' The pies were softening. He wondered if they really were roo meat. They stank like it.

'So many oppertunities.'

He felt the pastry warming, the juice melting out of the meat. They probably picked them up off the side of the road, he thought, smiling.

'No opportunities, really.'

'Oh, carm on,' she said, scratching. 'You don't appreciate what you could of had.'

'Arr.' If the customers only knew why they tasted of duco.

'No. You could of done somethink.'

'What?'

'I dunno. There must of been somethink. Yer mad if yer can't find somethink to do wuth yourself.'

'I have. I work here.' He unbolted the door. The bell clunked.

'Arr, yer mad. You must be stupid, or yer haven't looked.'

'How the hell would you know?' He slammed the Liquorice Allsorts on to the Laminex. 'Shit, Rosa, what would you know?'

Rosa fiddled pasties on to a tray, thick steam rising into her face. She lifted the damp hair out of her eyes. Her face was pink.

'You're weak as piss, Jerra.'

The bell clonged, a turd hitting the water. He braced behind the counter.

The deli was on a street corner. There were houses neatly spaced along the street, and in the next street there was a school. A street or two down, there was a factory that made doors. As lunch time neared, the mountains of potato chips crumbled, the milkshaker screamed without stopping for a breath, and aniseed balls scattered and clattered as more black-toothed children, smiling through their gaps, came and went on the lino that gripped their thongs, tacky with Coke.

Al scowled at all the customers, young or old, slamming their pies down on the counter in their brown bags, rattling the lollies into little white bags with careful underestimation, baring his teeth to the children humming and hahing over two for one, three for five, or how much can I get for two cents. Jerra knew it didn't matter a damn to Al, who gave them all the same and said he wished he was a dentist.

They worked under the tinny snaffle of the transistor that perched high on the back shelves. Jerra poured the thick shakes, watching the stuff unwind and settle like castor oil. He sorted ham and salad, sneezed wrapping curried egg, and slapped the beef and pickle together. He felt the coins, hot from the customers' hands, and cursed the twenty-dollar notes passed over, with Kingsford Smith smirking, for a Mars Bar or chips.

All day. All day. All day. Then wiping the Coke from the floor, and scraping the coagulated sauce from the counter.

He gave the old Veedub a kick, feeling the notes in his pocket, and spun her out of the dirt patch, hopping it off the kerb with a chirp.

'Why doesn't anyone tell him the truth?'

'It's between Sean and his dad,' said his mother, pegs between her teeth.

'Someone's gotta tell him!'

'He wouldn't listen, Jerra.'

'No, he wouldn't,' he admitted.

'He thinks his father's right. That's all he's got left.'

'And it's worse than nothing.'

She bit on the pegs, shaking her head.

'And he doesn't want to find out, Mum. Why doesn't anyone want to find out anything?'

'They get old,' she said, spreading a heavy, gently steaming sheet on the line, holding it with an elbow and pegging one end. 'And Sean's got old too soon.'

'No. It's giving up. No one gets old too soon.'

'I figured it out,' he said, putting two ciders on the table.

'What?' She seemed distracted.

She was wearing jeans and a quilted coat; the same stuff they made the old sleeping bags out of, he noted. Her boots were freckled with mud. A singer was howling about a big brass bed and the smoke poured on itself, boiling to the low ceiling. A different singer, all beard and eyes.

'Your theory.'

'Oh, that.'

'Yeah. I figured it was wrong because there was a . . . what do you call it? . . . a variable. The fish.'

105

'Eh?' She glanced at him over her glass.

'The fish. You said you had power over it; but it's not really true. Put him in the bag. Fine, he's dead; you scale him, gut him, eat him. But if you throw him back there's no guarantee he's going to live.'

She was still looking at him, an eyebrow up.

'You have been a busy boy.'

'The fish might survive the hook and the exposure and take off. Or he might be weakened and be easy prey for a bigger fish, or he might die in a couple of minutes, just from shock.'

'So, the fish decides its own fate?'

'Sort of. Maybe the fish's strength, or something else; but whether he lives or dies won't be decided by throwing him back.' There was nothing to him like that grunt of surrender, the gentle collapse from deep within, and the mate rolling off into the deep at the precise second. Nothing. Like knowing or believing in subtle defeat.

She smiled.

'So, what does it all mean?'

'Dunno.'

She was looking around, her lower lip uncurling, tongue pushing from behind.

'Geez, this is a weird joint.'

'Lost in the sixties.'

'Yeah, the sixties.'

'You'd hardly remember.'

'An' you admit remembering?'

'Oh, bits. And pieces.'

'Maybe I don't remember. Bit young.' He drank his cider. It was rotten stuff, really, sweet enough to make you sneeze. They drank it at school parties, hidden in their greatcoats, cold and hard against their chests. A bottle left them flat – stung, on the back lawns of mates whose parents were away. Chundering in the long grass, against the rickety pickets.

'Don't they sell beer?'

'Awful stuff.'

'This is worse.' Dugite phlegm.

They watched each other. She was making a lot of enjoying the cider. The bubbles in the glass were like raindrops falling up instead of down.

'He's playing bloody Bob Dylan, again,' Jerra said.

'Falling back on the party favourites.' She ran the edge of her hand along the grain of the pine. 'So, by putting the fish back, feeling you've done a good thing, you could be killing it, anyway.'

'Yeah.'

'Gets a bit hard to tell right from wrong.'

'I s'pose it hits you sooner or later.'

'I don't know your name.'

'What?'

'I don't even know your name.'

'Oh, Jerra. Jerra Nilsam.'

'Jerra?'

'Jerra.'

'What sort of name is that?'

'Dunno.'

'Sounds like wood.'

'Yeah, they reckon.'

'I'm Judy Thyme.'

She got up and bought drinks, jeans tight against her calves.

The music lapped around them, smoke and noise producing a closeness that half stifled, half excited him. He studied her face, her tiny freckles, the crack in her thumbnail, the way she moved him through an endless series of conversations, breaking them down, word by word, tracing back tiny links that became new topics themselves. He loved being guided, and went whichever way she did.

At closing, they picked their way through the fallen bodies

107

and tables, and on to the street, where the cold air fronted them, the gutters wet, and the take-away menus from next door plastered soggily to the footpath.

'You got a car?' he asked as he rubbed his hands together. It was colder than it had been for a long time. Parking meters gleamed.

She shook her head.

'Swanbourne. Too far?'

'No worries.' His toes were numb; he had only worn thongs. The cold air was making his nose run, and he sniffed quietly.

In the alley between the wine bar and the opp. shop there was a figure up against the wall, someone wheezing as if having just run a long stretch. He looked again and it was two bodies, one rasping the other against the damp wall, feet shifting as the gutters trickled, seeping.

. . . my Jeramiah.

The VW stood alone in a parking lot by the railway line. A train passed, slow and brightly lit, with no one inside. A procession of lighted carriages rocking through the city. Jerra wrenched the door open.

'How long have you had this?'

'A few years.'

'Given you trouble?'

'First country trip I ever took it on. Got as far as Williams and it passed out.'

'What was wrong?'

'Country air, I s'pose. Hay fever or something. Funny ol' bus.'

The upholstery was cold and the beaded windscreen misty with breath. The roads in town were glistening, lit red and orange in neon flickers, and it was hard for him to keep his mind on the blinking reds of the road and talk as well. The river was black, awash with the lights of the freeway and the Brewery.

Passing the Uni with its stopped-clock tower lit against the black of night, he felt a hand on his leg. It could have been on his knee, but it was difficult to pinpoint. He didn't look, and it was harder to drive. She was closer and the cab had warmed. He didn't feel much like talking. He watched the slick, glistening road, listening to the muted roar of the engine.

He pulled into the driveway she pointed out, leaving the motor running.

'Thanks for the lift,' she said without letting go his leg. 'Coffee?' Her face was green in the light of the speedometer that never worked.

'I'd better be off.'

'I can make it with whisky.'

'Some other time, eh?'

'Yeah, fine.'

He leant over and kissed her clumsily on her mouth or ear, he couldn't tell, her hair in his face.

'Ring you?' His lips were cold, and hard to get around his teeth.

'No phone. I'll ring you.'

He mumbled the number and she climbed down. He shoved it into reverse and the van shook a little as the headlights lit her. She went up to the front door, lit sharp in the shadows. She waved.

The sheets took a while to warm, and the pillow stung his ear.

A lot further down this time. Deeper than he had antici-pated. Strands of weed brushed his cheek in the dark, and as he felt his way down the rock bit cold on his hand. There was nothing. He went in darker and found something soft. It trembled, the skin almost tightening. He rolled it over, the legs fanning wide, and saw the open slit reflecting green on the backs of his hands. Scars of old slashes gathered, pale on the flaccid pulp. Navel a stab-hole. In a dowdy gown, she was arching

109

pathetically, spreading her speckled hair, clutching, and he was saying Baaaaaaastaaaaarrrrrds! inside; and she wanted him to say something nice because nobody did any more. But she wasn't her. Just a bald slit and light showing through. They hadn't made her different, or even someone else; just nothing. And he was smiling, hand beneath the open neck that was once curved like a beach, kissing. It giggled, then groaned like dying, but she was dead already, before the butchery, and he wished he was now. He hated himself because she wasn't properly aware, because she couldn't tell half the time, and he was no different from the others taking advantage, helping to destroy, helping her in the delusion.

NO

Each morning, Al's dunny was worse. Jerra could smell it easily from the dirt of the parking lot, as if each turd was calling out for a septic tank, dying from claustrophobia. He had never been in there. A whole day's wait was nothing to what must lie behind that fly-caked door.

'There he is,' called Al, almost friendly. 'The early boy. Ready to work hard, eh?'

'Dying for it,' he replied, watching Rosa opening a new canister of ice-cream. The shop was warm from the ovens, but never warm enough to take the blue out of your hands.

Jerra stacked the fridge with Coke, and clacked together blocks of pies. His hands wouldn't warm, even when slushing hot water over the floors. Rosa was silent. You have to feel a bit sorry for her, hiding those chockie drops in her puffy palms like that, he thought to himself.

Having his lunch break once, Al sat next to him smoking a putrid Italian cigarette, leaving Rosa with the after-lunch mob.

'Rosa tell me you been to the Uni.'

'Couple of years.'

'Why quit? Not smart enough, eh?'

It was on again.

'Didn't seem worth sticking at.'

Al sucked on his cigarette. The smoke knotted around the room.

111

'So you *were* smart enough. But not enough to stay. Leaving so smart?'

Jerra shifted on the boxes. KIT KAT stamped on the one under him.

'Thought it was the smartest thing to do.'

'Knockin' back the chance?'

'For what?'

'To *be* somebody.'

He felt the corrugations in the sides of the cardboard, ribs under his fingers.

'Nothing to do with it.'

'So you work 'ere, in a shop that I have to run to be somebody. Al the Ding. He runs the deli down the road. You waste time doing things like this.'

'Not a waste.'

'How would you know? You done nothink! Got brains – so you work in a lousy shop.'

Jerra bit. The gristly mince was going cold. He swallowed quickly, trying not to taste duco.

'*You* work in a lousy shop.'

Al grubbed his smoke out on the grey wall. Small rings crept around the bulb on the ceiling.

'I got no choice. There's nothink else.'

'Same. For both of us.'

Al stood and kicked the boxes, planting a hole in a red K.

'Rosa is right. You *are* stupid. You donna what choice is!'

Jerra took a breath. Al was gone. He finished the pie in the smoky little room.

Rods stuck out stiff from the granite of the mole. The sea outside the harbour was chopped by a sou'westerly. The sun was dropping quickly and, here and there, lamps began to glow. At dark there was no sound but the wind in the rocks and the slow click-click of the reels winding in. A launch passed, lit brightly.

Snatches of music stuttered in the wind. Jerra saw his mother's hands in the lamplight, the thick needles moving over the brown wool; she sat in the lee of a coarse boulder, out of the chill. Insects beat themselves on the hot glass. Next to him a reel clicked, the ratchet turning over slowly.

'Anything?'

'No,' said his father, hair ruffled by the wind, wisps of grey shining in the periphery of the light.

'See the paper today?' his mother asked.

'No.' He reeled in a little.

'More bad news.'

'Bloody Russians,' said his father, swinging the gang of hooks up onto the rock. 'There'll be war soon.'

'If the Yanks have their way,' said Jerra.

'Conscription, too, the way the Liberals are.'

'That'd be awful.'

'Could do some good. Absorb some of the unemployed, or something.'

'Send 'em off to the Middle East. Vietnam absorbed a few. Like a bloody Wettex.'

'Who needs a war?' his mother said. 'There's kids killing themselves these days. In a phone booth, last week or before.'

'It wasn't because he needed a bloody war to go to.'

His mother was silent. He could hear the needles clicking between gentle gusts. His father cast out, the mulie spinning out into the darkness. A small white splosh. Jerra reeled in, checked his bait, and cast out languidly, dropping just short of his father's splash.

'Bit more flick.'

'Don't worry, Dad, I'll get it one day.' He laughed, glancing over his shoulder. His mother was looking down at her hands. 'Who's it for?'

'You.'

'Oh?'

'Been knitting it ever since you got back from South.'

'Vee-neck?'

'Course. Learnt my lesson.'

'It itches my throat.'

'Father's the same. At least he'll wear his.'

Wham! Jerra's rod whipped down, almost into the water. He jerked back and took up the slack, but there was nothing.

'Strike?'

'Gone.'

'What was it?'

'Big an' fast, whatever it was.'

'Anything's too fast for you two.'

His father reeled in, chuckling. He turned into the lamplight to bait up. Jerra reeled in as his father cast out. Bait gone. He impaled a frozen mulie on the line of barbs.

'More flick, this time.'

'Yes, Dad.' He flicked the bail-arm over and drew the rod back. It bowed and snapped forward, line whistling. A white pock showed, quite a way further out than his father's.

'Better?'

'Not bad.'

'Clowns,' murmured his mother.

'Haah!'

Line unspooling with a whine, his father braked and dragged the big rod back.

'What is it?'

'Big.'

The rod arched, straining to reach the water. His father stepped back and took slack. Jerra could hear his little gasps.

'Get the gaff!'

Jerra went back to the rocks, still holding his rod, and grabbed the long gaff.

'Doubling back!' yelled his father, reeling. The rod straightened. As the fish turned again, it went back into the crook.

Jerra watched his father trying to straighten, hair in his eyes. His knees were bent and the baggy trousers were flapping.

'And again. Gaff.' He was puffing.

'Yeah.'

'Lost him again.' Straining.

Jerra reeled in, put his rod down, and stood ready with the gaff. Line hummed out again.

'Wassamatter?'

'Nothin', jus' . . .'

Reel screaming.

'Hold it!'

'I—'

Jerra dropped the gaff and grappled the rod away, almost losing it as his father let go and sagged back into his wife's arms. He dragged sideways to break the run, and reeled. The rod was alive, quaking. Jerra heard his mother behind. Water broke and there was a tail-slap. Then the fish ran at the rocks and he could hardly reel in fast enough. He gaffed it, one handed, up onto the dry rock.

'Bonito!'

The thin, whippy tail hit him in the shin.

'Give me a hand,' his mother said. 'Come on, Tom.'

'Hey, Dad, how's that?'

His father didn't look up.

'You OK?'

'Jerra—' his mother hissed.

'Bit of a turn's all.'

Jerra laughed.

'He did yer, orright, eh?'

She glared.

'Fifteen pound of 'im.'

'Nah.'

'Big *enough*.' Jerra laughed.

His father said nothing, grey faced, breathing short and shallow.

*

'How've you been?' Judy asked him.

'Orright.' He could never think of anything to say on the phone.

'The deli?'

'A ball. Make it a career.'

'Hmm.'

'And what've you been doing?'

'Nothing much.'

'Mm-hm.'

'Dinner?'

'Orright, sure.'

Bitten fragments of talk. He hung up, wondering. He shivered. Winter would be a long one this year.

It was so cold in the morning that Jerra wore gloves to drive to work. But he had to take them off at the shop. Hygiene, Al said. Jerra's fingers were bluer in a few minutes than they had ever been. They ached from working the ovens and fridges at the same time.

Al came in off the dyke, sullen.

'Move your arse today, boy. Friday they spend big.'

The morning ached slowly on. Near lunch time, the kids and the mothers with prams, and the overalled men from the factory began to straggle in, buying extra chips and cigs to last the weekend. The chips crackled, pies were slapped on the counter, bottle-tops jangled in the bin, and milkshakes were snorted up through straws by grimy children, arguing colour and length and three for one.

At the peak, the counter was writhing with heads and hands calling for a thousand different things and rattling change and lollies in bags. A big man from the factory shoved kids aside, forcing his way to the counter. A boy, short and dark, complained, glancing up at the man.

'Boofhead,' said the little face.

The man took him by the collar and flicked him under the ear. Spilling his coppers on the floor in a shower, the boy fled.

Laughing, the man scooped up a few coins, held them in his hand for the other children to see, and pocketed them. The children murmured. A lady walked out, muttering 'Bloody oaf' over and over. Rosa was busy at the other end of the counter. Jerra went over to the pie oven where Al tapped impatiently on the glass door.

'You see that? What a bastard. Shall I serve him?'

'Has he got money?'

Jerra looked away. If he didn't before, he has now, he thought.

'Yeah.'

'He's a customer.'

'You can't let a prick like that get away with it. What about the bloody kids!'

Al opened the oven door.

'Serve him.'

'An' you think I'm weak as piss,' he muttered, going back.

The big man was at the counter, leaning heavily on the Laminex in his greasy overalls, twiddling the straws in their chrome canister. Jerra avoided him, serving kids on either side. The factory worker tapped hard on the Laminex with a coin, that irritating, pecking sound.

'Arr, carm on. Serve some bloody customers!'

Jerra ignored him. Coaxing the little heads to speak and lingering over their orders, he fussed unnecessarily on their behalf. He was itching for something. From the corner of his eye he saw a blue arm reaching into the Coke fridge. Jerra knew now what he was itching for. He dropped his whole weight on the heavy lid, jamming the man's arm up to the elbow. He roared. Jerra saw the corned beef in his teeth and leant heavier on the lid.

'Getchafuckenandoff!'

'What's it doin' in the fridge?' he yelled back, smiling at the children who were more terrified than impressed.

The face brightened in its reds and whites as Jerra pressed harder, then the other hand, out of reach, smacked the straw canister to the floor, spraying straws and children in all directions. Then, despite Jerra's weight, the man dragged his arm out of the fridge, taking off a flap of skin, and threw a tall jar of penny-sticks on to the floor. It shattered, glass skittering on the linoleum. Jerra was no longer smiling.

'You little barsted!'

Rosa screamed. As he backed away, Jerra knew that Al was not there; he had an idea where he would be. He groped along the side bench for a weapon. Anything. As the big man straddled the counter, Jerra fumbled up a cold bottle of Coke, feeling the teeth of the bottle-top in his palm as he slammed it down onto the overalled shin. Another scream. Not Rosa. The man purpling. Blood from the arm. Jerra pounded him frantically on the buttocks as he continued dragging himself over. Very scared now, Jerra retreated behind the chocolate shelves where he caught a glimpse of Al, scuttling and locking.

Something shattered. Rosa screaming again.

'He's got a bottle!' she wailed.

As the bloody sleeve appeared, the teeth of glass held like a knife with many blades, Jerra moved back further, wanting to be sick and ready at the same time, backing into the dimness of a corner with a thirty-cent Coke chilling his palms. Overalls. He sprang out, rammed the bottle hard and high between the man's legs, and kicked wildly in the same place and others as the legs bent like paper straws. A hand went around his throat but opened as the man fell. Grunting and gargling, the body pumped on the linoleum, twitching, sucking in air.

'Rosa,' he called, very quiet, shaking.

'Is he dead? Where's Dad?'

Jerra kicked the broken bottle-neck from the writhing man's fingers. It slithered into a corner.

'Dad orright?' Rosa came.

'He's just locking the strongbox.' That bubbling noise sickened him.

Al appeared.

'Got a smart-arse, eh?'

'Oh, shit, Al.'

'Whatcher make trouble for?'

'Oh, come on!'

Al went back behind the shelves. Jerra leant against the counter, staring around the empty shop, keeping an eye on the stricken factory man. Al came back with the strongbox, unlocking it again.

'See you were lookin' after things,' Jerra sneered.

'Rosa was right. You're *real* stupid!' He flung the box open and snatched out a few twenties and some smaller notes. 'Here.' He dropped them on the counter. Jerra saw the sweat coming out of him. 'That's your pay, thassall!'

'Just like that.'

'Silly bastard,' muttered Rosa. 'Yer crazy.'

He snatched up the money and went carefully round the back, past the sweaty, vomity thing. Near the back door, he stopped and peeled off a two-dollar note.

'Hey, Al!'

Al's head showed.

'What?'

'Money for the Cokes.' He dropped it, swaggeringly, near the head on the floor, hand trembling. 'His is on me.'

'Hey,' called Al. He looked nervous. 'What about him? You can't just leave him there!'

'Your fuckin' customer,' he cried, eyes full, ashamed. 'Serve him.'

Al threw something on the floor. Rosa was sneering.

'Bastard! What am I gonna do with him now, eh?'

'Lock 'im in . . . in—'

Out the door. The stench forced fingers up his nostrils. He leant against the bricks. He wanted to vomit, but there was nothing.

'Crazy bastard!' From inside again. 'Thinks he's tough shit now.'

He pulled jerkily into the driveway. The man next door was harvesting dog turds. Jerra went upstairs, smelling cold pies and roos and puke, thinking of all the caustic one-liners now it was too late. And there was tonight.

'How can they see what they're eating?' she murmured. She seemed happy.

'Yeah.'

'What's wrong?'

'Nothin'.'

Picking her way, the waitress came with the wine, reds jiggling thickly in the bottles. The little gas lantern on the table glimmered on the glass. He couldn't read the label, though he didn't try hard.

'Hope you like Shiraz.'

'Mm.'

'You don't?'

'Eh?'

'The wine.'

'Yeah, fine.'

She pulled back her hair.

'Not the full biscuit tonight, are you?'

He put an elbow on the tablecloth.

'Gimme some plonk. I'll cheer up.'

At other tables, leaning into the yellow gravy light, people tilted glasses, pausing with the glint of cutlery in their hands. The music was thin. Jerra filled his barren throat with wine, watching her neck as she drank. She wore a thin brown shawl of coarse wool, an open shirt and boots. He felt the hard toes against his jeans. Her eyes were different. Make-up, perhaps, he guessed. Freckles, dusty and fine, glowed on her forehead. No, it wasn't make-up; he had seen those shadows in eyes before; he ignored it.

The waitress returned.

'What are you going to order?' Judy asked, touching his cold fingers.

The waitress held a torch to the menu. It was all a bit silly, and they must have made a mistake with the prices. Whatever happened to the Chinese joints with tile floors and sweet and sour pork for $3.50?

'I dunno,' he said. 'What about you?'

'Umm. Veal Whateveritis. Sounds good.'

'Yeah, but how does it taste?'

'Very good,' said the waitress.

He nodded politely, wondering what the hell about the veal.

'Rack of Lamb. That sounds gruesome enough.' He wasn't hungry.

The waitress snapped her little notebook shut and went off into the darkness.

'Should've had cray, I suppose.'

'Know anything about crayfish dishes?'

'Not much. Only cray à la boil-bust-and-bog-in.'

'Awful things. To look at, I mean. Tell me about your friend.'

'Sean?'

'Yes.'

'Nothing to say, really. Fathers close friends. Grew up together. Best mates. Us the same. You have many friends at school?'

'Not really. Girls aren't really friends at school – just bitches waiting to get you back for this or that. Girls don't make friends; doesn't do much for our image.'

'S'pose you'd know.'

'Yes. I would.' She eased her head back, showing the soft white beneath her chin that ran in a parting curve between the buttons shining like teeth. Her breasts quivered. 'Bet you spent your childhood in the pinball shops on the beachfront.'

'Oh, off and on. Surfing was big, then.'

'Peroxide your hair?'

121

'I tried lemons every summer, but it didn't work. Walking round, smelling like Air-O-Zone. Doesn't get a bloke anywhere, somehow.'

'Not much school, eh?'

'Why? Do I seem stupid?'

She put her glass down.

'I was joking,' he said weakly.

'Oh.'

'Tell you something about crayfish seeing's you're so fascinated by them.'

'OK.'

'You can float along in a boat some days – a calm day – and sometimes, if you lift a big piece of floating weed, there'll be a cray underneath, using it for shelter. They migrate during the growth season or something, under bits and pieces that give them shelter. If you keep a shadow over it, the cray won't notice the difference, and you can just scoop him up into the boat. No one seems to know much about those buggers. Reckon they travel hundreds of miles. Like pilgrims, or sumpin'.'

She was watching his hands move, he noticed.

'Ever been crabbing?' he asked, brightening, suddenly self-conscious.

'Oh, God, yeah!'

'Get bitten, eh?'

'No, but I dreamt it a million times.'

'Great fun, though.'

'Marvellous.' She didn't appear convinced.

'Really hot nights, the mud stinking like an excavated graveyard, the lights on the beach, people laughing and talking. Great.'

'Sometimes, even crabs.'

'Boilin' 'em up in big drums on the beach. Cookin' spuds on the fire. Beer. A girlfriend from school.'

'With braces.'

'Him or her?'

'Both, no doubt.'

'Her dad and others out with the nets. A quick grope on the beach with the Tilly down low. Mud squelching under the tarpaulin.'

'Mm.'

The imprint showing perfectly when packing up to go. Parents' eyebrows. Drop the tarp back down for a sec — shoelaces, yeah, just do the old shoelaces up. Looking down at thongs. The girl giggling nervously.

'Bet she was a younger girl.'

'They.'

'Oh, they? All crawling after you, eh?'

Catching only the distant silhouettes out in the water. Hearing her talk, back on her elbows, brushing mosquitoes, hair lapping back over her shoulders near his feet. Wishing, wishing. Watching all the way up from those little feet, brown thighs shining in the lamplight, to the snug, white shorts. Wishing. And hating that glint on her hand. Imagining the broader mould they would leave, wider scoops in the mud from her buttocks. Sand forced under his toenails. Seeing hers, white shells in a neat row. Wishing *she* had braces. That she wasn't Sean's mum.

'Did you ever have braces?' What was he saying?

'No.'

'Perfect teeth all your life, eh?'

'Yeah.'

Jerra sliced down the bone, stripping away the soft brown meat. He still wasn't hungry, but the wine had hollowed him out, reminding him of how little he had eaten. And the vomiting.

'So where did you go to school?' he asked.

'Methodist Ladies'.'

'Wonder your oldies didn't give you braces, just to show they could afford it.'

'Aren't we the righteous one!'

'Sorry. Was it a girls' school?'

'Girls only at a Ladies' College. You are bright tonight.'

'Like it?'

'You don't like it; you afford it.' She smiled.

'And what did your parents do to get you into a private school?'

'How, not what. They're both doctors with separate practices. Probably didn't know what else to do with their money. Got sick of buying and collecting, and decided to put a few shares into me.'

'Just like that.'

She speared the veal.

'You bet.'

'Did you pay off?'

'Oh, I topped classes and everything, but I think they were expecting something else.'

'Like what?'

'Love. Respect.'

'No chance?'

'I remembered their birthdays and things, but they're hard to love.'

Jerra continued to slice and eat. He was feeling a little better now, stronger, the wine burning in his stomach.

'Are they still together?'

'They go by clauses.' She pressed a fingertip against the bottle. 'Still, there's always a way round what's on paper.' She drank more wine.

Their faces rippled and wavered. Jerra picked at the label on the second bottle and noticed his nails, white in the blue tips of his fingers.

'Be running dry, the way we're going.' He was feeling sad, a little sorry for her, a little sorry for himself.

'Plenty at my place.'

'Yeah.'

'So. You had a friend. Be good to spend a childhood with a special friend.'

'Sometimes it's like putting all your eggs in one basket.'

Outside it had begun to drizzle, slow, floating wisps of moisture settling in the fibres of hair and wool. The VW was only a block away. She kissed him on the neck as he unlocked the door. He could feel the steamy heat beneath the buttons; the shawl was rough on his neck.

'Taking me up on the coffee?'

It was an old, solid house with white stone walls and a large open veranda, like many of the old Cottesloe-Swanbourne fortresses of the forties. The veranda was cluttered with hanging pots, ferns, picture-frames, a rusty tricycle, and a six-foot oak table, buckling in the centre. The outside light was on.

He followed her inside. A long carpeted hallway. On the left, with a lamp in the corner, was the living-room, strewn with mats and cushions. Other doors along the hall were closed. Jerra watched the swing of her hair. The kitchen was long and wide. There was a big combustion stove with swing doors, and a long window near the sink which must have overlooked a garden. Twigs and small boughs clawed the glass.

She went to the sink and filled the kettle, dropped wood into the slow-burning fire that murmured when she opened the door, then took off her shawl and threw it over a high chair.

'Come into the living-room. We can light the fire.'

In the living-room there was a large red-brick fireplace, with pine kindling and large pieces of split jarrah on the hearth. Over the fireplace was a mounted rifle, a weathered Lee-Enfield. Judy knelt at the hearth, sprinkling the wood. Jerra heard the *pfff* of the wood igniting as he ran a hand over the calloused stock.

'That's better,' she sighed, rubbing her hands. 'Pooh, this kero stinks. Just go and wash my hands.'

125

When she came back, a glass in each hand, she noticed him running a finger along the rusted sight.

'Like it?' She gave him a glass.

'Hmm?'

'The rifle.'

He sat by the fire.

'Nice 'ol thing. Can't get ammo for them any more.'

'My father gave it to me with the place. Used to take me shooting, sometimes. Took us to the Territory once, shooting buffalo. Shot donkeys once.'

'Shooting as well, eh?'

'When Dad was charitable with his time he used to do lots of things with us.'

'Hunting. Like it?'

Flames lapped round the base of the chimney.

'Better than fishing,' she said. 'Nothing much that beats stalking something big, waiting till you're close, sight him, then bang. He's yours for good. That's real stuff.'

He looked into the fumy reflections of the tumbler.

'Done much hunting?' she asked, poking something further into the flames.

'Only small stuff. Never real game,' he murmured, remembering those quiet drives along country roads with his father, waiting for a rabbit to show.

Ears like two fingers in the air, then the full silhouette as they round the bend. His father murmurs and switches off the engine. Jerra hears the gravel moving as he opens the door, wheels of the ute still rolling. Wedges the barrel in the V-space between the door and the car. Silhouette twitches, tiny head wavering, then settling again. Dirt up behind just before the crack of the .22. His father whispers, 'High and to the left,' and he pokes another round in, shaking, expecting the head to bob down any second.

A hit was little different. The head bobbed down anyway. And backwards a bit.

126

'You don't think hunting's all that good?' she asked idly.

'No. You're not talking about hunting.'

She moved over and sat next to him near the hearth. Her glass was empty on the bricks, blazing with firelight.

'Time for *your* theory, sonny-boy.'

He felt the breath of fire on his face. The whisky scalded the back of his throat.

'You really want to hear?'

'Educate me.'

Hand on his leg. The room warming.

'Animals are different alive and dead,' he began enthusiastically, blindly.

'No prizes for that.'

No moonlight. The rock was cold and hard beneath his buttocks. His father had the whistle in his mouth, sucking quietly. Jerra held the spot, the cord running across the fence to the tractor. Little weeping, shrill sounds came from the whistle.

'OK, turn it on,' whispered his father. 'See him this time.'

Coals appeared in the scrub about forty yards away.

'There,' murmured Jerra, holding the spot steady on the eyes. Like jewels. Nothing else shone like that. To have one in a little bag, to look at on special occasions, that would be good. To show Sean. Not the rest of the kids. They wouldn't know.

'Off,' said his father. He whistled again. 'He'll come further.'

'Why?' He switched out. The light was heavy, though not as heavy as the little rifle his dad called the pea-shooter.

'The whistle.'

'What does it do?'

'Sounds like a wounded rabbit. Fox thinks he's got quick tucker.'

'But he hasn't.'

He smiled. They would get this fox. His dad was smarter.

'On.'

He switched on. Gone. No, they were closer, in the long hair of wild oats to the left. He stood. His father moved behind, resting the slim barrel on Jerra's shoulder. He could feel his father's knees touching the heels of his boots and smell the oil on the barrel. His father took a long breath. He breathed with him. Crack! in his ear. The lights went out. Only the white circle like a moon on the grass.

Judy waited.

'Explain,' she said, touching his arm.

His palms were damp.

'You said that stalking and the kill were best, with animals. Stalking is good. That's hard; makes you work. But the kill is different. With an animal, killing changes it. With big things. Things that ripple and snort and you can hear them breathing, you're so close.'

'So?'

'No use hunting a buffalo or a roo, because you're hunting something you'll never get. What you get, even with a good kill, is different to what you were after. A roo, I know, won't have that hard, tough look; the eyes are different, like glass marbles. Just a sack of dead meat with blood snotting out the nostrils. A rabbit's like a rag doll when its bladder collapses. Foxes, they're the best thing. You hunt them for the eyes. You get him, the eyes go out, there's just the body of a dog with the tongue out.'

'Why fish? Isn't that the same, catching a big fish?' she said, moving in on him.

'Fishing isn't hunting either.' He knew now. 'Sitting out of the water, gaffing the sods up, it's luck with a bit of skill. Up to the fish to take the bait. All you do is pull him up, wear him out a bit on the way, and try not to get wet. The fish can rip the hook out, and his lips with it, or surrender.'

And die. With the mate sliding off deep, leaving you with it in your lap, covering the gaff holes.

'So there's nothing worthwhile in hunting?'

'Not animals, but fish—'

'You just said fishing was all luck.'

'Not spearfishing.' He grinned. 'That's hunting. Real hunting.'

'Oh—'

'Odds are nearly even. A few in the fishes' favour.'

'What about aqualung?'

'Slaughter.'

She curled around him. Hot by the fire.

'Now I *know* you're bullshitting.' She giggled. 'All that crap about things different dead.'

'Doesn't apply.'

'Crap! Surrender while you can.'

'A fish is different,' he continued, blurting, trying to explain. 'Doesn't collapse when it dies. The eyes the same, scales the same. Still a fish. A good kill leaves a small mark in the right spot. —Preserved.'

'Until it goes off.'

'It'll fight, a big fish. Try to drown you if he can.'

She pressed against him.

'I believe it,' he said.

'Mm.' Buttons.

'Do you know about the pearl?'

'Little hard—'

'Something you wouldn't believe.'

'Oh, I—'

'Made out of the part of the brain.' The aggregated life, the distilled knowledge of lifetimes, of ancestors, of travel, of instinct, of things unseen and unknown. His sluggish mind blundered on unaware.

'Silly—'

A hand at the back of his neck.

129

'The bit he stores and hides—'

'This way.'

'—in the back of his head, hard as—'

'Anything.' She breathed hot.

'And I believe it. Dad—'

'Mind the wall—'

'But lost it.'

'Here.'

'Fell between the boards.'

Floating on his back, the water moved under him. Shirt opened to hot fingertips, scalding, everything. A knee pressed into his side. Ends of hair in his face. Her giggles.

'Bloody fish. Tell me—'

'God—'

'Something nice.'

'No,' he breathed, empty.

'Hmmm?' Hands on him, opening everywhere.

'No! No!'

His face met the scorching breasts as he struggled, hair between his lips. She gasped as he levered her mouth off, flung her aside, groping for the far-away light of the doorway. And no breath.

All down the hall, staggering, he scrabbled with his shirt, chest burning. He tried to cover up, but there were buttons gone. Jumper, he couldn't remember. He wanted to puke. Anything. Opening the door, he sucked the chill deep and it stung all the way down in his chest. Stubbed on the rusty tricycle. Off the veranda.

Kettle screaming.

PART THREE

like men and boys

'I just am, that's all!'

'No sense in it!'

'I know.'

'What are you running away from?' asked his father.

'Nothing.'

'Something happened?'

'Plenty.'

'Tell us,' pleaded his mother.

'What the hell can I tell you that you don't know already?'

'Jerra,' she sobbed. 'We don't know anything.'

'Then it's the same.'

His father held his arm.

'Jerra, yer not making sense!'

'Course I'm bloody not!'

His mother crying on the bookshelves.

'Tom, what's he done?'

'Nothing! I got sacked, orright? Here's my board.' He held out some notes.

'We don't want that!'

'What do you want?'

'Whatever you want.'

'You can't. It's too late.'

*

He rolled the canvas tight. Rope lay in coils. He had done it well in the dark, not sleeping all night. Picking up the box of cans and cartons, he went for the door.

'Where will you be, then, son?'

'Fishing,' he said. 'Or something.'

'Jerra?' His mother held out her arms.

He slapped the flywire door back.

Boys don't say it.

The VW was nearly full. Next door, the man was starting his mower before breakfast. Drizzle drifted.

Boys don't.

All the way to the sea he could see the collage of city, misted with rain and latticed with sunlight where it penetrated the cloud, gradually losing focus, diminishing in the mirrors as Jerra sat in low gear up the winding hills. Drizzle spotted the windscreen, blurring, but not wetting it enough to use the wipers. At the top of the hill, the labouring VW was eased, and the road wound through hilly pine forests and gravel pits. It rained heavily. The tyres hissed and the wipers slapped spastically on the glass.

'Do you love me, Jerra?'

'Yes.'

Her gown was slipping; a nurse passed, eyebrows lifted.

She always asked before he left. He always felt the eyes on him in the corridors as he left, with her looking after him.

The monotony of pines diminished into hills and thick pastures clogged with huddling grey sheep. Gullies lined with trees furrowed through the hills, and already, in low paddocks by the road, flat black pools lay pocked with rain, fences jutting out with stiff stalks of cut weeds. Cows slapped their tails in the wet. He passed a tractor hub-deep in the dung-like mud. Cold air was piercing the panels of the cabin, and Jerra felt his feet numbing. He remembered the times on the farm when he had stood, barefoot, in the fresh green cowpats, warming his toes as he squelched.

'I'm old.'
　'No.'
　'Ugly.'
　'No.'
　'Do you love me?'
　'Yes,' he said.
　'Yes. Tell Jerra you said it.'
　'Jewel, I am Jerra.'
　She smiled uncomprehendingly.
　'I am Jerra.'
　She was watching him gaily as he plodded down the stairs, defeated.

A roo lay upturned beside the road, legs stiff in the air. Smears of blood disturbed the gravel, picked over by crows and magpies. Pie meat, the poor bastard, he thought.

Listening to the note of the engine, and tapping out its rhythms on the steering-wheel, Jerra tried to remember the things he had forgotten to bring, but it was hopeless; he hardly knew what he had, and, as always, he confused this with other trips, other forgotten things, other items to be remembered. He pulled in at Williams, coasting into the Golden Fleece roadhouse with the motor off, and sat for a moment with the silence.

'Yeah?'

135

A girl in a red parka, with black teeth, at the window. Jerra wound down. It was drizzling.

'Fill it up, thanks.'

She went around to the fuel tank as he stumbled out. His thongs slid over the oily tarmac, spotted with greasy spectrums, as he made his way to the -EN door. He peed into the crap-stained bowl and flushed away the scum of butts and paper. He had seen the flies and smelt this place in the summer, and for a moment the winter was not so bad. The deodorizing thing sat on the browning cistern, a sugary yellow jube.

Outside in the drizzle, he dug his hands into his coat pockets and watched the girl spill petrol down the duco as she tried to force more into the tank. A cow moaned. He got up into the cab shivering, wiped the mist from the windscreen with his hand, and glanced in the back at the jerry cans, the smoky canvas, the blankets, stakes, tins of food, bags, and boxes; the handle of the axe and the end of his spear protruded from the hessian bag. He reached over and dragged out a bag of peanuts. He shelled a few and ate them, stuffing the shells into the ashtray, already full with Judy's stinking butts and the foil from Lifesavers.

'Why doesn't he love me, I wonder?'

She was wandering again, and Jerra picked off a bud, feeling it between his fingertips.

'He does.'

'You think I'm an idiot, dear.'

He pressed the bud.

'He hates me, I think. Does Jim say things about me?'

'I don't know.'

'Sean hates me.'

'He hates this place.'

'He doesn't have to live in it.'

'No,' said Jerra, smiling nervously at the nurse who

scurried by at exactly the same time each morning, to watch them.

The girl came back to the window, hands wet with petrol.

'Six fifty-three.'

'How much in the tank?'

'Eh?'

He gave her the money, noticing the black underneath her nails. When she returned with the change he had the motor running.

As the country flattened out, opening on to wider slopes of green, the cold crept up from his fingertips, blueing his knuckles. He felt the tyre blow and the van list as he rounded a bend, and he stopped at the gravelly edge of the road. Thongs flicking spots of mud up on to his back, he went round to the rear tyre. He dragged the dusty spare out and rolled it on to its side in the mud. He found the toolbox and left it out on top of the gear in the back. Opening the heavy jarrah lid, he pulled out the jack and wheelbrace, tossing aside something wrapped in a smelly old flourbag.

The spare on, Jerra wiped the punctured tyre as best he could, shoving it under the canvas. He sat at the edge of the sliding door for a moment, scraping the mud from his jeans, then wiping his hands on the flourbag. Something heavy inside. He pulled it out. Small flakes came off in his palm. The ringbolt without a bolt. Funny old thing. He dropped it back in.

Rain was falling heavier in big thick drops that left welts in the rusty mud. He climbed back into the cab, shaking off the water. It was midday. He shelled a few peanuts, left them in a little pile on the seat beside him, and drove off.

*

'Come on, read yours.'

They lazed in her backyard. Sean was standing under the hose, cooling off.

'It's your turn, Auntie.'

'That was yesterday.'

'OK. This is the end of the one I was on last Saturday:

> And so everywhere I go
> I know
> That there's ships and planes
> And football games
> And bubbles to blow.'

'What bubbles?'

'Snot.' He grinned.

'Oh.' She laughed palely. 'Jem-Jem, you're so corrupt!'

Echoing.

Clouds gathered choppily over the southern edges of the sky, thicker and darker than the nondescript overcast spreading behind. Rattling across the small white bridges, he caught glimpses of the creeks with that energetic, muddy complexion of winter. Beaufort, Balgarup, Kojonup, Hotham, Crossman, Arth-r, Abba, Orup, Kalgan: little white signs, rough faced with blisters, fighting out of the strangling weeds of the banks. Jerra ate the peanuts slowly, spinning them out. He passed through the one-street towns, hardly slowing down as he whipped past the diagonally parked utes rusting outside the co-ops and pubs.

In a flooded paddock, with the low, weepy-clouded mountains in the background, Jerra noticed a flight of ducks skidding on to the water. He slowed as he neared the paddock, pulling over on to the gravel. A few hundred yards away, the ducks haggled on the water, and he watched them poking their heads into the black, coming up again and again with gobs of mud slushing from their beaks. He shelled a few more peanuts, tearing the brown film that looked like cigarette paper off the kernels, watching the ducks pecking each other behind the neck. He blew the horn and drove off as they lifted away together, a dense cloud, into the grey sky.

> *Petals fall like scales on to my hand,*
> *My love seeps like water through sand,*
> *– Nothing.*

He smiled, feeling his unshaven chin.

'You remember?' she asked.

'Yes.'

They strolled in the yellow sunlight between stiff buds of Geraldton wax, bees hopping from flower to flower.

'Wasn't a very good poem, was it?' She trembled.

'Better than some I've read.'

'But not as good as yours.'

'Better. Yours was true.'

'. . . *And bubbles to blow.*'

He looked away, flushing at the waxed petals. Other women walked by with husbands and children.

It was late in the afternoon when he passed through Albany, its little houses set into the gully between hills. The main street over-looking the shoals of the inner harbour was clogged with cars and children. He parked beneath the shadow of the town hall clock and went into the Wildflower Café and bought some milk, making his way out of town in a light rain that swept the dark bitumen. The hilly roads wound through fences of trees through which Jerra caught glimpses of the Porongorups on his left, and the coastal hills, low and scrubby, to the right. Gradually the hills subsided, and the trees became rugged scrub. Farms were smaller and less frequent. Cleared land was set further back from the road, the kerosene-tin mail boxes gaping in flat scrub with little sign of farmland behind.

'Don't let them, Jerra.' Eyes direct, of a sudden, then gone again, out of the window, to the dressing-gowns strolling the lawns.

Light weakened and the sun ignited the mirrors. Jerra found a truck bay and parked under some ghost gums. His eyes ached and he was hungry. There was a barbecue fireplace under the trees, and a table with benches screwed on to it, but the ground and the wood in the pile were wet. He climbed over into the back of the van and did his best to separate the mattress from the boxes and bags. He found a can opener and hacked open a can of peaches. He speared them with the end of the opener. They were sweet and soggy in his mouth. The milk burnt cold as it went down. He shelled more of the peanuts. They weren't too bad with the milk, but he was getting sick of them. He left some milk for the morning and drained the sugary juice from the peach tin.

Still drizzling outside. He stuffed the can and the peanut bag into the barbecue and hurried back. As darkness came, the inside of the van warmed with his breath. He found a blanket and lay with his head on his sleeping bag, the heat of the engine underneath his back. It ticked as it cooled. Rain beat on the roof. Dripping from the cab. He had forgotten: the dash leaked. Little drops; one, another, again, more, each a different shape and weight and tone – *drop!*

From his patch of black, words dropped, sank and swam his way, bending, involuting scarry letter-faces, some sounding, others just lighting up, burning into the empty space behind his eyes.

jellyfish	blood . . .
boys	. . . witness
no	jerra
corrupt	jem
don't	jem
clover	jez
leaves	crazy bastard

coming and going, streaming out, a bubble trail uncoiling to the invisible silver of the surface.

In the middle of the night, the whole world lit up, as if by an explosion or a fire. A truck engine knocked. He heard it pull in. Darkness returned, then silence. A moment later, Jerra thought the dash had given way altogether, but then the gush stopped and he heard a zipper and footfalls.

He was warm inside the blanket.

He woke in the twilight, and it was cold in parts of the blanket; places that hurt they were so cold. As light pretended to come, shapes and outlines emerged, and he saw the clusters of droplets on the ceiling. His breath, no doubt. Shivering beads, ready to fall at any moment.

The sky was low and heavy. The rain had stopped. No wind, no sound. He staggered out into the cold. The gravel was soft. His breath clouded grey before him. His feet were stiff and heavy with mud as he hobbled round the car, noticing the Kenworth further down the truck bay. He climbed back inside, scraping the mud from his feet with a stick.

The Veedub spluttered, backfired, and growled. Jerra saw a head appear behind the fogged windscreen of the Kenworth as he slid out of the mud and chirked hitting the bitumen.

He passed the turn off and almost didn't go back. He braked, sliding off into the loose edge, sat for a moment, then reversed up. The dull gravel strip led down to the coastal hills. There was nowhere else.

He slid on the surface. In the gullies, ochre puddles lay across the road. The deeper ones slopped up into the windscreen leaving mud and grit on the glass. Ruts and holes deepened. Jerra slowed down, wincing as the old bus was jarred and shaken crossing the hollows and washouts.

The black sand was hard, packed down with rain, and the tyres ran whispering over, the wide ruts curving up gently to a smooth hump in the middle. Dark wet roots protruded, and grass grew high, rasping the underside of the body. Trees had grown thicker, leafier. Below in the stillness, the sea through the trees was grey and opaque. Boughs and leaves brushed squealing against the fenders and the roof, showering heavy drops on the ground. A bird slapped skyward.

He passed the shack, furred with grass and leaves. He saw the truck in the mirrors as he rolled carefully down the track, avoiding stumps and jags of limestone. A sapling poked through the truck window. He rolled.

NO, said the tree.

The clearing was smaller and greener. The thick grass grew in hairy tufts. Black stones lay scattered, some in the clearing, others in the edges of the bush. He turned off. Birds tittered. He got out and unfolded his legs, tasting the salt.

It was a struggle to get the annexe up alone; it had been difficult enough with Sean. Rope bruised his hands and the axe handle roughened his palms. The ground wasn't quite dry, but he couldn't wait and risk further rain. Because of the sea-winds he knew would come, he faced the annexe away from the beach, behind the van between two thick-trunked gums.

For lunch he ate braised steak from a can. It tasted of gas and fat. Rain looked inevitable later in the afternoon. He gathered wood and shoved it under the VW to dry and, while he still had time, he gathered stones for a fireplace. It puzzled him that the blackened stones from the previous fire had been scattered. He left them alone, foraging in the bush for clean lumps of limestone, avoiding the granite because it often exploded. He set them in a knobbly circle and dug a shallow pit in the centre. Then the rain came, spattering the shivery leaves, and he sat in the annexe stacking food and utensils. Gulls passed over, heading inland with vacant cries.

Rain fell constantly the next day. Jerra sat inside, listening to the pattering on the canvas, drops making animal scampering sounds, trickling softly to the ground down the sides of the annexe, and ate sloppy things cooked on the stove. In the afternoon he made rigs, stringing together hooks and swivels, tasting the whale oil as he held them cold and brassy in his teeth. He decided to fish the lagoon, but turned back, thinking of the drizzle and the cold granite and blue hands. He sat inside, knotting line.

Clover tickled his ears. They couldn't see each other, it was so deep. Above, the tree spread thick and green against the sky, the scratchy gumleaves shining in the sun. Jerra sucked the sweat from his upper lip. He held his thumb tight.

'How's yours?'

'Orright,' said Sean.

'Hurt?'

'No.'

'Mine neither.'

'Hot.'

'Yeah.'

They looked up into the scabby boughs.

'What if a maggie swooped us 'n' pecked our eyes out?'

'Who cares?'

'Yeah, it's OK here.'

'Too hot for maggies.'

'Ya couldn't see, anyhow.'

'Yeah.'

Jerra wiped his thumb on the clover, big flat leaves smearing.

'Gonna tell anyone?'

'Nah,' said Jerra.

'Secret.'

'Yeah.'

'What if we got different blood?'

'Nah, same blood.'

'Is now, anyway.'

'Yep.'

'Here.'

Something cold landed on his chest. A closed safety pin. He put it in the pocket of his shorts.

'Like Indians,' said Sean.

'Yep.'

'Our dads did.'

'Dad told me.'

'Mates.'

'Yep.'

Stringing hooks, thumbs on the barbs . . .

His father's face, soft in the lamplight . . .

He was reluctant to go out at all the next day, under the dull skies. Although there was no wind, the air was cold and sharp. Jerra walked down to the beach. The sand was wind smoothed in flat hummocks and ridges, the sides of the dunes ribbed and fluted on their bald patches. The bay was calm, the water dark. He looked down towards the rocky end of the beach. There were no footprints. He went back up to the clearing, threw some gear into the hessian bag, screwed his spear together, and made for the lagoon.

The water was clear and cold. He floated, stunned, on his chest, letting the streams shoot up his arms and legs inside his wetsuit; he clenched his teeth, head aching, pushing along the almost oily calm of the surface, and under him brown, green, yellow weed stood upright, lank and motionless. The water quickened him, making his movements easier as he felt his arms come alive with gooseflesh. His head burnt and his breath burst sharply from his snorkel. He sucked in the air, burning his throat.

Everything below in sharp focus, Fish hung in thick clusters, like knotted weed. Jerra wafted through the shallows, pulling himself, with his fingers dug in, along the sandy patches of the bottom. Tiny whiting darted away, almost invisible against the sand, and as they went he could see their veins and gut showing through their transparent bodies. He ran his fingers through the sand as he glided along, turning every now and then to see the billowing clouds settling behind. For a few yards he slid along the bottom, nudging the sand with his chin. A garfish passed on the surface above, snooking along with its bill out like an ice-breaker.

Following the declivity of the bottom, Jerra moved out to the reef. He surfaced, *bff*ing the water out of his snorkel. He felt it on his legs. Ruts and potholes opened in the carpeted rock. He dived along a gently sloping bank of turf, soft under his hands. Pomfrets scattered, flashing silver and gold. He could have caught one, wide eyed in his hands as they passed. The trenches in his palms were darkening, and little welts lifted in crinkles where he had swung the axe.

He kicked out to the hulk and hovered, looking hard. Even knowing, it was difficult to see where rock and timber separated. He swam out to the edge of the reef, a hundred yards further out, and floated over, looking down into the pale blue. It was too deep to see bottom, great schools of buffalo bream patrolling, thirty, forty feet further down. He turned back over the reef.

At the entrance of a long, low cave, a group of scalyfins twitched and banked nervously. He came down from behind them, but they were too quick, their green and black flanks gone under the ledges. He poked his head into the cave, no bigger than a forty-four gallon drum. A small squid, all bulbous eyes, floated against the back wall. Nothing to cook it properly with, he left it, quivering, turning its big eye.

Without sunlight, the water was an oily colour, and the reef was dull with even the most flaming reds and oranges of weed appearing cold and faded. A large bream floated over a weed bank. It was harder to see without sun, without silver flashes. The bream was feeding or asleep. Jerra sank to the bottom, letting out quiet burps of air as he stalked through the weed. About five or six feet away, he aimed for the spine behind the gills. The spear flashed, the fish balked and avoided the prongs. He tried again, but the fish streaked into open water.

It was cold and his jaw ached from clenching. He took out his knife and prised a couple of abalone from the reef, peeling them off with quick flicks that left them twitching for a grip. He held them in his hand as he swam for the flat rock where he had left the gear. The shellfish twitched, their flesh writhing in spasms. He swam without holding them after a few moments, big discs sucking, welded to his palms.

Steam hissed on his shins as he stood closer to the flames, wood cracking and popping. His hands and face and feet were numb, pricking with blood as the fire warmed him. In the bay, the water was still flat as ice.

He gouged the meat from the shells and threw gobs of guts into the flames, watching them sizzle. He found a clean rock and bashed the meat on it with the flat of the axe. Wiping the dust from the pan with his sleeve, Jerra dropped in a pat of butter and melted it over the fire, flames wrapping back and forth. He could smell the hair singeing on the back of his hand. It curled off in little wisps. The pan hot, he dropped the abalone in, watching them buckle and turn in the butter. He fried each side until the milk oozed out and they were the same colour as the butter.

He heard it faintly, but clear.

> Out in the longboats, then sailors,
> Put your backs to the oar,
> Mind a big bull don't
> Come up an' nail us
> Or we will be sailin' no more.
> — We will be sailin' no more.

There was no surprise this time; he had been waiting. Jerra saw through the trees but pretended.

'Smells good.'

'For sure.'

'So you came back.'

Jerra scooped the abalone out onto a plate. The pan fizzed on the grass.

'Want one?'

'Oh, no.'

'Only need one. Be a waste.'

The old man scuffed. Jerra went in and got him a stool.

'There you go.'

The old man sat.

'Looks cold, the water. Dunno how you could stand it, this weather.' His hair was thin and plaited with knots, his beard seemed greyer. He wore an oilskin, dried and cracked in the creases, open at the front, stinking of fish. There were two buttons on his shirt, which was bleached almost white.

'Not too bad once you're in. Gets to you after a while, though.' He looked at his purpling hands.

A stink of burning meat from the fire.

'Rotten smell,' said the old man, chewing. 'Never get it out've yer clothes.'

Eating, squeezing hot butter out with each chew.

'What you been doin'?'

Jerra cut a slab of bread and buttered it, giving it to the old man.

'Went back to get a job.'

'Yeah?'

'Got a job an' now I'm back.'

'Doesn't sound too good.' He moulded his rubbery lips around the bread, butter glistening on them.

'Worked in a deli.'

'Why'd you chuck it in?'

'They chucked *me* in. Or out, the silly bastards.'

The old man chewed slowly, his feet rocking inside the crusty boots. His face was dried hard with sun. His eyes were moist and clear under the dry lids, moving from object to object in Jerra's new camp.

'How's this place?'

''Asn't changed. Colder with the winter, and wet, but still the same, jus' the same.'

'Hut holding up orright?'

'Leaks a bit, but I fixed the roof with a strip of wire. It'll last long enough.'

Staring into the fire.

'Where's yer mate?' he asked, holding his hands to the heat. His oilskin steamed.

'Working.'

'How is he?'

'Orright, I s'pose. Dunno, really.'

'Any different in the big city.'

'Just the same.' Jerra grinned. 'Still full o' big-mouths.'

The old face creased, whitening in the wrinkles.

'Come down to do a bit of fishin'?'

Jerra nodded, filling the billy.

'Might do a bit.'

'Not much round, really. Buggers 'ave pissed off on me. Nothin' decent for a while.'

'Couple of whiting around.'

'Could be.'

'What about crays? You could make a couple of pots and sink them in holes in the reef.'

'Too dangerous, walkin' out on that reef.'

Jerra put the billy into the flames, hands stinking of burning hair.

'At low ebb, you could wade out and drop them over.'

The old man was looking on, watching the steam rise from the blackened outside of the billy as the metal handle glowed gold and blue and green, *pfff*ing quietly.

'Like a woman,' he murmured.

'Hmm?'

'The fire.'

'How?'

'Dunno. Just is.'

Jerra wondered. Other things, too. Like men and boys.

'Saw a few fish today.'

'Yeah?'

'I was too slow, though.'

'All slow down a bit, this time o' year.'

'What you been living on?'

'Rabbits. A roo every now an' then. There's carrots, radishes, spuds.'

'Wouldn't think anything'd grow in ground like this. Bit sandy, isn't it?'

'Ah, there's a rich patch behind every shed.' The old man laughed. 'Been ripenin' a while.'

Jerra smiled.

'Bury rubbish, anything that rots. Makes orright dirt. At first it's a bit hard to eat what grows out've yer own shit.'

Jerra laughed.

149

A SHIT SANDWICH.

'But it's the best stuff,' said the old man.

'Eating the same thing over and over.'

'Right. But it doesn't do too badly. When you've got nothin' else, there's still things that grow out've shit. Doesn't taste so bad, if it's yer own.'

A light wind was dribbling in off the bay.

'Hard living.'

'Brought it on meself.'

'I haven't told anyone.'

'Some people got bad in 'em. More 'n most.'

'Who knows?'

'Me.'

'I mean—'

'But I *do*. Yer can't burn it out've yer on yer own. Some days I've got along the beach with a stick, squashin' crabs on the rocks, poor little bastards. Jus' pin 'em down an' shove the stick through. Crack, an' out comes the froth. They still bite, though, the buggers, even when yer rip the nippers off the body they still get yer an' won't let go. Crazy buggers.'

Jerra poked the billy with a green stick. It would boil soon.

'We all get that,' he said. 'But there's good things.'

'Maybe. Some things are too bad to let any good come any more.'

'Some people never do anything at all. Maybe it's better doing something bad than never doing anything all your life. At least it's trying. You make blues. You gotta try.'

The billy began to rattle in the flames. Holding the stick through the handle, Jerra drew it out and dropped in some tea, watching the brown stuff spread on the water. He poured it into the mugs, a scum of leaves floating on the top.

'Had a mate used that as a motto. Said yer gotta hit a good patch, sooner or later. It was north, in me younger days. He was jinxed as a three-legged dog, but he kept at it. We was superstitious bastards. He died broke.'

'Maybe he just wasn't any good.'

'Never fished with 'im.'

'Why don't we make a pot and try for the crays?'

'Bloody reef. It's a devil.'

The tea was hot. Jerra stirred lots of sugar into it, seeing it dissolve in the coppery stuff.

Quickened by the wind, the clouds had darkened out in the bay.

'Rain tonight,' he said to the old man who was hunched over by the fire, sucking the hot tea.

He breathed into his mug and finished it.

'I'd better get back.'

'Want some supplies? Plenty of tea, sugar, flour, tinned things.'

'I'm orright.'

Wind ruffled his trousers as he went.

Sunlight glowed in the moisture on the windows. Brilliant strings of beads hung from the van and the trees. Wind rocked the leaves in little tremors and round drops pattered on to the detritus as the sun shifted through the trees, darkening the sky, browning the earth. Through the webbing of boughs and trunks the ocean glittered, dazzling fingers of light clenching and unclenching. Frosted breath of mist hung in the bush, wavering, the colour of ash.

Jerra pulled on his jumper and greatcoat. The cold gauze of mist burnt his nostrils. Water spilled from the canvas as he opened the flap, and droplets ran down in clusters on to the rough arms of his coat. Leaves were cold and gummy beneath his toes. A tiny bird glanced off the gilt branches of sunlight that forked and tangled in the clearing.

He prodded the ash and coals with a stick. Underneath the ash was white and warm; he felt the heat on his palm.

With a dirty fishing bag under his arm, Jerra stalked across the cold sand, feeling it, almost petrified with cold under his heels, remembering as they numbed the days when he and Sean would beat the sun to the beach, avoiding the morning traffic, and walk across the stiff sand with blue curling toes, surfboards cold glass under their arms. They would sit in the swell with mates, paddling furiously to beat each other to the biggest of the set, feeling the breeze on their faces as they dropped down into the trough, zig-zagging through the swimmers in the bathing area. On big days, after a cyclone had carried too far south, they would paddle out to the reefs that boiled and thundered as they neared.

NO carved in the hard sand. Jerra kicked it over.

The tide was lower than he had seen it. He walked out over the dry reef, over the rocks soft with algae and kelp. The drying weed was beginning to stink. He picked off a couple of small abalone and sliced the white meat from the little ear-shaped shells. Mother-of-pearl snatched the sun. Spectrums quivered as he turned it in the light. He punctured a piece of the tough meat with a hook, and cast into a hole in the reef. Green water surged as he watched the sinker and white blob of meat disappear.

As the sun rose further, weed dried and Jerra sat on a flat rock that normally frothed with breaking waves. The hole glugged as the water rose underneath the ledges and slapped ceilings, the edges lined with fleshy clusters of kelp. Whitebait stung the surface like grapeshot.

Wrench on the line. It trembled. He dragged in and it cut into his fingers. The fish came shuddering out of the water, scales lit in the sun. Jerra pulled the hook out, fin spines pricking his palm. The gills flapped as he held the fish up to the sun with its pectorals unfurling. Breaksea cod – black-arsed snapper, his father called them – not much bigger than his hand.

He wet the bag and put the fish in, scales and mucus clammy on the cloth. The tough meat was still on the hook. Cheap way to fish, he thought, as he dropped it into the hole.

A crab marched slowly across the rocks, opening and closing

its orange claws. It would make better bait. He held the line with his left hand, caught the crab by its back flipper, and with the knife dashed the claws off and dropped them into the hole. The crab struggled in the bag as he fished. Another bite. A sweep, big as his foot. He held it under his heel as he unthreaded the hook. The sweep was knife-thin, chromed on its tight flanks underneath the black bars. Sweep were one of the best to see underwater, quick and curious.

Jerra sat until the sun was above the hole. Lips and nicks in the grassy rock brightened in the direct sun and, near the surface, heads retracted into the snug dark. He had caught a half-dozen small fish; sweep, some cod, and a leatherjacket. There were no more bites. He scaled and cleaned the fish, slicing neat behind the gills, disconnecting the narrow little heads of the sweep, slitting the turgid sac of the black-arsed snapper, and did what he could with the hide of the leatherjacket. The unravelling guts went into the hole. He took out the crab and put the fish in the bag. He broke it in half, an eye and battery of legs either side, and crushed the shell with his heel. Tobacco-coloured juice ran out. He took the abalone off the hook and sank the barb into half of the crab. There was probably nothing left down there, unless something wandered through, but it would have been a waste not to have used the crab.

He lowered the bait into the hole. Before it hit bottom, the line whipped into the water, the spool chasing it all the way in, zizzing loops, vanishing in the water. He stood for a few minutes with nothing in his hands but a red welt, seeing nothing but the hole.

He wet the bag afresh and picked his way to the beach.

. . . IT'S A DEVIL

That afternoon, Jerra took three of the bigger fish in the bag, and made for the rocks at the other end of the beach. He followed the crowded little marks, and ran a wide perimeter around the beam halfway. There was still a stink, green as ever, in the sand where the seal had been. It would be there a long time yet. Sand cracked under his feet.

No sign of the old man from the front of the humpy, only a humming from somewhere behind, and the gulls in the trees around. He went round the back. In the few yards between the rickety back wall and the bush, there was a moist black strip of soil, stirred and turned in heavy sods. The old man crouched in a net of flies.

'G'day,' said Jerra, swinging the bag.

He looked up, blood wet on his hands.

'How's things?'

Wiping his knife on a tuft of grass, flies clinging, the old man looked over.

'Not too bad.' Smiling with blood in his beard. 'A good mornin'. Got this big bastard.'

The hindquarters of a roo, fur tarred with blood.

'Not bad goin',' said Jerra, feeling foolish about the headless little fish in the bag. 'A big buck, isn't it?'

'Buck orright. Hairy ol' bastard. Snared 'im in the hills. Most of 'em give it a wide miss – smell me on the snare – but this ol' hopper wasn't the full quid this mornin'. Fall for things like that when you get old.' Flies dug into the corner of his mouth, a twitching scab.

'How'll you keep him?' Jerra asked, eyeing the neck and head on the grass a few feet away, glass eyes open.

'String 'im up in a spud sack an' let 'im bleed for a day or two.'

'It'll go off.'

'This weather? Nah. One fine day in a hundred. Flies only out with the sun.'

The old man ran the knife up the stomach from the anus, letting the coils spill on to the ground. Steam from the opened abdomen.

'One way to get yer hands warm.' He laughed.

A bit revolting, really, smelling the steam, the bowels open. Jarra noticed that the knife had only half a blade, but it looked very sharp.

'Caught a few fish this morning. Six. Thought you might like a couple. Too many for me on my own.'

'Wouldn't be right.'

'They'll only go off.'

'You got ice?'

'No room.'

Rubbed his bloody beard. He peeled off a section of fur, flesh pink underneath.

'Do you a deal.'

'Orright.'

'I'll take a couple of 'em, and you take some o' this bugger.'

'Fair enough.'

Jerra reached into the bag.

'You don't have to give me the meat, you know.'

'Deal's a deal.'

He lay the smooth, softly boned fish on the grass. Something else in the bag. He pulled out the half-crab.

'Any good to you?'

The old man looked up, a strip of sinew in his teeth.

'Good for the brew.'

'What brew?'

'Good things grow outta shit.'

'That brew.'

'Keep it in a drum up the back. Got all the produce in there. Anything comes to hand. Bled this feller in there, 'smornin'. Drop what's no good in as well, after. All good ammo. Plenty o' rain. Good for the carrots an' spuds.'

'And they grow orright?'

'Enough to keep the scabs off me arse. She always told me to eat me greens, like me mother.' He chuckled. 'No bloody choice now.'

'Was she good?'

155

The stunted black blade opened flesh in the flank.

'Good lookin', orright. Spent our weddin' night on a boat we borrowed, a launch with a big open afterdeck. Married in December, hot as hell. We slept out in the open on a big kapok under the stars, with some bottles and a sheet.'

'On a boat.'

'Didn't sleep, that night.'

'And stayed with boats.'

'Reckon we liked 'em better 'n each other. An' her little pianner. Couldn't play it.' He relaxed on his haunches. 'Was a goodun, our boat.'

'Big.'

'Enough for us.'

'And the fish.'

'Yeah, the fish, orright. We lived like bloody royalty. Thought we was the only people in the world. Gawd, I believed in 'eaven, then. But it was a bugger when it went no good. So she had the licker. And her friends in town.'

'Lousy.'

'Nothin' else to keep us from each other's necks. Nothin' to share 'ceptin' the boat. A boat can only be a boat, said and done, only a boat. Not the same. I just couldn't give 'er what she wanted. We went bad. Her worse. But I didn't stop her, she was her own girl. She got what she wanted in town.'

'Hard.'

'An' some days I dunno nothin'.'

Scaly fingers peeled back the limp skin. It sounded like sticking plaster coming off as the old man sliced upwards, holding the stumpy knife like a pencil, and laid two long pink fillets on Jerra's bag.

'There's a fair swap, seein' I've got a weak spot for leatheries.'

''Squits.' He looked at the long tongues of flesh, side by side on the bag.

The old man continued his cutting and peeling.

'Thought you'd go gogglin' today. Good day for it.'

'Bit cold.'

'Not as cold as yesterday.'

'No good yesterday.'

'Get it while yer can. Bad weather comin' soon.'

Gulls stirred, bitching in the trees.

'Take long for a roo to die when you snare it?'

The old man stretched a flap of skin, seeing the sun through it.

'Not if you do a good job. There's ways.'

'What do you do for a snare?'

'Pianner wire.'

'Must be painful as hell.'

'If you make a mess. Bad to mess up an animal. Killin's bad enough without mutilatin'. This one went down with his legs caught, see?' He showed Jerra the raw patches in the fur. 'Lucky I heard 'im go down, or I wouldn't've found him till later in the day. Just slit 'is throat while he was stunned. Didn't take long.'

'Still, a pretty awful way to go, especially if you don't hear. Could lie there for hours.'

'You can only try to be around.'

'And if yer not?'

'Some things 'ave to be done.'

He laid some organs on the grass.

'If yer want 'im bad enough, yer do everything you can and still do the best by him.'

Liver jellyfish-wobbling.

'Ever go into town?'

'Questions.'

'Bloody hard life.' Jerra shrugged.

'Said before.'

'Ever thought about goin' back to town? To live. Normally.'

'This is normal enough.'

'What about when you get too old to look after yourself?'

The old man bit an intestine in half.

'Too old to look after meself?'

Jerra covered his steaks. Flies were bad.

'One day you'll be too old to fish or hunt any more.'

'Reckon I'll know what to do.'

'And you could die trying to think of something.'

'Not too many choices.'

'And just die?'

'Others are dead an' still walkin' around. You know why I won't go back.'

'If anyone had any idea they would've been out years ago.'

'They've been out, orright. They must've seen the driftwood the day they came – wouldn't've known she sank it before – they think I'm drowned, both of us. Sometimes they're right. I take the punishment every day. Why the hell go back for more? Any'ow, they wouldn't make much fuss over the like of her. Better out've the way, for some. One bastard 'specially, if he knew. Why go back for more?'

'And lockin' yourself away here, isn't that runnin' away? Chuckin' it in?'

'Not chuckin' it in. Any'ow, look who's tellin' me.'

She kissed him, gown open, by the hedges at the south end of the gardens.

'I've been writing poems again, Jerra.'

He nodded. It was hard now. She wasn't getting any better. Sometimes she was worse, carrying herself like a queen, dainty in slippers that scuffed the lawn.

'About my babies. The ones you never saw. You never knew them, Jerra. They loved me. Brothers for Sean. He'd have liked brothers I think. His father didn't want them, though. Not even the last one. It was *his*. I was an animal, Jim said. But I was only a mother, Jerra.'

She pulled Jerra to her breast. His tears wet her, but she didn't seem to notice. There was nothing he could say.

'But he doesn't do it on purpose, Jerra, I know it. He couldn't. It hurts.'

He cried.

'My baby,' she whispered.

He looked up. She was smiling. She liked talking about her babies now. Jerra couldn't bear it. He decided, then, in her arms, that he would go away. A job. Anything.

Sun was gone from the trees. It lit the sky over the hills. Smoke and hints of mist hung in the boughs. Jerra sat looking into the fire, smelling the flesh cooking in the pan and pulling his coat about him. The cold shrank even the fire a little, though the flames sprang out at unexpected moments, the greens and blues so pure and inviting that Jerra sometimes longed to touch. A moment later, a tongue of flame would leap out and burn the hairs off his hand.

He turned the curling meat, sizzling in its fat, darkening. It was too fresh to cook. When it began to burn, he took the pan off the fire. It was hot in his mouth, still bleeding, and tough as hide; he could not tear a piece free from the rest. It tasted of smoke and blood. Spitting out what he could, he threw it into the fire with the piece he hadn't cooked, and went for some water.

The tea was strong and scalding. He sat chewing the half-bitter leaves from the bottom of the mug, watching his shadow move in the pearly moonlight. He breathed the cold air deep.

Better out of the way. He wondered about the old man's Annie and whether the old man knew what he was saying. How could anyone be better out of the way? Perhaps he was like all the rest. Sometimes the old man really got his goat.

'Orright, eh?'

'That's how people get married.'

She smiled, long legs shining in the sun.

'Yes.'

He took the ringbolt out of the VW and sat by the fire, just looking, picking bits off. He hung it on a short branch and looked at it for a while longer.

Then he went to bed.

He would stay down till he exploded; bring it up to know, wrenching it out of its black watery recesses to end the whole thing. The pearls. He wondered.

. . . It's all fisherman's bloody superstition . . .

hunting

Birds were making cautious sounds in the half-light of morning as Jerra carried spear and bag through the trees. His feet were cold under the fleshy wet leaves, and he was hungry.

Smooth rocks colder under his feet. He felt his heels brushing the pores of granite as he hopped from shoulder to shoulder until he came to the flat rock where Sean and he had dived and caught their fish. He undressed slowly and was stung by the air, naked, fumbling in the big hessian bag for the wet suit. He pulled it up over his legs, damp and mouldy from the last dive. The zip burped all the way up his chest and the black skin was tight on him. Stooping, he clipped the weights on, then the knife on his leg, cinching the little rubber straps over the hairs on his calf.

White feet in the water, he swilled the flippers and pulled them on. He left the flourbag with his clothes in the big brown sack. He wet the mask, spat on the glass, and washed it out. Leaning his head into the water, wetting his hair, feeling the cold fingers run down the back of his neck. He pulled the mask on, snug to his cheeks.

He pushed off into the icy green and it ran down his back inside the wetsuit, gripping him as he floated. The water was shallow with the ebb tide. In about ten feet of water, Jerra saw the greenish shadow disappear behind a clump of rocks and weed. He dived steep, ears popping. As he neared the place a

161

great tail, like a giant waving frond of weed, lashed out and was gone under a tight ledge. Jerra surfaced and dived again, but there were only a few small fish staring bubble eyed. The ledge narrowed into darkness, too small to turn in, probably impossible to get out of. He followed the line of the fissure, gliding on the surface, to where it was obvious. A splattering of rain on the water. Drops perforated the glassy surface.

The crevice gaped in the side, shrouded with the palpitating weed that bristled around it. Jerra pushed down, weed brushing face and arms. Tiny cracks and holes in the encrusted walls shed spines of light into the twilight. On the bottom, the fanning blue-green tail. As Jerra sank closer, it moved into the darkness of a crack. Holding his nose through the mask, he cleared his ears and sank, settling on the bottom. Breath tight in his chest. He circled the flat, curving floor, pulling himself round with his free hand. The bottom moved under his hand. Peering carefully into the cracks, he saw small fish in most. In the biggest crack, under a sagging beam, was the big fish.

It pinned itself against the back of the hole, gills rising and falling, the eye staring roundly, lip glinting as Jerra came in. It stirred. Jerra lunged and slammed the spear into its broad side, but it was too far back from the head. Too far! The fish lurched, buckled, and sprang out of the crack, ramming Jerra up against the far wall, bludgeoning breath out of him. The wall moved, he heard it creak. Pieces of grit fell, and flakes of rotten ply came off as the fish whipped its tail, pectorals and mouth twitching. Scales rasped against him. Frantic, he took out the knife, almost dropping it, and sank it into the soft place behind the gills, and there was blood; thick, oily stuff. It curled in whorls before him as he dug the knife in more, twisting, feeling the blades of pressure turning inside himself.

The great thing went limp, arched its back, sagged, gills pumping. Jerra dragged it up by the gills, his vision pulsating with a galaxy of spots. Feeble kicks.

Surface. Gobs of blood, crimson. Jerra whooped in the air,

coughing his own gobs, gasping, treading water hard to keep his head out. He got the head to the surface, flat teeth gleaming. The tail thumped his legs. It was like wrestling in the schoolyard, he heard himself think, crazy with gasping, breathless. The spear bent and the prongs were tearing flesh, barbs exposing white meat under the scales. He thrust a whole hand inside the gill to get a grip and to give the groper pain. The fish steadied. He found the embedded knife somewhere in the body and shoved it in more. It trembled and shuddered, rolling him on his back. He fought to the surface again, screaming with panic, dragging up through the spirals and clouds in the water. The spear broke off, barbs left sunk in the meat. Clubbing him with its tail. Jerra found his feet on the bottom and pinned it to the rocks. Rain falling lightly, ruffling the sack and clothes. As Jerra was dragging it up the flat granite, shaking the water out of his eyes, the fish gave a grunt, snorted up a gout of blood, and died.

Jerra laid it out on the rock, a bellowing in his ears. His nose was bleeding and his hands were cut. Thick streams gushed from the gills and gouges in the side, pooling on the rock. Jerra heard gulls, but didn't look up. The stub jutted from the flank, showing tattered white. He pulled the barbs out, ripping the meat as little as he could, and did his best to close the holes with his hands. He turned the fish over and smoothed the scales of the undamaged side with the back of his hand, feeling the little terraces settle into place. A little silver hook lodged in the upper lip.

He took the knife out and made a deep cut behind the head. He wished he had the old man's stub of a knife as he pushed through cartilage and bone, through the black cavity, and then the flesh of the other side. When the juices had run and gone, he cut around inside the head. He found nothing. Only the grey little brain and the black lining behind the eyes.

He sat back for a moment seeing the turrum of his childhood trembling in his arms, against his chest, and the fish's mate scything loyally through the water beside the boat – just ruffling the flat surface in which Jerra saw his reflected face – until the fish grunted and died and the mate became a shrinking black diamond silhouette diving deep, beyond the limits of breath, with an old fisherman's myth and something of Jerra Nilsam locked in its conical head.

Squabbling, the gulls settled on the rock as he made for the clearing, ignoring the figure moving up the beach.

Like water through sand
– Nothing.

'Didn't have any choice, did I? It was bigger than me, almost. It wasn't easy, you know, it wasn't easy! I beat him!' he yelled at the old man, knowing different.

The old man clenched his fists that were black with dried blood as he paced by the fire.

'Bad enough you hack the poor bastard up; but you just left it there for the bloody bastard seagulls! A beautiful blue thing like that with those sad-lookin' eyes pecked out.'

'I was crook. Had water in me guts!' Jerra couldn't get close enough to the fire. He was freezing and his head pumped.

'An' the fish? You left it with *no* guts!'

'Arr.'

'Eh?'

'I said—'

'So, you got 'im – big deal!'

'Yeah, I—'

'Jus' left 'im out there.'

'Well, what—?'

'No *head*!'

'Don't be so bloody—'

'With those bastard birds!'

'Shit!' Jerra shivered.

'What are you? Gotta mutilate fish to find out what you want? Why don't you hack yourself open?'

164

'And what—' He spat in the fire. 'What the hell sort of animal are *you*? Talk about mutilation! Like burning women! And with what she was carryin'!' he shouted with triumph and dread.

The old man stopped dead and turned to Jerra, eyes wide.

'Yes.' His eyes shrank, withdrawing into his head. 'Yer got a fish, boy.' He kicked a black lump of dirt into the fire and left. Jerra didn't watch him go down to the beach.

He heard the seagulls screeching until well after dark. He would have jumped into the fire, but he was too cold to burn.

The fire almost out, Jerra brought from the van the bundle of letters he had brought with him. He flicked through the envelopes addressed to him without opening any of them, least of all the last in the bundle, the one about the Guy Fawkes night he now knew so well he might have lived it himself. He had been on a fishing boat six hundred miles away from her. By then the letters were not love letters, nor insane poetical screams, but long, sad, friendly letters – kindly, almost – full of her hopeless advice and explanations and reassurances. He read some of it:

> . . . was a beautiful craft, Jerra. Your father would
> have loved it. And I loved it as much as Jim. I can't
> deny that I convinced myself to love it, but I thought
> such an hypocrisy worthwhile . . . well, because of Sean
> and the hope with the new child. I thought that the
> only important thing, regardless of how I did it, was to
> be loved.
>
> And the party. Well, the party. We were drunk,
> drunk with pretence and enthusiasm and reunion and
> optimism and much fear, no doubt. I was highly
> regarded by all as the recovered woman, even though I
> looked repulsively expectant. Expectant. Such a word,
> dear Jerra. Take note of it. One must always be
> expectant, but one must not be stupid and mess it up.
> You only have a right to be expectant if you are doing

true things. Do you understand this? I'm not sure I do myself, though I know I have wanted things the wrong way, pretending too much. Oh, we've all cheated so much! It's the way you go about it. And I can say that all too safely now, because I have nothing else to go about. And I have an inkling I will not even go about that properly.

Please excuse this silly talk from an old lady you are (I know) dearly tired of. I wrote this to clear up the matter of Guy Fawkes night because I know Sean believes I lost the baby on purpose. As I started telling you, we were all very drunk – the Watsons, the Courts, all of 'em – and Jim wanted to show off the new boat, and it was after midnight. We went out without a crew. Too far. It was black. I was helplessly burdened, and drunk – I will not pretend I wasn't – and we kept drinking . . .

Jerra did not read on. He knew it well enough. He saw her, heavy and turgid on the deck of the brilliant white vessel and felt for himself the grinding, shrieking collision with the reef, the settling, the jarring rattling her as if to make her spill her burden on to the boards. It was as if he was there. He saw the red lights in the sky, fizzers and rockets cartwheeling red, red, red up into the vast blackness with their spent, smoking carcasses hitting the water with quiet smacks. And Jim calling 'ohgodogodogod!' as if he believed in one other than himself. Jerra felt her breaking up from within, short razors of pain shredding her as she watched the house lights on the beach. The hull shuddering with her. And the screaming. He saw her stricken, pulling on the long bottle shoved in her face for the pain and to shut her up. Eating on the glass . . . The tide rose, edging them off the reef and into the deep, sinking quickly as Jim fired flares up into the sky with all the other gay lights, and was, for once in his life, perfectly ineffectual. Hurrahs and hoots on the beach . . .

Jerra had lived those scenes in his imagination innumerable times. How they reached the beach was beyond imagination and, apparently, beyond her recall.

Jerra rebound the envelopes with the elastic band.

With all her silly talk, all the stupid advice, he thought, all the insane things she dreamt, I'll believe that part for ever. Jerra hated. And he would not forgive – not even her – that grinning slit that cleaved open the skin of her throat which was cracked, black and green, with her seaweed clump of a head half-buried in the sand that the storm had heaved up. On the same beach.

'Didn't they know she would?' he called out to the darkness. 'She was gonna go back all the time!'

Green plastic peeled back to show her grins.

'Been in the water a long time,' said the man next to him.

Jim, up the beach in front of the summer house, wept into Jerra's old man's duffle-coat. A crowd gathered on the sandhills, perched on the horizon, waiting for the news.

Jerra looked down at the naked legs and scarred, slack belly. A jade tinge to the blown fingers.

'Slit herself and went for a swim,' said the man beside him, adjusting his coat in the drizzle. 'Crazy.'

'Yes,' said Jerra. 'They reckon.'

'Know her?'

'No,' said Jerra.

Gulls hovered. The other man cocked his head at him.

'Not personally, no,' said Jerra at the man. He kept talking after the man went further up the beach where seagulls flagged in the breeze. 'No,' Jerra said, more than once.

He dropped the bundle on to the smoking coals, and until – at length – it ignited, he did not regret it.

the sea-winds

Rain fell all night. Out over the ocean, a thunderstorm cracked and clashed. Lightning lit the inside of the van as Jerra lay awake, shivering under the blankets. The leaves were still chattering at dawn when the sky was dark as wet soil. His hands were fishy, and blood had dried brown under his fingernails. He lay under the blankets all day, getting up only once to leak in the fireplace. The stinking steam rose and made him sick. He wondered again for the first time in a while, why? Was it Jimbo? The booze? Sean? Or was it him? 'No,' he said once, listening to it in the dark. 'She was crazy.' And he knew someone else who was crazy. The old man was, he just knew it.

Just before dark, the rain cleared and he cooked a damper in the coals he rekindled. The damper was doughy and burnt on the outside, but it was hot and it cleared the taste from his mouth.

He slept in bits, chased down into the pale depths by schools of roe, wriggling mucus, green and leering, calling verses he didn't remember.

Dawn, another grey. More damper in the slow fire. The wet ground was almost frozen in places. Still hungry, he put sandshoes on and walked up the track to where the prints of rabbits were most obvious, droppings showing in the damp. He veered into the bush for a warren. If that old fool can do it, he thought . . .

*

Gathering his snares, he made his way back to camp, holding the rabbit by its ears as he and his father had, letting the stuff run out as he walked. There was sand in its eyes.

With the brown-stained diving knife, he slit the rabbit up from the anus and pulled back the skin, trying to ignore the putrid steam. He drained off some blood, cut the head and paws off, and hung it with a cord from the fork of a tree where the ringbolt hung. Then he collected some firewood and shoved it under the VW to dry. He sat by the fire all morning, drinking tea and pussy-looking soup from a packet, looking up occasionally to the slow drip from the carcass.

Midday. He stoked up the fire and took the skinned carcass down from the tree. He took a stiff piece of fencing wire and ran it up the anus to where the neck had been. He secured it, bending the ends, and sat waiting for the fire to die. On either side of the fire, he sank a forked stick. Waited.

When the fire was ready, the carcass was no longer a rabbit. It had curled pink on the spit, naked and unformed. Coals clucked and hissed as he took it in his hands, running, running in case it whimpered.

Morning was hard and brittle with frost. The stillness of dawn was buffeted by a sharp wind off the ocean. The bay, as Jerra crunched across the sand, was beginning to roughen like goose-flesh, tiny bumps rising from the smooth grey. Horizon and sea were dark, hard to separate.

N O in the sand.

Jerra listened to the shells under his shoes. The wind was making his nose run. His sleeve was rough. His hair, stiff, weedy, rubbed against his neck. He saw handprints, flat knee-marks.

N O again, wobbly and hurried.

Halfway along the beach, ash white, perched on the bleached beam sticking out of the sand, the old man sat naked and shuddering. As Jerra neared, he saw that the old man's buttocks and feet were blue, and that there were brown stains in his beard, sand all over his body.

'Hey,' cried Jerra. 'What're you doing out here in the cold? You'll bloody freeze to death.'

The old man stared out into the prickling ocean, knuckles bleached, his penis and testicles shrivelled and grey with cold. A shoulder twitched.

'No good sittin' out here. Gonna rain. Go back to your place.'

'Can hear 'em, you know.'

'Eh?'

'Both of 'em blisterin'. An' the boat before . . . never seen anything like it, swimmin' around in the bits 'n' pieces of yer life. An' it's always the junk that floats. Real things're 'eavy. She was racin' me in. She wanted the truck. She wasn't comin' back. I got in first. Gawd yer swim like a bloody fish when yer desp'rate. An' I knocked the livin' crap out of her when she told me 'er . . . condition. Man's a bugger at times, a bugger. She was leavin' in the morning. I give in to her after what I did. An' hit the grog plenty. Can never do the things wanted of yer. Gawd, but she was orright, me Annie . . .'

'Come on!' Jerra tried taking the bony arm, but the old man would not be moved. 'Come on up to the fire, eh?'

'An' I wus burnin' inside . . . I couldn't let 'er go! I *loved*! But . . . she laughed. An' as she wus down there on the beach in that little shack makin' ready for town, I wus up the hill, drinkin' and thinkin' hard . . .'

'Come on up to the fire, eh?'

Creased and shabby in his greying skin, the old man was immovable. Rain began to fall lightly, opening up tiny pores in the sand. Jerra left him there. He'll come up when it really begins to rain, he thought.

He was uncertain how long the old man had sat in the rain. It had been unbearable to watch. Jerra dug himself into the blankets after covering the fire with a piece of tin in case the old man should come up. Rain spattered, *suss*ing on the hot tin in sharp breaths. When the rain finally stopped, Jerra went down to see; but there was no sign, only a windblown set of footprints wobbling all the way to the rocks at the end of the beach.

The wind was much stronger as he trudged through the sand, doing what he could to keep his hair out of his eyes. The sea was the colour of spit, bubbling and foaming. He followed the staggering prints to the pile of granite and began to climb around, the spray from the lumbering waves stinging his cheek, leaving little trickles that ran down the back of his neck under the collar of the coat.

From the top of the rocks he could see smoke from the wobbling chimney. Flecks of weed and dried sponge blew up across the sand, and some were pinned to the walls of the humpy.

Hunched over a drum, the old man wore the cracked oilskin and a black cloth cap. Jerra watched from a few yards away as the old man ladled some of the slush on to the dark, turned soil. Gulls fought in the trees. Jerra was upwind and didn't smell it much. The stuff slopped on to the ground and was largely absorbed, leaving small mallee root turds on top of the soil.

The old man looked up. He dropped the ladle, an old saucepan. He came forward a step, squinting at him, then spat and backed away to the drum.

'Won't give me peace, I smelt yer cracklin'. I knew. She tol' me. That's why, not just 'cause o' the boat. Could o' forgiven her, but she never will. An' you?'

No use this time, either, he knew. It was the same.

'Just thought I'd come over and give you a hand with the veggies.'

'Say it.'

'I said—'

'Come on!'

'Geez.' Jerra sighed.

'Arr, yer can't spook me, any more. Yer can piss off, whosever's yer are! Go on!' He reached into the drum.

Something landed in the sand next to Jerra's foot. Another splattered further away. He could smell it, even in the wind. As he walked away he felt one burst on his back. The stink followed him. Back at the camp he scraped it off, but the smell would not go away.

He looked between the gnarled railway sleepers of the jetty down into the dredged green, green that went for ever down. The pearl was there, somewhere at the bottom. He felt his father's breath in his ear; they were both looking and neither said anything.

It was dark and the wind was too strong for him to keep the fire going. He went inside, listening to the canvas rippling and snapping, the flurries of leaves falling onto the roof of the VW. Rain came and he heard gulls floating over, going inland with the wind. Rain pattered, then sprayed and pelted the canvas and Jerra moved what he could into the van, seeing trickles creeping inward from the ground edges of the canvas. He sat by the blue flame of the Primus, heating spaghetti in a can, bleached every now and then by bursts of light from the sky.

Surf thundered above the tearing sound of wind; the creaks of trees and leaves plastered themselves to car and annexe. Before going to bed, he went outside to the angry night and secured all ropes and some loose gear that was out in the open. Rain showed, driving down steeply, in the light of the torch. Ropes sang in the wind, taut and wet. A dark rivulet was coming down the track into the clearing, black pools appearing on the ground.

Jerra went inside and dried. Already the annexe roof was bowed heavy with water that failed to run off. He left it, knowing that the pores in the cloth would open if he touched it. The rain must ease off soon, he thought. The beach would be being eaten by surf. He wondered how the old man's humpy was faring. Jerra pictured him by the fire, babbling wildly, the ply walls shuddering in the storm.

The little notebook opened in his palm: *All the severed men . . .*

It looked at him. He scribbled, stopping occasionally to listen to the wind and rain, surveying what he had written.

> *All the severed men*
> *Clutching themselves*
> *Butchering*
> *—And the guilt.*

He wondered what the stuff it was supposed to be, closed it to have another go tomorrow. It seemed a waste of time.

Warm inside the blankets. He slept a little.

C. J. Dennis, his birdlike grandfather, and a mealy-mouthed Sentimental Bloke pursued him into the depths with lines he only recalled in his sleep.

> *What is the matter wiv me? . . . I dunno.*
> *I got a sorter thing that won't let go*
> *Or be denied—*
> *A feelin' like I want to do a break,*
> *An' stoush creation for some woman's sake.*

It must have been after midnight when he heard the tent-poles collapse. He sat up and saw the roof of the annexe sagging to the ground. Outside in the wind there was the sound of rain on water. Lightning crackled. A lot of water on the ground.

There was no use doing anything until morning. In the

distance there was the creaking, grinding sound of a tree falling, falling. He pulled the blanket round. He felt his head going through things, crashing in his ears, a pinging, slapping surge of sounds that drove his head deeper, further under grey water out of the rain and the noise; and he was laughing, singing and finding strings of words that were never strong enough to stay together pinging around in his brain. Deep – *of 'ope an' joy an' forchin destichoot* – and he tasted the bitterness of beer.

The surface returned in choppy waves, bringing the whipping of cloth and wood back into his ears. Breathing hard in struggling gulps, and he spat things before going down again, feeling the sappy weed stroking his face, eating into his cheeks.

Gulping up into the grey again he heard the shrill whistle of wind and the rabbit squeaks of boughs on the paintwork. Morning soon and he would have to clean up the mess.

Jerra saw a lot that night. He sprinted in the dark with screaming in his ears and lights bursting green around him until his vision was reduced to a mottled opaque green like dense foliage. He smelt the bush. It made him drunk, drunk and floating until he was soaring between vast gorges and over water like a great sea-bird. He flew like this for some time before his wings began to fail him, tearing with the pressure of wind. He began to sink. He saw pollard-gloved hands pierced with hooks, and arms outstretched calling 'Jerra!', reaching up through the mottled webbing of net. 'You can't chuck it in!' the old man said, rolling over and over with his tongue out. Flares burst around, forcing Jerra down to the water, green water, and he slid in and cruised like a shark, savaging, feeding off a struggling creature that swam out to sea leaving a red chalk-line like a diligent Gretel. Excited, he plunged his head into weed, plaited, matted strands, found a slit, and furrowed greedily down into the warm sap-green until sated and ashamed. Then, in retreat and revulsion, he saw the shredded corpse jaded under plastic and the Sentimental Bloke called out:

> *... I'm sick*
> *Of that cheap tart*
> *'Oo chucks 'er carkis at a fella's 'ead*
> *An' mauls 'im ... Ar! I wish't ...*

'No!' Jerra cried.

> *... that I wus dead! ...*

He bit his tail turning perfect, frenzied circles, ripping pieces away from himself in fury and frustration and he came to pieces, each tiny piece stabbing the other with knives and safety pins and eyes and words and cactus spines. Something swam slowly past making for the rarified deep – a muscular diamond – secreting tears of grief that became solidified gems encrusting the outside of its skull like the boil-cased face of Job.

His head went tight between his knees as he retracted, wishing for escape, speed, a bigger engine. Blood between his knees, on his legs. A coughing gout. He hugged the beautiful, sleek, dead creature, afraid to follow the muscular diamond into the depths to see. He cried, left with the dead and dying.

'Don't let them make you old before you're young, Jerra,' she said, trembling as he went back down the corridor. 'Don't let them make you give up. You don't have time to get that way.'

He went out into the sunshine.

Hands had been softer, and drier. There was breathing and the exhalation of weeping trees. Glass tinkled, falling like shells and jagged stones. The brace moved on his chest. Fingers bit into him – twigs. Cold flatness on his cheeks; he was floating up against the ceiling. A cough, bubbly with phlegm. Hot breath

175

on his forehead. Ribbons of grey floated past in the breeze. Still outside. Thunder of surf. Then – now and then – a painful travelling. His body contorted, manhandled.

Coughing racked the grey silence again. He might have remembered a lurching dinghy, a boy crying, face turned; but it did not fit. Something solidified under his back.

'Son?'

It shifted the black. The blanket folded back.

'Yer awake?'

The blanket ruffled. More coughing. The overcast lightened.

'Yeah.' Throat dry. Blood, tasting the way it smelled.

'Hurtin'?' The voice reverberated a little.

'Dunno. Yes. Something holding me round the guts.'

'Hmm.'

'How'd you get in? Annexe's a bit of a mess, I think. Bit of a blow last night.'

The old man coughed, apparently uncomfortable.

'Your shack hold up orright?'

A strange twilight. Windows were higher. Only cracks of light coming through. Jerra felt odd.

'It opened up an' blew away,' said the old man.

'What? Gone?'

'I felt water on the bunk first, in the blankets. The roof was leakin' in a few spots an' then it was pissin' down the insides of the walls, down the chimney. Heard that go later. Went outside and the whole lot blew away like a tent. That ol' drum was rollin' around, sprayin' everythin'.'

'Come here to get out of the rain, eh? Thought I heard some noise. Find a blanket orright?'

'You what?' The old man's voice sounded strange again, as if he was taking another crazy turn off on his own.

'Hard findin' yer way in the rain?'

'Bloody oath. Water was up to the sandhills. Thought I was gonna get sucked in, a couple o' times there. In the bush, stuff rumblin' everywhere. An' gettin' you up the track with all the water comin' down, like wadin' upstream.'

He coughed, rattling. 'Heavy bastard you are, too.'

'Hang on—' It was crazy talk to Jerra, who did not understand.

'Oh, you—' The old man laughed.

'How'd you get here in all—' Jerra became impatient.

'Stumbled into the tree. Bloody great tree stickin' through yer bus. Crashed through the roof, pinned you. Bloody mess. Bit of a shame about yer bus. An' yer a bit knocked about by the looks of it. Nothin' busted, I don't think.'

What the hell?

'So where are we?'

'The old hut. Up the hill. Nowhere else to go.'

Jerra lay, going through it again. Then the VW is gone, he thought, or maybe the old coot is exaggerating. He decided he would have to see for himself. He could feel the old man next to him on the dusty boards. It hurt under the damp blanket.

'Dawn soon,' Jerra murmured. 'I'll go down an' check the damage.'

The old man wheezed, shuckling up some phlegm.

'Night's only just come.'

Jerra listened to the gentle burr of bark on tin, his back aching. He thought he caught a word or two, but they were gone. It was all beyond him.

'Will you stay here, now the other hut is gone?' he asked a bit later.

'Have to think,' breathed the old man.

'Not much timber around. To rebuild.'

'I got this one. Last as long as needs be.'

'Pretty safe up here. No one's gonna look for you.'

'Just can't fight 'em any more, that's all. Just keep goin' till I can't.'

Ocean hammered in the distance.

'Don't s'pose there's anything to eat,' said Jerra. 'Thirsty as hell, too.'

Old man scuffing around in the dust.

'Went down this afternoon and found some things. Matches . . . knife . . . here, some biscuits. Soggy, I expect.'

Jerra ate a couple. They might have been gingernuts.

'Saw that groper, too,' the old man said, carefully.

'Mm.' Jerra closed his eyes.

'Stuck up in the rocks, above the watermark. Crabs been at it.'

'Made a mess o' that. Didn't I?'

'Yeah, a mess.'

'Nearly took me with him.'

'Did good to beat him, I s'pose.' Cough coming from deep within him. 'But not good enough, son.'

'Beat him, didn't I?' said Jerra, suddenly arrogant.

'No.'

'Some things you can't get around. Your words.'

'Yer can have anythink and it'll likely be no good. It's how yer get it and what yer do with it, that's what counts. Havin' it's nothin'. Everybody's got things. It's nothing.' The old man paused and spat. 'Go to sleep. Some water here if you need it.'

Jerra closed his eyes.

'I was after the pearl, you know,' he whispered. 'It didn't have one.'

The old man chuckled in his throat.

'Keep tryin', boy. You 'ad the wrong fish. Spear an open swimmer, they're the ones. Cave fish see nothin'.'

'An open swimmer.'

'They're the ones.'

Morning was a long way.

. . . or see this great fire any more, lest I die

The pool of yellow slag was dry and hard beside the blanket left in a crumpled ball. Green, fleshy leaves protruded through the tin. Out the window, the sky was the colour of dead skin.

Pain was more distant than he anticipated, much of it from lying on the wooden floor so long. His back was tight. On his forehead there was open skin, hard already with drying, and he found grazes on his arms, and a thin pain – like little barbs – in his hip. He limped out into the pale light.

Guttered with washouts, the sand track wound slowly – NO faint and puffy wound in the bark – until he saw the knotted masses of foliage in the clearing; a shred of canvas impaled on a branch; vomity flour pooled on the mud. Wide black puddles reflected the thin clouds. The VW, toppling on its side, was fused to a thick gum, fenders crushed. Unmelted hailstones of glass lay on the ground. He peered in. The steering column a splintered tangle; panels buckled; boxes spilling. Black blood, stinging scent of eucalyptus, wet blankets. He reached in for his shoes. He found two oranges and his coat. Matches. The shoes might have been anywhere. He put the oranges in the pockets of his coat. The old man will be hungry, he thought, wondering where he might be.

Weed and shells were strewn up on the sand; heaps of piled weed, buzzing with little insects. The bottoms of the dunes were eaten away and deep gouges ran part of the way up the beach. Jerra heard the gulls. The old man was not here.

He went up the track, stumbling barefoot in the deep open veins in the mud, pulling his coat tight around him, the shit-stink following. Bird noises. He thought perhaps the old man would be back at the shack. Gulls hahed high in the trees. Others were skirting the treetops, crowding in.

'Ah, bastards.'

He cut into the bush.

The gulls moved back without blinking when he came close. The old man's face was in the mud, feet in the air, ankles pecked raw where his trousers had crept up, skin open, sunk with piano wire that gleamed dull. A little puddle of blood and mucus bathing the old face. The ringbolt on the ground, next to the puddle.

Jerra sat keeping the birds away for a while. He knew what he would do.

A single witness shall not prevail . . .

On the beach, he wrapped the old man in the tattered canvas sheets. He tied his diving weights around the middle, threaded the ring through. He undressed. He took the old man's boots off the cooling feet. He waded out to the shallow part of the reef, the icy water gripping his shins. Beneath his numbing feet the fur of algae yielded softly. He steered the bundle out, stopping every few moments to unsnag it, until he manoeuvred it over a hole, using the ring at the waist as a handle, and lowered it over the edge, watching it sink slowly into the green, grey hole. The water stung his cuts. He watched the green.

Seagulls were gathering on the water as he pulled his clothes back over his blue limbs. The old man's boots were rank, but soft inside. He went up to the clearing. Digging into the mess he found sultanas, and socks for the boots. Packets, boxes, coils, blankets spilling. Birds in the trees, mostly gulls, were showing their pink tongues, one close in the fallen tree that crushed the VW. It laughed at him with those red Sean-eyes, squinting, edging closer.

'Bugger off, yer bastards!' he yelled.

The gull came closer. Blinking.

Jerra lit a match, smelling the dead breath of its smoke, dropped it into the fuel tank, and ran.

THAT EYE,
THE SKY

For Simon White

From the otherworld of action and media, this
interleaved continuing plane is hard to focus;
we are looking into the light –
it makes some smile, some grimace.

Les A. Murray, 'Equanimity'

I

chapter one

Dad has the ute going outside. I am behind Mum. Her dress has got flowers all on it, none of them much to look at. Her bum moves around when she laughs. Dad always says she has a bum like an angry mob, which means nothing to me but a lot to him, I reckon. I can hear the rooster *crork*ing out the back. He's a mean rooster – goes for your pills when you collect the eggs.

'Seeyaz.' That's Dad going. He revs the ute up. He's in a hurry, going to town for Mr Cherry.

'Wave him off, Ort,' Mum says to me. She always reckons you should show people you love them when they go away because you might never see them again. They might die. The world might end. But Dad's only going to town for an hour. It's business for Mr Cherry. And there he goes, out the drive and on to the road.

Mum puts her hand on my shoulder and flour falls down my arm. The rooster *crorks* again. That's a mean rooster. Dad drop-kicks him on Saturday mornings just to let him know who's boss.

'Hop inside and do your homework, Ort,' Mum says.

'In a minute,' I say.

'What you learnin'?'

'Burke and Wills.'

'Uh-huh.'

Mum doesn't know what Burke and Wills is, I bet, but she

won't let on. But that's orright. I don't know what it is yet, either. Gotta learn it. That's why it's homework.

'Well, get in there, my second man,' she says, putting up her dress a bit for some air. It's hot.

'In a minute.' I pick at the flap of skin on my stubbed toe. Stubbed toes are something you have to live with in this life.

That mean rooster goes again. I can just see his red dishmop hairdo wickering around all over the place as he yells his lungs off. The sky is the same colour as Mum and Dad's eyes. When you look at it long enough, like I am now with my nose up in it, it looks exactly like an eye anyway. One big blue eye. Just looking down. At us.

My name is Morton Flack, though people call me Ort for short. Ort is also a name for bum in our family. It means zero too (you know, like nought), but in my case it just means Morton without saying all of it. My dad's name is Sam Flack. Mum is called Alice. Her last name was different when she was a maid. Tegwyn in the next room with her magazines is my sister. She finishes school next month. Grammar lives in the room behind with her piano she never plays. She never does much these days. That flamin' rooster going again.

The light slants down funny on my desk from the lamp Dad fixed up there on the wall. I should be doing Burke and Wills. They don't seem very bright blokes. Instead I'm listening to the night coming across from the forest – all small sounds like the birds heading for somewhere to stay the night, the sound of the creek tinkering low when everything gets quiet, the chooks making that maw-maw sound they do when they're beginning to sleep all wing to wing up under the tin roof of the chook-house. Sometimes in the night I can hear their poop hit the ground it's so quiet. Sometimes it's so quiet, Dad says you can hear the dieback in the trees, killing them quietly from the inside. At night the sky blinks at us, always looking down.

The sounds of the night aren't really what's keeping me from Burke and Wills, though. It's Dad. He's not back. But I'm not worried. Fat Cherry is my best friend. He's got a head like a potato, eyes like a baby pig's, and his belly shimmies all over the shop when he walks. Until we got separated, Fat and me sat together in school. His real name is James, but even Fat is better than that. Fat Cherry is a good name all round. So's Ort Flack. All the other kids in the district have got names like Justin and Scott and Nathan and Nicholas which are piss-poor in anyone's book. And no kid wants to be called Mary or Bernadette if he's not a girl. Even my chook (my private chook – my pet one) has got a better name than the kids at school. Errol is my pet chook's name. Mum says it's a sacrilege but I haven't figured that out yet. When Errol was a chick I found him outside the chookrun with his leg all busted up and caught in the wire. I put tape on his leg and kept him in bed with me for a week until Mum went off her face about the sheets.

Wait . . . wait on . . . I can hear a car. No, it was someone passing. Someone leaving the city. If you climbed the dying jarrah trees down there towards the creek, you'd see the lights of the city. From here, the only lights in sight are from Cherry's roadhouse a hundred yards along the highway on the other side of the road. You can see their bowsers glowing, and sometimes you think you can actually see the numbers rolling in them, but you're just kidding yourself.

The tail-lights of that car burn the bush up and go slowly out. Burke and Wills.

Ah, another car. That'll be the old man. He's late. Boy is he late. Mum'll be mad.

The car comes up the long drive towards us, but the engine noise is all wrong. Mum is going out. If I could, I'd go out too, but I'm all stuck, like the chair has hold of me. I'm scared, a bit. I am scared. I'm scared. There's fast talking out there. *Isn't anyone gonna turn that engine off?*

'Morton? Morton!' Here she comes, setting all the floorboards going, there she is, my mum, with those eyes full up and spilling, the dress shaking enough to shed all those dumb flowers off it.

The big, strange car shoots us down the driveway and out on to the sealed road with Mum and me rolling across the big back seat that farts and squeaks under us. Headlights poke around in the dark. A man with a bald moon at the back of his head is driving and talking – both too fast. My belly wants to be sick. Mum's eyes are making me wet.

'How far, Mr . . .'

'Wingham, Lawrence Wingham,' the man pants.

'How far?'

'A couple of kilometres, only a couple.'

The speedo is like a clock gone mad. I don't know why, but I feel like I just swallowed a whole egg, shell and all. I can tell something bad's happened – I'm not stupid – but no one has told me yet. I don't know. If my dad is dead, we just won't live any more.

The moon sits over the road like a big fat thing. It looks useless as hell tonight. I never felt that about the moon before. As the road goes downhill I can see the pale lights of the city far away. Trees hang all over the road.

'Where's Tegwyn?' I ask.

'She's home looking after Grammar.'

'I could've done that.'

'I want you . . . with me,' she says. I know she's crying. All the door handles glow in the dark. It's like I can see her face in them and she's crying in all of them. Tegwyn will hate looking after Grammar.

Now the road is winding down towards Bankside, the place where my school is. There's two shops, a pub, a bowser, a big church place, and a post office as well. It's not as big as the city.

The orange light makes me jump. I can see it through the

trees and it gets stronger as we round the bend. Mum's arm is around me, pushing all the air out of me. A tow truck. Some cars on either side of the road. A big mess in the bush. The flashing light makes the road and the ground and the bush jump. It makes the men walk in jerks.

No one even looks at us when we pull up. Mum is out and running. Dad's ute is all pushed back on itself something horrible. I can see Ted Mann from the Bankside Garage shouting at Bill Mann his brother. It's their tow truck making the orange light. There's not much for them to tow. I stay in the car. Mum has Ted Mann by the singlet. They shout.

'The ambulance has been and gone,' he says.

'When?'

'Ten minutes ago.'

'Tell me, tell me.'

'What, Mrs Flack?' Ted Mann does not like us because we work for Mr Cherry who is competition.

'Is he all right?'

'Looked pretty bloody crook to me,' he says, turning back to Bill Mann to keep up the argument. They're always arguing. Their wives went away to live in the city. Or so Tegwyn says.

I'm all sick. But I can see all right. I'd be sicker if Dad was dead. I know he's not. I know it. But I feel sick enough.

The man in front of me, the man who has driven us here with his bald moon of a head coming up out of the seat, is still here. Mum comes back to the car.

'Can you take me into the city?' she asks the man who starts the big car again.

'That's where I was headed in the first place,' he says, moving around on the seat.

She ges in front with him and then twists around to me. 'You get a lift back with Mr and Mr Mann. I won't be back till late. You've got school tomorrow.'

'School? Mum!' I can't believe it.

'You've got one week of term left. You've never missed a

day yet and you're not gonna. If you start something, you finish it. If I'm not back before morning, you get a lift in with Fat and Mr Cherry. Tegwyn will cut your lunch.' She kisses me on the nose hard enough to make me eyes fog up.

Outside the car, there is the dry smell of wild oats and the brown smell of the paddocks and the talk of Ted and Bill Mann. I get in their truck. The big car pulls out and passes and I see Mum wave and fix her hair. Her hair is the colour of white wood. Ted and Bill Mann argue. I get out because it's hot in the cab. Ted Mann looks at me and shrugs.

Dad's ute is so small. I look inside. The seats are all back and forward and up and over everywhere. Everything inside is sticky. It's blood – I'm not stupid. I go round the side to where the open tray is. A bale of hay has come loose and split itself all over. There's his big tool box still there, and on it, the big rag that he wipes his hands on. It used to be a pair of my pyjama bottoms until the bum came out. I pick it up. It smells of turps and oil and grease. It smells of my dad. A long way away there is a siren. That will be the police. It's a long way for them to come. I suppose they will look at the skid marks and those trees over there that are all flat and sprinkled with glass.

Mr and Mr Mann are arguing about how they'll tow the ute. I stand here waiting. The sky blinks down at me.

chapter two

In a couple of years they're going to pull this school down. It's only a tin shed, so it won't take much. Next year I have to go to high school in the city anyway. That means I'll get home at six o'clock like Tegwyn; six o'clock when there's only three hours of light left – and that's in summer. High school. I don't like thinking about it. Tegwyn's been there three years and she *still* doesn't like thinking about it. Funny to think this school will be gone. Bankside used to be the country. Now you can see the city at night. Soon the city will be here.

Across the classroom I can see Fat. He's trying to get me to look at him. One little pig eye winks, and I want to wink back but I can't. He keeps winking a message in morse code but I can't even look properly at him. His dad was all strange in the truck this morning when he gave us a lift. Tegwyn kept looking at me as we twisted down the hill in low. Mr Cherry didn't say a word. Sometimes he drives us nuts with his talk and showing us his funny eyes, all black and shadowy. He says he looks like Eddy Canter whoever that is. Bores us dead. But today not a word. When the truck bumped around and I hit my head on the door, he gave me a funny look as if to say: 'Don't even say ouch or I'll dump you out on the side of the road.' Tegwyn burped then and giggled and Fat got a clip on the ear as if *he* did it.

Mr Cherry isn't very big. He looked even smaller this morning, as if the steering-wheel had grown. He hadn't shaved and his chin was full of little grey iron filings like the ones on his workshop floor. He didn't say one word about my dad.

'James! James Cherry.' Mrs Praktor has seen Fat's spastic winking. Praktor-the-tractor. Good ol' Max Factor. That's what we always say. 'Sit up straight and do your work.'

Someone giggles. Someone always giggles. There's all grades in this class. It's the only class in the school. Nathan Mann is year six. Bernadette Mann is year four. Mary Mann is year four, too. Bernadette and Mary are twins, but you wouldn't know it. One like a horse, one like a camel. Billy Ryde is only year two. There's all grades, but me and Fat are the only year sevens.

It's hot in here. You can hear the bush moving around outside like it's tossing and turning in the heat.

At lunch Fat and I play french cricket under the big tree with the bits of lumpy lawn under it. I keep chipping the ball away near his feet and when he dives for it, his whole belly goes nuts.

'Have you heard about my dad?' I say, knocking one a bit too high.

He snatches the ball.

'Gotcha.'

'Made it easy for you.'

'Ah yeah.'

'Did ya hear anything?'

'Carn, gis the bat.'

'Well?'

He takes the bat and faces up. Across the yard the Mann twins are playing skippy. Their plaits jump around like propellers. They look like they're gonna take off any moment. Chuck-chuck-chuck, a camel helicopter and a horse helicopter chopping across the paddock, over Mann's Garage and the Bankside Arms down towards the city. I take the ball. It's a furry old six-stitcher Fat's dad gave him. I put it at him high on the bat and Fat jumps back out of the way.

'Well?' I say, grubbing in the lumpy grass for the ball.

'My dad told me not to talk about it.'

'Don't then.' I throw low and he hits sideways and I miss the catch and I'm angry all of a sudden.

Errol and me sit out on the back veranda. His beak is all hooky and busted. His eyes are pink. The way he looks at me, sometimes, you wouldn't know he was a chook. My schoolbag is all hot and leather-smelly from being in the sun. I toss Errol across the veranda and he garks and fluppers and I go inside to the cool of the house.

'Is that you, Lil Pickering?' Grammar calls out.

'No, jus' me, Grammar.'

She makes mumbly, spluttery noises and then goes quiet. As I pass her door I look in. There she is with her feet up on the windowsill and the breeze up her nightie.

'Lil Pickering?'

'No, just Ort, Grammar.'

In her hand there's a big red apple. She likes to have things like that around, bright things she can still see. Sometimes she just looks at her feet which are the colour of boiled crayfish and stink twice as much. Old people are a bit boring and a bit scary. But I go in because something makes me. And there she is, all tears down her face, big branches of them. You'd think they were our family tree. Her arms are all old and bag down under. I just shine her apple with me hanky and leave our family tree on her face and go out.

There is a bit in me, you know, that tells me my dad is not dead. But it isn't enough. Fat won't come over to muck around today – I just know it. I don't want to muck around anyway. I'm just sitting here in the cool kitchen thinking of all the things I don't want to do. It only takes one thing to make you unhappy.

I should go down to the old sawmill. I should be thinking of all the funny things that have happened to us. I should chop some kindling and start the fire for Mum – Tegwyn will be home in a minute. I should . . . I should figure out why all . . . Mum's glass jars along the shelf above the stove are all full of . . . jewels. Crikey! In the flour jar there's big red stones like the big lumps you get with a blood nose. And in the rice jar there's diamonds! Eight big, fat jars with their lids pointing at me, all full of shining things. Jewels!

'Oh, Ort.' There's Mum standing in the doorway with her arm against the frame. Her hair is across and up and all over the place and her eyes are red. 'Thought you might get the stove going for us.'

I don't say a word. I've still got one eye on those rubies and gems. I point at them. Mum looks and then looks back at me.

'What?' she whispers.

And then they're gone. Flour and rice and lentils and icing sugar and tea are back in their jars.

'No. Nothin'.'

Mum looks at me and I look at Mum.

'Is that you, Lil Pickering?' Grammar calls from down in her room.

'No, Mum, it's me,' Mum calls. 'Come on, Ort, get the stove going. Tegwyn'll be wanting her bath.'

'Is Dad dead?' My mouth just says it – I can't help it.

'No,' she says, tying an apron on, the one with Sydney Harbour Bridge on it. 'No, he's not dead.'

'Is he crook?'

'Pretty crook, yes. He's in a coma, Ort. He's not awake. In a coma. Like you were once. You probably don't remember.'

But I do remember. I was only small, but I do remember. I was dead. Twice. Two times my heart stopped and my brain stopped.

'You had meningitis. Your head was all full of water. You screamed like you were on fire. And then you went asleep and didn't wake up for two weeks.'

I remember. It was like a sea, up and down on waves, and the light was like after the sun has just gone down, and voices called.

'Twice, you know, they said it was all over. But I didn't listen to them and neither did you. In hospitals you just don't listen to them 'cause they don't know any better than us. They don't really know what it is that makes people work. They just guess.

'In the end there was me and these three nurses – rebels they were – and we just kept talking to you, talking about the weather and how's yer father' – she stops for a moment and I look at me toe-scabs – 'and the doctors went crook and tried to keep us away. He can't hear you, they said. But we just kept on chatterin' away there until one morning you just woke up. You were a baby all over again. You were born all over again. Had to have you in nappies. Three years old – in nappies. God, I cried.'

All of a sudden Mum is at the sink doing absolutely nothing at all except having her shoulders jump up and down.

'I remember,' I say to her.

'Your father'll remember too. When it's all over, he'll remember.'

I don't sleep that good. Never have. Even when I was little and Mum or Dad put me to bed, I'd lie awake until they'd gone to bed themselves – longer even. It's lonely in the middle of the night with just you and the sky and the noises of the forest. There's no one to talk to except that big sky. Sometimes I talk to it. Sounds funny, but I do. Ever since they brought me home from the hospital the time I was so sick, I haven't slept good. It's like those two weeks of sleeping in the coma were enough sleep for one person in their life. Strange to think that Dad's down there in a hospital in the city asleep, hearing all those voices and seeing all those colours like I did. He won't sleep much good when he gets better, that's for sure. Still, he's not much of a sleeper anyway.

I can hear Tegwyn talking in her sleep. All night she was playing Grammar's piano. She hammers up and down on it with her brown plaits hanging down forward, her long fingers going at it like mad, her back bent like a slave. She bashes that piano, Tegwyn. I don't know about her. Sometimes I see her in the shower through the hole in the asbestos. She sings to herself. She's got big boobs – they look like pigmelons – bigger than Mum's. Mum's are like two socks full of sand. Tegwyn isn't happy much. When she's in the shower she soaps her legs and in between like she's trying to hurt herself. She looks at her soapy brown legs with a sad look. And sometimes she looks straight into the shoot of water that comes out of the shower head. She lets it go right into her eyes. For a minute, sometimes, looking straight into it and letting it hurt her. I don't think she feels it until she goes to sleep. That's why she groans and calls out in her sleep. Those noises make me cry for no reason, sometimes. Night time is like that. Crazy things happen and you just can't help it.

I was born at night. In this house – out in the living-room. Mum and Dad talk about it now and then. It was winter and cold. Dad said he could hear a dog barking somewhere all night. Mum was all fat with me inside and in those days there wasn't any ute. The people who owned Cherry's Roadhouse in those days had a car, but they were out seeing people in Bankside. Mum started to hurt with me, and Dad put her in the living-room where the fire was going hot and red. All the time he was looking through the curtains across to the roadhouse to see if the people had come back with their car. There was no phone. Still isn't – Mum and Dad don't like them. It was a long drive into town and the hospital. Dad was starting to get jumpy. Mum said he kept stoking the fire up for something to do until the room got so hot that the wallpaper started to come off. Then Dad was running around trying to put the wallpaper back up and while he was doing that Mum had me on the sofa and the first thing I must've saw was those lousy brown flowers on the sofa and my dad chucking a mental.

Mum said I came out all blue with that cord thing all round me neck. She bit it. Ugh! And pretty soon I went all pink and she gave me some milk from her boobs which probably weren't so socky in those days. Well that's what Tegwyn says.

I've always lived in this house – even from the first day. Maybe that's why I like it so much. Tegwyn was born in hospital. I know enough about hospitals to tell you that you don't want to be *born* in one.

Mum was born in a truck coming across the Nullarbor Plain. She just got shook out. The Nullarbor has the worst roads in the world. Dad got born on the enquiries desk of a police station. He says they just cut his cord and put him in the OUT basket. Grammar used to talk about it once. I think she was born on a farm up north where all the ground is red and it rains in summer and is warm in winter.

Being born is hard work. Mum says people scream. Errol came out tapping. His egg just opened up and there was no screaming, but I suppose it was hard work all the same.

People die, too. Even stars die – you see them falling out of the sky. Mum used to say it was the sky shedding a tear.

Tegwyn is asleep now. Everything is asleep.

Before I go to sleep, I go out and pee off the back veranda. The ground smells summery. That stupid rooster is at it. Middle of the night. A long time after I'm dried up, I stand out there looking up to see if maybe a star might fall.

chapter three

The summer holidays came so quick – here they are. I'm in them! And here I am with Fat, walking along the top bank of the creek down towards the sawmill with everything jumping in the trees, and the pods snapping and popping in the heat. I've got one eye out for snakes and the other out for something different. Down here, you always find something different. Holidays do that to you, you know. You see better, you smell better.

In the reeds along the edge of the creek, frogs churk and gulp and catch flies. The water is still and brown. By the end of summer there'll probably be no water at all and there'll be roos and rabbits sniffing out pools all along here at dusk. Tadpoles scribble away across the surface. Birds tip-toe here and there like old ladies. There's tigersnakes about, but you just don't think about that.

'Can you see it?' I ask Fat. His shirt is off and his belly button is full of flies. Fat squints. When he moves, his belly button squints too, but those flies won't move for anything.

'Nup.'

'Should be along here somewhere. Was 'ere in winter. 'Member that time you nearly drowned us?'

'That was your fault.'

'Ah, pull the other one.' Fat capsized us. I can't say anything. He knows he's fat – he doesn't need me to tell him.

'There,' Fat says, 'there it is.'

We run along for a bit and then edge down the bank on our

bums to where we can see the brown corner of that car roof we had last summer.

'It's pretty rusty,' I say. We try to pull it out. Grass and pigface have grown all over it and it's half buried in mud. There's even roo poop on it. But there's no holes in it, and pretty soon we've got some long sticks for poles and we're out on the water. The creek is only six foot wide or so, but it's deep in places. After pushing away and making a lot of noise – what with shouting at Fat to keep in the middle, and nearly losing my pole – we get going smooth and quiet and the only noise is the water moving aside to let us pass and the mosquitoes playing their sirens all around.

When it's like this, and you're doing something quiet with someone, like when Dad and me are walking through the forest, or when Mum and me have stopped reading a book together 'cause it's started to rain all of a sudden, it's then that you feel like you know what both of you are thinking and you don't have to talk. Fat's back is pink already from the sun. I can hear him breathing. He hasn't been over for a while. We've done some things, me and Fat.

'Mum an' Dad had a fight las' night.'

I look up from the water. He talked.

'Yeah?'

'Mum kep' hittin' 'im with the *Sunday Times*.'

I laugh. The *Sunday Times* is what Dad used to hit his dog with, before the dog got caught in a rabbit trap and had to be put down.

'He was . . . cryin'.'

'Oh.'

Fat steers us away from the end of a log all clotted with ants. I don't say anything.

'Like a baby.'

We keep poling quietly down the creek until we get to the sawmill.

For a long time they cut the forest up at the sawmill. Down

around Bankside you can see stumps everywhere, little grey toadstools. All the farms in the district used to be forest. Now the forest is only this small bit behind our place and along the main road for a mile or so. It goes down to the edge of the scarp – another mile – and that's all. And now there's dieback eating them all to death. My dad talks about it a lot. He loves trees. He had a fight with a logger once, but that was a long way before my time and Mum reckons it's not true anyway. The sawmill hasn't been used since I've been alive – that's twelve years. We pull up near it, and shimmy up the bank.

Fat and me kind of stand around, picking through things, but our hearts aren't in it. I climb into what's left of the old furnace and shout. My word jumps back at me and goes across and up in an echo: You!   You!

You!

Everything is rusty and when you touch it it falls apart or makes your hands red. The sheds are all falling over. Some saws are still left, but you couldn't move 'em with an earthquake. There's big wheels and cogs and pistons, but nothing fits together any more. Possums live up under the roof. They must get used to the flapping tin. It wasn't such a good idea to come here. Everything is too sad.

'Why were they fighting?' I ask Fat as we push further downstream. Flies and mozzies dive-bomb us. Something crunches off into the bush. 'Your mum and dad.'

Fat doesn't say a word. He hardly moves. Maybe he's trying hard to keep balance. His pink legs come out either side of him like wings.

We float on down, pushing ourselves over logs with our poles bleeding sap where we broke them off.

He doesn't say a thing.

*

Where the creek meets the main road, there is a wooden bridge with white rails and big black piles driven into the bank at either side. Sometimes Fat and me like to lie under there in the cool with all the insects singing and listen to the cars going across, setting all the boards going like a xylophone. There's a high note at one end, and a low one at the other. Cars come up the scales or down them. Tegwyn says it's not real scales at all and we're jus' kids. Fat usually makes a fart with a hand under his arm and that makes her go away. 'I'm so disgusted,' he'll say, walking after her the way she walks with her bum going from side to side.

As we get far enough around the bend to see along the high banks, Fat says: 'There's someone under there.'

'Who?'

'How do I know?'

'Let's get out and go over, see who it is.'

'No,' Fat whispers, 'it's quieter on the water. Let's float down closer. They won't see us if we keep to the bank.' He's right, you know. He's not dumb, Fat.

From behind a fallen log, we watch the person under the bridge. I can hear Fat's heart. Small birds wink past. It's a man. Older than my dad. His pants are grey and baggy. He's on his knees with his hands in his lap and his head is all back so that his black hat kind of hangs off and looks like it'll fall any moment. Sometimes he looks like he's talking because his mouth moves. Beside him is a blanket and a little brown bag. Fat looks at me and I look at Fat.

A car, a station wagon, rushes over and sets the bridge xylophoning up the scale but the man on his knees under the bridge doesn't seem to hear.

'He's been sleepin' here,' Fat says, very quiet. We're close enough to hit him with a stone, an easy underarm throw. His face is brown and looks like the old saddle Dad has out in the shed – all cracks and lines that change when his lips move. His teeth are very white. His hands are big in his lap. He looks clean enough. Suddenly he reaches behind and pulls up a head of grass and squeezes it in his hands until all the soil falls away, then he just holds it to his face and his lips keep moving.

We sit here for a while, hardly breathing, not taking our eyes off him for a minute.

The sun is almost down by the time we get over to Fat's place, and in the driveway of the roadhouse there is a man in a Ford flat-top with the horn going on and off and his face all red above a shirt and tie that are both undone as if he's been tearing at them he's so angry.

'How the bloody hell does a man get some service around this godforsaken place?' he's yelling between honks.

'How much do you want?' Fat says, his eyes going thin very quick. He pulls the nozzle off the bowser and takes it over to the Ford. 'Your petrol cap's locked.'

'Leave it alone, Slim. I want your father.'

'You won't fit him in there,' Fat says, pointing to the petrol tank.

The red man with the pulled tie and open shirt says to me: 'You think that's funny?' His eyes are white on his face. He looks like he might open the door and climb down any moment.

'No, sir,' I mumble.

'How much do you want?' Fat asks again. He looks like nothing could make him laugh. But his belly gives him away; I can see it just beginning to shuffle around.

The man puts his sunglasses on and looks like he's going to do something any moment. Then he's leaning forward a little – going for the door handle. No, he's winding the window up. The bowser rumbles. Fat points the nozzle on to the truck's tray. With a sharp kick the Ford starts up. The man looks at me for a second and then he drives off with a squeal. I can't believe it. And there's petrol pouring off the tray as he swings out on to the road and heads down towards the city. Pouring off. Like the back of a council water truck.

I turn to Fat. He's got this cheesy grin all over him and there's still drips of petrol running down the steel tip of the nozzle. 'Fat!'

And then we're both laughing our teeth out.

For a while we fossick about in the workshop, once or twice putting the hydraulic lift up for a dare. There's a calendar on the back wall from 1969. That was the year after Tegwyn was born. On the calendar there's a girl with big brown boobs and a dumb look. *Pirelli*. Pirelli is tyres. All over the floor there's tools and parts and gobs of oil and bits of rag. This is where my dad works. Sometimes I come in here and see his bum sticking out of the bonnet of someone's car. The radio always plays and there's revving and the chink of spanners. *Y'canna hand a man a grander spanner* ... SIDCHROME. But it's not so friendly in here with him gone. It's kind of cold and dumb and dirty.

'I better go in,' Fat says.

I nod. I follow him round the side of the house to his bedroom window and give him a boost up. The flywire is all busted. He flops in on to his bed and the springs twang. You can hear Mr and Mrs Cherry yelling in the kitchen.

'Seeya,' Fat says from inside.

'Seeya,' I say, not wanting to go.

'It had nothing to do with me ...' Mr Cherry is yelling. I can't hear all the words, but I listen as hard as I can. The sun is gone now and the bush is all blue with twilight.

'You work the man ... and then expect ... like a bloody errand boy ... just ... your little weakness. You're a weak man, Bill Cherry ... so weak ... can't even bring ... admit it. Your bloody gambling will ruin us one day – I said that.'

'Oh, look, the man was an innocent. He ... liked ... never

said a . . . even offered . . . take the bets in and collect for me. Anyway, he always drove too fast for his own good.'

'. . . about him as if he's something in the past.'

'Well.'

'You're a weak man, Bill Cherry. You use a man so you can save face and all the time he gets the reputation in town of a compulsive gambler . . . me sick. You hear? Sick!'

'. . . said enough.'

'Never.'

'I said that will be all.'

'That poor woman.'

'You never cared a black damn for her.'

'You . . .'

'. . . you . . .'

'You!'

From here I can see our porch light on, getting stronger with the darkness, and very softly I can hear a voice calling my name. It's not Mum or Dad, but someone kind of familiar, and anyway it reminds me to stop listening to Fat's privacy.

Mum'll sting me for being so late, but her heart won't be in it. None of us can get our hearts in much, these days.

chapter four

Today is my first visit to the hospital and even though it's only ten o'clock in the morning, the noise of Mr Cherry's truck is making me sleepy because I was up before the sun. Honestly, I spent all night trying so hard to be asleep that I woke up more tired than when I went to bed. Today I will see my dad.

Mum and Mr Cherry don't talk. They haven't said a thing all the way. I want a pee real bad but I am too scared to ask. They look like they might blow up. I just watch the stumps and fences and the billboards and hold on and get dreamy.

This morning I stood out on the back veranda and listened to the birds wake up. The little sleepy, cheepy sound they make is the same sound chickens make under their mum just after they've hatched. I listened till they started to sound like grown-up birds and then I went inside to check on everyone. I check on everyone all the time. Fat calls it perving, but it's really just checking on them. I like to see them. To see that they're all right, that they're still the same. This old house is full of holes. The asbestos is cracked and none of the doors fit so it's easy to check on everyone. I just sit and watch for a while.

Grammar was asleep with her lips going rubbery with snores. All her silver hair was on the pillow. When I concentrated, I could make out everything in the room: the dusty piano, all her pictures of Dad and some of Mum and other people I don't know, the dresser with combs and Pop's old medals and yesterday's apple. A swallow appeared on the windowsill and looked in, too. Some breeze moved the curtain at the side and the swallow was gone.

Tegwyn's room was darker, with the curtains drawn. All her walls are crowded with people. It must be like sleeping in a cage in the zoo with all those people watching. Piles of magazines hold each other up under the window. Her bed was all piled with her sheets and her legs, and her hair was like Grammar's all over the pillow, except black. Over her sheet, one boob poked its nose. She slept quiet.

Mum and Dad's room is easy to see into. The door handle is missing and the hole is big enough to see just about everywhere inside. Sometimes I wonder about checking on people. That's when I see Mum and Dad without clothes on actually *doing it*. You kind of wish they didn't have to do that, but lots of people do. Fat says he thinks his mum and dad probably do. And other kinds of things do it. You see the drake hissing and chasing one of the ducks, wings smacking around until she gets caught and bashed into the ground and jumped on and all the feathers bitten out of her neck. It's natural, but I don't reckon that's any excuse. At least Mum and Dad only hurt each other in small bits. They make little hurting noises, but pretty soon after that they stop, like they know when they've had enough.

It's hard to watch. And hard to stop. Sometimes I just see them talking to each other. Might be about the day or about Tegwyn and me. I can watch all night when they do that.

This morning it was only Mum asleep with her bum up and her face down. A big white bum that got pink with the sun. A bum like an angry mob (still don't get it). I came out of that bum. Gotta face facts.

Fat reckons it's wrong. Checking on people, I mean. Mostly I reckon it's the best way of making sure you know how your family is getting on. You get looked at all day and all night anyway. That eye of the sky sees you – why worry about your kids or your brother looking? It's honest enough.

Funny, I keep thinking about people getting born and things getting born. Things die, too – I'm not stupid. Grammar will die before long because she's lived a long time and has just about had enough. Chooks die. Forests die. I had a brother once. There are scars like train tracks on Mum's belly. She was big with a baby when I was nine. Dad used to put his face on that big parcel and listen. When it came time to have the baby, she went into hospital in the city and came back a week later with nothing, only stitches and full eyes. I used to watch her squeezing milk from her tits into little bowls. I didn't know what it was all about then. I can't remember everything from that time, but I do remember Mum squeezing milk. And I do remember Dad on the bed when no one was around, crying, crying. I know how Fat feels. It's scary when your dad cries.

Here I am, half asleep in Mr Cherry's truck with houses and shops going past. Traffic lights, billboards, people out on their front lawns with hoses, cars, cars, cars . . . it's the city all right. And none of us is saying a word.

Here I am mumbling in my head. Here I am on the way to see my dad asleep in hospital.

I'm glad I live just out of the city. Mum and Dad moved out before Tegwyn and me were born. Dad said he wanted to live near trees. Mum said she wanted to live near Dad. I reckon it's made them happy. The trees all being chopped down made them mad, but even dying trees are trees. I don't know everything about us Flacks. Only what I hear and what people tell me. You spend your whole life trying to work out where you fit.

Here I am.

'Here we are,' says Mum, pointing to a big, long white place smothered in car parks and signs and people with bunches of flowers. 'This is the hospital he's at.'

Mr Cherry says nothing. His dark eyes look even darker today; he seems to be getting smaller. I'm pretty certain now that I don't like him. He makes us feel guilty for being in his truck.

We scoot into one of the driveways and as a toll gate comes down in front of us, Mr Cherry digs into a pocket, but before he comes out with anything, Mum puts fifty cents on the dashboard. He takes it and gives it to the man in the glass box. The gate goes up. We're in.

Zigging and zagging up the bitumen car parks, Mr Cherry finds a space in the end and when he's fitted us in the space, he turns the engine off.

'I'll wait here,' he says.

'You sure will,' Mum mutters. She opens the door.

It isn't like I remember. This hospital is like the State Government Insurance Office that Dad took me to once: long halls that go nowhere, paintings on the walls that don't make sense, people rushing past without looking at you. No sick people anywhere. We go through a place where everyone is smoking. It stinks. There's music, soft and weak. Lifts bong like clocks. Still no sick people.

'Why didn't Tegwyn come?' I ask Mum, who is walking very fast. Her dress is yellow as a duckling. Her shoes are black and a little bit dusty. When she looks down her hair falls into her eyes which are never the same colour twice.

'Tegwyn came yesterday. She didn't want to come today.'

'Is there something wrong with her, do you reckon?'

She looks at me. Her teeth are straight. 'Ort, I don't know what's right and wrong, sometimes.'

Then we're down another corridor. Down the end on a door it says ICU.

'ICU.'

'Intensive Care Unit,' she says. 'That's where he is.'

Now my heart is jumping around in me.

'Before we go in, I just want to say something.'

'Yes?' I say, wishing she'd said something all the way down in the truck.

'He looks different to last time you saw him.'

Last time, last time. Geez, it's such a long time ago, since before the start of the holidays. Last time. There he was, kissing Mum on the face and walking out to the ute with no shirt on and his back the colour of red mud. He had shorts on with elastic in the back, the ones that make your hips crinkly. When he got in the ute and looked out, I saw a gob of grease on his chin. His black hair was tied back in a plait. He was smiling. That was last time.

'How different?' I ask.

'Well, he's asleep for a start,' she says with a halfway grin. 'And he's been in a terrible accident, of course, and to help him stay alive the doctors have put tubes in some places for food.'

'For food?'

'It's called a drip,' she says. 'It's water with . . . things in it that feed him. And . . .'

'What else?' This is getting scary.

'His mouth doesn't look very nice, but that's because he doesn't use it much. He gets ulcers and sores in it. Things like that.'

'Oh.'

'You'll have to be a bit brave.'

'I'm not a baby,' I say, with my own halfway grin. We walk to the door. 'Mum?'

'Yes?'

'What's a compulsive gambler?'

'Someone,' she says, 'someone who gets people hurt.'

ICU. Here it is. And in we go.

The room is quiet, oh geez, so really very quiet. A nurse comes up and smiles. She looks real lonely in here. There is a big desk, high like a stage, in the middle of the room. All the walls are glass halfway up. There's beeps and quiet whooshes.

'Mrs Flack.'

'I've brought my son.'

'Only for a moment, then.'

We follow her. My feet are real heavy. It's hard work walking. I can't see into any of the rooms. The glass bit is high. We go in one. Everywhere there's machines like big computers and TV screens.

'Here he is, Ort,' Mum whispers.

'There's some visitors for you, Mr Flack,' the nurse says to a long thing on a table. She smiles at us and goes just outside.

Mum bends down and kisses it. When she moves out the way I can see it's him. His eyes are half open like he's only half asleep. Tubes come out his nose. Down the side there's tubes in his leg and arm. His mouth is all black and horrible. Scabby. Everything stinks of cleaning stuff. Everything is shiny. My Dad looks crowded and small in here.

'Hello, love,' Mum says, 'it's me. I've brought Ort with me. He's come to see you. He's a bit nervous 'cause they cut off your hair.'

That's it! His long plait is gone. His hair is all spiky. Mum brings me in close. I can hear him breathing. His hair. His hair.

'Hello, Daddy,' I say like I'm a baby or something, 'it's me, Ort. You got a nice room here. All computer games. They're gonna make pinball with computers, Fat reckons. Don't think you'll like that, eh? Errol says hullo. I'm going to high school next year. Reckon I'm too young yet. I could stay down for a year, eh?' Mum touches me on the shoulder. 'Well, have a good sleep. But wake up, eh? When yer ready.' Me eyes get hard to see through. 'Well, Dad, over and out.' The nurse comes in and gets us.

Before she goes to bed, Mum comes into my room and sits on my bed. I've been reading a book I read when I was ten. Mum pats the sheet near my leg. Her gown is loose and I can see the edge of one of those socky boobs of hers. Her hair is up like a big knot of pine and she looks kind of sleepy and I can tell she's been doing some hard thinking.

'You were brave today,' she says.

'Didn't need to be. It was still Dad.'

All of a sudden she's up on the pillow with me and putting her arms around me like she used to when I was really a kid. She is warm and her gown is fluffy and her breath smells like cough medicine and my head is on her shoulder looking down into that long dark crack between those bosoms.

'I'm proud of you, Ort. You know I love you.'

'Yes,' I say real quiet. 'I know that.'

'Can you tell me something?'

'Me?' It's a surprise.

'There's something I need to know.'

'What can I tell you?' I feel all silly.

'It's something no one else in the world can tell me.'

And that gets me all frightened and flappy inside.

'You see . . .'

'Yes?'

'Well. What was it like when you were asleep in that coma when you were so little? Maybe you don't remember – I don't s'pose you do – but I need to know real bad. Can you remember any little thing? You see, people talk, they say all kinds of things, they give you pamphlets and forms to sign until you don't know your bum from a mineshaft, and . . .'

'I remember,' I say, before she starts to cry properly. 'I remember.'

'Were you alive?'

'Course. Course I was alive.'

'But inside your head. In your sleep. Did you think things? Did you hear things?'

'Yeah, I heard things, I saw things.'

'Because some people say your father's not really alive.'

'He's alive. He isn't dead!'

'Hush a bit. You'll wake Grammar up.'

I feel really messed up. I pull my book out from under her leg; it's all crumpled.

215

'What you reading?' she asks, sniffing.

'It's about some kids who go into a weird kind of land through a wardrobe. It's a Poms' book. The kids are wet and they talk funny, but . . .'

'But what?' She picks the book up and bends it back into shape.

'It's not really all that make believe. Things happen.'

'What things?'

'Crazy kinda things. You hear things sometimes. See things. You think sometimes you're somewhere else.'

'In dreams, you mean?'

I look around the room, at my leaning wardrobe, the picture of Luke Skywalker, at the bits of wood I keep because they look like animals and stuff, the plane Dad made me out of balsa, and then I look at Mum and see her worried face.

'What if they're not dreams? What if you're awake when you go to sleep and dreaming when you wake up?'

'What if, eh?' She smiles. 'I dunno, Ort. I just don't know about that. I can't even get me mind to think about it. Maybe it's all the same thing.'

I shrug. Maybe it is. I don't even know what we're talking about any more.

'Is Dad coming home?'

'Yeah, he's coming home.'

'When?'

'When he's good and ready. He only ever does things when he's good and ready.'

'He's not dead.'

'I'll tell them that.'

She kisses me on the cheek and goes, walking a little bit wonky.

Out on the back veranda I can hear something moving around in the grass down past the back fence. Could be a fox or a roo or anything. The sky is very clear tonight. Kind of the

216

same colour as my dad's poor mouth. Stars look like they're moving and still at the same time.

The wind makes a kind of noise in my ear that reminds me of a bell. Not a school bell. Deeper. Bong, in my ear. It makes my toes tingle.

A word slips out of my mouth.

'Please?'

chapter five

Tegwyn and me are walking into Bankside this morning because it's Saturday. I don't know why we go in on Saturday mornings. We've been doing it for years. We just do. Because it's hot as hell out in the sun, we stick to the shade of the forest edge which makes walking harder with all the logs and holes and bushes to get past, and the snakes to look out for, but it's not as bad as having your brain casseroled by the sun out near the road. A lot of the time Tegwyn walks in front of me – it's to save talking. Her hair is back in a big long bready plait that flaps against her shirt. The plait comes down to my eyes; that's how tall she is. She's as big as a grown-up woman. Her pink shorts grab her bum and push out half moons at the edges. Sweat all runs down her legs. The flies paddle in it.

Birds crash through the tree tops and now and then a car goes past out on the road. When Dad was home we went with him in the ute. He used to like sitting out the front of the pub to drink his lemon squashes in the shade and watch us. Or play pinball in the shop. It was sure faster getting to Bankside in those days. Doesn't it sound like a long time ago, November.

Flies suck my toe scabs. My thongs smack my heels. Saturday morning. Mum is still asleep, I'll bet. Never seen her sleep so late in my whole life.

'Mum hasn't been in to see Dad for a while,' I say to Tegwyn's bouncing plait.

She makes a wet sound. 'Because that bastard Bill Cherry

won't take 'er in any more. They had a blue on the way back last time. Couldn't you see that one coming a mile off. Pah! He's a greasy little bugger. Like to stick his nose in a mincer and then stuff it in his mouth.'

I just keep walking. She talks like that sometimes.

'Feels frigging guilty, that's why. Slimy little bit of cockroach snot.'

Gawd, she makes me guts roll sometimes. 'Fat reckons they fight. Mr and Mrs Cherry,' I say.

'Fight? Course they fight. Wouldn't you fight if you had to kiss cocky snot in your bed at night? Listen, Small Thing, there's things you just don't know.'

'And there's things I do,' I say, quiet, real quiet.

'Eh?'

'Nothin'.'

She stops and turns and I walk straight into those big hard lumps on the front of her. She laughs and pushes them together round me ears.

'What do you know, Small Thing?'

'Yer tits stink, that's what I know.'

'Up yer bum.'

'Won't fit.'

Next thing, I'm stuck in a blackboy with me legs in the air and spines up me shirt. By the time I crawl out, she's way ahead up the track, moons flashing white out of them shorts. She can still be funny, Tegwyn. It proves anyone can be funny, because she must be the saddest, angriest person in the whole world.

In a while we come to the place by the side of the road on a bend where all the dirt and bush is cut up with drag marks and a tree is broken off at the base. We just walk past it like we don't notice a thing.

Feels like a real long time getting into Bankside. We pass the big sign with its bullet-hole freckles, and the forest is way behind and the sun right on us. Mrs Mack waves from the shade of her veranda as we pass, and pretty soon we're coming up past the pub. There's always a strange buzz coming from that pub. It goes: I-I-I-I-I! A man comes out to spit in the drain and look at the sky, and then he goes in again, pushing his hat hard down on his head.

Next to the pub is the drapers which Mr and Mrs Watkins run. It's got all balls of elastic and bits of material on rolls in the window. And a dummy with no head. And a little cardboard sign that says: *Gospel Meetings Sundays 11 a.m.* The drapers is always clean and unfriendly. Next to that is the shop. It's the post office, too, and also a couple of banks. There's a big veranda with an old sleepy dog and a pinball machine in the shade, and inside the flywire door there's the proper part of the shop – rows of cans and packets and bottles and boxes. Up the far end is the counter, a long shiny thing with the post office and banks on one side and the cash register at the other. Mr Firth is at the post office with his pencil in his black teeth and his hair all oily and sitting back. Mrs Firth is shaped like an ice-cream cone, fat at the top and skinny at the bottom. When it's hot, a map of the world comes up on her face. Africa goes right across her nose. She always seems to be smelling Africa and not liking it one bit.

Tegwyn and me sit out on the veranda for a bit. Malcolm Musworth is playing pinnies with the machine. He is back from boarding school in the city and his hair is short like his dad's. His dad owns the pub and a farm twelve miles out with its own manager.

'G'day,' I say.

'Hi, Tegwyn,' he says, without even looking up from the flashing silver ball.

'How's boarding school?' I ask.

He looks at Tegwyn's legs. 'Shithouse.'

'Doesn't he look like his old man?' Tegwyn says to me with a kind of pig-snort and goes inside. The bell tinkles on the door. Malcolm Musworth looks at me.

'Well, what about it, Ratface?'

I just stand there and can't say anything. I wonder if he's gonna belt me up. He's embarrassed.

'Piss off, Ort-the-Abort.'

I go for the door.

I get inside to the airconditioning where it's cooler and closer to Tegwyn. She's up the corner where the make-up is.

'Can I've a drink?' I ask.

She gives me a dollar from between those boobs of hers. 'Get me a Coke,' she says.

Mr and Mrs Firth watch us. They always watch you to make you nervous and clumsy. From the fridge I get a Coke for Tegwyn and a Weaver & Lock ginger beer for me. Mum says Weaver & Lock make the best ginger beer in the world.

For a while we stand around sipping our drinks, looking at things, just being cool in the airconditioning, listening to the clatter and ring of the pinny machine outside. The big freezers have got cold fog coming up out of them. I walk very slow past the rack of comic books. There is a sign: THIS IS NOT A LIBRARY. IF YOU WANT TO READ THEM, BUY THEM. I walk past so slow my knees shake.

Then I notice in the far corner of the shop, up near where Mrs Firth sits, a great pyramid of red cans. ARDMONA TOMATOES. The stack goes right to the ceiling.

'Wow,' I say.

'She's got the decorative touch, my wife,' Mr Firth says without moving his lips.

'Cor,' I say.

'Four hundred and twelve cans,' Mrs Firth says.

Right up to the ceiling. You couldn't put another can up. All red and shiny. The best thing I ever saw in this shop.

The door tinkles. I look around. A couple of yobbos come in. Black T-shirts, black beetle-crushers, hair all cut short. The kind of yobbos that drive loud cars with fat wheels. They kind of wade up the aisle with their boots going oink-oink on the floorboards. They see Tegwyn.

'Ooor,' one says. He grins and elbows his mate.

'Oooright,' the other says. They both laugh kind of dirty. My guts goes all tight and all that ginger beer fizzes in me and it kind of hurts.

'Can I help you two gentlemen?' Mrs Firth calls.

'Not as much, no,' one says. He's got a tooth missing. The hole is somewhere a mouse would go to live in. They both kind of wade over to near Tegwyn.

'Piss off, bumface,' Tegwyn hisses.

'Miss Flack,' Mrs Firth calls from the cash register, 'there won't be any language like that in our shop.' She gets out from behind the cash register and stands behind me, right near the pyramid of tins, like she doesn't trust me near it.

My guts hurts. I wish I could get out. The pinny machine clatters away outside. The two yobbos just kind of hang around near Tegwyn like two fat blowflies until the one with the mousehole touches her shoulder with his finger and suddenly I let go a terrible fart and Mrs Firth makes a crook sound. Oh, that ginger beer! Weaver and flaming Lock! And there goes Mrs Firth swaying back with fingers pegging her nose. Tegwyn hisses like a cut snake. I look for somewhere to go.

'Get away!' Tegwyn yells.

'Listen here, love,' Mousehole says.

Oh, geez! The cans! Here they come and I'm running for the door. Tegwyn is running and laughing and the two yobbos just stand there and look like dags. The sound is like a volcano. Mrs Firth screeches. Running, running. We get to the door as the whole flaming lot comes down and one can comes out through the door with us and lands on the pinny machine and sets it ringing and the dog howling like mad and Malcolm Musworth is yelling: 'Free game! Free game!'

*

So. The walk back. We hardly got to Bankside and here we are going home. Still, it made Tegwyn laugh. She's walking just in front and it's hotter than it was on the way in.

'Wanna swim?' she asks all of a sudden. Even the sound of it is cool.

'Geez, yeah,' I say.

There is a deep swimming hole in the creek on the other side of the road from our place, just down from the bridge, and we head for it, sweating like pigs all the way. Every year there's the same deep spot in the creek where the bank shoulders out under a big redgum, where it's shady and thick with leaves under your feet, with an old rope hanging down that used to be for swinging from before it snapped and broke someone's neck. Now it hangs out of reach and looks kind of sad and funny.

After about a million years, we get to the bridge and go off down away from the house. The bush here is raggedy and only thick near the creek. There is even some green grass under that big redgum with the rope tassel. I take my shirt off and dive in and go right down to the bottom where it's all mucky and dark, and then I shoot up and come out yelling it's so good. It's cool but not cold. The water doesn't move much. You can see the redgum reflected in it, and even that silly little bit of rope. I breaststroke around in circles.

Tegwyn takes off all her clothes and gets in slow, bit by bit. Toe . . . ankle . . . shin . . . knee . . . thigh . . . waist . . . and then she ducks under and a moment later I'm under too without expecting it. I kick her off and come up coughing.

'Just pullin' ya leg.'

'Yer just a kid,' I say, angry. 'No more grown-up than anyone else.'

'Ah, don't get snooty.' She spouts water and floats on her back.

After a while we go over to the bank and lie with our heads in the grass and the rest of us out in the water. Midges and dragonflies come and go. A crow calls from somewhere. Mostly it's real quiet.

'That was a good trick back there, boy,' she says. 'Saved by a fart.'

I can't say a word. I feel so important. I could go to sleep right here.

A bit later I ask: 'Are you happy?' But she doesn't say anything. Probably asleep.

When we get home, Mum has jobs for us. Jobs! On a Saturday! Tegwyn has to help hang out the washing. My job is different.

'What do you mean?' I ask.

'Go out and have a look at the chookhouse. Then you'll know what your job is,' Mum says, steam in her face.

I go out to the chookhouse and there is that lousy rooster with his neck sticking out of the wire. His neck is out, but there's no head on it. The only thing holding him up is his feathers in the wire. Oh, geez. Foxes. Or one fox, anyway. Must have just lay there waiting for that big dumb rooster to put his head out and . . . whack, no head.

Out by the fence I dig a hole with Dad's shovel. The rooster is stiff and hard and smelly and stuck to the wire so that I have to kind of rip him off. Errol walks behind me as I take the rooster over to the hole. I wonder if Errol knows what I'm doing; he doesn't look all that bothered. Errol sleeps out on the dunny roof. I wonder if that's why foxes never get him. My brainy chook!

I know Mum'll ask me anyway, so I shovel out all the chook poop from under the roost and put it into bags for the veggie garden. Poop makes things grow – don't ask me why. It's one of those facts. All the hens go berserk as I shove stuff out. The little chicks jump and squeak and look stupid. Chooks just eat and lay eggs and hatch babies and that's all. I wonder if they ever talk to each other.

I'm just tying off the bags in the shed when Fat comes over.

'G'day,' he says.

'Hi.'

'Playing with yer poop again?'

I shrug. 'Watcher been doin'?'

'Nothin'.'

Funny, you know, I feel a bit awky with Fat just now. Can't tell if he's looking me in the face because my eyes are on the ground, but I bet he isn't. The ground is all dried and cracked like Grammar's cheeks.

'Wanna muck around?'

'OK,' I say.

I run up and tell Mum and she comes out on to the veranda with her arms all red and just looks at Fat, not real friendly.

'Be careful of snakes,' she says, looking right at me and then a long time at Fat. 'And mind how you walk.'

Fat and me walk slow through the forest, munching leaves and sticks and bones and dead grass under our feet. The air in you is hot as a baked dinner – you have to kind of chew it before it'll go down.

'You ever been to the beach?' Fat says.

'The ocean beach?' I scrape skin off my peeling nose. 'Nup.'

'A lot of people in the city go to the beach on a day like today. And all last week. Every day I can remember, they'd be down at the beach. Wish I had a surfboard.'

'You ever been to the beach?' I ask.

'Coupla times. If you get up in the morning and drive down there and through the city – and boy that's hot – you get there just in time to get wet and get home by dark.'

'You'd have to live in the city to go all the time.'

'I used to when I was a kid. I wouldn't mind living there again. I mean I wouldn't mind all that much. In the morning you wake up when it's real hot. You get up and go down to the

225

beach. The sand is white and hot enough to make blisters on yer feet. It's really wide, a long way. Geez, the water is blue. Blue. And you have waves all around and lifesavers to look after you. Afterwards, you go up with your oldies to the beer garden and you get a lemon squash and sit in the shade and wait for the Fremantle Doctor.'

And now I know he's starting to bull me.

'What do you want a doctor for? Blisters?'

'What?'

'The doctor. You're bulling me 'bout a doctor.'

'The Fremantle Doctor, you dill. It's a wind that comes in the afternoon off the sea. Cool, it is. People open all their windows. You can see it coming; makes a dark line on the water. You can see it coming in from Rottnest Island.' He looks at me like I'm real stupid.

'I know about Rottnest Island,' I say, 'there's quokkas on it and Vlamingh discovered it.'

We come down to the creek, sweat all down us, and Fat is shaking something in his hand. Sounds like a baby's rattle. Matches. A box of Redheads.

'It's bushfire weather,' I say, kind of half-hearted.

'There's water close,' Fat says. He lights one up. I can smell it. Reminds me of lots of things I can't remember. He chucks it at me. I hit it into the creek.

'Don't be a donkey,' I say, a bit scared.

Fat lights another one.

'Don't be a stupid mongrel!' I yell as he flicks it at me. But it's dead before it reaches my hand. Fat looks all mean. His face is all bunched up.

'Don't, Fat. Don't! You'll make a bushfire!'

'Ya chicken, are ya?'

'No.'

'Reckon you are.'

What's he saying this for? What the hell's going on here? Fat has this ugly look. He looks like an angry porker going to the yards. I shouldn't have called him a mongrel or a donkey, I know it. But everything I say makes him worse.

'I reckon you should shut yer trap,' I say. It's like me mouth is angry and the rest of me doesn't know what the hell is going on.

Another match comes my way. I stamp on it.

'You Flacks,' he says with a hard laugh. 'You think ya hot shit. Butter wouldn't be yellow in ya mouth.'

'What's wrong with us?' My throat is real small, too small for words.

'Ya sister's a slut. Ya old man's a vegetable, and ya mum's a pisstank.'

And that's it. I'm going forward like some bit of a train that's busted loose and I'm rolling forward at him and he throws a match that I knock down hot at the ground and then I hit him and the matches go all over. His bum hits the ground. He kicks at me and one thong comes off. I kick him in the leg and then in the side and he's up like a ball, like a turtle, like a caterpillar, like a snail, crying, crying.

'Yer a fat slug!' I yell at him. 'I hate yer big flubbery guts and yer pig face and yer crybaby old man who thinks he's so funny and yer scrawny plucked-chook-piece-of-poop old lady. I hate yez!'

With a whoof! behind me, something else happens. I turn around. Flames. I turn back and there's Fat Cherry up and off into the forest heading home.

'Come back here, you . . . !' But there's no time.

The fire is as big as a forty-four gallon drum and running up the bank. I take my shirt off and wet it in the creek and run up behind the fire and hit it. The flames hurt my face and my arm and I hit them all, swinging around half crazy and not knowing properly what the hell's going on. It crackles and spits. I'm hitting and hitting. I go for it like I'm attacking it, like I hate it to death. It goes on and on. Swing, hit, and then nothing, only black ground and smoke.

For a while, I dance around in the big, black patch, burning my feet, and then I fall in a shallow bit of the creek on my knees and just lie there.

A long time goes past before I move. I'm sore and hurt all over, like half of me has died. Bits of smoke still lift off the bank above. I roll over and look up at the sky between the trees, big branches like eyelashes across it.

The skin of the creek is black. Little things skip across it. I float downstream. I push off snags and rocks. I dogpaddle and breaststroke down. You don't need an ocean beach or a Fremantle Doctor to know how to swim. Sometimes I pull myself along the bottom, it's so shallow.

I know when I pass the sawmill – there's our car roof still there on the bank. Down I go. I don't want to get out till I feel better. It's cool. The air is the only hot thing in me now. Even my brain has cooled down. Kookaburras gargle up in the jarrah. Stroke, stroke.

At the same log as before, I rest and peer across at the man under the bridge. There he is, still, on the bank in the shade with the bridge piles on either side of him. My hands hurt when I hold on to the log. I get back in under the water, crouched, and peer round the log. I look careful at him. How does he live? What does he eat? What's he doing so close to our place? Did he hear us this morning when we were swimming at the hole on the other side? I forgot about him.

Funny. I can see . . . his . . . I have to look real hard. I'm not far away. It's his thing, his old feller. It's real big and fat, up out of his pants like a periscope. And he's just sitting there in the cool looking at it. Looking at it!

Cor.

Reckon I better tell Mum about him. Real quiet, I swim back a bit, then get out and walk back barefoot.

*

We're all eating tea real quiet when there's a thump at the front door and shouting. Mum looks at me scared. No one's ever come to the front door before, except the Mr Wingham that came to tell us about Dad. Tegwyn sighs. It's steak for tea and I was halfway enjoying it.

'Tegwyn, will you go?' Mum says as Tegwyn gets up.

It's sad at tea with just the three of us. With two at the table it makes you feel real crummy.

'What's the meaning of it, eh? What's the meaning? Explain to me. Where's your mother?'

There's yelling coming from the front door. Mr Cherry, clear as day. He bursts into the kitchen, his singlet all wet and the black hairs on his shoulders all plastered down.

'Good evening, Bill,' Mum says. Sick-looking.

'Mrs Flack.'

'Well, what's all this?'

Tegwyn is behind Mr Cherry pulling dogfaces.

'I want your son disciplined,' he says.

'You smell of beer, Bill Cherry.'

'You're a one to talk.'

'You are in my house, Bill Cherry. I don't want to throw you out. You'll speak decently to me under my own roof, thank you.'

'And what's gonna stop me? Bully boy here?' he says, pointing to me. I stop chewing, gob full of steak.

'What's gonna stop you is me.'

'You're only a woman!' he laughs.

'It's a shame we can't say you're a man, Bill Cherry.'

He looks hit. 'What?'

'Any real man would've made arrangements for an employee of his who was maimed running personal errands. For a favour. Any real man would've owned up to it and took responsibility. A decent man would've offered compensation.'

'Bugger you, woman, I've driven you to hospital near on twenty times in my own time, on my own juice. Leaving me wife to run the place on her own. Bloody place is going to ruin—'

'Because my Sam's not there to keep it alive. Get down to the point of your rudeness, Mr Cherry.'

More banging on the front door. I go out to see. Mrs Cherry comes in like a runaway tractor.

'Oh, Mrs Cherry,' Mum says, back to the fridge, 'come in and join us. Your husband—'

'Come home, Bill Cherry.'

Tegwyn snorts. Mrs Cherry looks ready to kill. Tegwyn nicks off.

'Your children could do with some discipline, Mrs Flack. The whole lot of you could do with some gratitude, I reckon.' But she looks half-hearted about it.

'Your snivelling little son—' Mr Cherry starts.

'Now listen here,' Mum goes.

'No, you listen!'

'Bill Cherry.'

'Let go, Leila.'

'Get out.'

'Mrs Flack, there's—'

'You'll get no bloody help from us when they pull—'

'Bill Cherry!'

'Out!'

'—him off the machines!'

Mum grabs a handful of mashed spud off the table and I get the hell out.

The forest moves quiet tonight. Jarrahs move a long way up and out of sight. Now and then I hear little animal noises. All these trees are dying, and all these little animals will have nowhere to live. One day the whole world will die and we'll die too. My back hurts and my bum stings and the backs of my legs too. I've got no clothes on out here in the forest. Prickles and burrs and twigs stick in me all over. I rub them, squirm and shake around. It hurts a lot. I'm hurting myself. I want to hurt myself. I want to.

Over there I see the house lights. I dunno if they are still fighting in there. I hate all of this. None of this is fair. Somewhere I can hear a bell, a deep clonging bell, like the big bells in churches on the movies. Bong. Bong. Rings in my ears. Sometimes so loud it hurts.

I look up and see bits of the sky through the trees. None of this is fair. Not one thing.

I get sleepy. I grind on the prickles and burrs and sharp pieces of wood so it hurts me awake. It hurts.

Oh. No. Right before me eyes it comes up on its own. It's not fair. It's the last straw. It makes yer sick. There it is, me old feller with its nine black hairs, sticking up just like that old man's under the bridge. And here I am looking at it. Makes you sick.

There. I'm bawling. There. I can't stop bawling.

For a long time I cry, until I feel sleepy and that bell comes back. I hear a car, close. The lights cut up high in the trees all around. The engine runs for a long time real close and I look over at the house to see it leaving the drive. Red tail-lights leaving. Oh. I hope it isn't the cops. I hope there hasn't been a murder in there.

I get up.

There is something over the house. Like a cloud. *Like* a cloud. It glows, just sitting over the roof. Hell! It's bright as the moon. I start running towards the house, hit the wire fence like a truck and go flat to the ground and get up again all wonky and go like hell.

Mum is out on the back veranda, screaming her lips off. And I'm running. Feel my old feller flapping all over. Here I am in the nick, raw as a prawn, me shorts back in the bush, here I am running across the backyard.

'Moorr-toon!' Mum is yelling.

Oh. Not a murder. Please.

'Morton! Morton!'

She sees me coming. All of a sudden and out of nowhere, something hits me in the gob and I go down again. It's Errol. Jumped off the dunny roof at me. Me mouth's full of feathers and stink.

'It's your father,' Mum says, looking at me like she's not sure of anything in the world any more. 'Ort, he's awake. He's awake.'

I get up on one elbow, all embarrassed. Errol shakes himself, poops on my hand. Errol is a hen. A she. I never thought of it before.

II

chapter six

From up the road I can hear a car coming. It's a sound like a waterfall from a long way off. Tyres make that water sound on the road. I'm up on the big fat fencepost here, looking. A bunny bounces out of the bush and on to the bitumen. Out the way, bunny, you'll get chundered by the car that's bringing me dad home. Some ants crawl up my leg but I've got no time for them. Have to hope they behave themselves. A long time I've been waiting for today. Feels like I been waiting all my life, like I been waiting since before dads were invented.

There. I see the sun off the windscreen and hear the engine sound. Real quick, I pull the comb out of my shorts and push my hair back off my face. Never wanted to comb me hair before in all my life. Hear that engine – a big six. Dad likes a big six. Roomy, he reckons. Give you room for your elbows under the bonnet. But a terrible waste of juice, he always says.

Here he comes, slowing down now. But as they pull into the gravel drive I can see another man driving, a man with short red hair and a white jacket. I jump down and run beside the car for a while, and before it leaves me behind up the track I get a look inside and see my dad lying in the back with the sheets and short hair and a kind of nothing look on his face.

By the time I get to the house they already have him out on a stretcher thing and are carrying him inside and the bloke in white is talking.

'We'll have to see if you can manage. And of course there's no promises.'

'The doctor has explained it all to me,' Mum says, kind of flustered.

'And who's this athletic young man?' He looks at me. I don't like red hair.

'This is my son Morton.'

'Well, hullo, Morton.'

'Why isn't he walking?' I ask. 'Why wasn't he driving the car? What are you carrying him for?'

They stop walking with him and the sun hits us hard and the white sheet and the white suit make us all squint.

'I think we'd better get Mr Flack out of the sun.' They get walking again. Tegwyn opens the door looking squinty like she's just got out of bed, and I follow them in.

I didn't know this was going to happen. I thought he was going to be all right, but he looks pretty crook to me. From up the back of the house Grammar is calling.

'Is that you, Lil Pickering?'

'No, Mum, it's me. We've brought Sam home.'

Why didn't he bring himself home? What the hell's happening here?

'Shame about his hair,' Tegwyn says.

'Yes,' Mum says, 'he had beautiful hair. It'll grow back.'

'Took him years to grow it,' I say. 'He told me it took him years.'

'Well, he's got plenty of time to grow it back.'

'He looks like a punk with it all standing up like that,' Tegwyn says with a laugh.

'Short hair looks more manly, anyway,' says the man in white.

I pull a face at him when he looks away. I hate red hair. Short *and* red. Him and Mum go into the kitchen and talk quiet for a bit and I get a good look at my dad. His face is pale and thin and it makes his whiskers stand out like pig-bristles. I pull the sheet down and what I see on his neck makes me yell.

'What's going on?' the red-headed man says, running in.

'Ort, what's wrong?'

'His neck! What they do to his neck?'

'It's a tracheotomy, son,' the man says. 'The doctors had to open his throat to let him breathe. He was all smashed up.'

Mum touches me on the arm but I don't look up from the big gob of sticky plaster that goes up and down with his breathing. A whistling comes out. Like the wind through the crack in a door. It makes me cold all over. Makes me bum tingle. A hole in his throat.

'Anyway, Mrs Flack, as I was saying, hospice workers will visit if you like and we'll rely on you to keep in touch. I'll bring the wheelchair in and show you how to set it up.'

While they go outside, I get a good look at Dad's face. One eye is all wonky and white at the edges. His mouth is all right and his teeth look OK. He looks at me with his one good eye and his one wonky eye as I open his lips with my finger. I can't tell if he knows me. I pull the sheet down further. All his chest is covered with sticky plaster. He has big white undies on that look like they come from the hospital. His legs are skinny and a bit yellow. There's all stitch marks on them and mercurochrome painted here and there.

Mum and the red-head come in with the wheelchair. Just the look of it makes me frightened. They hoist Dad up and slide him into the big armchair in the corner and prop him up with pillows, put a blanket on his knees, and Mum kisses him on the cheek.

Then the red-head goes, revving up his hospital's big six Holden. I sit there for a long time just looking at what's left of my dad, listening to that cold draught whistling in and out of him.

*

'I'm not going back to school,' Tegwyn says, eating her tiny piece of steak. She starves herself something terrible.

Mum looks up. You can hear the whistling from in the lounge-room. Mum looks at her fork. 'Why not, love?'

'I wanna get a job.'

This kind of talk turns me guts. It's like a fight without blood or fists. Words going back and across. Makes you wanna keep your head down.

'You'll get a better job if you stay at school two more years, you know.'

'I don't wanna better job. Anyway, in two years there'll be no jobs.'

'Where will you work?' Mum says, looking real tired. 'There's almost no jobs now.'

'In the city.'

Mum sighs.

'You did,' Tegwyn says, kind of whining. 'You got a job early and that was in the city.'

Mum nods.

'Don't you like us?' I say. The words just come out of my mouth. I wasn't even thinking of them. It scares the pants offer me.

Tegwyn spits a bit of fat on to her plate. 'I hate it here.'

Then Mum is crying, hands over her face, elbows on the table, and Tegwyn goes to her room and I just sit there feeling useless.

'I thought Dad was going to be all right,' I murmur, after a long time.

'He will be,' Mum whispers, snuffling. Some snot shines on her lips and her eyes are angry with tears. 'He will be, Ort. I won't let him not be.'

Here I am up in the middle of the night, watching through the door cracks and the holes in the wall. There's an old sticker on

Mum and Dad's door that says GET THEM OUT OF VIETNAM. There's a good hole right next to it. On the big bed, Mum is asleep with the sheet up to her ears, and Dad lies there with his eyes open, his toes moving a bit like they're dancing in the breeze that comes in the window. The house is quiet except for breathing in Tegwyn's room, snoring from Grammar's, and that cold whistle from in there. He's still all busted up. He hasn't been fixed. He should be fixed.

It took me and Mum ages to put him to bed. Flamin' Tegwyn wouldn't come out of her room. We had to roll him and drag him like a feed sack, push him, pull him. There's his heel marks in the dust on the floorboards in the hall. How are we gonna keep it up? How? What do we do to get him fixed? He's not bad, you know. He's done nothing bad. My dad kisses me goodnight and he puts his fingers in me hair and tells me stories and shows me how to do things that you don't normally think of. He sits out on the veranda at the back and plays his old guitar with the LIVE SIMPLE sticker on it and teaches me chords that are too big for my fingers. He kisses Mum all the time and calls her 'Babe' like on the movies. He knows about trees and cars and chooks. He knows everything. He's flamin' better than everyone else's stupid dad, he can run faster and his hair is long like a Red Indian's. He never, ever, ever hits me. He loves us. He's good! Good! Crap! Turd! Shit! He's good, you hear me?

'Ort! Stop all that shouting. What are you doing out of bed? Get back to bed. You'll wake the dead.'

It shakes me up, you know. I thought I was only thinking. I reckon I'm going nuts. It's real embarrassing. But I don't go to bed. I can't sleep. It's lonely when you can't sleep.

This used to be a happy family. Everyone loves everyone. Why does it go like this? It's all stupid.

Outside, the ground is all bright like there's a full moon. I go out. There's no moon. The sky is clear and winking at me a thousand times. There's no moon. The light is coming from the roof. I walk out into the yard and look back at the house. There it is, that little cloud, small and fat like a woolly sheep, glowing bright. It looks like it's in exactly the right place there just above the roof. It's crazy, but inside me it feels like that shining cloud is the most normal thing in the world. And I bet no one else can see it. It just shines down at me and it makes me smile and I stand there until I feel tired enough to go inside to bed.

My porridge looks like fresh sick with all steam coming up out of it. I feel tired already. Dad is in his chair at the end of the table and Mum is giving him his porridge, feeding him like he's a baby. Makes me angry to see that. It took us so long to get him in here to the kitchen out of bed. Mum won't let him stay in bed. 'I'm not having him waste away in there,' she said. She won't use the wheelchair; it's still in the lounge-room. I'm with her on that. It's a horrible-looking thing. But it's so much work moving him. We can't keep it up. I know it.

'Eat your breakfast, Ort,' Mum says. She looks real tired.

'Can't.'

'You'll never grow up big and strong.' What does she think I am, a baby?

'Like Dad, I s'pose.' And straightaway I wish I didn't say it. Mum's face goes all crook and white.

Tegwyn comes in with an empty plate.

'She ate it all. Like a pig.'

'Don't say that, love.'

'I'm sick of her. Why do I have to feed her? Why do I have to look after her?'

'You're older.'

'No, I'm a girl. Ort doesn't have to 'cause he's a boy, 'cause he's got a dangler and I haven't.'

I look at Mum. She looks surprised like she's never thought of it before.

'You and Dad always talk about boys and girls being equal. You're hypocrites. I'm leaving school.'

Mum still has that surprise on her face. 'Well,' she says, 'now we've got two people to look after. You'll have to look after one of 'em. I'll have to find some work to get us some money. Maybe Mrs Musworth'll give me some laundering. Now there's two people, an old woman and her son.'

'You don't think you're hypocrites, then?' Tegwyn puts her nose up in the air.

'I don't know.' She looks worried. 'Maybe we are.'

Tegwyn sits down to her porridge like she's not real happy with that answer. I keep my eyes away from hers. I didn't know she hated me for being a boy.

Mum sighs. The kitchen is warm. The fire I lit in the stove is going good. Lunch time, it will be too hot to sit in here. I look at Dad's eyes, try to see where they're looking. Wonder what he saw when he was in that coma. It's like his eyes are looking in and not out. Wish he could tell me about it.

And then there's a thump at the front door. We all look at each other.

'If that's Mr Cherry, you call me straightaway,' Mum says, looking like one more thing will be the end.

I go through to the front door that we never used until lately, and I open it with a pull and there at the door is a big man with old clothes that you could buy at a school fête for fifty cents, a real long face with a big hoe chin, funny eyes, a book in his hands, and grass seeds all over him.

'Hello, Morton, is your mother there?'

I don't say a flamin' word. I know him. Me mouth must be way open but I can't help it. It's the joker from under the bridge.

In the end, Mum comes up behind me and says, 'Can I help you?'

'I'm not selling anything,' he says, then looks like he'd like to change that but can't, so he shuts his mouth.

241

He's big, tall. Wide hands. He could do with a wash.

'Yes?'

'I've come to help with Sam.'

Mum grabs my shoulder hard like she's trying to pop a boil out of it. 'Are you from the hospital, then?' Oh, look at him, Mum, does he look like he's from the flamin' hospital?

'No, I'm not from anywhere in particular. Nngth.'

I look up. What was that? He said this funny word at the end then.

'No, I'm here to help you bathe Sam. It must be time now.'

'I didn't ask anyone to come,' Mum says.

'No,' I say, 'we didn't ask anyone to come.'

'I understand that. Nngth.'

There he goes again.

'Are you from the Social Security?'

He shakes his head, smiling.

'Council?'

Mum looks at me. She wants to let him in, I can tell. She's mad. He's a stranger. He's dirty. We don't know who he is. We didn't ask him to come.

'We didn't know about any of this. Who's paying you?'

'I'm a voluntary worker.'

'For nothing?'

'Yes. More or less.'

She looks like she's decided to close the door on him, like she's suspicious after all, but then she just looks kind of scared and lost and she gives me a dry smile that says 'I'm sorry'.

'Well, you might as well come in, now you're here,' she says with a sigh. 'He'll be finished breakfast in a moment.'

We go inside to the kitchen, where Tegwyn is feeding Dad his porridge like she's the angel of the house. Mum asks the bloke to sit down. He puts his black book down on the table and he's so big he makes the chair disappear.

'G'day, Sam,' he says to Dad. Dad swallows porridge and his eyes don't go anywhere special.

'This is Tegwyn,' Mum says, kind of nervous. Tegwyn just looks him up and down. 'And—'

'He knows, Mum,' I say.

Mum looks embarrassed. She's only got on the big T-shirt of Dad's that she wears in the mornings before she gets dressed proper.

'I'll just go and get changed,' she says.

'No need. Really,' the man says. But she's gone.

Then the kitchen is quiet. I look at Tegwyn and Tegwyn looks at me. Now's the time I feed the chooks. I should be out there feeding the chooks. Mum comes back in with a pair of shorts on and a shirt.

'My name is Henry Warburton,' the man says.

'You've been sleeping under the bridge,' I whisper. He makes like he doesn't hear me. His eyes don't ever look at the same spot.

'Well,' Mum says.

'Come on, Sam,' Henry Warburton says, getting up. 'You could do with a bath, I'll bet.'

'He's not that dirty,' I say.

'I meant he might feel like one,' Henry Warburton says. He picks Dad up in his arms like he's a little kid, and asks, 'Where to?'

'You mean you don't even know the way to our bathroom?' Tegwyn says with a halfway grin. Henry Warburton smiles.

'Your Mum'll show me.'

Outside the bathroom door I listen. The water is running and it makes the walls hum. From Grammar's room comes the sound of Tegwyn playing the piano. She hasn't played in the morning for ages. Dad always wanted her to play it in the mornings. Grammar always did. She was the one what brought Dad up because his old man died when he was five. Grammar looked after him. She used to play the piano at dances in country halls all over the place. He used to sleep on the lid in a little fruit box. That's what he told me, or Grammar told me, I forget.

Tegwyn is playing some old song that Grammar used to sing. Makes a lump in yer throat.

In there, in the bathroom, they're putting Dad in the water. No, they're testing it. The water's still running. Someone farts. Must be Dad. Henry Warburton goes 'Ahem'. I reckon they're embarrassed. Good old Dad.

Grunting, lifting noise. Putting him in the bath.

'Not often you see a man bathing another man,' Mum says. No sound from Henry Warburton. I can hear the water moving. Dad and me used to have baths together. In the winter when it was cold, I used to snuggle down into the hot and his big legs with all their black squiggles came up high out of the water. He used to sing songs like:

> *You can get anything you want*
> *At Alice's restaurant*

and he would hum and I would look at his old feller and wonder about it. You can hear the wind through the holes in the wall. Mum'd yell at us to get out, but Dad would keep singing and I would snuggle down in the water.

'Why are you here?' Mum asks Henry Warburton. 'Why are you doing this?'

'Does there have to be a reason? Nngth?'

'There has to be a reason for everything.'

'Yes.'

'Well?

'I don't really know why I'm here.'

'I don't believe that.'

'Your husband is sick.'

'He'll get better.'

'Not on his own, he won't.'

'What are you saying?'

'I . . . Nngth. Nngth.'

I put my eye up to a hole and look. Why does he do that

sound? Mum looks real worried. She watches Henry Warburton rubbing Dad's chest with a flannel. Dad looks like he's fair enjoying the bath.

'What are you?' Mum whispers.

'A man. A servant.' He runs his thumbs over Dad's wonky eyes. 'Only a man. Like Sam here.'

'What are you going to do?'

Henry Warburton looks at her and smiles kind of thoughtful, looks at her hands. 'I really don't know.'

Well that puts us all in together. Not one of us knows what the hell's going on.

'Lil Pickering? Is that you, Lil Pickering?'

chapter seven

He's out there digging in the vegetable garden. The sun is up over the trees but it's not too hot yet. The dirt he turns up is all dark and wet underneath. Mum's corn wobbles in the wind behind him. Cucumbers, zucchinis, tomatoes, lettuce, eggplant: it's like a picture, and he's out there in it, like something in the middle of a picture.

Mum comes out on the veranda with me. Her hair is all over.

'Is he staying, then?'

'Looks like it.'

'He's a bit weird.'

'Ort, you should hear 'em talk about us.'

'He sleeps under the bridge.' Mum says nothing. I look up and see her with her hair all crazy everywhere and her eyes squinty in the light, and I know she hasn't heard me.

At lunch in the lounge-room, where it's cool, we're all eating salad as quiet as you can eat salad, and Henry Warburton says to me:

'Want me to teach you how to set a rabbit trap, Ort?' He has a big smile and a piece of lettuce on his chin.

'I orready know. My Dad taught me when I was six.'

'Oh.' He laughs. 'No teaching *you* any new tricks, then.'

I don't look up from my plate.

'Sam . . . is very good with him.'

'That's because he's my father.'
Everyone laughs and I dunno what's so funny.

All afternoon he works in the vegetable garden and the weeds pile up on the ground outside the wire that goes around it. The whole yard smells of fresh dirt. Reminds me of being little again, when I used to eat it. He ties tomato plants up straight and pinches off little buds. In a box he puts long zucchinis and eggplants, a lettuce, some onions, and a carrot. He doesn't sing or anything when he works. His back is white and wet in the sun. His daggy pants get real dirty. At the end of the afternoon I go and help him throw the weeds in to the chooks because I know Dad would be ashamed of me watching someone else work in the sun all day. When we are washing the vegetables under the tap at the tank, he looks up at my bat on the veranda.

'Wanna hit?' he says, pulling a face at the eggplant.

'Can you play french cricket?' I ask.

'I invented it.'

'Bull.'

'Well, I can play it, anyway.' He laughs.

We leave the veggies to dry on the back veranda and get the bat and the ball and start to play. He hits out of my reach. His big long chin digs into his chest and his funny eyes go everywhere so you don't know where the ball will go. He plays good and it makes me a bit mad and makes me feel OK. Then he hits an easy catch. I get it in one hand.

'You're not trying,' I say. 'You let me get that.'

'Yep.'

'That's not fair.'

'You shouldn't ever knock back a bit of help,' he says, pulling up his awful, dirty pants.

'I don't need it.'

'Everyone needs it,' he says. 'Sooner or later.'

I take the bat from him. He grabs my hand and it makes me

247

look at his face. He's kind of smiling. He doesn't look so bad, really. My hand is small next to his, but harder and darker.

'You're a good man, Ort,' he says. The ball is in his other hand. It's just the cork guts of an old ball. In his hand it looks like a fresh bird's egg, like it might break if he squeezed it.

'Why did you work in the garden?' I ask. 'No one asked you to.'

'It needed doing,' he says, holding my hand and the ball, looking from one to the other.

'What's that book you got inside?'

'A wise book.'

'What's it got in it?'

'Dreams, stories, poems, advice, jokes.'

'Nothing about cricket, I s'pose.'

He smiles at me like I'm really dumb.

'That was a joke,' I say. He lets go my hand.

'You *are* a good man. Wait'll they publish your gags. *The Portable Ort.*' Then he bowls quick, underarm and high on the bat, and I kind of jump out the way and the ball nicks the edge of the bat and runs away on the hard dirt. He grabs it and lobs it across to me and I turn like a baseballer and hit it high. It goes up into the blue so you can hardly see it, but Henry Warburton is running across the yard with his big hands up and those dumb dirty pants flapping. He yodels as he runs and it kind of makes me laugh. His feet flop across the dirt. He runs backwards. The ball comes down. He leans back and gets it in one hand and then his feet go up above his head and he goes over the fence backwards with a yell, and comes down hard and laughing thin like a loonie. When I get to him I stop dead and look at the hole in his head where an eye was.

'It's orright,' he says, winded, 'it's glass. It's a false. Eye. Just come. Out with the fall.' I find it for him in the dirt. It looks like an ace marble, a tombola or something. He wipes it and puts it back in. It doesn't look so bad.

'How'd it happen?'

'When I was at school. Nngth. Was playing first slip. Ball hit me in the face. Crushed the eye.'

I help him get up. I feel sorry for him about the eye. Half his pants are still on the top barb of the fence. Mum is on the back veranda laughing.

I love it when we sit out here at night feeling the hot day go away and listen to the forest making its night noise. Sometimes when a car goes past out on the road, you get kind of surprised that there are other people in the world. Before his accident Dad used to sit out here with us and play sad songs on his guitar and tell stories. Like about the time Grammar had a fight with a man at a dance where she was playing piano and she knocked out his teeth with one hand and kept playing the bass part of 'On Moonlight Bay' with the other. He used to sleep in a box with *California Navels* written on it on top of the piano. He reckons that's why he always sleeps with music in his head. On nights like this Mum and Dad remember things and tell us. It's like the forest and the sky make them remember. Mum has stories, but she only lets them out in bits here and there.

'Be Christmas soon,' Tegwyn says. She files her nails.

Henry Warburton moves his bum to get comfortable. He's down against the veranda post. Dad is next to me on the lazyboy. Mum is in the cane chair. Tegwyn is in the hammock. It's dark, but I can see them all in the light from above the roof.

'What do you do for Christmas here?' Henry Warburton asks.

Mum sniffs. 'Oh, get a turkey. Go down to the creek for a swim. Muck around.'

'Get bored,' Tegwyn says.

'Not me,' I say.

'That's 'cause you're still a kid.'

'He's going to high school next year,' Henry Warburton says. 'He's half grown-up.'

249

'He's too immature.'

Hope I am. Then I'll stay down and get out of high school. I don't want me head put down the dunny.

'You know what they call first years?' Tegwyn says. 'Melons. Yer gonna be a melon, Ort.'

'Least I'll be a watermelon,' I say, thinking of all those dunnies, 'you were a pigmelon, Tegwyn.'

'Cut it out, you two.'

Henry Warburton laughs and then he says that strange word, 'Nngth.'

'What's that word?' I say.

'It's nothing,' he says.

'Ort.' Everyone gets embarrassed.

'It's a thing I have,' he says. 'A speech impediment.'

'Oh.' Geez, he's got troubles, eh.

'Time for bed, Ort.'

'But it's holidays, it's early.'

'Well read, then,' she says. 'You can go too, Tegwyn.'

'Are you staying the night?' Tegwyn says to Henry Warburton. He doesn't say anything.

'Yes,' says Mum. 'He'll sleep in the lounge-room.'

Tegwyn sniffs. We go in. She slams her door. Me too.

I open my window. It's too hot to sleep yet. I can hear talk coming down in bits from the back veranda, and I wonder what they're saying out there where it's cool and good. So I do it. I climb out the window, crouch on the warm dirt for a minute, and then scrub along to the back of the house and sit in the dark at the corner. I can hear Errol scratching on the dunny roof. The light from that cloud makes the dirt in the backyard look mysterious, like the face of the moon.

'How long you been out here?' Henry Warburton asks my Mum. I can't see 'em because I'm just behind the corner of the house.

'Oh,' she says, 'sixteen years, more. Since just before I had Tegwyn. Sam and I came out from the city to try to get away from a lot of things. We were optimistic. Everyone was in those days. You know, there was Bob Dylan and the Beatles and everyone. We were hippies.' She keeps talking like she can't stop, like she hasn't done it for a long time. Which isn't true, 'cause we're here to talk to all the time. 'Sam and I met back in '67. There was a house in Subiaco where lots of people used to crash and come and go. Some got permanent. I'd chucked my job in; I'd been working as a secretary for a mining company. I just got fed up with being handled from behind.' She laughs. 'So I was living off savings. Running away from my father, too. He and me didn't get on. He was getting pretty rich from this fleet of hire cars he had. He thought he could treat Mum and me like we worked for him. Mum swallowed it, but I couldn't. She was used to it. Women of her age were used to it. Sorry, I keep getting sidetracked.'

'Keep talking.'

'Well anyway, I was living up the back of this house and Sam was living up the front. The house was full of muso types and people doing drugs. There was a guy who wrote poetry — what a prick. All of us used to sit around the fire in winter and just talk and talk like it was the most important thing in the world to be doing. People argued and cried all over each other. Sometimes it was fun. Other times it was just scary.

'You could tell there was something up between me and Sam 'cause I could never look at him and he could never play guitar in front of me. He was playing in a band called The Grasshoppers. This is gonna sound dumb ... but one night when the talk got really intellectual and I couldn't understand it any more — I tell you, people who write poetry are such pricks—'

'I've written a bit myself,' Henry Warburton says.

'Oh.'

He just laughs.

'Well, it mightn't be true for everyone. Anyway, this night I got sick of it and went outside. I felt really thick, going out, like

I was stupid or something, but I couldn't take it any more. And I bumped into Sam on the front veranda in the dark. He'd been out there longer than me. We were both really embarrassed, but I cracked a joke about poets and that made it easier. Well, that was all it took. That was the start of it all. We went walking, walked all night talking about things, telling stories about ourselves, bitching about the others in the house, till we found ourselves walking around Kings Park. That's a great place, you know, a big slab of bush right in the middle of the city. And there we were, walking around in this big bit of bush with all these trees around us and animals moving around, and Sam says, "You know, Alice Ann Benson, when we get married, we'll go and live amongst trees like these. People should always live near trees." And then we came out of the bush and there below us was the city with all the lights and cars and those big buildings and flashing signs. It was like looking over the whole world all of a sudden. We had a fight straightaway. We argued for hours.

'But I married him. We hitched up here into the hills. I still had some money. We found this little place; it used to be a ranger's house before they opened the national park for felling. We've tacked rooms on to it over the years. We came up here and lived like hippies, growing our own veggies and milk, living near the trees – it was pretty romantic, you know. But it was hard to keep it up. I got pregnant and we got scared and Sam got work pumping petrol over the road. He had no trade or anything, but the Parkinsons – the people who owned the roadhouse in those days – taught him how to be a mechanic. He still hasn't got his ticket, or anything. It was crazy, a hippie working on machines. He even got to like it. He likes fast cars. It . . . doesn't make any sense.'

'You OK?'

She's sniffing.

'I'll be all right.'

'He can hear us, you know.'

'How do *you* know what he can hear?' she says, real angry. 'Who are you to say? He's all busted up because of that greedy little pig Bill Cherry and fast cars and because he's a good man. Are *you* gunna fix him up? What right have you got?'

Then it's real quiet. After a long time, Warburton makes a hawk sound in his throat and says, 'She's got me there, Sam.'

For a while they sit there being real quiet and I push my toes into the dirt to feel it go cool. It's funny, you know, even though I'm immature and too young for my age, I feel older since Dad had his prang. I haven't tried to be, though I should've. It's just come on me and I didn't even know it. Well I think it has. How do you tell? These holidays better last. I don't want them to go quick. High school keeps coming up in my mind. I can see it at the corner of my eye sometimes when I'm thinking, and I keep it there. Geez, I don't want to grow up. Being immature is OK.

Mum sounds like she's finished her story. If I was her, I'd ask him for his. It's time he said something that makes sense.

Sad about Fat. I still like Fat. But I never see him now.

'So,' Mum says with a sniff. 'That's how we got here. Right now it looks like a nice dream turned bad. We weren't even real hippies. And now look at us – local yokels. We're more country than the country. But what about you? You're not giving much away.'

'Oh . . .'

'It's rude to let people spill their guts and then not do the same.'

'Have you done that?'

'Yes.'

'You don't talk much with people, do you?' he asks.

'Sam is all I need. He's all I put my trust in.'

I reckon Henry Warburton wants to keep us in the dark. From here you can hear Dad's whistling throat. It's not such a

253

bad sound, kind of familiar and reassuring now. Reminds me that he's listening in, too. And they talk like we're both not here.

'Well,' Mum says, 'where and when were you born?'

'Geraldton, 1942.'

'You're older than us.'

'You sound surprised.'

'Living around Ort and Tegwyn, you feel like you're the oldest thing in the world. No, I'm not surprised. You don't wear it well.'

'Shame I can't slight you so gently in the same manner,' Warburton says. 'But for a woman living like you, working hard, away from cosmetics, roughing it, you've done well.'

'I wasn't meaning that,' Mum says, kind of cool with him. 'I meant you look tired and sick of things.'

'I am. But you're the one who should be tired and fed up.'

'I've got no reason to be. I live a good life.'

'And you guard it jealously, like your pride.'

'I don't like people speaking to me like that.'

'Well,' Warburton says, 'you've got a cheek. You just finished telling me how decrepit I look. A man has pride, too, you know.'

'Don't I know it,' she says. 'I live with two of them.'

'Geraldton must be the windiest town on this earth.'

'What?'

Talk, talk, talk!

'Geraldton,' he says. 'The trees grow at right angles to the ground. There's miles of sand dunes. Everything is clogged up with salt. A hell of a town.' He laughs. Across the fence and over the road, the lights are still on at Cherrys' Roadhouse. AMPOL, the sign says, THE AUSTRALIAN COMPANY. You can see the lights on in the bowsers. The bowsers look like little robots waiting for something to happen.

'I went to Geraldton once,' Mum says, sounding a bit

happier now. 'I had an uncle who was a crayfisherman. He got rich quick and lost the lot. Went to Indonesia.'

'Hell of a town.'

'What did your parents do?'

'Tried to stay married. My mother was a sculptress and my father was an Anglican priest.'

'Yeah?'

'Yes. And there was I in the middle,' Warburton says. 'I think they both tried hard to be what they thought they had to be. I don't know. They were in competition. My father was a very popular priest. People used to drive in from miles out to hear him. Mum was successful too, in a small way. I was a believer, you know . . . well, a kind of believer.'

There is quiet for a while.

'Why did you say that?' Mum says. I can hear her sandals scraping on the boards.

'Don't know. Think I'll go in. I'm really tired.'

'Oh.'

'I'll help you with Sam.'

As I scoot down the side of the house to my window, I see my shadow, fat and grey, running beside me. It's like running under a full moon. But, of course, there's no moon, only that crazy cloud up there.

chapter eight

My eyes open, and morning comes hot and white in the window. A dream is going out of me, out and away, leaving me awake and kind of sad. It was a crazy dream. I thought it was real, I really did. It as a crazy dream but it seemed right.

I was out at the edge of the forest just lying on my back, looking up at the moon. The moon was pale – it was daytime. Birds mucked about in the jarrah trees. It was nice there. I could smell the leaves on the ground. I could smell myself. Sometimes I can smell myself and it's OK. (It'd be awful to smell bad, like Malcolm Musworth.) As I was lying there with ants going past, feeling good because there were no jobs to do, I felt the ground go all funny, like it was shivering. The shivers went into my back. It made me feel cold and strange. I stayed there for a bit and it went away. A white bird flew past and went over the house. No one was around, not Mum or Tegwyn or anyone. Then it came again, the ground shivering like it was cold or frightened or finishing a leak, or something. Fences jangled around and twigs and leaves came down out the trees. I stood up. The house was kind of puffing and panting. I saw it from where I was – walls going in and out. So, I started running. I was thinking about Dad. I jumped the fence and Errol came flying at me and hit me in the chest and stayed there, and I stopped to look at the windows going up and down and the doors flapping. The ground shook. It made my legs all funny. I looked around for everyone else but there was no one. The sky went cloudy and dark. Then there was a crack like a tree splitting and falling and the back door came open and the house sucked me off me feet, sucked me in, and I flew in, feet first into the dark house. Inside, everything was shaking. Like the house was taking off. I moved around, falling everywhere, kicking things over. Plates and cups came out of the cupboards and smashed on the floor, the piano was going like a cut cat, playing something I never heard before, the TV was on its face, smashed, sliding across the room. That sofa with the crummy brown flowers was running around the lounge-room and I got the hell out. I could hear nails squealing out the floorboards. I lay in the hall. Suddenly, all the doors opened and closed and everything went dark and quiet. It took a while to get quiet, like it was winding down. Scraping noises went on for a while and something smashed and a nail hit the ceiling and then it was quiet except for little bits of plaster coming down on the boards. And then nothing. I was in the hall. All the doors were closed. It was dark. I was near pooping meself. I could hear me own heart whacking away. And then the lights started, blue, green, red, white, purple, blue, green, red, white . . . and it was like the inside of a fire. I couldn't tell where they were coming from, those colours. They got brighter and brighter till I could see all down the hallway to the back door, and then down the hallway came Dad. He was in the raw and asleep, and kind of sliding along the floor on his back, like he was being sucked along like I was, only slower. When he got to me, his feet touched mine and he stopped. That's when the lights slowed down, got fainter. I didn't know what the hell to do – I didn't know it was a dream – so I didn't do anything. The hole in Dad's neck was open and I heard him whistling. And then out of the cracks and holes in the walls and doors, all the holes I watch the family with, this white, thick light came, all going above us near the ceiling till it made a ball, a fat, mushy ball of white light. It stayed there for a bit and I just looked at it and felt like I wasn't frightened any more and didn't care that I didn't know what the hell was going on. I watched as a little finger of light came out of the ball, getting longer, coming down to us. It pointed around – at one wall, the back door, the other wall, me, then Dad. And then it slid down to Dad and poked around for a bit and went in the hole in his throat. The ball of light got smaller and smaller as it kind of untangled and went into Dad and he started to shine white. He got so white I could hardly look. He was really white, like, like, like ... really, really *white*, and I thought he was getting up, full of this light, but then I woke up ... and here I am, kicking the sheet down, awake, and knowing already that today is gonna be a scorcher.

I lie here for a while. I can hear the chooks fussing. Someone is walking around. Someone is chopping wood. Listen – you can hear the split bits falling to the ground.

Two days Henry Warburton has been here now. Reckon I can't make up my mind about him, but. He's been fixing the place up and helping Mum and even playing with me and trying to teach Tegwyn some piano even though she doesn't listen. He's big, you know, and kind of ugly and got one eye and that thing that stops him talking completely right, but he's got a good laugh like a horse and he has a look sometimes that says maybe he could tell good stories. Long time since anyone told stories around here. Grammar is too old and in herself, and Mum is too worried and busy, and Dad can't talk any more. The only stories these days are the ones you listen in on, or the ones you figure out for yourself.

Yesterday, he walked into Bankside and came back riding an old yellow bike, a crappy old crate with a girl's carry basket on the front. In the carry basket was some clothes he said he scabbed from Mrs Musworth at the pub. They were old bits and pieces that men left behind in their rooms. Some had been there for years. They were awful and I reckon he didn't know.

His hands have got blisters on them. They are all soft and pink. What was he doing under that bridge?

*

'Do you think the bloke across the road would be likely to give me a bit of work every now and then?' Warburton asks Mum at breakfast. He eats toast with big, quick bites, like he's not sure if it's alive or dead.

We all look at Mum. She has a white shirt on, one of Dad's. It's too big for her but it makes her look young.

'No,' she says. She sips her tea.

'Not even a day here and there?'

'No. He keeps an eye on this place, you know.'

'What do you mean?'

'Him and Leila jump to conclusions. Anyway, they're both too damned guilty to give anyone the time of day just now. I think he's hit the grog a bit.'

'What do you think, Ort?'

I shrug. I dunno. I don't really get what they're talking about much.

'Why don't you and me go over after brekky?'

I nod. 'OK.' Tegwyn is still in bed. Grammar is singing in her sleep.

Henry Warburton and me go through the fence and the bush clicks and ticks. There's a hot wind this morning. It makes the brown grass lie over and it makes the dead leaves fly and it brings the smell of the desert, or so Dad used to say. He said the easterly brings little pieces of the deserts and the goldfields and the wheat-belt: red dust and gold dust and yellow dust. The country is a nomad, he says, always going walkabout.

Cherrys' Roadhouse doesn't get used much now. People go to Bankside for their juice because it's cheaper and there's a pub. Cherrys' gets people cut short or people who don't know about Bankside, or people at two o'clock in the morning when Bankside's shut. They used to sell lunches, too, but no one buys 'em. It's a sad place.

• 'What's he like, this Mr Cherry?' Henry Warburton asks. He puts his hand on my shoulder.

'Bit of a dag.'

'Ort, old son, you have the gifts of concinnity and concision.'

'Yeah?'

'Most definitely. Is that Mr Cherry over there? In the full-blown flesh?'

Fat's dad is working on his front bowser with a screwdriver. His black pants hang off him until you can see the crack of his bum. He sees us coming, you can tell.

'Yep. That's him.'

We go across.

'Er. Mr Cherry?'

'You've found him. What.'

'I was interested to know whether you had any need of help.'

'Help?' Mr Cherry hasn't looked up from his bowser yet. Me and Henry Warburton just stand there and look down his hairy crack.

'Of the hired sort.'

'A job?'

Warburton looks at me and his eyebrows go up and up and up till they nearly drown in his hair. I almost laugh.

'I think you have my meaning.'

'I've got your number, too, smart-arse. Piss off.'

Henry Warburton unzips his pants real loud. *Then* Mr Cherry turns around real quick.

'Oh, hello. You're with us, then?'

'Get off this driveway.' His face is all blue with not shaving and his eyes are red.

Warburton zips up. 'You have no jobs?'

'She's got a bloody hide sending you over here. She's got a hide, full stop. Her old man still in the house, under the same roof.'

Henry Warburton moves real quick and has some of Mr Cherry's shirt in his hand and he looks very much bigger all of a sudden, but then he stops and lets go and stands back.

'I'm sorry,' Warburton says, 'that was silly.'

Mr Cherry looks frightened. I can see Mrs Cherry and Fat behind the flywire door and I feel all sick.

'What about my dad's tools?' I say, without even expecting it. It happens all the time now.

'What tools?' Mr Cherry looks at me like he hates my guts.

'Some of my dad's tools are still in there.' I point to the workshop.

'Rubbish. Anything in there is mine, you cheeky little bugger.'

'Come on, Ort,' Warburton says, taking my arm.

'You're a piece of poop, Mr Cherry!' I yell. 'My dad is nearly dead because of you!' Henry Warburton yanks me away. We run across the road, jump the fence, and then walk home. The ground is flat and hard and brown and hot. Grasshoppers hiccup all over the place.

'That wasn't a good thing to say,' Henry Warburton says. I don't say anything. I feel all tight and sick and hot. 'How do you know it was his fault?'

I don't say a word. Not one.

Later in the morning I stand outside the bathroom door and listen to Warburton washing Dad and talking to him.

'You can be washed in the blood, Sam,' he says.

I can hear Mum coming in from out the back, so I slip across into my room.

'. . . whiter than snow . . .'

I drag out the box of *Mad* comics from under the bed to see if they cheer me up. One says RONNIE REAGAN HANGS LOOSE. There is an old man on a horse. The horse and the man are

261

smiling and have ropes around their necks. I dunno what it means. I wish it would make me laugh.

The hot white day swims along real slow like the sun is breast-stroking through that blue sky when it should be going freestyle. Everyone hangs around the shade of the house listening to the trees in the east wind. The ground is wobbly with heat. The house ticks. You can hear seeds popping, grass drying up and fainting flat. You can hear the snakes puffing.

Henry Warburton pokes around in the big shed all day. Hear him moving things, dropping them. Dad's Chev truck is out there. He bought it before I was born. It's older than any of us, except maybe Grammar. Every now and then Dad will go out there in the evening with some lamps and his tools. Me and Tegwyn and Mum sit out on the veranda waiting to hear the sound of the motor. But we've never heard it yet.

All day out there in the hot, Henry Warburton bangs around and we sit here inside wondering if we can even be bothered going down the creek; all day until the sun is gone and the east wind stops and we come out with Dad on to the back veranda.

But the same happens again: Tegwyn and me get sent to bed early so they can talk. Tegwyn slams her door and I slam mine; then she does it again, and so do I. I hear the springs going as she jumps on her bed. I knock on the wall.

'Piss off, Small Thing,' she says.

So I go out to listen again.

'Seemed there was more life in what my mother did. Out of clay or stone she made things that were alive. My father's conjurings with wafers and wine seemed more mechanical than her chipping away with chisels and bits of rock.'

'What was she like?' Mum is asking.

'Oh, I don't know, really. I never took the time to find out.

She had long black hair she used to wind up in a bun, big red lips; she was thin. I suppose she could have been one of those Darlington wives whose husbands are bone marrow specialists with lots of money and near perfect accents. I don't know — I was so young. I left at seventeen. Went to university. I didn't even go back for holidays. I was supposed to be studying literature and music, but I don't know what I did all those years. It was fun, though. I wound up teaching. Lasted three months at a public high school. I knocked the headmaster over in the staffroom. I was in a hurry. He fell over on to the principal mistress and they ended up on the floor together. It was an accident, but I cracked a dumb joke about how she now qualified as the principal's mistress and that we should apostrophize her. I got the sack. They found some excuse and I didn't fight it. That was '65.

'Then I just started hitching around. Thought I was Jack Kerouac himself. It was really something to be young and not committed to anything except having a good time. I met lots of people, got into some interesting situations, did a lot of dope, experimented a bit. '67, I shagged out all of a sudden. Lived in a commune. North Queensland. I thought I was going to be there for ever. I used to write poems and look after the kids. My book came out in '69.'

'What was it called?' Mum says. 'I've never met an author before.'

'I thought you lived with a poet.'

'Oh, he never had anything printed.'

'You'll laugh if I tell you.'

'It was a long time ago. I'll understand.'

Henry Warburton is quiet for a while. Dad whistles in the dark.

'It was called *Heavy Dream-Jazz from the Tropic of Capricorn—*'

'Oh, no,' Mum says, with a laugh.

'—*and Other Verse Statements.*'

'Oh. Oh, dear. Did you make all the poems look like flowers and motorbikes and things?'

He laughs. 'Yes.'

'Did anyone buy it?'

'Not that I know of. The publishers made papier-mâché briefcases out of them, I think, and sold them to Chinese diplomats. I don't know, really.'

The night seems cool with their laughs.

'What made you stay at the commune?'

'Oh, a woman.'

'What was her name? Was she nice?'

'Her name was Bobo Sax.' His voice goes all funny. 'No, she wasn't nice. She had the voice of a man and she smelt like a Labrador.'

Across the road Cherrys' lights go out. The roadhouse is closed early.

'Why did you stay with her?'

'Um. I couldn't not stay. I don't know. She was the exact opposite of my parents. She thought nothing, believed nothing, did nothing, pretended nothing. She wasn't nice or decent or restrained. I really couldn't say with any conviction that she was even human. She used to lie in her mud hut in the dark. The smell of her . . .'

'Yes?'

'Well, I stayed. 1970 I left. I don't know why. That was the year Jimi Hendrix died, wasn't it. It was as though I came out of a trance. I just dropped everything one day and walked off. I hitched back across the continent and went home to Geraldton. I got a shock. My mother and father didn't live there any more. It had been eight years since I left. The priest there told me my father was in Perth, and that he was a bishop. And my mother was dead. Brain tumour.

'I hitched back down to Perth as though I was stoned. I didn't know what I was doing. Someone showed me where my father lived. I found his office – it was fairly plush with lots of leather-bound books and dark furniture. My father was in. He didn't look surprised to see me. He poured me a drink. We stood there in his bishop's office with the sun coming in the high window, just looking at each other. He was wearing civvies – sensible cuts, sensible colours. His hair was grey and shiny. He probably couldn't believe the sight of me. I hadn't cut my hair for eight years. I didn't used to wash much then. I wore home-made clothes. He just looked at me and I just looked at him. Then he said, "Now neither of us has anyone on this earth," and then he showed me out.'

'God. What did you do?'

'Oh, I worked for a while, saved some money, and went over-seas. Easier to do then. Europe. I met a girl in Frankfurt. Married her and came back to Australia. In '73 our baby boy was born. We were living in Sydney. I had a job in advertising. Martha and I were happy enough. In 1974 she and the boy died in a rail accident. I drank myself stupid, got sacked, and went back up to northern Queensland.'

He talks like it's someone else doing all these things. So many things.

'To Bobo Sax?'

'Yes. I took a lot of acid and spent a lot of time with her. It nearly burnt me out completely. She died in 1977. It was a . . . bad affair. Our farm was burnt down afterwards by the locals. I ended up with nothing again.'

'That was seven years ago. What have you been doing all this time?'

'Oh,' he says, laughing, 'learning to live with nothing.'

I tell you, I don't know if I'm firing on all six. I just got this crazy idea and before I even decide about it, I'm up and off and doing it and the house is behind me as I cut across the firebreak toward Cherrys'. These days I just do things, like me parts don't need permission from me brain. It's real scary, like when I say things without giving me mouth the nod. Maybe it's growing up – or going whacko.

I move along real quick and quiet. The road is still warm when I cross it. The driveway of the roadhouse is oily and gucky under my feet. The big tin doors are down over the front of the workshop. AMPOL, THE AUSTRALIAN COMPANY. Round to the side window. Some nights I used to come here and watch my dad's legs coming out from under a Chrysler or a Ford, listening to him sing and make noises with his spanners and I stood there for a long time knowing he couldn't see me, just watching his legs for no reason.

The window near the front is closed, but further down, the louvre windows are open a little bit, so I start working away at them. The first one comes out real easy, and I put it careful on the dirt and have a go at number two. Hard to see good. No moon. Stuck. I push and pull, try to work the glass out. Oh, geez! It breaks and comes away and I catch both pieces and feel the glass go in the skin and blood come up quick. I put the pieces on the dirt. The next louvre comes out easy, but with blood all over it. I scuff up on the ledge, get my head in the hole and kick in.

Suddenly there's lights and stars and rainbows and me head hurts like hell. The vice! I shuffle away from it with my hands on the bench, and then I get my feet in and I'm like a dog on the bench, sniffing around. I get down on the floor. Something chinks in the dark. Parts, tools. Up the front past the hoist I find the meterbox and try the lights. They all come on sudden and the place is so bright I cut them down to one little one low to the floor that gives everything a soft light. Radiator hose curls up near me feet. Boxes of old parts. An air filter. Fanbelts. Carbies. Tools, tools, tools, everywhere. Just tools. I can't tell whose they are. They all smell the same now; there's no telling one from the other. Some of these tools are my dad's. He should have them back. But I can't tell which ones so I just stuff some into the old pillowslip on the bench that they use for a rag. Spanners, screwdrivers, things like that. On the way back to the window I see the Pirelli calendar from 1969 with the brown boobs pointing at me, so I grab it just before I decide to and stuff it in the pillowslip. There is a light green square on the wall where it was. I go back to the fuse box to turn out the lights.

The louvres go back in like they came out. They look all right except for the crack in the middle one and the blood all over. The tools chink and ring on the way back. All the way across the paddock and up the firebreak I watch the light above the house. It shows me where to walk.

'The first Christmas we were married, I wanted a Christmas tree,' Mum is saying as I sneak up the side of the house. 'Sam couldn't understand why, and anyway there was nothing like that around here then. That was before they tried re-foresting down near Bankside with all that crappy pine. Christmas Eve I come into the lounge and there in the corner is a sunflower in a bucket of sand, decorated with old pieces of foil and bottle tops. Oh, I cried. I really love him, you know. People say they don't know what love is. Everyone says it now. They're scared to know. I'd suffer for him and be humiliated for him. I'd be ashamed for him and let people hate me for him. I have and still will. People don't want to know love. They might have to get dirty.'

Then she goes quiet, like she's said a whole lot more than she thought she would. I can hear Dad's slow awake whistle. Henry Warburton's shadow grows out across the dirt of the yard. He must be standing up at the edge of the veranda with the inside light behind him.

'Yes,' he says, just loud enough to hear. 'You're close to things, Alice. Close to all things.'

'And what does that mean?'

'Hmm? Oh, sorry. Nothing. I'm just waxing a bit lyrical tonight.'

'Oh.' She doesn't sound sure.

All of a sudden I'm real tired. This talk is way over. I climb back in real slow, pushing the curtains and the flywire away, holding the tools real tight so they don't chink.

chapter nine

Yesterday I saw Henry Warburton and Mr Cherry down at the fence. Their faces and hands were going like mad but I couldn't hear what they were saying. This morning I found Errol hanging off the clothesline with his neck wrung, and I'm not coming out all day.

Before lunch Henry Warburton carries Dad down the hallway to the bathroom in his arms. Dad looks so small, like he's my little brother now and my new dad's taking him to the bath. When we were small, Dad used to come in the night and take us to the toilet in case we forgot. He used to say to me: 'This is how I picked you up when you were still wet from Mummy's belly. So big now,' and I would still pretend to be asleep so he might talk more but all he would say was 'So big, so big now' as we went down the hallway with the wind going outside and the rain rattling hard on the roof.

I hear the water running and Henry Warburton's voice bouncing around in the bathroom. Later, when the water stops, those crazy words come out, too big and weird to understand. Always those strange words.

A knock. Mum comes in with a tired face and her hair all down. Her face is so brown that when she looks tired or sad, white lines cut her cheeks up.

'Hi.'

'Hi,' I say, making room for her on the bed.

'Don't be angry. It doesn't help.'

'I know Mr Cherry did it.'

She puts her hand on my face. 'He drinks a lot, now, you know. He doesn't know what he's doing.'

I don't say anything.

'Henry's going over to speak to him later.'

'Tell him not to.'

'Why?' she asks.

'Don't let's even talk to them any more.'

'Well, I'll talk to Henry,' she says. 'He's not feeling well this morning, anyway. Says he feels funny in the head.'

I push my pillow in two and lie back on it. Mum puts my feet in her lap and squeezes all my toes, one by one. Her green shirt has got patches on it.

'What does he talk about in there with Dad?'

'Henry? Oh, I don't know. I never noticed really.'

'He talks to him all the time.'

'I notice you don't any more.'

'I forget,' I say, looking at the wall with its cracks and holes. 'Sometimes I even forget he's here. Why isn't he normal now?'

She sighs. 'They don't know. You know what doctors are like. Talk a lot and say nothing. I reckon they don't know. And if they did they wouldn't bother telling us.'

'He doesn't look like a spaz or anything. He just looks like he's far inside like Grammar.'

'Sometimes he looks so sad.'

'Are you sure he'll get better?'

'He came back from the dead, didn't he?'

'Yeah.'

'Have some faith, then.'

'Faith?'

'Just don't give up on him.'

*

Lunch is quiet and I feed Dad his salad. His hands are going white; even under his nails it's white.

After lunch Tegwyn goes off into Bankside on the old crate Henry Warburton brought back. Mum sits in the lounge, mending clothes. Henry Warburton just sits with his eyes closed. I lie on the floor; it's cooler there.

'What was it like when you went to high school?' I ask him.

'Best years of my life,' he says without opening his eyes.

'Did you like it?'

'Hated it.'

'But you said—'

'Listen, leave it, will you?'

Mum raises her eyebrows at me. Henry Warburton sighs and gets up and goes outside.

'What's up with him?'

'I think he's crook, Ort. Don't bother him.'

'I just asked him a question.'

Mum shrugs. She pushes the needle into Tegwyn's jeans. I get up and go out. From the back veranda I see Henry Warburton going into the forest. All over the backyard, Errol's feathers muck around in the wind. Makes me angry again, and the dark patch that shows where he's – she's – buried makes it worse; I pass it on my way to the fence. Only a chook.

I follow Henry Warburton, keep behind him a long way so I can see him but he can't see me. His white shirt flashes in the red and brown trees. Birds scoot across. I walk careful over logs and dry sticks, make myself small to go through prickle bushes. I stop sometimes and look at him through a blackboy or around a tree trunk. He walks without thinking of snakes, and he doesn't mind making a noise. You'll never see any animals if you walk like that. In the bush you walk real wary, real slow. You put your feet down like you're not sure it's quicksand or not. You listen with your eyes and see with your ears. The same as when you walk through the house at night, keeping an eye on everyone.

We go down near the creek and pass the big black patch from the fire. He doesn't look. We go past the old sawmill. He doesn't look. Then I know. He's going to the bridge. But when he gets to the bridge he doesn't stop. He walks under and along the bank for a while till he comes to the swimming hole. I stop back quite a bit, high up the side of the slope, and get in between some blackboys. Henry Warburton stops at the swimming hole. On the other side, the bit of green grass and the piece of rope look kind of funny and out of place. Henry Warburton sits down and takes off his shoes and socks. Then he takes all his clothes off and folds them and puts them over a log. Midges move over the water. Little helicopters. He walks into the water with his white back and bum showing. Then he slides under.

Flies get in me shorts while I'm watching and it nearly makes me giggle. Two of them going like a duck and drake, buzzing together all the way down me leg and into me shorts. I watch Henry Warburton float and swim and blow water. He gets out once on the grassy side, takes a run-up and chucks a bombie. He hits the water curled up like a baby. Water goes high up, almost to that tassel of rope in the big redgum. He comes up laughing. Makes me wanna get in too.

When he gets out he stands in the sun a bit. Then he picks up his clothes and walks back under the bridge. I follow him down and come closer because it looks like he's gonna stay for a bit. I breathe with my mouth wide open — it's quieter that way.

Under the bridge he just stands there in the raw, talking. Talking! To no one. His bum wobbles when he talks. Water still drips down his white back and arms.

'I hide and you see. I run and you follow.' I get squeamy; maybe he's having a go at me, like he knows I've been here all the time. 'To the ends of this earth, to the limits of the pit of myself, you will see and know me. Your love is terrible. Its gentleness a blow, its patience a judgement. Its silence thunders all about. Help me, Giver of All, I am unfaithful to men and to you, and even myself. Make my great weakness your strength. O God, my Father and Mother, help me, let me love them, make me love them. I . . . I . . . carry . . . carry . . . you like a live coal in my chest . . . my . . . my . . .'

He's puffing like he's gonna cry or be sick and his bum cheeks go mad shaking and his legs all shivery. He holds his head with his hands.

'. . . my . . . God . . . save . . . take . . . wh . . . wh . . . whaa . . . ghh . . . nghh . . .'

He falls down and gurgles and his back goes like a bridge trying to come up through his belly. His hands dig in the dirt. All his muscles come up like polished bits of wood, popping out his skin. He's hard all over like a piece of wood and sap comes out his mouth like he's turned into a tree.

'. . . nngth . . . nngth . . . ogh . . .'

While Mum is in the lounge-room watching Henry Warburton sleep on his mattress on the floor, I stash the pillowcase of tools and the Pirelli calendar under Dad's side of the bed. I look around, too, for Christmas presents, just in case, but there's none under there yet. Probably too early. I go back into the lounge-room. Henry Warburton is still asleep under the sheet.

'Get the mercurochrome, Ort.' Mum looks tired and dirty and her scratches are worse than mine. There's a cut under her eye, skin missing off her knees and elbows. I bring the little bottle from the bathroom and a clean rag from the bag in the linen cupboard. Mum puts the red stuff on me. It stings and makes the scratches look worse. When I put it on her it makes her look like she should be in bed herself. It was a long, long way back with Henry Warburton. I was already stuffed from running home and then back with Mum to the bridge. We could only carry him a little bit and then we had to rest. We dropped him sometimes. Mum fell over a stump and hacked her toes. I was crying 'cause I was frightened and sore. All stuff had gone dry on his face. He looked dead.

'Now we've got another one to look after,' I say.

'Don't get it in my eye,' Mum says. She tries to show how much it doesn't sting.

Tegwyn comes in, sweaty and red from riding. 'What's up?'

'Henry chucked a mental,' I say, 'down by the bridge.'

'It was a fit.'

'Is he an apoplexic or whateveritis?'

'An epileptic, Tegwyn,' Mum says. 'I don't know.'

'Lucky he wasn't swimming,' Tegwyn says, putting her bag on the sofa.

'He was in the nick,' I say, with a grin that won't go away.

Dad sniffs; it makes us all look around, but there's no kind of look on his face that's special.

'Beaudy,' says Tegwyn. 'Now there's three.'

She goes down the hallway again and soon we hear music from the piano. It's kind of nice: up and down sounds, up and down.

'That's Grammar's music,' Mums says, just sitting there. 'She used to play it all the time when she first came here. It's the kind of music they never let her play at the socials and in the dance halls.'

'It's nicer than plonky-plunk music.'

'Yeah. It's German.'

'How long's Grammar been here?'

'Since the day after you were born.'

'I don't get some things.'

'Understand, you mean?'

'Yeah.'

'What don't you understand?'

'Why Dad's crook. Why Grammar is so old and inside herself. Why *he's* here, and why he baths Dad and talks funny and chucks a wobbly in the bush so we have another one to look after.'

273

'Is that all?' Mum says with a laugh.

'Why Tegwyn doesn't like us. Why Mr Cherry is . . . Mr Cherry . . .'

'You've got me there, mate. I don't know either. Crazy, isn't it?' She's got wet eyes. 'Bloody crazy.'

Henry Warburton wakes up and doesn't know who the hell we are. He walks around real soft. He doesn't remember. He's all arse-about. Doesn't know his own name. He starts laughing and then bawls his face out into Mum's Sydney Harbour Bridge tea towel. We put him back to bed and he sleeps and sleeps until morning.

Just as the sun is up I find ten chicks under the chook I call Bruiser. She pecks me away but I get a look and count 'em real quick. I go to the shed and get them some mash. Bruiser gets off for a while and I grab a little pecker and take him inside.

'There's chicks,' I say at the kitchen table. I open my hands.

'New life,' Henry Warburton says. He looks at the chick like it's hard to see. He goes on eating.

'That means there's chook for dinner tonight,' Mum says with a smile.

'Why?' asks Henry Warburton.

'Because we always do,' I say.

Mum shrugs. 'A kind of celebration, I s'pose. Will you do it for us?'

'What?'

'The chook.'

'*That?* Kill it?'

'No.' She laughs. 'A big one, silly.'

'No.'

'You eat chicken, don't you?'

He nods. 'I won't kill.'

'Sam always says everyone who eats vegetables should grow their own at least once, and everyone who eats meat should kill it at least once, so they know what it means to be responsible. And so they remember who and what they are and why they keep living.'

Henry Warburton gets up and goes into the lounge-room. Mum looks at me, and I know what it means. Me guts goes funny.

After breakfast I put the chick back and catch a fat young hen. I tie her up like Dad does and hang her upside-down from the clothesline so she goes calm. I bring the machete from the shed, take the chook down the back, and take her head off on the block. I don't let her go. Dad says it's an abomination to let an animal run round without its head. Mum brings the hot water out. The feathers come off easy. It stinks. I pull the guts out, wash it, and it's all over. Henry Warburton can go hungry tonight for all I care.

For two days he walks round like he can't remember what he's doing in our house. He shouts things in his sleep like: 'They have given the dead bodies of your servants as food to the birds of the air, and the flesh of your saints to the beasts of the earth!' He cries in his sleep. Mum washes his sheets every morning because of the sweat, and then one morning when we're looking at the little chicks running around on their own, yellow and brown, he comes out in his pyjamas and says, 'I'm better now.'

Mum and Tegwyn and me just look at him. The pyjamas are too small; the leg ends are nearly up to his knees. Tegwyn says to him, 'Are you sure?' and we all laugh because he looks such a dag and the chooks stare at us like we're dumb animals and don't know any better.

chapter ten

And then out on the veranda in the warm dark he blurts it out. We're all quiet, just sitting listening to the night in the forest and the chooks sleeping and Dad whistling in–out, and Warburton starts talking like it hurts him but he won't stop. I look at the stars and try to see what they're saying with those bright little mouths going open and closed all the time. The sky goes way back tonight; it's like looking into water, and you wonder why you can't see your reflection at the bottom, but you know you can see *something*. Henry Warburton makes us all jump with his quick words.

'It's time I stated my purpose. I haven't meant to be deceitful; God has sent me here.'

Dead quiet. At the end of the dead quiet Mum says, 'What do you mean?'

'So very hard to explain. I know you won't believe me, but I had a vision.'

'What's that?' I ask.

'It's something you see that no one else sees. It's real, it's there, but only you see it.'

'Like the light,' I say.

'What light?' Mum says.

'The one up the roof. It's a cloud kind of thing. Look, it lights up the yard. You can see rabbits' eyes in it all round the fence.'

'Don't talk crap,' Tegwyn says. 'There's no light, there's no rabbit eyes. It's pitch black out there. If your brain worked as well as your imagination you wouldn't be so thick.'

'Tegwyn,' Mum says, 'leave off.'

'Well, what did *you* see?' Tegwyn says to Henry Warburton.

'It's not important. I just saw.'

'Oh, bollocks.'

'Tegwyn, another word like that and you can go to your room. Don't be so damned rude. Go on, Henry.'

'God told me to come to you.'

'Who's God?'

'Ort, be quiet.'

'No, it's all right,' Henry Warburton says, sounding like it really does hurt to talk like this. 'God is who made us and made the birds and trees and everything. He keeps things going. He sees all things. He is our father. He loves us.'

'I thought it was just a word. Like heck. Is he *someone*? Mum?'

'I never really thought about it, Ort . . . I, I—'

'So what did he send you here for?' I ask Henry Warburton.

'To love you.'

Tegwyn groans. 'I thought you said you were all right.'

'Did you get our names from God?' I ask him. 'How did you know our names? You knew all our names, and you knew about Dad.'

'He was living down at the bridge spying on us. He watched us swimming—'

'But—' I start.

'And I had no clothes on. Did God tell you what me fanny looks like, too?'

Mum stands up, skraking the cane chair. 'Tegwyn, go to your room.'

Tegwyn slaps the back door against the wall. The flywire pops out the frame. We hear her door slam. After a bit, Henry Warburton keeps talking and we listen. He talks and talks about this bloke Adam and this bloke Eve who had no clothes on and

277

it didn't matter 'cause they ate fruit and talked to a snake and it was a bad thing, and everything went wrong-oh. And how you can see God but you can't. And all these stories about God in burning bushes and piles of fire and tornados and little clouds. Stories! Piles of 'em. He tells stories like you've never *heard*, boy. About God getting sad when no one loved him, and him just waiting around keeping things going, waiting for someone to like him, and then getting angry and crying and making a flood with his tears. This bloke Noah and his boat. I know that story from school. Another one about a kid fighting a monster, and this one about a bloke trying to run away from God and how he got swallowed up by a big fish and chundered up again. I saw that on telly. All the time he's talking about this bad in people and God wanting people to love him but they can't because of all this black bad in them like in an apple. And this real long story about God making a kid in a girl's belly. This kid grows up and some like him and some don't. He can do crazy things like walk on water and then make it into plonk, make crook people better and dead people alive. People didn't like him because he was so good to them. They killed him by sticking him on a tree. They put him in a hole but he got up afterwards and went up into the sky with God.

At the end of the story it's real late, but I feel like I just got out of bed. My head's ticking away and me hands are all tingly. All the red eyes of the rabbits out near the fence are dancing. Mum sighs.

'So. You're a preacher.'

'Yes. An evangelist, I suppose you'd say.'

'Well, why wait until now to start preaching?'

'I've been preaching since the moment I arrived. I'm sorry, I don't do it well.'

Mum sniffs; she does when she's thinking.

'So, God's up there?' I say, pointing to all those wonderful stars. 'A someone?'

'Everywhere, Ort. He's in everything. The trees, the ground, the water. Everything stinks of God, reeks of him.'

'But he's up there a lot?'

'Well, they call him the Father of Lights.'

'He sees *everything*?'

Henry Warburton sighs, and then again. 'Yes, Ort, every little thing.'

'Then he knows the secrets.'

'What secrets?' Mum says; she sits up straight.

'All the secrets. All our secrets.'

'Yes,' he says.

'And he saw who killed Errol.'

'Ort.'

'And what happened to Dad. What he's thinking. And he knows what Grammar's always thinking.'

'All . . . all the mysteries. All secrets.'

Sounds right to me.

Mum sniffs. Henry Warburton laughs. Out over the forest, a star tumbles out of the black eye into the trees. Tomorrow I'll go and look for it.

'Did you make a wish, Ort?' Mum says.

'Yes.' Not true. I forgot.

For a while it's quiet, like everyone's thinking. There's lots of questions in me, and this feeling right down that makes me feel like I'm jumping in the air, or like when you hit a bump going real fast in a car. Butterflies, bellyrolls.

'You never mentioned any of this before,' Mum says to Henry Warburton. 'When you talked about yourself. Not a word. Why did you do that?'

'Because,' he says, real quiet, 'because . . . I'm weak.'

'Yes, I can see that now.'

'You don't like weak men.'

'No,' she says, 'all men are weak. A woman's got no time to be weak. It's not that I don't like weak men. I just get sick of

279

them. Bill Cherry, for instance. He takes out his weakness on children.'

'And Sam?'

'I count Sam with the children.'

'I don't understand.'

Mum sniffs. 'Sam is a child in a man's body. He trusts people. He thinks the best of them. He sees the way things should be, not always the way things are.'

'And he can hear every word, Mum,' I say, grabbing hold of his hand. 'You forget.'

She looks at me. I can see the water in her eyes in the light from the roof. Her hands are all tight and twisted together the way two brown, fighting spiders would be. She nods, real slow.

'Even kids've got ears,' I say.

'Sometimes their ears are too big for them and they hear too much,' Warburton says, like he's not in a good mood.

'Not as much as some,' I say, pointing up there into the night.

Henry Warburton gets up and for a sec I don't know what he's gonna do, but he just steps off the veranda on to the dirt and walks out into the middle of the yard with his hands in his pockets, kicking with his feet, whistling some tune or other. He stops and turns around, looking up, looking round with all that black and white winking behind him.

'Afraid I can't see your light anywhere, Ort.'

'It's there,' I say.

'I can't see it.'

'I can't see what you see, either.'

'I'd say you've got a match here, Henry,' Mum says, laughing like she feels better all of a sudden.

I squeeze Dad's hand, worm me fingers between his and squeeze. There's no squeeze back, but that doesn't make me feel different.

'Anyone for a cuppa?'

We all say yes except Dad, who never says no to a cuppa.

We go in when the kettle's boiled, and bring out the pot and the cups and a tin of Mum's bickies – the ones made of bran and oatmeal that go through you like the charge of the life brigade. We sip and dunk and I help Dad. It's not that his hands and mouth and eyes don't work; it's just like he's not interested in using them any more. It's like he's given up. We eat and drink and go quiet again; the tea and bickies makes us friendly.

Mum makes herself a second cup, and me too; makes you feel real grown-up, two cups. She looks like she's gonna say something for a sec, and then she looks at Henry Warburton and then at her cup of tea and says nothing. He smiles.

'I was converted, if that's what you were going to ask.' Mum smiles and looks kind of embarrassed. 'God is a mystery. He plants his love in the path of all our plans.'

'Aren't you tired, Ort?' Mum says.

'No, is this secret?'

'Of course not,' Henry Warburton says. 'Of course not. What was I saying? Oh, our plans. I had a lot of plans after Bobo died. Plans to get a job. To go away again. To buy a farm. To kill myself. One morning I woke up with this awful haze in my eyes. It was like looking into a sixty-watt bulb. I had it for three days before I went to the first doctor. This terrible light in front of my eyes. It hurt. I had headaches, I couldn't see properly. I couldn't continue a normal life, couldn't keep a job. I went to doctors, eye specialists, even a psychiatrist. None of them could help, though they all had different explanations for the same phenomenon. It went on and on. I was staying in this boarding house in Brisbane. The landlady was a crazy old thing with a hearing aid like 1950s TV – almost big enough to have to strap it to her back. She used to climb the stairs day and night, shouting: 'In my father's house are many rooms!' I just thought she was a nut. I ended up completely immobile in my room with this shocking light and pain and this feeling of not quite being attached to myself, and she came in, morning, noon, and night, nursing me and cashing my dole money for herself. I got worse. I fought it, thought I was going blind, so I fought against it, and it was like a cramp when you're swimming – the more you fight it, the worse it gets, the quicker you drown. It brought on nightmares and I must have been out of my mind in the end, fighting it, fighting it, all the time this white light burning into me. I don't recall much of it. It was a week or so of it. I think I just gave up, something inside of me just broke and surrendered. I was utterly exhausted and it went away. I looked around for a moment, at the cobwebs in the corner of the ceiling, the brownish curtains, and I just fell asleep. Woke up two days later and there was the landlady – Mrs Sims was her name – with a bowl of soup, ready to feed me. She didn't smile. She just said, "God has been with you," and stuffed an iron spoonful of her awful soup in my mouth.

'Recuperating was almost as bad as going through the experience itself. I was constipated to the point of no return. Concrete laced with razor blades.

'When I got better, I went out and stole a Bible from a shop that sold heavy Catholic theology and plastic Marys. I started travelling again. Met farmers, wanderers, bush philosophers who were believers. Blokes in road gangs. Barmaids. And I realized that the Church did exist. The kingdom without walls. Family of Man, or whatever. It was a terrible shock after being brought up by a High Church agnostic. I learnt a lot of things. Lived in a community in Gippsland for a year. There we were, God was with us and in us, without us having to say the secret formula. We didn't need to conjure God up with wafers and wine. He's always been there only we never look. All you need to do is open your eyes. You see, and then you either want it or you don't. If you believe, the Spirit helps you to believe more. Helps you to love more.'

'But you had to have them opened.'

'Sometimes we need a bit of prompting.'

'And now you're out here prompting the Flacks,' Mum says smiling over her cup. I suck on tea leaves.

'Yes, here I am. Proselytizing the heathen Flack.'

'You could actually say you've seen the light,' Mum says, with a laugh.

'I suppose so.'

'I can't figure you out,' she says, shaking her head.

He laughs. 'You know what my middle name is? Esau. I think it was a joke my father thought I'd appreciate when I was old enough to understand. He used to call me Esau the see-saw. Up and down. Yes and no. Good and bad. The blind leading the blind.' Again, he laughs. 'Esau selling his birthright for a pot of lentil stew. Literally. We ate a lot of lentils in northern Queensland.'

'They're good for you,' I say.

'Yes,' he says grinning, 'but they make you fart something awful.'

'Everything has a price,' Mum says. We all laugh. The chooks shuffle on their perches and the rabbits move red eyes in the dark.

chapter eleven

It's real early in the morning. The creek is flat brown and the swimming hole looks like someone just painted it for us, like God just did it. Down here at the bridge it's real quiet. Mum, Henry, and me are standing in the water, and Henry is talking. Everything's stopped except us.

'Do you believe, Alice?'

Mum looks at me. 'Yeah. I reckon.'

'Then I baptize you in the name of Father, Son, and Spirit.' And under she goes, with Henry holding her. When she comes up, her dress sticks and her hair is flat. She splutters and laughs a bit.

I stand there, nervous. Think about what Henry told us that night a couple of days back. Yep, it still sounds right. He turns to me. I feel the mud in my toes. I see a bird frozen still in a tree behind Henry and, up by the bridge, Tegwyn hiding to watch. I feel sad a bit.

'What about you, Ort?'

'Yeah. I believe it.'

He crosses my hands on my chest and holds me big and strong and I go back like I'm falling out a window, out into the sky for ever, and I keep my eyes open under the water and it's like tea and it all goes up me nose and then I'm rushing up to the surface like out of a dream. And there's the sky. All over. And it all starts again. That bird calls out and chops off somewhere, and it's quiet under the sky. And I laugh a bit too.

chapter twelve

This morning when all the birds were starting to make their heep-beeb waking-up sounds, Henry Warburton rode off on the old yellow bike. He had a white shirt on and black pants, and shoes. He rode down towards Bankside. I saw him go, and I don't think he saw me. A couple of weeks, he's been here now. Things are different. The sky was all pink. Everything was still. I knew then it would be a cooler day; could smell it in the ground. Mum was up and getting breakfast when I went in. I told her Henry was gone and she looked like she was worried but trying hard not to look like it.

'What about the Lord's Supper and the praying and the Bible story?' I said.

'Oh.' She sighed and put more wood in the stove. 'I s'pose we can do it ourselves. That's what Henry said. Don't need anyone to do it for us.'

I was a bit nervous, but we did it. We sat down at the table while the eggs were on and the bacon, and I read.

'In this you greatly rejoice, though now for a little while you may have to suffer grief in all kinds of trials. These have come so that your faith – of greater worth than gold, which perishes even though refined by fire – may be proved genuine and may result in praise, glory, and honour when Jesus Christ is revealed. Though you have not seen him, you love him, and even though you do

not see him now, you believe in him and are filled with
an inexpressible and glorious joy, for you are receiving
the goal of your faith, the salvation of your souls.'

The bloke who wrote that once cut off someone's ear. You'd
think that someone who went round cutting off people's ears
could tell a better story. Anyway, the eggs and bacon were ready
by then, so I stopped and Mum said a prayer.

'Thank you Jesus for this good food please make us good
and Sam better Amen.'

And then we ate breakfast. At the end of breakfast we did
the Lord's Supper like Henry Warburton's been doing with us
since we got baptized last week. Mum got the sherry and some
bread. Then she said the words she could remember.

'Take it, it's my body.' She gave me some bread and took
some herself. We ate it. 'Drink all of it,' she said, pouring some
sherry in my tea mug. There were tea leaves floating. 'It's for
forgiving sins.'

Then I said: 'We love you God Amen.'

That was this morning. We did it all again at lunch 'cause
it's as often as we meet, like it says. It's not really the blood of
Jesus. Any dumbo can see that. Henry says it's just to remember.
It's no use eating Jesus. Ha! He's in you already.

And now I'm here wiping up for Mum. Christmas is five
days away. Maybe Henry Warburton's gone off to buy us
prezzies, eh. I can hear the forest sighing like it sleeps in the day
and wakes up at night. Mum scrubs away at a pot, her arms all
red.

'How big's a soul, you reckon?' I ask. She blows a bit of
hair out her eye.

'Oh, I don't know,' she says. 'Big as your fist.'

'He fits in small places.'

'Who?'

'God.'

286

'Well, he's a mystery,' she says. 'That's what Henry reckons.'

Getting baptized was real weird, but kind of fun. Henry asked if we were into it, if we believed all the stories and stuff, and I said yes real quick, 'specially after him talking about being born twice and coming back from the dead. I know about that stuff. So does Dad. We've both come out of comas, and I was dead twice. I had to learn to walk and talk again. Dad will too, if he ever gets better. So, I was into it. Mum said yes in the end. She said she didn't know. He explained it all again. Took ages. In the end she said yes. Tegwyn said it was a load of crap and ran out the room. Henry Warburton shrugged and looked sad.

And now we're Christians. Things change fast round here. Henry Warburton turning up out of the blue like that, giving us all this stuff about Jesus, me going to high school next year, busting up with my best mate Fat Cherry. And Christmas real soon. Feels like I'm growing up. You can't be immature for ever.

We finish up the dishes and then go in and get Dad out of his bed for a bath. With Henry Warburton away, it's gonna be real hard looking after Dad again. He's hard to move; he falls all over like a bag of chook poop. Mum and me get him on the floor and drag him. The wheelchair is in the corner, but Mum won't have a bar of it.

'Berrrrgfh!' Dad burps.

'Beaudy, Dad.'

'Morton,' Mum says, 'pull your weight.'

We drag him down the hall and leave tramlines in the dust with his heels. The water is going already – thunder in the bathroom.

'Is that you, Lil Pickering?' Grammar calls out.

'No, it's just us, Grammar!' I yell.

We get Dad out of his PJs and in the water. His head goes under. Mum pulls him up by the hair.

'Yer swimmin', Dad,' I say.

'Sorry, love,' Mum says.

We get out the flannels. Dad's chest hair goes like grass in the wind.

'You think he knows about his soul?' I ask.

'He used to always talk about his heart speaking to him,' Mum says. We always say 'used to', like he's in the past now.

'He must know about God,' I say, soaping his face. He looks at me with those inside-of-himself eyes. 'He's into trees and animals. And *you* reckon he's like a kid. Henry says we're s'posed to be like kids. It's easier for kids to be like kids, though, isn't it?'

'You talk too much.'

'You mean I hear too much.'

She chucks a flannel. It hits me in the gob. I chuck it back. Then it's on, me and Mum mucking around like kids, chucking water and sending it all over the asbestos walls and flying in Dad's face.

Then I get an idea. I stop flicking water.

'All these baths Henry gives Dad. You reckon he's baptizing him all the time?'

Mum wrings out her flannel, puffing a bit.

'I thought you only got it once,' she says. 'Any more questions, Morton Flack?'

'Will that scar always be there, where they cut his throat open?'

'Some things never go away.'

After tea and all the praying and reading and doing the Lord's Supper with sherry and bread, we drag Dad out on to the veranda to watch the sun go down. Grammar sings to herself in her room. Tegwyn goes in and plays the piano hard like she's poking all its teeth out.

We sit out here and see the night coming, and wait for Henry Warburton. Mozzies come around. The light up on the house shows the eyes at the edge of the forest, but Henry Warburton doesn't show.

Mornings and nights go past. Tegwyn won't talk. She beats the piano up and it makes these kind of yells that are music. Maybe Henry Warburton isn't coming back, like he's baptized us and now he's off for good. Just dumped God all over us. Things are bad, real bad. Everyone's thinking the same thing, I reckon. And Christmas getting closer, and Dad so heavy to carry to the bath every day.

'You think we could wash him in bed?' I say to Mum as we go in to get him.

'He's not in hospital now,' she says. 'Sam Flack can take a bath like any normal man.'

Every day we drag him out. I don't sleep good. Worse than normal. All night I lie on my bed, looking up at the daddy-long-legs hanging off my reading light. Makes you feel like the only person left in the world, like everyone else is dead. Sometimes I read the story about the Pommie kids going through the wardrobe into a strange land, and once I even try myself; I get in my wardrobe and close the door and wait, but all that happens is the stink of old socks makes me want to sick up.

In the days I help Mum or muck around in the forest or down at the creek. And some nights, when I don't sleep and can't think myself away, I get up and walk quiet around the house to check on everyone. I go down the hall and look in on Tegwyn. Her light is still on. Through a hole I see her on the bed. In her mouth is a smoke. A *smoke*! She sucks on it and makes kind of smoke doughnuts that go up to the ceiling and squash flat. She has no clothes on, sitting there smoking. On her tits there's red marks – all over – like she's got chicken pox or something. She has another puff. I wonder if I should tell. No.

289

Real careful she takes the smoke out of her mouth and looks at the hot end and puts it on one tit and shivers. Burning! Oh, geez. Oh, geez. I go down the hall and out the back and a bit of sick comes up. I don't get it. I don't. Why does she do things like that? Why is she unhappy all the time? Why does she hate us?

'Is that you, Lil Pickering?'

I go inside and see Grammar. I sit next to her and pick up her old yellow hand from off the sheet.

'Who you listening for, Grammar? Who you hearing all the time?' She snores. In olden days she must have been beautiful, old Gram. And her music, too. She was married to a policeman, that was my Grampa who I never saw. Dad says they lived in country towns all over. Margaret River, Bridgetown, Manjimup, York. He kept getting transferred and she went with him, playing the music and having babies. That's Dad's brothers and sisters. Not worth a zac, he reckons.

'Is? Is . . . ?'

'Who's there, Gram?'

'Walking near . . . oh, biscuits . . . jam . . .'

I go up the hall and check on Mum and Dad. They have the sheet down. Mum has Dad's hand on her belly.

I go back to bed. I take the Bible off the kitchen table with me. I turn my light on. The daddy-long-legs runs off. I read for a bit to get sleepy.

> *You are beautiful, my darling, as Tirzah,*
> *lovely as Jerusalem,*
> *majestic as troops with banners.*
> *Turn your eyes from me;*
> *they overwhelm me.*
> *Your hair is like a flock of goats*
> *descending from Gilead.*
> *Your teeth are like a flock of sheep*
> *coming up from the washing.*

What a poem! This bloke taking the Michael out of his girlfriend for being ugly and for dropping her falsies in the washing. What a book. Stories! Pompous Pilot, Juders, Holly Ghosts. Doesn't get me sleepy at all.

Christmas Eve comes slow enough, waiting out on the veranda each night after tea, but it gets here. Mum is so tired when she gets up, she can't stop crying. We try to get Dad out the bed for his bath before breakfast because there's lots to do for tomorrow. But we're too tired and Mum can't stop crying. So I get the wheelchair. I jam me fingers in it trying to open it and that makes Mum cry worse. We get Dad in it, and wheel him down the hall with Mum blubbering on him. She hates the wheelchair.

I pray at breakfast. 'Jesus fix us up. We're breaking to bits here. Make us happy tomorrow on your birthday, Amen.' Mum pours big cups of sherry for the Lord's Supper and we are a bit happier. Then she starts cooking the cakes and I go out to do the chooks for tomorrow.

Not so bad when you've done it before. I kill two chooks with the machete. I'm holding a chook with no head, letting the blood go on the dirt, when I look across and see a big, high, green truck at the roadhouse and men bringing mattresses and chairs out to it. Out the front is a FOR SALE sign. I see Fat carrying a box and I look away.

All day you can smell cakes and bickies cooking. By late in the day, the Cherrys have gone, moved away. I go over and do something I can't stop. I piddle under their back door. I used to piddle in the middle of the road at night, going round and round like a drill. It made a piss ring that dried and would stay there three days. Don't know why I used to do it, but. Piddling under the Cherrys' door is worse, but I don't stop – just keep hosing it under. Then I snoop around the back for a bit, looking at the pieces of newspaper under the clothesline, an old shoe, the

291

empty bit of dunny roll. And then I see something for Mum and grab it and carry it back real careful.

After tea we bring out Dad and even Grammar on to the veranda. No one says anything. Tegwyn sits on her legs with her eyes closed. I listen hard to the forest. Think I hear something. Yes. A bell. A bell ringing: *bong*, *bong*, in the forest. I've heard it before.

'Can you hear that bell?' I ask everyone.

'More crap from you,' Tegwyn says.

'Bell?' says Mum, kind of ratty.

'Yeah, hear it?'

'Oh, that.'

'You *hear* it?' I can't believe it. Someone else gets my visions.

'It's a big piece of steel or something down at the mill, Ort,' Mum says, like she's got no time for this. 'It bangs around in a westerly. Used to give me the willies once.'

I can't say anything. It hurts, you know. I don't say one thing. All me guts goes tight and hot.

For a long time it's just quiet out here on the veranda.

'Well, this is bloody cheerful,' Tegwyn says.

'Tegwyn, please—'

'Happy Christmas, everyone!'

'Let's ... let's sing carols, then,' Mum says. She's almost bawling.

'Oh, Gawd.'

'Well, what do you suggest, Miss Smarty Pants? You got any better ideas? You got any ideas at all in your bloody selfish head? Life isn't tailor-made just for you, you know! There's other people to consider here. Sick people. Tired people. There's better people than you here.'

Tegwyn stands up. 'Go to hell. I'm getting a job.'

'What, you're gonna wait in your room till a job comes out here asking you to do it?'

'I hate your guts,' Tegwyn says. 'You're weak in the head, pathetic. You're a hick, a burnt-out hippy from the olden days. And now you're born-again, bashing the Bible and Holy Jesus. I think you're crap.'

Mum's face is moving in the dark. You can see it jumping around. 'Come here,' she says. Tegwyn stays put. 'Come here, please, Tegwyn.' Tegwyn is smiling.

'OK, beat me up. Make bruises on me, make blood come out everywhere. Show 'em how pathetic you are.' Then she walks across to Mum with a white smile in the dark. Mum stands up. I squint, wait for it. Suddenly, Mum grabs her and her arms go round her hard so you can hear the air coming out of Tegwyn. Mum's hands lock like they'll need bolt-cutters to undo. She's squeezing.

'I love you,' Mum says. 'I love you. Love you. Love you.' And then Tegwyn is bawling and all saggy and smaller-looking, and they stay like that for a long time.

Later we sing 'Silent Night' and it makes me sad. In my brain I can see Jesus getting born, but I can't see his face. In the end I give him my face. Could be worse for him; there's uglier people than me.

The bell rings. That light still glows. I have a bit of a bawl in the second verse.

Christmas. We give our presents. It's pretty weak, this year. Mum gives me Dad's walking hat, the one with the budgie feathers in it. She gives Tegwyn a brooch; I've seen it before, it's one of hers. I give Tegwyn the black smooth stone I found down at the creek once. We both get real embarrassed. I give Dad the tools in the pillowslip and the Pirelli calendar – Mum looks like she's gonna chuck a wobbly until I go out and get her present.

It's the sunflower I pinched from the back of the roadhouse. She kisses me. She cries. Now I know for sure – we really haven't got much money. The dole isn't a lot of money.

Mum puts the chooks in the oven and I scrub the fresh little spuds and Tegwyn picks peas; it starts to smell like Christmas. I bring Grammar and Dad into the lounge-room. The stove growls.

Suddenly there's a bang from somewhere. We all stop what we're doing. A car noise. I go outside, and down the long drive comes a yellow car, old and farting, rolling down the drive towards me, and there he is – Henry Warburton at the wheel.

'Well, Morton, old son,' he says, pulling into the shade behind the house, his elbow out the window, 'what do you reckon?'

'It's a heap.'

'Cut it out, it's an original 1958 FC Holden Special.'

Mum and Tegwyn come out. Mum is wiping her hands on the hem of her dress and you can see all her legs. Tegwyn walks like she's in no hurry for anyone. Henry Warburton gets out and leans against the 1958 FC Holden Special. It groans a bit, sniffs, and ticks. It stinks of burning oil. The back door is wired on with coathangers. The red seats are all furry and busted. The tyres are balder than babies' bums.

'Where the hell have you been?' Mum says, real quiet and angry.

'Doing business,' Henry Warburton says with a smile. He looks clean, with new clothes on. 'Working on your behalf, I might say.'

'What've you done?' Mum looks real worried and nearly as old as Mrs Cherry. 'Where'd you get this heap of rubbish?'

'No one's taken to the old FC yet, I see.'

'It's a heap of crap,' Tegwyn says.

'I sold the wreck of Sam's ute and bought this.'

'But how . . . without . . . because . . . papers and things—'

'All organized.'

'How?'

'Today, people, we're all going on an outing. It's Christmas Day, day of rest and rejoicing, day of contemplation – though not too exhaustive – and day of thanking the Lord for what is. Where to, kids?'

'The reservoir,' Tegwyn says.

'Yeah,' I say, 'the reservoir.'

'But lunch isn't ready,' Mum says, kind of smiling.

'We'll take it with us,' he says.

'Let's do it!' Tegwyn yells.

'At least wait until it's cooked,' Mum says.

'Righto,' Henry Warburton says as he puts up the bonnet.

New pine forests pass by. Henry Warburton's 1958 FC Holden Special farts and rattles and takes us up the road real slow, but it's enough to make you feel rich anyway. Bees splat on the windscreen; honey gurps out of them and spreads in the wind. The smell of hot grass comes in the windows. There's the smell of Christmas lunch all wrapped in tea towels in the cardboard box on my knees. The wind gets in Grammar's hair and it goes all grey and white everywhere so you can't see how old she is. Dad is next to her, awake and blinking in the wind. His shirt is yellow, flapping, with the sun on it. I muck around with the ashtray that's in the back of the seat. There's butts and ash and bits of lolly paper in it and a mean kind of smell. I look at the back of the heads in front. Henry Warburton's hair is flat-greasy with snowy bits of white sticking to it and getting on his shoulders. He's singing and thumping the wheel. Tegwyn's hair is down and kinky from being plaited, and pouring all over the seat with little worms and snakes of it dancing in the wind and tickling my nose. I can see over her shoulder she's mucking around with knobs and vents and things. Mum's hair is down too and brushed; it looks like white wood and smells good enough to eat.

We turn off on to a smaller road and go downhill where trees are thick and shady and make big pools of shade on the road. Silver water. The dam. Brown stones. Some barbecues. And no one around at all. Next to the water, in the shade, we spread tarps and blankets and bring out the box and Dad and Grammar, and Henry Warburton has four bottles of beer. He says a prayer and flicks the tops off. We lie back, push Dad and Grammar back to back, and get into it. Birds go mad in the trees and the water flashes and the ants come and everyone is eating and laughing and sighing and blowing the white off the top off their beer with gravy under their noses and peas in their laps. Wishbones, the parson's nose, baked spuds, long burps, and me guts sticks out like I swallowed the 1958 FC Holden Special itself.

III

chapter thirteen

I sit up in bed so fast it cracks my back. He's screaming, calling out. Fall out of bed. Down the hall to the closed door of the lounge-room where Henry Warburton still sleeps, ever since Christmas. Put my eye to the keyhole, and there he is, on his mattress in the raw with his sheet kicked down and his old feller sticking up like a flagpole again, and in the moonlight there's tears on his face, and he says real quiet:

'Go away.'

I step back from the door.

'No. Away.'

Can he see me?

'Bobo. Oh God! No. Hmph!'

I go back to bed and lie down and watch the light from the full moon and the cloud on the roof come pouring in through the curtains like it's milk from a bucket. What makes me think milk is the cow Henry Warburton bought for us. She's called Margaret and she's brown and white with big tits hanging down. I'm learning to get the milk out of 'em. When you got your ear against her belly when you're pulling milk out, you can hear sounds you'd think came from *Star Wars*. Ooowup-wup-wup . . . owkss-ut . . . gbolp . . . reeet. It's like cows talk five languages in their three guts.

Six weeks we've had Margaret. Mum reckons we're all getting fat from the cream. Dad's drinking it with a straw. At least he's doing that much. Henry Warburton sells things, bits of stuff from the sheds, to buy feed.

Down the highway we go in the 1958 FC Holden Special, farts, squeaks, smoke, and all, three of us across the front seat like real hoons with our elbows out the windows. If there was a radio we'd have it going flat-chat, boy. Down the highway, through Bankside, past the paddocks full of stumps, and down to where you can see the city going all the way to the sea.

'I think you're supposed to go to your nearest suburban office,' Henry Warburton says. 'I know. I've been on the dole more times than you've pouted at yourself in the mirror.'

'I don't care,' Tegwyn says. 'I wanna go to the big one in town. I don't wanna work in the foothills or out on the limits. I wanna get a job in the city, in the offices, the skyscrapers.'

'Regardless—'

'Look,' she says, putting her feet up on the dash, 'you said you'd take me. Anyway, this car belongs to the Flacks. Me and Small Thing here are Flacks – that's two against one.'

So we go all the way in, through the places where there's houses and lawns and cars in cement drives, and trees all along the roads, past factories and streets and streets of car yards with little plastic flags out front, to where you can't see anything but walls and windows and red-orange-green lights and people walking and cars bumpered up as far as you can see.

And then up in this car park that's like the inside of a big cake, round and round, up and up, until we get to the roof in the sun and find a spot. We get out and look across the city. The river is fat and blue and buildings come up white out of the ground like they're brand new.

'Let's go,' Henry Warburton says.

'Wish Mum was here,' I say.

'She hates the city,' Henry Warburton answers.

'All right by me,' says Tegwyn. Her jeans are so tight you can nearly read the size of her undies.

'I don't wanna be a bloody check-out-chick at Woolworths!'

'That's if you're lucky,' Henry Warburton says as we get into the 1958 FC Holden Special.

'Are we still going to the beach?' I ask, putting me feet up on the glovebox.

'Shut your face, Small Thing.'

'Your sister is learning slowly, Ort, that her services aren't in any more demand than those million and a half others who're trying to get a job. But don't worry,' he says with a laugh, 'she knows what she's on about. She's an adult now.'

'Up your bum, preacher.'

Henry Warburton winks at me and starts the car. 'I think the beach would be lovely, Ort. Might even cool someone off.'

The beach is the whitest flaming thing you've ever seen in your life! Black car parks, green water, and white sand that goes for miles. You squint as you walk across it, through oily brown people on blankets and under brollies with radios going and babies crying. Some girls with their boobs showing, brown things with eyes that watch you go past. Geez.

Tegwyn and me get in the water with a run and a dive like all the other people are doing. I come up with me mouth full of sand and me nose all skinned. We swim out to where everyone is standing. It's quiet and flat and people talk, but they're always looking out to sea. Maybe they're looking for Rottnest. Tegwyn and me duck-dive and swim around. Tegwyn stands on her hands so her legs come out the water and people whistle. Then the whole place goes mad. People swimming out to sea, wading, paddling at the water with their hands. Blokes on surfboards

301

turning round and going like hell. Takes me a while to see the big lines coming in like a convoy of wheat trucks, some with bits of white blowing back off the top like wheat dust coming off the load.

The first wave lifts me off my feet and puts me down again. I hear it thump behind me but I don't look 'cause this other one's coming. And two behind it. The second one makes me kick like crazy to climb over. The third one drops on me like the side of a house. There I am on the bottom, with sand in me gob and water thumping me up and down on the back, turning me in circles so I don't know me left from me right, and me lungs saying: 'Get up, Morton Flack, you dill. Get out of the water or you'll die!' And in the end, without doing anything, I pop up, head first, with all this white stuff around like the soap bubbles from the washing, and Tegwyn is laughing her box off next to me. It tastes funny. Like blood. It's crook water!

Everyone else catches the waves when they come. They swim with them and shoot along to the beach. But I stay put. I get run over by surfboards. I get run over by fat ladies with prickly legs. I get run over by bigger waves. I get run over by my own sister. And then I reckon I've had enough. I think all the knocks have ruined my brains, 'cause I turn around and catch the next wave that's coming. I kick and go freestyle like mad. The wave comes up behind me like a brick wall. Then I'm flying. Really flying. Most of me isn't even in the wave. I'm hanging out over a sandbar that's a long, long way down and I hear me own voice going: 'Oooooohhhh!' Like jumping out of a tree. On to your head. Hohh! I come up with more sand down my throat and music in my head and another wave tumbles me over. Another one fills me up with water and sends me along the bottom. The last one drops me on the beach. I get up and then I know. Me shorts! Here I am standing in the middle of the city with nothing on. Henry Warburton is there, laughing.

'Had an accident, old son?'

There's people everywhere, looking. Never seen so many eyes in all me life. I walk. My legs are all wobbly. Feels like I been run over by a truck.

'Here.' Henry Warburton takes off his shirt and ties it round me. We walk up the beach and sit on the towels. I kind of feel numb. For a long time I sit watching more waves come. Water runs out of my nose. Next to us, a girl rubs oil on her boobs and makes them move in funny ways and it gives me goose-bumps, like when you scratch a blackboard with your fingernail. Henry Warburton is looking too. I can feel it.

'Dirty old sods.'

I look up real quick. It's Tegwyn, dripping, wiping snot from her chin. I get up off her towel, and then she looks at me and sneers.

'Got a rock in your pocket, Ort?'

I look down. Out the front of the shirt Henry Warburton lent me, there's the outline of my old feller sticking out like a handle. The girl next to us is smiling.

Then Henry Warburton takes a step, and *slap!* across Tegwyn's face and her eyes go wide and full and then she's off, running up the beach towards the car park, kicking sand all over people, her bum jiggling; people whistle and hoot and Henry is after her, calling: 'Tegwyn, Tegwyn, listen, I—'

So here I am standing in the middle of a million eyes with this thing sticking out like it's made up its mind to point rudely at people for the rest of its life.

'I wanna go to Kings Park,' I say as we drive along in the traffic, still wet and salty. Tegwyn isn't saying anything. Since Henry Warburton caught her out in front of the hamburger place, in front of all them people, and said how sorry he was and everything, she has not said one word.

'Why Kings Park?' he says, looking at me kind of strange.

'Oh, I just wanted to see it. I dunno.'

But he takes us. He's in a kind of mood where he has to; we could make him take us anywhere.

From Kings Park you can see the whole river and freeway and buildings and parks and causeway. This is where Mum and Dad got to know each other. This is a bit of the reason I'm here. This is a bit of me. I s'pose it's different at night, more ... romantic? I can just see Mum and Dad coming out of them trees back there and coming on to this bit of grass with all the cannons pointed out towards where we live behind the hills, and him saying, 'You know, Alice Benson, when we get married, we'll go and live near trees like them. And our kids'll be called Ort and Tegwyn, and it's gonna be great.' All the lights, all the ...

'Ort!' Henry says. 'Are you with us? Time to go, mate. Back to Flack country.'

I walk back to the 1958 FC Holden Special with a big grin on me face that a doctor couldn't get off.

'The breeze is in,' says Henry Warburton, looking at the trees bending as we creep along towards the hills.

'Fremantle Doctor,' I say, and just the words make me feel good and sad at the same time.

All the way up through the foothills, no one talks; it's a kind of sleepy, tired feeling, listening to the 1958 FC Holden Special squeaking and popping in second gear.

chapter fourteen

High school's getting closer, you know. Not that I'm worried about it, but. Bad enough going to high school at all, but there's not going to be one person there that I know. Fat is gone and he was the only kid in my school who's in my year. Last year I knew every single kid in our school (there's only ten). There's a thousand at Outfield High – that's what Tegwyn says. Three weeks. That's all. All I do now is muck around on me own, walking in the forest, playing armies, finding little creatures in the bush, talking to myself and sometimes to God. Funny when you talk to God. He's like the sky (well, he is the sky, kind of). Never says anything. But you know he listens. Right down in your belly, even in your bum you know.

Yesterday I took the car roof down the creek to the bridge and back, but there was no fun in it. Fat's fatness was the best part of it – you didn't know when he was gonna capsize you. And it was someone to talk to and see things with. When you see something, a rabbit running away, a dugite in the grass, a fox watching you from a long way off, you say 'Look! Look at that!' Even when no one's there, you say it. Sometimes I hang around the back of Cherrys'. Sometimes I chase Margaret around. Sometimes she chases me. Sometimes I stay inside and read *Mad* comics.

Out there today Henry Warburton is walking Dad in the wheelchair, up and down the yard, all day, talking talking talking about I dunno what. I reckon Henry's got something crook that makes him yell out at night and go quiet sometimes. And there's those fits, and that speech thing that's gone away now. And his glass eye. He's taught us how to pray the Lord's Prayer. He teaches us little things. He's not that bad. He says things that are right. But he hit Tegwyn. Maybe he did it for me. She was ragging me in front of the whole city. But he never said anything. My heart works better than my brain. Me brain says Henry Warburton was sticking up for me, but me heart doesn't believe it, and when me heart makes up its mind, that's it.

Mum is kind of different these days. She doesn't seem so sad any more. You don't see her sitting out on the veranda crying over Dad and combing his hair with her fingers. She's wearing all her bright dresses with feathers and things in her hair. She wears the shell earrings she used to wear a long time ago. She looks young. She washes her hair a lot. She lets Henry Warburton have Dad to himself all day. It's good to see her happy, I s'pose. Can't tell if it's Jesus or Henry Warburton she's happy about. I wonder how long it will last.

Days and nights are the same for me now. Both kind of lonely. There's no one to hang around with.

Out there, Henry Warburton walks Dad up and down and Dad has this no-frown-no-smile look on his face like he can't do either. There's wheelmarks in the dirt that get deeper and deeper.

Some new people have moved in over the road. Makes you feel sorry for them, moving into that sad place. The man and lady came across this morning and said hullo. She had big teeth like fenceposts; they looked like they could chew steel. Her hair was all frizzy and grey and she smelt like lemons. He was tall and had a loopy back and he looked at you out the top of his head which was small as a softball. He didn't stink of anything. I thought he was all right, but *she* talked like she thought she was the king's bickies.

'Hel-loo. We are the Alfred Wat-sons. Wee have as-sumed

proprietorship of the traaans-port establishment o-ver yon-der.'
I dunno why she talked so funny. They look just as daggy as us.
She said:

'Those previous owners must have been a tri-al for you
people. Everything smells awfully of u-rine.' Mum and Henry
talked with them a bit. Mum looked cocky again, like she used
to. They looked at us like they were dead sure they weren't as
daggy as us.

February. School tomorrow. And here I am out on the dunny
for the sixth time tonight. My teeth chatter even though it's hot
as hell. I sit here till it all runs out. Going past the bathroom I
hear Henry Warburton talking, and stop.

'Hell, Sam, how can you listen to me day after day? Guess
you don't have much choice. Sometimes I wonder if I'm not here
for my own sake more than yours. You're the perfect priest,
Sam. You don't believe, you listen, and you don't say anything.
You . . . what the hell am I saying?'

I go to my room. He talks that kind of stuff all the time,
and then he cries at night. He doesn't muck around much with
me any more, doesn't play french cricket or anything. He argues
with Tegwyn and wheels Dad up and down the yard and leaves
me and Mum to ourself. And sometimes Mum looks at him,
kind of hungry.

For a while I lie here on my bed trying not to think about
tomorrow. Then I get up and go and listen at the bathroom
door again.

'I know you're waiting, Sam. God is too, I can feel it. I'll do
it, Sam. Soon. But I'm so scared, so . . .'

Talk talk talk. The other day Henry Warburton talked to
Dad for so long the bath water went cold and Dad was shivering
and blue and Mum came in and went crook something awful.

He only sometimes does the Lord's Supper with us now;
after meals he goes and sits on his own, or takes Dad for a walk,

or tries to teach Tegwyn something on the piano, and Mum and me are left to do it on our own.

Talk talk talk.

I go outside, walk right into the middle of the yard, and look back at the house. That cloud-light is still there. Now that's a mystery. Little clouds that shine like moons don't sit on everyone's house. Or maybe they do and not everyone can see it. Mum can't see it. Not even Henry Warburton can see it. If you chuck stones at it they go right through – nothing happens. Every angle, it looks the same. It's like a dream that's always with you. But it's there – it's my vision. I know God's in it somewhere. He *is* waiting for something.

Bong! There goes that bell in the forest. Like a school bell. Yuk!

Not even the chooks are up yet, not even the birds, not even the sun, and here I am jogging around the house, lapping, going round like I'm tied to it, like I'm a model plane with feet going round and round on the same track. Jogging is the dumbest thing in the world to do. I can't think of anything dumber. Except eating olives and going to high school. Round I go again. Can see my own footprints in the dirt now. As I come around past the back veranda I see Mum in her sleeping T-shirt of Dad's, standing there, rubbing her eyes. She looks at me and her eyes make me stop dead like there wasn't another step left in me anyway.

'Morton-flamin'-Flack, what the *hell* do you think you're doing?'

'Jogging, Mum.'

'*Jogging?* From my bed it sounded like a bloody stamp*ede*! Get inside, you'll give the world a fright.'

'But I'm nervous.'

'What the heck you wanna be nervous for? God looks after you, you know that.'

'He doesn't stop me going to the dunny fifty times a night.'

'We'll have to sew your bum up, then. Anything. Just don't surround the house with yourself at four o'clock in the morning.'

'I'll go for a walk.'

'OK, do that, then.'

'You wanna come?' I say.

'At four o'clock in the morning?' She steps down off the veranda with her thongs clacking. 'I think the Lord must have been cracking a joke on us when he gave us children,' she says as we walk towards the forest. There's all crackly bits of sleep in her eyes, and her hair is all over. She knows how to love people. I can feel the warm from the bed still on her, and the smell of Dad, that Flack smell.

The forest has got the light in it that comes before the sun, and you can hear things moving in grass and bushes. We walk down past the creek and into the real thick part of the forest where it tumbles over the edge of the hill to a tricky slope where the loggers couldn't cut trees down. You can see the edge of the city in tiny bits between trees here.

'How come we live up here, Mum? Everyone else lives in the city.'

'I dunno. It's just where we are, I suppose. We liked the trees, your Dad and me. You know that.'

'How come we stay here if Tegwyn hates it?'

'Kids hate everything when they're sixteen. Even themselves. It was like that for me.'

I think about that for a while as the sun makes a dot of pink through the trees behind us. Then we make a turn and come around with the little pink point of sun in our eyes.

'What does God really look like, you reckon?'

'Why all the questions?'

'Get them all out the way before high school. Tegwyn said if you ask questions kids'll think you're a suckhole.'

'But you don't care what they think, do you?'

'Oh. No.' Funny how when you get older you can easy say things you don't mean.

'What does God look like, then. Heck, Ort, you ask toughies,' she says, picking up a stick with a fork in the end and a black leaf skewered on it. 'Now. Henry was talking about this a while back. He said that no one has seen God except Jesus. No one else knows what he looks like. He always comes with something to cover himself up. Like people couldn't handle it if he showed his real self. Remember that story about the whirl-wind and the one about the burning bush? We'll see him soon enough. When we're in heaven.'

'Are you still into it?' I ask, squinting as that pink sun gets stronger.

'Into what?'

'This believing.'

'Well, yeah.'

'I just wasn't sure.'

Mum smiles. 'We don't know much about it all, do we? It's made us different, Ort, this believing. It's like we weren't even alive before. It doesn't stop us hurting. But ... but you know the hurting's gonna stop one day. Everything's gonna make sense. One day we'll understand.'

I break off a dead stick and suck the end. 'Why don't we go to a church? Is that what people do?'

'I s'pose so. Never thought of it. There's that sign in the drapery. Gospel meeting, they call it. The one the Watkinses run.'

'But they don't like us. I heard Mrs Watkins talking about us. Called us hippies. What's hippies?'

'It's people who lived in the olden days. Don't worry about it.'

'I'm not worried.'

'You? Course not. It's normal for you to go to the dyke fifty times a night. Morton Flack never worries.'

'I don't wanna go today.'
'You have to.'
'That's why I don't wanna.'

The school bus is an old tub. Fifteen kids all sit up the back. I sit up behind the driver. The bus crawls down the long hill in low. In my bag there's a lunch box, a *Mad* comic, and a tennis ball. Some kids up the back are smoking. Don't they know it kills you? Big globs of slag come down the aisle. I read my *Mad* comic, or just make out I am, till the bus gets to Outfield High.

The school is down at the bottom of the foothills where the city has crept out to take over the country. There's some parts with houses all together, and parts with chook farms or flower farms and some factories. When I see the high school me heart goes blah. Looks like a gaol. Two storeys high, all brown from bore water, people with bags walking around like they're in for life.

Well, then it starts. Everyone is looking for melons. You can tell the melons. We all look scared to death, some of us have shorts on, and we're all in little groups on the oval. I don't know anybody. I've got no one to make a group with, so I have a look around, keep walking like I know where I'm going to, like I'm a group of my own. Girls with pink hair point at me. Classroom doors everywhere. I go up to the drinking taps and put my head under so it's all wet. But it's no good – further down the quadrangle four big kids yell: 'Melon!' and drag me in the dunnies and pick me up and shove my head in the crappiest bowl and flush. They pinch my *Mad* comic and my tennis ball and nick off. Another gang of kids push some melon into the pisser and I take off.

I'm late for five classes. I get lost seven times. Someone calls me a poofter and a teacher tells me to get me hair cut. I get flushed again just after the last bell.

311

Mum bawls when I get home and tell her. I stink like hell. Tegwyn laughs. I stay under the shower till I half turn into a prune.

All week it's the same. I go for runs in the morning to get ready for being called a poofter and being told by old poopheads to cut my hair. The bus ride is awful, kids killing 'emselves up the back with smokes, pink-haired girls showing me their braces. I get everywhere late and have to do scab duty at morning recess. Scab duty is picking up wet tissues and brown apple cores in the quadrangle. Mr Frost sends a letter home to Mum telling her to get my hair cut. Mum writes one back telling him to mind his own business. I do scab duty a lot. I don't listen much in class. It's hot and flies sing you to sleep, and I always think about swimming in the creek.

The second week is the same. And the third week. The fourth week I'm used to it. And Mum gets me some long pants, so that's something. Home at nights I do some of my homework and then sit out on the veranda with everyone else, but it's not the same any more. I feel different. I feel like I live out in the middle of nowhere. I pray to God and hope he hears me. All I get is deadly quiet from him. I'm kind of stuck. I don't feel like a kid any more. I'm not even a proper teenager. I'm not a grown-up adult. I'm not in the city. I'm not properly in the country. I dunno what the hell to do with meself.

Sometimes I stand out in the forest after dark, thinking about me poor crippled Dad, and the way Mum is . . . I dunno . . . not the same, and how I find Henry Warburton out behind the sheds sometimes, saying through his teeth, 'Help me, damn you. Do something.' And him not saying much to me these days, and him wheeling the old man up and down like a bloke who's waiting for someone to come and get him. When I'm standing out there, thinking of all those things, it all looks pretty bad, the whole show. Mum said it would this year. It's puberty or some dumb thing. Everything is just so dumb. Sometimes, some nights, it's just so stupid. And I just go out and look back at the house, and that little cloud of light that came on the house the day they brought Dad back, it stops me from bawling. It makes me stop everything. Something in it says to me, says to me soul in me belly and in me bum, *Hang on, Morton Flack.*

Crazy, eh?

chapter fifteen

Sunday morning. It's cool. Summer is about over. Margaret makes ork, pork, goilk noises in her guts. Her milk comes out hard and thin and makes the bucket growl. I can see sparrows watching us from the window ledge. I wonder if cows like their tits pulled. Margaret always comes whingeing up to the back door for it. She eats Tegwyn's undies on the clothesline like it's just for something to do. Glad Henry Warburton didn't bring us a goat.

When I take the milk in, Mum says to me:

'Why don't we go to the Watkinses' church this morning? It's good to go to church, isn't it?'

'I dunno,' I say, pouring off the milk into the big pot on the stove, 'I s'pose.'

'It says where two or three are gathered . . . where two or three . . . something something . . . oh, whatever. Henry, what do you think?'

Henry Warburton shrugs and doesn't look up from his newspaper. He gets them from Bankside now, tries to get me to read 'em. Not even the comic section is any good.

'Henry?'

Henry Warburton looks up. 'If you'd like to.'

'Is that to say you're not coming?'

'Well, obviously you can't take Sam and his mother, and someone's got to look after them.'

Mum thinks for a bit.

'Tegwyn will look after them, won't you, love?'

'Always me,' Tegwyn says. 'Why the hell should I?'

'I'll stay,' Henry Warburton says.

'Maybe you'll be able to teach my daughter some manners.'

'I don't think there's any hope of that,' he says with a grin.

The sun is out but it's kind of cool. When we go inside the back part of the drapery shop that Mr and Mrs Watkins run, it's like walking into a fridge. It's a kind of storeroom where the rows of chairs are. Up front there's a table with a lacy table cloth that looks like it's got a big parcel under it. On the wall is a flag, the Australian flag. There's a reading-stand thing up there, too, and a picture of the baby Jesus. I count nine people. Everyone talks in whispers like they don't wanna wake up baby Jesus. They all look like they're going to a dance or something; all got their best clothes on, and there's me and Mum in our thongs. We sit down at the back. Mr Watkins gives us a little blue book and a big thin book. They got songs in them. Hymns.

'What's hymens mean?' I whisper in Mum's ear.

'Hims. It's hims,' she says. A lady is looking at me all red. 'Just old-time songs, Ort.'

Hims. Makes me wanna giggle.

'Welcome! Welcome! Welcome! Here we are, it's the Lord's Day and here we are in the Lord's House, so let's offer unto him our prayers.' Everyone closes their eyes and holds their noses with their fingers like they got a headache. Everyone bends over like they dropped something on the floor. 'We praise and thank Thee our Father that Thou has given unto us plenty . . .' He goes on in this funny talk, like he comes from another planet and talks a little bit like us, but not enough to let us understand right. Thee and Thou. Dunno where they fit in, but the bloke up there in the blue suit and oily hair knows 'em pretty well.

'The text for today, brethren and sisters, is taken from the book of Revelation, chapter sixteen. Ahem. Hurumph.

315

*'And I heard a great voice out of the temple saying to
the seven angels, Go your ways, and pour out the vials
of the wrath of God upon the earth. And the first went,
and poured out his vial upon the earth; and there fell a
noisome and grievous sore upon the men which had the
mark of the beast and upon them which worshipped his
image . . .'*

Geez. On and on. This gutsy story with drinking blood and
scorching and earthquakes and no reason for it. Then Mr
Watkins gets up with his blue suit and his hair oiled too, and he
stands behind the table and starts talking about the Lord's
Supper, which me and Mum know about. He tells a little story
that I don't get, and then he takes off the lacy table cloth and
there's two trays. He passes one to two blokes in blue suits who
pass it to each other across the row. When they get to our row
they stop passing and go back to the front. Mum looks at me.
There's only us in our row.

'Only crackers, anyway,' she says. 'Can't be doing too well
with the drapery.' A lady with fruit in her hat looks around.

Then the other tray, full of little glasses, comes up and down
the rows. This time Mum leans across the row in front when the
tray goes past and she picks out two little glasses. When she sits
down again, she gives me one. I drink it. The fruit lady gives us
a dangerous look. Her apples go redder.

'It's only grape juice!' I say. I look up. Everyone in the room
is looking at us. The men passing the tray are red in the face.

'And I thought *we* were poor,' Mum says with a giggle.

Then they bring round another plate that people put little
envelopes on.

'What is it?' I ask Mum. 'Letters? Don't they *say* their
prayers to God?'

'Sshh!' the lady in front says. Her moustache goes all stiff at
me. Her fruit jiggles.

This time the plate comes to us. Mum smiles and passes it

to the man in the blue suit and oily hair who is still red in the face.

All the ladies have got hats on. Some with flowers in them. Some like cowboy hats. Some like crash helmets. Some like little pink zits on the top of their head.

Then Mrs Watkins warms up her accordion and everyone sings:

> 'The Son of God goes forth to war,
>   A kingly crown to gain,
> His blood-red banner streams afar:
>   Who follows in his train?
> Who best can drink his cup of woe
>   Triumphant over pain . . .'

Mrs Watkins has an orange dress on, and her arms are all orange too. They squeeze and push and the accordion sounds a bit like our 1958 FC Holden Special.

After the singing, the first man with a blue suit and oily hair gets up and shouts at us. It's like algebra and arithmetic and geography and story-time all wrapped into one. There's 666 and dragons and beasts and seven heads and four angels and 144,000 and Babylon and Russia and China and a thousand years and seven seals and Sodom and Gog and Magog and Mr Arafat and Com-munism and Blasphemia and Lambs and more blood drinking.

'Read the signs! Read-the-signs! The Antichrist himself comes. We have no doubt of it. The prophecies are fulfilled daily. For all nations have drunk of the wine of the wrath of fornication with her . . . the fornication of Babylon. John's own words from Patmos. We-have-no-*time*! The-need-is-*great*! *Press*-ing. *U*rgent. How will we stand in the *tri*bulation? How? How? How will we stand in that time of woe and *tur*moil and crushing of spirits? How?'

The man shouts at us like he's angry, especially at us up the back. But I don't know what he means. He asks us questions and before we can answer he asks another one.

Real sudden, Mum stands up and jerks me up and pulls me along the row of empty chairs and just at the door on the way out she turns around and says:

'You don't have to shout. We're not animals, you know. And not even God's animals should be shouted at like they're made of mud!'

And then we're outside and we get in the car and Mum rests her head on the steering-wheel and sighs. The horn goes on. The men in blue suits and oily hair come to the door and point their red faces at us.

When we get home Margaret has got into the vegetable patch and is trying out the tomatoes and treading on everything else. Dad is stuck out in the driveway on his own in the wheelchair, and Henry Warburton and Tegwyn are in the kitchen fighting.

'Don't try your religious crap on me, boy. Don't come the crapper with me. You just leave me alone, you big gawky galoot!'

Henry is standing by the stove, dodging all the lemons she's chucking at him, smiling away, shrugging his shoulders. Mum just goes real angry through the flying lemons to her room. I go out to Dad.

'Hi,' I say, taking off the brake and wheeling him down the drive. His hair is growing back and there's a good beard on him that makes him look old and real wise. I put my hand on the back of his head and feel how warm it is from the sun. The wheels crackle in the dirt. At the end of the driveway near the road, I turn him around and then I walk around and sit on the dirt in front of him. I look at his face. It's a good face, not real handsome, but straight – a telling-the-real-truth face. He looks kind of old and wise sitting there with his PJs on. I reckon that's what God looks like. Dad's eyes look like they see everywhere today, all over the world.

I look up at the faded sky with its warty-looking moon. It goes on for ever up there.

'Do it, God,' I say. 'Make him get up and walk.'

I sit back on the warm brown dirt and wait. And Dad sits there waiting, too. Birds land in the trees close by. They watch us. A little wind comes across, makes the leaves go silly. I keep waiting. The bush just sits there. The whole world goes on. Margaret moos like mad up behind the house 'cause no one's bothered to milk her. And nothing here changes. Then, after a long time, Mum starts calling us in for tea.

When I get up it's nearly dark and Dad's shivering and I feel scared as hell.

chapter sixteen

Two weeks. Three weeks. Every day after school I take Dad out to the end of the driveway with a blanket on his legs 'cause it's getting cool, and every day I pray. Every day I wheel him back in for tea.

Homework. Here I am sitting in my room trying to write an essay on the prime minister, and it starts raining. Rain! It just comes out of nowhere, belting down on the tin roof. I get up and go into the hallway. Across the hall Henry Warburton is talking to Dad. I put my ear against the door, have to listen real hard because of the rain noise.

'. . . they used to anoint the sick person with oil, and lay hands on him and pray. I've never known you as your real self, Sam. I'm afraid. I'm a weak man, Sam.'

I go outside to the veranda and see the ground boiling in the dark. The light on the house makes milk ribbons in it.

And then it's April, real sudden. April Fool's Day I get told the principal, Mr Whipper, wants to see me in his office. I go to his office and say who I am. He looks at me kind of strange.

'Is this a poor joke?' he says.

'No, sir,' I say, nearly crapping myself.

'What did I want to see you for?'

'I thought you'd know, sir.'

'You are insolent, Mr Flack.'

'You mean you didn't want to see me?'

He doesn't wanna see me. I get six of the best to show how much he doesn't wanna see me. April Fool. Beaudy.

Henry Warburton works on the old Chev in the evenings. He works real late, banging, shouting, trying to get it to go. One of us goes to the back door every now and then to listen for the sound of the engine. It would really be something to hear that Chev after all these years of waiting. Like raising the dead, it'd be. But there's nothing.

Flowers have come out with the rain. Tiny yellow and pink ones all over and 'specially thick in the forest. On Saturday I follow Tegwyn into the forest and keep a long, long way back. She sings to herself and it's like the trees drink it up. I keep low and follow the pink of her jeans. She picks flowers and puts them in a bag. She looks so happy, picking flowers; never seen my sister Tegwyn so happy, and singing some dumb song that doesn't mean anything much. Makes me happy to follow her round.

I follow her back to the house. Henry is building a bigger fence for the vegetables. Some twenty-eights fly over, green as grass, looking for places to nest. Mum is washing. I let Tegwyn go inside with her little bag of flowers. Then I go in to see what she's up to. She looks like she's up to something. I walk real careful down the hallway. Look into Grammar's room. Grammar is asleep on her own. No one in my room. Tegwyn isn't in hers. Real careful I put my ear to the wall outside Dad and Mum's room.

'How's that, then, old boy?' she's saying. The door is half open. I look through the crack next to the GET THEM OUT OF VIETNAM sticker, and there is Dad with all pink and yellow flowers in his hair. He looks like a king or a prince or something. I can't help meself; I burst in and say:

'Oh, Tegwyn, it's beautiful.'

She goes all stiff with pink and yellow flowers in her hands, and already her face is changing.

'It's lovely,' I say.

'It's a heap of crap,' she says, and pulls the flowers out, ripping at Dad's hair, chucks them into the box, opens the window, and dumps 'em all out.

Later, Henry Warburton brings in some flowers for Mum and she goes all silly.

'This thing with Bobo Sax, Sam. Ngth. It was like nothing else you've ever been through in your life. She was like a bitch in heat. She was filthy. She stank. She never came out of that hut and I used to go to her. I'd hate myself. I hated her, but I'd go into that hut and sometimes I wouldn't come out for days. She was slippery, lithe, she had you like a vice. I tell you, that woman, that creature fed on my weakness. I drank and smoked myself into it. I forgot myself and my place, sometimes, and I was happy. But I'd wake up in that filthy, foul darkness sometimes, ngth, and want to tear myself to pieces.

'They said she was a witch, the local people. Maybe they were right, I don't know. That's why they burnt the place . . . after she was dead. Why do I need you for a priest, Sam? Why do I need a priest at all?'

He leaves Dad in the bath a long time these days. It's getting colder. He's gonna make him worse.

Sometimes instead of my homework I go through the back of that big black Bible of Henry Warburton's where it lists the words. I keep going back to OIL. I read all the stories about it, how they put it on people's heads who were kings, and how it was like gold and people argued over it. And here's this bit that Jesus' brother wrote down. Henry Warburton showed Mum a long time back.

*Is any one of you in trouble? He should pray. Is anyone
happy? Let him sing songs of praise. Is any one of you
sick? He should call the elders of the church to pray
over him and anoint him with oil in the name of the
Lord. And the prayer offered in faith will make the sick
person well; the Lord will raise him up. If he has sinned
he will be forgiven. Therefore confess your sins to each
other so that you may be healed. The prayer of a
righteous man is powerful and effective.*

Oil's what you do chips in. Oil's what those blokes at the
drapery had in their hair.

The first night it's cold enough, I light a fire in the lounge-room.
Makes me feel good. I was born in this room with one ripper
fire going. Mum irons clothes. She's real angry still about that
church. She says she's tired of taking crap from people. We look
at the busted telly every now and then. There's a funny story
about that telly. It's been bust for two years. When Grammar
was OK, when she used to help Mum with the cleaning and the
cooking and the two of 'em used to laugh together, she had this
thing about the telly. She hated it. Used to shout at Mike Walsh
and Bert Newton. 'You don't fool me!' she used to say to them.
'It's all fake. Fakers!' It used to make us all laugh because it's
true. On TV they all pretend. But soon Grammar started to get
sick and inside herself. One day she came in when Mike Walsh
was on and she got Mum's secateurs and started cutting up the
back of the telly. The electricity chucked her into the fireplace.
'Do that to an old woman, will you? Shameless!'

'Henry's in there with Tegwyn again,' I say. 'What's he
doing?'

Mum looks up from the steam. 'Trying to save her soul, I
think. She's a hard nut, our Tegwyn.'

'She hates him.'

She nods.

'Do you like Henry?'

She flinches. Doesn't look up from her ironing. 'Oh, yeah.' Looks like she's got to thinking all of a sudden, like I knocked something out of place.

You can hear them shouting from here. At it all the time. In a while, Henry Warburton comes out and sits down by the fire. He covers his face. Looks like he's gonna cry, but no, he takes his hands away and he's taken one eye out and he's got it between his fingers, showing it to me.

'Henry, put it away, for goodness sake,' Mum says.

'See, Ort,' he says. 'This is like the eye of God.' He moves it all over the place. 'Sees everything.'

'I know what it sees.'

'Yes?'

'Bugger all.'

'Morton!' Mum says.

'That's glass. Doesn't see anything. God sees everything, and he's got two real eyes. I think you're full of crap. You don't even believe what you're talking about.'

The room is deadly quiet. Mum looks at me and then her face changes and she looks at Henry real cool. The fire crackles. Tegwyn is yelling from her room.

'Well how would you like to be called Tegwyn? How would you like to have to be out here in this dump living off yer own shitty veggies like a caveman? How would you like to look after children and crazies and cripples? How would you fucken like it?'

Henry gets up and goes outside.

After a while I get up and make some tea. The glass canisters along the shelf are full of eggs. *Eggs!* I go and get Mum. She looks but she doesn't see them. All she sees is rice and tea and flour and lentils. She goes back to the ironing. I make a pot of tea with those eggs looking down at me.

We sit and sip our tea and listen to the sound of breaking glass from the shed.

'He's busting up the Chev,' I say.

'Yes,' Mum says. She looks stuck, like she can't decide something.

And we drink our tea, and I just wonder what the hell's going on.

chapter seventeen

I stuff my essay on 'The Brave Anzacs at Gallipoli' into me schoolbag and Mum stuffs in a bag of Vegemite sangers. It's a rank essay; most of it I copied straight out of books I got from the library. The library at school is the only place I go to out of class. I even eat my lunch in there up between the L–Z shelves. There's books on trees and cars, other countries, even a big Bible with pictures. Sometimes I go to the encyclopaedia and look up the one on 'S'. It's nearly falling apart, the one on 'S'. Looks like a lot of kids want to know what the hell's going on you know where.

Anyway, I grab my bag, get a kiss from Mum, go out on the back veranda, and there's Henry Warburton chucking up on the ground next to the 1958 FC Holden Special. He kind of yells as it comes up. Then he rests for a bit and looks at me, and then he wipes his mouth on a hanky and opens the car door and gets in. I go over and get in.

'You crook?'

He doesn't even look at me. The 1958 FC Holden Special drops its guts and we're off. All the way into Bankside he says nothing. I look at him a lot of the way; he's got this look on his face like he's scared. He's all bristly from not shaving and his eyes are red. His hair is greasy and all over. His clothes are dirty. I can smell the sick on him. He drops me off at Bankside outside the pub where some other kids wait. He doesn't even say goodbye.

I stand out close to the road away from the other kids. They're mostly older. It's boring, waiting for the bus. I look around. The pub and the drapers and the shop and up behind the pointy bit of the church. Boring. Over the road I see something moving. I look hard. It's a bobtail goanna. Looks crook, like it's trying to move but can't do it right. I go over and see that it's got one flat leg. Reckon it's been run over by a car. I pick him up. You can tell when a bobtail's real crook – it doesn't bite. He just looks at me and doesn't even open his mouth. I stuff him in me bag. The bus is coming.

All day I keep him in my bag. I check on him during every period, feed him bits of my sangers. Social studies and maths aren't so boring with a lizard in your bag. I call him Bartholemew 'cause it's in the Bible and it's a crazy name for a goanna to have. But by the last period it's shortened to Barry. With one leg flat as a popstick and mushy pink. I wrap a bit of Glad Wrap around it. Gonna fix this lizard up. I just sit there in English as Mrs Trigwell reads that dumb poem 'Jabberwocky' at us, laughing at herself all the way through, and I wait for school to be over. This school is full of kids who talk like people in the movies. They're not even like kids. Makes me feel like a baby.

Henry Warburton drives me home and doesn't even say hello.

'Do animals get into heaven?' I ask him.

He looks at me. 'S'pose so. Can't see why not.'

'Trees?'

'Probably.'

'Are you crook?'

He drives careful. Slow on the bends. He's had a shave and his clothes are clean, but it doesn't help much.

'Why?'

'You look rank.'

'Oh? Nngth.'

327

'You should pray about it.'

'Sure, Reverend.'

'I think there's something wrong with you.'

He looks at me with his eyes all red and a sad smile on him. 'God only knows what goes on in your brain, boy. Do they give you a hard time at school?'

'What do you mean?'

'For being . . . the way you are.'

'I stay in the library.'

'What're you gonna do when you bomb out?'

What's he mean? 'I dunno. Help Mum.'

'You're a singular sort.' He laughs. 'You are one in a million, boy. How did they make you?'

'In the bedroom,' I say. 'Sexual intercourse in the nude.'

He doesn't stop laughing all the way home. The 1958 FC Holden Special rattles and parps like it's laughing *its* box off, too.

I slip Barry under the wardrobe soon as I get home. Tea's on. Henry Warburton reads something short and prays something short. Mum dishes up the curry. I take some up to Grammar and feed her. When I come back Mum is talking.

'Sam and I built a pyramid out of logs before the kids were born. Out the back. Wasn't for any reason – just for the fun of it. We dragged old logs over from the forest and piled them into a triangle together. Sam got some white paint he found somewhere and tossed it all over. It used to glow at night. It was a laugh. I don't know why we ever did it. It went in the bushfire we had in '74. The fire jumped the creek, came up towards the house, burnt down the fences and the sheds, and then it took our pyramid before the wind changed. Thirty yards, that was all. Last night I thought I saw it glowing out there,' she says, looking real strange. 'I could have sworn it was there. I was praying for Sam.'

'I always pray for him,' I say, 'but I don't know the words.'

Tegwyn makes a fart noise with her mouth. Mum looks at me kind of sad.

'You still pray for him, Henry?' Mum says. She looks hard at him like never before.

It's quiet for a while. Henry Warburton looks like he's got a splinter somewhere. And frightened. He's got frightened listening to us.

I eat the rest of my curry. It's nice and hot; makes me ears burn. Henry Warburton sits there looking at Mum real scared.

After, when we bring the sherry out for the Lord's Supper, Henry says he has to go to the toilet. Mum says it without him. 'Help us to be more than we are,' she prays. 'Help Henry.' We sit in the lounge-room by the fire. Mum sits with Dad's head on her lap. He lies across the sofa with a blanket. She rubs his face and looks at his wonky eyes and then looks at the fire a lot. Henry comes back in.

'I sometimes wonder if I haven't come to the end of my tether,' Mum says to no one exactly. 'Sometimes.'

I look up from the fire. So does Henry Warburton. Tegwyn is going to sleep on the floor with a pillow and blanket.

'Yes,' he says.

'What right have you got to agree?' she says, real quiet. 'You're not in my position.'

'I've got my own surviving to do.'

'It's not survival we worry about, Henry, it's healing.'

'Isn't it the same thing?'

'No. Healing is what you do for someone else. Survival is for yourself. You can eat people if you want to survive bad enough. Or you can die if you want to heal someone bad enough.'

'Well, you have been thinking, Alice.'

'Don't talk to me like that.'

'Death is a healing, too, you know.'

It's quiet for a long time. In the end I get up and go to my room. I check Barry and give him some sultanas from my pocket. Then I pray.

'This lizard is crook, God. I reckon you should make it better. I really do. What else can I say?'

In the morning I check on Barry and find him stiff under the wardrobe. I open the window and chuck him out.

chapter eighteen

'One week to Easter,' Henry Warburton says.

'More crap from you,' Tegwyn says.

'Tegwyn, please,' says Mum.

It's Sunday and raining and we're all stuck inside together. Henry Warburton goes on about Easter. How today is Palm Sunday when Jesus galloped in on the donkey and they all had leaves for him. After that he got arrested and the soldiers whipped him and put prickles in his hair and killed him by making two pieces of wood and sticking him to it with nails. When he died some bloke put him in a cave. Three days later he came back from the dead. People went beserk. Later he went into heaven. Then people talked a lot about it.

Tuesday it's the Passover. That's when God came over and people put blood on their door. When Jesus did the Lord's Supper, it was on the Passover. Think that's right. There's so much stuff to remember, I can't keep it all in me brain. Least there's a story to it which is better than school.

When it stops raining, I go out on the back veranda. Tegwyn comes out too.

'Do you really believe that garbage he tells you?' she says. She doesn't look at me; she looks out over the wet yard. Chooks fight for good pozzies in the roosts.

'Yeah. I reckon it's true.'

'Even though Henry Warburton's such a dickhead?'

'It's not him we believe in – it's, it's Jesus.'

'And you still think Warburton knows *mysterious* things?'

'Oh, yeah. Some things. He knew all our names and everything about Dad.' I look at her. There's a smile on her face. It's not nice.

'Do you think it's easier to believe because you're – you know – a bit . . . slow?' She grins and her teeth are pointy and aimed at me. 'Warburton's a bloody fake. He knew our names because he was skulkin' round the place for weeks. He asked people all about us. He saw us swimming. I was in the nick. Remember, buddy-boy?'

'That wasn't your fault, then.'

'Oh, come on, Stumblebum, wake up.'

'We went for a swim,' I say. 'You asked me to. I got you out of the shop that time. You—'

'Oh, don't be pathetic. I knew he was there. I knew what was going on. I didn't need to go with *you*.'

I can't stay. I go inside to my room and get under my pillow and just bawl and bawl. It's all horrible. I stuff the pillow in me mouth till it near makes me sick.

When I wake up it's dark. I can hear the hot water hissing in the pipes. I had this dream. I was here in the house and white birds were coming over, hundreds of them coming out of nowhere. They came around in a circle and then started to land in the trees. Pretty soon they filled the forest. Like snow. The forest was white and moving. And then it was over and here I am listening to the pipes.

I get up and go into the hallway. Henry Warburton's talking.

'. . . why I can't heal you, Sam. I'm unclean. I wake up at night with her smell on me, it's thick in the room. A succubus, Sam. That's what it's like. Bobo comes back to have me. It suffocates me, I tell you. I want her and I want to escape her. It makes me desire her and the thought of her makes me ill. Is it her? Or the other half of me? Is it the Powers? Is it my fault it's happening to me like this?

'I haven't told you something about her death, Sam. Oh, God, how can I say this? The reason I'm tainted, Sam, is because she died while we . . . were . . . while we. She died on me. Over me. I wonder if the bitch didn't do it on purpose, to mark me for life. She marked me with death, Sam. The same part of a woman that brings forth life. In the act that makes life. She died on me.

'I want to love. I do love. I want to love purely. I want that kind of love that heals, that soothes. I want to love properly. I want to *heal* you, Sam Flack. You will save me, Sam. Your healing will heal me. Or, Goddamn it, I'm lost.'

I go up into the lounge-room, where Mum is sitting by the fire looking into it. I sit down next to her.

'Mum?'

'Hm?'

'Do you still love Dad?'

'Of course.'

'I thought maybe you loved Henry. You started to dress up.'

She puts a hand to her throat and there's tears coming in her eyes. 'Oh, Ort. I'm so lonely. A woman needs a man.'

'Dad's still a man.'

'I know now. I'm growing up, Ort. You can't see on the outside, but I am. Be patient.'

I really want to say 'I love you, Mum' but it sounds so crummy I can't do it.

'Are we supposed to put blood on our doors on Tuesday, do you think?' she says.

'I don't think so,' I say.

'Good. I didn't feel like doing something like that. It's barbaric. If only I was a smarter person. Maybe then I'd understand things.'

'Both of us must be a bit dumb, then.'

She looks at me and smiles.

I go out and look at the sky but it's blank; no stars, nothing.

Today is Thursday and tomorrow will be Good Friday. Mum said this hospital person came today and did tests on Dad and asked Mum all these questions about the colour of Dad's pee and how many times he went in a day and did he this or that. She said this girl poked him all over with her fingers and put a torch in his eye and shouted at him and hit him with a little hammer. She tore all the plaster off him – took his hair out. The woman went crook at Mum for not looking after him better. Mum is restless now. She walks around the house like there's ants in her pants.

'I just resent it, that's all,' she says, 'I resent it.'

Tegwyn and Henry Warburton are arguing again. They fight all the time in her room; he uses all the big words on her like *salvation* and *sanctification* and she yells at him and tells him to go stuff his head up Margaret's bum.

Later I come out after scrubbing potatoes for Mum, and I see Tegwyn throw the potful of tea leaves all on Henry Warburton, on his face, in his hair – everything. He picks her up and puts her over the rail of the steps and smacks her. Her dress is all up over her head and her knickers are black and he smacks her and smacks her until she screams and bawls.

After tea I go into the bathroom to brush my teeth to get out all the bits of meat and there's Henry Warburton bleeding into the sink. Blood's all coming out his nose and it runs all over his chin and into the white sink. He looks at me in the mirror.

'Not a word.'

I go out.

Before bed I go out and stand in the yard and look at that crazy light on our house. It just looks like it's sitting there waiting for a bus or something.

*

In the middle of the night I wake up. There's someone here in the room. Can feel it. I stay still, like a bit of firewood. I wait. No one moves.

'Who's there? Who is it?'

Down the hall I hear Grammar's voice: 'Is that you, Lil Pickering?'

I turn my bedside light on real quick. No one there. I get up and go down to Grammar's room. She's all up in a ball with the sheet on her head and the blankets all around.

'Is that you, Lil Pickering?'

'No, Gram, it's me, Ort.' I sit on the bed. 'Who do you hear, Grammar? Who came just then? I heard them. Who was it?'

'Pickering? Biscuits. Springtime? Mozart? Will you bring them? Am I ready? Will you come for me?'

Poor Grammar. Who? But I heard them. Someone has been here, you can feel it.

I go out into the hall and go down to Mum's room. She's in there crying. I go in.

'What's the matter?'

'Oh, Ort. I can't be expected to hold everything in.'

'The hospital person?'

'No, it's something else. The hospital girl was an excuse.'

'What, then?' I sit on the bed. Dad is snoring.

'I got a letter today. The wreckers want to know a few things. They're giving us early warning, they said.'

'What? What?'

'It looks like Henry didn't get the car in the proper way. It looks as though he's stolen it. Our car doesn't really belong to us. Henry lied.'

When's it gonna stop? God, when's it all gonna finish and leave us alone?

chapter nineteen

We're not eating today. Mum and me just can't. Nothing happens all day. It's Good Friday. There's bugger-all that's good about it. We do nothing all day, me and Mum, except in the morning we wash Dad. It's my idea to get him before Henry Warburton does. Tegwyn and him fight all day. The noise of it gets to you after a while.

At tea Mum says to Henry Warburton will he do something special for Easter tonight, but he says he's too busy, that something more important is calling him. He looks sick as a dog and that 'Nngth' is back real bad. Mum gives him and Tegwyn their tea with cold looks, and I take Dad's to him and she goes to Grammar.

'We're going to church tonight, Ort,' she says, real quiet in the hall. 'If you want to.'

'Not the one with all the greasy hair and grapejuice!'

'No, the big one. The Catholic one. I never thought of it before, but I have to do something. I have to.'

I shrug. 'OK.'

We organize Tegwyn and Henry Warburton to look after the sick ones, and we get in the stolen 1958 FC Holden Special and drive in to Bankside.

Well! What a place. Right away we get in there we don't know what the hell's going on for a minute. There's candles all up the front and dark everywhere else and we go up the front so we can see. There's only a few people there. No one says one single word for a long time until this bloke with a dressing-gown and a party hat comes down the aisle. Then there's stuff happening all over the place – people in white sheets, music coming flat-chat out of these pipes up the front and some bloke singing or talking like nothing you've ever heard before in your life. Scary, boy! This talking and singing going on and on with candles going out every now and then. It gets darker and darker. I can feel Mum grabbing me arm. Me fingers start throbbing. I don't know what's happening. No one talks to me or Mum – it all just happens. And all the time I'm looking up at this statue up on the wall, trying to figure out who it reminds me of. It's Jesus on the cross in the statue, I s'pose, but it reminds me of someone I know better.

More candles going out. Creepy singing. Mum is bawling now. That long hair, those wonky eyes, those holes in him – it looks like my dad. That's who it is. Then it's real dark and I get Mum up and take her out and people go 'Ssh!' at us and I tell them up their bum and take Mum out to the car.

'I. Can't. Drive,' she sobs. 'Can't. Drive. State. I'm. God.'

So I put her in the back, get her to lie down on the seat, and I drive the stolen 1958 FC Holden Special all the way home. In one gear. I thought it would be easy, but it's not. The car goes all over the place. I knock down six fenceposts and go into the storm gutter at the side of the road twice and get out again. Mum bawls in the back. I can hardly see out the windscreen. Rabbits run all over the road.

I keep it straight all the way down the drive, but I don't stop properly and I take a bit off the back shed. I get Mum inside and put her in bed with Dad and she cuddles up to him, still crying. Everything is dark. Me brain is going flat-chat and I can't keep still. I look in on Grammar. She's asleep. I look in on Tegwyn. I see the big lump in the bed. I see Henry Warburton's hairy arm. I see them in bed together and I go to my room and think.

337

I lie there thinking for a long time. I think about my dad being a good man and him being smashed up for no reason. I think about God and Jesus and Henry Warburton and his dreams and his false eye. And I think about my sister Tegwyn who can't love us. And I think about Grammar punching someone in the teeth with one hand and playing beautiful music with the other . . .

In the night I wake up.

'Who's there?'

I turn the light on. Grammar is calling.

I get up and go into the hall. I look in on Tegwyn and her and him are biting each other and hitting each other, with his hairy bum up and her making hate noises at him and the bed squealing.

I go down to Grammar.

'Coming for me. Waiting a long . . . old I am. Too old.'

I go to sleep there.

Everyone is very quiet today. Henry Warburton works on the stolen car. Tegwyn paints her nails on the veranda. Mum cooks, quiet, not speaking. I see her hands shaking. The whole day goes away like that. Except that I see things. Those canisters change all day. The rubies and diamonds and things come and go all day. Mum doesn't notice; like she's seeing something far inside herself; birds look in the window. One flies against the glass and kills itself and I bury it. The fire in the stove keeps going out. And I keep lighting it. In the evening everyone stays in their rooms. I go to sleep early, like I haven't been asleep all my life.

chapter twenty

In the morning I know. Mum is crying. I get up and do a check. My whole body is heavy, like I'm wrapped in a blanket. I can hardly walk. There's this mist, like me eyes've got something in them. Cloudy. Through all the holes and cracks in this old house there's stuff coming in. It's like cloud but it's light. Coming in the cracks. Mum is in Grammar's room. She's half on the bed and Grammar is grey and all gone in the face and I know she's gone.

'She's dead,' Mum says, without looking up.

I feel sick and heavy, and all this light is pouring in like smoke and I go out into the hall again and open Tegwyn's door. The bed is empty. Even the blankets and sheets are gone. I open a cupboard. Empty. I go into the lounge-room and see all Henry Warburton's stuff gone and only his Bible on the sofa. Me heart is smashing around. The cloudy white light is coming in – I breathe it in; it's warm and it tastes good. Me head's nearly bursting. I go to the window. The car is gone. Big skid marks all over the drive. Birds shout in the trees. The smell of bush flowers comes in real strong. I can smell milk. I can smell the honey from the bees. The dying trees look strong and thick and all the colours come in the window like someone's pouring them in on us. A bell ringing from the forest – it makes the china rattle in the kitchen and it puts tingles up me back and makes me hair electric. Everywhere, in through all my looking places and the places I never even thought of – under the doors, up through the boards – that beautiful cloud creeps in. This house is filling with light and crazy music and suddenly I know what's going to happen and it's like the whole flaming world's suddenly making sense for a second and I run to the kitchen and grab the big bottle of SAFFLOWER OIL and back into the lounge-room and snatch up the big black Bible and burst into Mum's room and there's my dad with these tears coming down his cheeks, pinpoints of light that hurt me eyes, tears like diamonds, I tell you. His eyes are open and they're on me and smiling as I come in shouting 'God! God! God!' His face is shining. I'm shaking all over. 'God! God! God!'

I get the lid off the bottle wading through the music, and the oil splashes all over him and Mum comes in laughing and the cloud fills the room till all I can see is his eyes burning white and I know that something, something here in this world is gonna break.

IN THE WINTER DARK

For Denise and Jesse

and for the Nannup Tiger
wherever you are

ACKNOWLEDGEMENTS

The author thanks the Literature Board of the Australia
Council for senior fellowships in 1984 and 1987 when
this book was written. Final revisions were made in
Paris at the Australia Council Studio while the author
was a recipient of a Marten Bequest Travelling
Scholarship.

A portion of an earlier version of *In the Winter
Dark* has appeared in *Antipodes*. Characters and events
in this story are fictitious.

There is such a thing as the pressure of darkness.
Victor Hugo

It's dark already and I'm out here again, talking, telling the story to the quiet night. Maurice Stubbs listening to his own voice, like every other night this past year, with the veranda sinking and the house alive with solitary noises the way it always is when the sun's set on another day and no one's come to ask the questions they're gonna ask sooner or later. I just sit here and tell the story as though I can't help it. There's always something in the day that reminds me, that sets me off all hot and guilty and scared and rambling and wistful, like I am now.

This morning I found Jaccob down at his boundary fence drunk as a mongrel again, and I carried him up the hill to his place and lit him a fire, fixed some food, cleared away the bottles and that shoe he leaves around, and I left him there in that big old house before it drew breath and screamed my name. An old man like me can lift him now, for God's sake. He's always drunk or silent and skyward as a monk. There's only me and him left, but he doesn't speak.

So I'm the teller. But why don't I keep my mouth shut? Why? Because someone has to hear sooner or later. Because the bloody dreams don't go away. Because today I saw a real estate agent sniffing around across the valley at the girl's place. Because I'm alone, I'm alone here on the farm, the carrier of everyone's memories. So when the dusk comes, in that gloaming time of confusion when you can't tell a tree stump from a kangaroo, an owl hoot from a question in the night, the dark begins to open up like the ear of God and I babble it all out, try to get it straight in my mind, and listen now and then for a sigh, a whisper, some hint of absolution and comfort on the way.

This is what I remember, but it's not only my story. It happened to Ida, too, and Jaccob and the girl Ronnie. It's strange how other people's memories become your own. You recall things they've told you. You go over things until you think you can see the joins, the cells of it all. And there's dreams. I have these dreams. Dead people, broken people bleed things into you, like there's some pressure point because they can't get it out any more, can't get it told. It's as though the things which need telling seep across to you in your sleep. Suddenly you have dreams about things that happened to *them*, not to you, as if it isn't rough enough holding down your own secrets. I don't know how it works — I'm no witch-doctor — but I know I remember things I can't possibly know. I'm not mad. Not yet.

They call this valley the Sink. Well, they did when I was a young man. From my veranda of an evening you can see mist on the dark sheen of the swamp and the river bend below. Ducks spatter round the old white bridge. Frogs come on with the sound of marching. The jarrah forest takes the westering sun as a prick of blood on its brow. There's still only three houses. On the stony pasture across the valley there's the little house surrounded by fallen fences where no one's lived since Ronnie, the girl. Weird thing is, I got to like her in the end, but everyone likes the helpless and the vanquished. To the left, on the slope just up from here, Jaccob lives in the limestone place that's been there nearly as long as I remember. We used to call it the Minchinbury place. God, how I hate that house. Jaccob's chimney smoke rising like a spirit against the gloom. He'll be sober enough to start drinking again by now. Since the day we dug a grave and drove to the hospital, the day we sat together like friends and drank half a case of Japanese Scotch and talked and talked it all out, we haven't said a word to one another. It's a year.

My neighbour Murray Jaccob used to push a lawnmower for a living. Just before it sent him deaf, he retired to nurse his crusty little crop of skin cancers. He sold up the business, left the city, and came here. Jaccob wanted to devote his retirement to the growing of grass. He was a big man in his late forties with streaky bleached hair, a kind of worn-out stooped look about him, and a way of looking at you as though he could never be quite certain where you fitted in; it might have been the way he squinted, or maybe the habit he had of speaking to a point just to the left or right of you. But I could understand that after twenty-five years of cutting lawns, a man'd want to grow long, scruffy, weedy grass, the sort you could wade through and see lapping in the wind. He never wanted to see lawn again as long as he lived. He bought the old Minchinbury place amidst run-down orchards, some good pasture, and a lot of uncleared thickets and forest. When I was a boy, a Doctor Minchinbury made it his country residence. When he died, he left his daughter there to grow old and crazy. I remember her too well. The house had to be rebuilt since her day – the wooden bits, anyway, but it's still the same grand, fatuous-looking joint dominating the hill with its wide timber veranda and white-washed stone. There's nowhere you can be in the Sink where you'll miss seeing it.

Jaccob was no farmer. I noticed how late he got up. He had a policy of doing nothing. He was rigorous about it. From his place the river bend was obscured by a hump in the lower slopes of his land, but as he walked daily between rows of scourged fruit trees he could see the black sprays of birds rising from it to curve out over the swamp. It was a kind of ritual, that walk in the morning. The rest of the day he'd involve himself in trivial tinkerings that chewed up the time and left him at dusk, looking down through the broken ranks of orchards with the satisfaction of knowing that he hadn't done a damn thing all day, hadn't begun to put the place to order, hadn't learnt any more about orchards, and above all, hadn't had his ears thrashed by a machine and his nose stung with two-stroke fumes while his brain broiled in the sun. One more lawn-free day.

Jaccob was the first to notice something. I know it so well now, it's like I'm there myself.

Walking in the orchard late in the day, Jaccob saw the flash of a windscreen across the valley. The few months he'd been here, he'd kept clear of his neighbours. Ida and me seemed friendly enough in a stiff sort of way. We were the old couple who'd been around for ever. Jaccob felt the amusement of those yokels, the way they saw his presence, his kind of life. But he couldn't know what hatred there was in me, what fear.

His other neighbours, across the valley, were a young pair. He wouldn't have called them hippies; they were kind of modern types from the city. He'd spoken to them a couple of times. The girl was pretty enough, though she wore clownish clothes and had her hair in spikes. The boy wore overalls, but you could tell he belonged in a leather jacket. Jaccob didn't know a thing about them and he was not curious, though that afternoon as the sun caught the windscreen of his neighbours' car over the valley, he watched it wind down to the road. He heard the unreasonable note of the engine and the muffler grinding as the station wagon left the gravel and pulled away towards town. He caught himself staring after it and it made him laugh. An event! Good Gawd, he thought; what a life to have found.

He turned to go back up to the house. The light was failing and he had wood to chop. He set off, but something stopped him still as a stump. Between the trees he saw something. A movement. A silhouette. It was travelling. *Loping*, that was the word that came to him. He squinted. All around him, birds were roosting, or stirring, or something. He heard the tick of his own body. The shadow seemed to stop, slip sideways between apple rows. And then there was nothing.

It was the evenings that took getting used to. Jaccob was teaching himself to do very little and to be content. In the city he'd spent evenings by the TV with a beer and a buzz in his ears. As he'd got older, it took more beer, more repeats of *High Chaparral* to soften his nerves. His bones ached, his sunburn stung, blood chugged in his ears. And the last couple of years there was that other twinge too, but only dreamless sleep could rid him of that.

Here at night, Jaccob was becoming a reader. To his new life he'd brought his carved jarrah rocker, some old Marty Robbins records, and a pile of big novels by people he'd never heard of. With its great awkward stylus like a plough, his ancient hi-fi was probably, he thought, the only agricultural implement he was ever likely to use.

That night he made a fire, put old Marty's 'El Paso' on repeat, and sat rocking with *Look Homeward Angel* over his knee like a fat little lapdog. He was good at not letting shadows and suspicions ruin everything. He was new to the country; there was no point worrying. He poured some whisky. Before long he slept.

There was a dream he had, an old one flashing the colour of lightning in him. A yowl of grief, the panic rising in his chest like locusts on the wing as, in another life again, he threw the newspaper aside and began to run for the nursery door. Now

349

Marjorie was screaming, shaking the cot as he came. I know this dream. It's Jaccob's, but I have it too, these days.

Jaccob slept on.

As that station wagon wound down the gravel drive in the sunset, someone else had been watching too. She saw her great herd of Muscovies scatter from its path. She saw the KEEP MUSIC LIVE sticker on the rear window – she'd stuck it on herself. The car left in the only direction it could – away. There were no passers-by here, no through traffic. These farms form a cul-de-sac at the end of a back road. The car disappeared around the first bend and was gone. The young woman found herself standing alone out in the cold, hugging herself until her breasts hurt. Her name was Veronica Melwater, though the man who'd just left her called her Ronnie.

She shivered. The kind of shiver you have when you cut yourself, in that moment before the blood springs, when there is only the shock of the open wound and the anticipation of pain or maybe outrage.

She'd helped him load guitars and amplifiers into the car, listening to him say how it was only a couple of weeks. We need the cash. You don't wanna go back to the suburbs, do you? Jesus, it's not like the old days, you know. Be reasonable, Ronnie.

Her Muscovies scuffled behind the troughs for night shelter, and she could hear the geese somewhere coming up from the river. There was the goat to milk and night was ready with the sun setting the trees afire up behind the old people's place over the way, but she stayed there until it flared briefly and went out altogether. She looked up to the great white house on the hill, the Minchinbury place. Now, that was a place, all right. Mist formed on the valley slopes below it. Looks like a movie set, she thought. But her eyes wandered and her mind came back to the huge empty space she seemed to be walking in. Who the hell needed to empty their wardrobe for a two-week trip? She knew what that meant. She wasn't stupid. Well, not in that way, boy. She knew things weren't like they were in the old days. Didn't she, though.

It was dark when she went inside. The little house had been an old soldier settlement place they'd repaired and filled with potted plants and posters. There were a few lumpy hand-woven rugs, a spinning wheel she'd never really learnt to use, a pot-belly stove, some simple furniture. The walls were scabby with stripped wallpaper. They'd never got around to finishing it off and putting some bright paint on the walls.

'Ah, Ronnie,' she told herself aloud in that dark, small place, 'don't panic. It's all right. It's just two weeks.'

She rested her low, full belly against the windowsill in the front room and felt the baby slip and kick inside her. All the Valium made her light enough to move without muscles, to float, like him or her, in warm fluid. She looked out into the dark and suddenly she was afraid. She had no car, for Godsakes. How would she get to town if she needed to? What was he doing to her? The money was gone, sure, but what else was going on? What about the staying out of music, what about the promises? Oh, Ronnie, you are so dumb, girl.

The room was dark and the faces of dead musicians and dead actors peered down at her. She held her belly. It was sinking in and it was like the pills were great white clots in her veins. Too many, Ronnie. She didn't even know how many she took, these days. But any of it had to be too much.

She felt this swimming creature in her, and she wanted to speak to it, to explain it all, but she was ashamed. She'd read the books, she knew what she'd been doing. Jesus, she thought; one minute you're paying some rich bastard to cut one out of you, and the next thing you're wanting one and you poison it.

Out in the dark she saw the anaemic cheek of a full moon rising from the forest. Stumps, windrows, clumps of gravel queued behind their own shadows.

Stuck. With everything, with everybody, she was stuck. It was quiet and she stood there feeling the strength go out of her. Always, she thought. Always when everything looks like coming together, just when you get up some guts, you get stuck. In the old days there was no problem. Then there was always a bit of acid to drop – keeping tabs on yourself, she called it. You stepped sideways and said fuck it. Ah, the old days.

It gave her an idea.

In the bedroom she knelt and pulled out a drawer beside the bed. She took it right out and put it on the floor. She reached into the hole it left and felt around the frame of the cabinet until she felt the little cellophane package taped to the wood. Old stock. A memento, really. She looked at it a while. No, things'd have to be black. She sat on the bed, getting strength back. She wanted this place, she wanted this baby, and she was gonna have them both. She made a fist in the half-light until she couldn't even see the tab in front of her. And then everything crumbled and went the taste of shit in her mouth, the taste of blotting paper. Fuck it, she thought; I deserve something.

When the walls began to breathe, Ronnie got up off the bed and went outside. It looked nicer out there. She felt the cold in an academic sort of way. Mist sifted past. It was like walking in the clouds. Better than breathing walls.

The sounds of the night were sharp. Crickets sounded like weapons being cocked. Her boots hissed in the grass. The bloated moon followed over her shoulder; she didn't like to look. The incline steepened toward a ridge of granite. The rock fairly pulsed in the blue light. Ronnie heard her own gasps, too loud to be hers.

The twisted trunks of redgums walked past, writhing. The ground was billowing now. Never do it alone, Ronnie. Oh, you never needed to in the old days.

She came to a delicious bank of grass and lay down in it. Up through the shreds of mist and the towering wet blades, the stars glowed. No, she saw, they glowered. I know, she thought; I know, you don't have to tell me. Cold beneath her, the earth soaked up her heartbeats and the stars showed blood in the dark contusion of sky. She heard a snapping, slapping deluge of footsteps, and turning her head she saw an army of ghosts marching upon her. They shrilled and squawked and sprayed shit.

'Oh, God! Nick? Nick!'

They closed on her with their great infernal pink bills pointing down at her from the end of looping white necks. And wings, evil white wings. There was purple fire in their eyes. She knew what they were, but they were more than that, you only had to use your eyes. She covered her belly and then they were gone. She got up and ran.

Ronnie stumbled through the granite boulders.

This wasn't the proper world. Tiny marsupials smashed through the bush. All the colours, all the dyes came unstuck and she walked through them.

A dam, huge pore in the flesh of the earth.

A fence. She plucked a riff crawling through.

There was forest.

There was forest.

Forest.

Forest.

Half the night there was Ronnie and there was jarrah forest, and yet it was no time at all.

There were places here the moon could not follow. No time at all but fast-time, quick-time, hurry-time that she dawdled in. She came to thickets. Thickets and thickets of thickets.

A year into the night there was sudden pasture again. Fog still. She coughed. Someone's hack. She swam through grass, played fences, began to find an incline. Big white house full of music. Trees like a graveyard. The road was a ribbon in the wind. She climbed aboard and surfed it, rode road bronco. It was fun enough to die. And in mid-step she fell asleep and went down into a softer dark. No, it wasn't like the old days.

Ida and me were married thirty-six years. We thought of ourselves as good country people; we knew what we knew, and tried to mind our business, or at least to be discreet when we minded someone else's. That night, as Jaccob slept, as Ronnie lurched around out there, Ida and me waited for dinner to cook. It was late because I'd worked through till dark, fooling with a fuel line in the ute.

She was a cunning woman, Ida, and I liked that about her. It was cunning that got her married to me. Our families look grim in the wedding photos. Everyone, including me, thought our Ida was with child. Her people disliked me, and now they had the chance to hate me, but there was no way they could avoid a marriage. Or so they thought. Lord, didn't we all get a surprise! There was no baby in *that* girl's belly – not for a year or two.

Pork chops spat and sizzled on the stove. It was warm in our big kitchen tonight. You could tell Ida had ideas for later when she cooked pork, but after nearly forty years of falling for it every time, a man has to pretend he doesn't know when he's being seduced. In those days, after a hard day's work and before a good meal, I liked to get by the stove with a volume of my *Pictorial History of Australia At War* and a bottle of beer and some bread and butter so I could get inside myself, all sullen with pleasure. I spread the big book on the table and listened to the urn hiss on the stove and sank into the comfort of history, the terse outlines, the facts, the bare black and white photos. I was never in a war, but my interest was deeper than that. In a way I've lived my life by the weather (that faithless bitch), and history, it seemed to me, was something solid, truthful, unswerving. Well, that was those days. I sat there airing my feet in their socks, and Ida tinkered with the chops in the pan.

Outside, the dog whined. It wasn't a farm dog, but a silky terrier, that useless kind of dog with a yap that sets a man on edge.

'What's that dog chained up for, woman?'

Ida sniffed. 'He's done business here on the lino and I'm punishing him.'

'I warned you about buying that dog.'

'Gawd, that was ten years ago, Maurice. He's old, that's all.'

'Well, there's three hundred acres out there he can crap all over.'

'I'm aware of the problem, Maurice. It's all in hand.'

I shifted in my seat, smoothed a page, and the dog found a keener note to whine upon. It was dark outside, and cold, and if it hadn't been for the dog and the chops and the stove and our crotcheting, you might have heard the water-snore of the valley, that strange sound of the river moving and the damp air settling on it in the hollows.

Ida sighed and served up the pork chops with a splash of peas and a hillock of mashed potato, and we ate in the silence we were used to. The food was good. I could feel the irritation and the weariness back off. Neither of us had really got going before the scream began. It wasn't a long scream; it stopped before I got to the door. Ida bellowed the dog's name, and the cold backhanded me as I stumbled outside.

I turned the light on. Saw the chain trailing down off the edge of the veranda.

'Maurice, what was it?' she said, sounding like she'd made the effort of being calm.

I heard her coming from behind me, and I kept my back to her. I held the bloody dog-collar in my hand.

'Get the shovel, love,' I said. I heard the awful quietness in my voice. 'Keep away. Go and get the shovel.'

I heard a thick noise in her throat, and as she moved away I looked out into the darkness. There was a light on up at Jaccob's, but no lights from across the way. My palm was hot with blood. In my hand was the severed head of Ida's silky terrier, still with nerves enough to flex its jaws foully in my grip. That was how I found it, the head left in the collar, the chain snapped, blood pushing out hot. And nothing else.

I heard Ida coming back and it struck me of a sudden that maybe we should never have stayed on here, maybe I should have taken Ida out of this valley thirty years ago and never come back. To spare her the hardships, the hidden things, this night.

We'd spent some time together, me and Ida. The children had grown and gone, and over the years Ida had fattened up. She sort of spread, like a garden gone wild. I think she was richer, better for the years. She'd developed a big, wide laugh and her memory was gentle. She wanted the best for people, to think the best of them. She gave me the benefit of any doubt, and she'd had a few, because, looking back on it, I see I'd grown in, gotten smaller, meaner with age. But she stayed, even so, though sometimes I wonder why. We loved each other, but I gather sometimes it's less than enough. Things had been cool between us sometimes, even stony quiet, but never in thirty-six years had there been an evening of such sick silence as this turned out to be.

We went to bed early, in the end. We lay beside each other, straight as coffins. Moonlight forked in through the curtains. We were there like that about an hour, maybe two, before Ida spoke.

'Was it a fox, you think?'

357

I listened to our breathing.

'I don't know.'

But she heard me open the bedside drawer, and she heard in the dark the heavy metallic sound as I placed the rifle bolt on the table. It was the only way I could tell her what I thought and not lie.

I dreamt I ran downhill full of holes in the creeping blindness of night, aflame and screaming. I lit up the valley like a torch and everything saw, everything knew I was being punished. I found the river, dived in, but it was just fuel to the flames. My mouth was a hole. There was nowhere to go.

We all dreamt that night – the four of us – as though our insides were all tight and grinding with rent chunks of secrecy shivering up to the surface.

I remember every dream from that night: Ronnie's floating nightmare, Jaccob's terrible memory, I even know what Ida dreamt. Like that old Bible story about the wild man chained up in the tombs, ranting and foaming in all those voices. Call me Legion, he says, because we are many. And the pigs screaming down into the water, remember that? What was he having, delusions? Or was he having everyone's recollections, was it history that tormented him? What had the wild man done in order to be mercilessly visited by everybody's dreams? Well, I can't speak for him, but I think about that poor bastard when I sit out here talking to the dark, or when I wake in the night from a dream that belongs to someone else. The wild man had someone come to cast out his demons. But here tonight, like every night, I sit here, and no one comes.

Jaccob went through his orchard in the light of morning. He looked about, but he most definitely did not search. His neck was sore and his bones ached from sleeping in the rocker. From over the Stubbses' place he heard the low gearing of a motor. Kookaburras whipped up a brassy chorus back in the trees, and he saw fresh roo scat between the fruit trees which he ground moist into the earth with a smile. He smelt grass. He remembered the day he retired, the day he was a little mad with sun, when he mowed that rich bastard's lawn and then his herb garden, and his azaleas, made his garden gnomes into amputees, until the place looked like a UFO had landed on it in a careless manner. Yes, it was good to have at least one memory where you took destiny into your own hands.

He went down to the roadside boundary from where he could see birds engraving the platinum surface of the river. The little bridge shimmered in the sun, and he could smell the muddy sweetness of the swamp. He knew this place was good. Even if he died here alone, it would be good. It was morning, light had come and he had nothing to do but live his life.

He stopped, though, when something caught his eye. Something red. The wet-stiff grass seemed to shiver. Jaccob reached for a stick. As he climbed through the fence, the stick snagged in the wire and he fumbled a second and left it there. From across the road, in the tall grass, he heard panting. Well, it might have been panting. He stood there in the road, wishing he could just walk away, but he was afraid to turn his back. Whatever it was, it was moving again. He could see its slow passage through the grass. As he crossed the road he listened to the stones mashing underfoot, then the quietness of the macadam. A duck bawled in the distance. Jaccob hardened up. He saw everything quite clearly: gravel at the edge of the road, wild oats, the black gloss of beetles. And, knowing it was a stupid thing to do, he waded into the grass. He felt weirdly calm, or perhaps calmly weird. It was morning and there was light and sound and it was his land.

It hit him behind the knees so hard he went down like a sack of wheat, steeling himself, even as he fell, for the pain to come. It had hold of his legs, but his nerves hadn't caught up yet. His nose ploughed the ground, his mouth was full of grass stalks, and he tasted whisky at the back of his throat, waiting in that awful timeless calm before the pain.

'Dad?'

Jaccob lifted his face from the dirt.

'Daddy, is that you?'

'What the bloody—'

He twisted over and saw behind him, grafted to his calves like a rugby player, the girl from over the valley. Her hair was wet across her blue-pink face, snarled in drifting snot. Her red parka was torn and twisted. She was a mess.

'Jesus Christ!'

'Don't go.'

He felt laughter and relief gushing up in his throat and he hit her.

Ronnie didn't dare breathe. Sometimes the man carrying her looked like her father and sometimes he didn't at all. His face seemed to grow and shrink. The ground raced below her, like a runway. Yes, he hit her, he was her father all right. Yeah, now he'd take her up to her room and beat her and that hopeless twat of a mother'd shout at him but not stop it and he'd leave her in the room and she'd tear her clothes and smack her face against the wall while they ate their dinner downstairs.

There was a big place coming up, all elephantine and distorted. White. A white place. Oh, God, not a hospital! No, not this trick. Oh, they had it all organized. So this was the doctor. With his knife, his fish scraper, his pig-sticker or what-the-hell-ever.

She was inside, like it swallowed her. White walls, dirty white walls. So why did he put her on the floor? On a rug? Sometimes the rug was all crawly and sometimes just a rug. She lay there. No she couldn't let them, but she couldn't move any more, no she couldn't. Here came those great shudders again, and then she was hot and prickling and there was orange light and the doctor was pulling at her parka. Oh, God in heaven must know she didn't deserve this; she didn't deserve much, but this . . . this! This all went purple and grey and this became that. Or something.

On hands and knees I went over the wet grass, combing the ground beyond the veranda. I smelt woodsmoke and eggs, heard birds, felt the angry drive of blood in my ears. I was looking for tracks and getting madder. Everywhere I found my own stockinged footprints where last night I'd trampled the place like a fool in a fit. There was a rut where grass and dirt had been uprooted: something stopping fast. I laboured on for an hour. I cursed myself, I felt the old back and knees complain, but in the end I did find a single, clear print. Fifteen feet away from the veranda. I sat there on my haunches and set my teeth to just look at it.

At breakfast, a beeswax cast of the print stood between Ida and me on the table. We ate in silence. The early cold blue of the sky was giving way to grey and it felt as though a westerly was due. The footprint tilted, catching a bit of light. I could smell honey from it. I caught Ida looking at it. She sipped her tea. She brewed the stuff strong enough to shrivel your tongue.

'It'll rain d'rectly,' she said. 'Better get to it.'

I watched her get up and push into her gumboots by the door. I saw the blue veins of her legs and felt grateful and sad and as old as hell.

That morning we drove around the property, moving from one minor task to the next, putting some feed about when it wasn't really needed, shifting steers from paddock to paddock. Ida drove the ute and I got out for the gates. The pastured hills were the colour of the sea, and the sheep and steers like islands on it. Crows hoyed from the trees. We saw Jaccob on the edge of his orchard. He was stiff and small in the distance. We rode the boundaries, as they say, and we didn't know quite what else to do.

On the northern boundary closest to the forest we came upon the carcass of a roo caught in the fence. It was a doe, fresh-dead with its neck broken in the wire. I motioned Ida to stop and I pulled the skinning knife from its sheath beneath the dash, thinking of meat for the dog, but Ida just looked at me and drove on and it caught me stunned a moment before I sank back like a fool, too ashamed even to say sorry.

Jaccob got the fire going and felt it hot on his face as he began to undress the girl who lay rigid with cold. Her eyes were wide, pupils like bullet holes. All she seemed able to do was shake her head. She was blue as a bruise. He peeled two shirts from her and her small breasts moved like . . . like things. Her jeans and boots were slicked with mud and his fingers had become fat and clumsy, but he got everything off and threw it on the hearth. He felt her eyes on him as he shucked down her panties, the way he might have done if she was his child, and the thought hurt. From upstairs he brought the feather quilt to wrap her up. The fire cracked and spat.

Jaccob sat down and thought. No, he wouldn't call a doctor, not yet.

The girl began to cry.

All morning Jacob tended the fire while the girl slept. He was agitated like he hadn't been for a long time. He tried not to prowl and pace lest he wake her, so he confined himself to the rocker. Hell, this was his neighbour, naked on his living-room floor. He didn't know her, and he sure as eggs didn't want trouble. He rocked by the fire. This was not good, but it was no reason to panic. It was just something silly and unexpected. Nothing.

Late in the morning when the girl still hadn't woken, he hid his whisky bottle and his novels before going out into the chill to clear his head. He felt like he had a decision to make. Like maybe something was happening and he should identify it in order to square it away and get on with being happy and alone.

At noon, he bundled the girl's clothes up and took them out to the wash-house. They stank of sweat and stale deodorant. Cleaning the small, silly-looking boots, he caught himself smiling; it reminded him of his own father. He remembered his father used to clean all the children's boots. It was like a devotion, and the thought made him unaccountably happy. He knew he'd wanted it for himself. There'd be no little shoes to polish now. The sudden warmth went and there was bitterness in him. He scraped swamp mud from the little green pointed toes.

By the fire, the girl slept white lipped and muddy in the quilt. He knew he should take her up to a bed, but it seemed somehow just too much.

Now and then she moved a limb. Once, a white foot slipped out from under the cover to reveal ragged toenails and a crusty heel. He wondered if maybe he could get her in the car and take her home. Surely she'd wake up soon.

*

After lunch I went up to the northernmost reaches and into the forest. The smell of a good stand of jarrah is enough to make a man sing. Sink people over the years came to call the scrofulous bald patch on our side of the valley Dick's Hill, after my father. Dad was a tearer and burner, cleared damn near everything he could find, but he had to stop at the northern boundary because it's state forest, Crown land. He was frightened of trees, my old man. Never sleep in the forest, he would say; everything is above you. And I know what he means. I've seen twelve-foot boughs fall and spear so deep into the earth that they looked like small trees in their own right. Being under that in your plastic tent – imagine. The old man had his practical side, but there was more to his feeling about the forest than that. Well, there's all those fairy tales for a start, all those stories we brought with us from another continent, other centuries. Whatever it was, the old man did what he could to bash and burn it into submission.

You get that big church feeling up there in the forest. We were running out of fuel early this winter, so I took the chainsaw with me to feel like I was working and not just farting about. I dawdled the ute along the muddy tracks in the broken light, looking for windfalls. It didn't take long to spot a toppled tree. I stopped and got out. The wind sounded like a choir way above. I grabbed the axe from the rear tray, picked my way through the undergrowth with its crush of bracken and creepers and ferns and bright orange fungi and beds of soft wet pungent bark, and when I came to the tree, I scrambled up its great flank and stood panting a moment.

The axe rang out sweet and clear, and I made a bigger notch than I needed to, just to feel the weight of the axe and hear that *thock!* a few times more. The timber was good and dead, the colour of honey.

I went back for the chainsaw. The air was full of the smells of eucalyptus and gravel mud and dew. As I hefted the saw off the ute, I saw something along the track, something red and quickly gone and I felt a thump of excitement in my chest. This was it. I put the chainsaw back on the tray and reached into the cab for the rifle.

I moved as quick and quiet as I knew, cutting an imaginary line through the timber to where I thought I might get another sighting. Birds shuttered away up into the wind. My feet sweated in the clumsy gumboots. I remembered to cock the .243. I didn't understand my sudden anger. Things began to happen too quickly; everything was breathless.

When I saw that red blur ducking away in the bracken only forty metres away, I got off two shots in a hurry. The forest rippled with the noise, and I heard a slug smack home. Strange, but the first thing I did was pick up the shells from the ground and sniff the cordite. As though I was putting off any investigation. Up there in the bracken, there was a scraping sound.

When I got close I saw blood, a smear on a fan of bracken. Ground litter rustled. I went forward behind the barrel of the gun. Then I all but trod on the quivering body of a fox, and I leapt back with a shout, and then let out a nervy little laugh. The beast had terrible mange, which would make it look bigger and stranger from a distance. I'd hit it twice: in the front paw and in the back hip. It shook with pain and didn't even look at me. I killed it with another shot and heard the crack tear up into the light. Then I went back to sawing wood.

Ida Stubbs heard shots and flinched enough to drop the preserve jar and it smashed at her feet. She leant against the sink a moment and looked out the window to the forest up the hill. Another shot; she heard it soar over the valley and it gave her a flittery feeling she didn't often get any more, that sense of being small, of not really belonging. She'd had it in her chest the day she'd come here after the wedding. And she got it each time she brought a baby back from the district hospital. She'd stand here at the window and feel new and strange, as though maybe she should get back in the car and take this helpless child to a town, a city, somewhere where the trees didn't stand over you, where the swamp didn't sit there brewing at your doorstep, where people might drive past occasionally and wave on their way to somewhere else.

She tucked a wisp of hair behind her ear and sniffed. That gun's just a bit big for our needs, Maurice, and besides, you couldn't hit a barn with a handful of gravel.

Ida didn't like guns. Her father went out one day five years after we were married and shot himself dead. And there were always accidents, stupid things. She had a cousin (an old man now) who blew his own ear off climbing through a fence.

She got on her knees and swept up the slurry of chopped apple and splintered glass. That was another thing; she hated waste.

What was that fool of a hubby doing up there?

I have an Ida dream all the time. Some nights I have it so bad it has me waking up thinking I *am* Ida. In the dream she stands at the last rise before those thickets which web the hills just beyond here. The children are there, picking mushrooms. They call out and throw cowpats and are happy. She holds their cardigans and watches them play, but in an instant she imagines them being drawn into the thicket, snagged deep beyond the light, as though the place will not yield and if it will not yield it won't be still. She stands there shuddering with apprehension. She clutches their sweet-smelling garments and watches her children. I am not there, not anywhere in the picture. She never told me about this fear. Maybe I wouldn't have listened. You understand yourself late enough to discover you're the sorriest bastard who ever was.

*

Jaccob woke at the sound of the shot. He got out of the chair and went out into the grey afternoon light. He waited but there was nothing else. Before long he heard the bawl of a chainsaw and he relaxed a little.

Guns. Jaccob had a rifle of his own, a .22 repeater which the estate agent had given to him as a sign of goodwill when he handed the keys over. To Jaccob it seemed an odd gesture of goodwill, and he'd never even fitted the magazine to it. He kept it in his wardrobe.

Jaccob yawned. Strange, but he was bored. With someone else around all day, just being uselessly there, the day seemed truly long and pointless. He poked in all the sheds behind the house with their chaff and rodent and diesel smells. He fed his pullets and watched them scuffle and bluff. He pocketed eggs. He chopped wood in the hope the noise might wake the girl up and it would seem accidental that he should disturb her, so he chopped until his back ached and he felt like a complete dolt.

The light went. Jaccob slunk back into the house and showered. Then he resolved to be neighbourly and set about roasting the leg of lamb he'd been saving the past few days. A roast dinner, a bottle of red, that might do. He crept around in the kitchen, basting meat and peeling vegetables, mixing mustard and finding some mint for a sauce.

But the dinner cooked and the girl slept on.

Jaccob ate alone as always, only now with someone else in the house he felt more lonely than he'd felt in all his months here. Mostly he'd been all right here on his own. Only a couple of times, usually when drunk, he'd given in to sadness and taken out the photo albums and looked at the pictures of Marjorie and him, Marjorie and the baby. But not tonight; he was damned if he'd cave in tonight. He listened to the sounds of his cutlery. Oh, how the clink of knife and fork spoke its own language. Yes, he remembered those evenings at dinner after the shit had hit the fan, when they were still married but with nothing between them but grief and recrimination, when her scraping knife would say: it wasn't my fault, so don't look at me like that, and his fork would rattle and mutter: for Christ's sake, leave it be.

Jaccob pulled his novel down from behind the old kitchenette and opened it beside his plate so he could read and make some normality. He took a mouthful of wine. The novels were Marjorie's. She read serious books and listened to serious music, and late in the piece she didn't even hide her contempt for his penny-dreadfuls and his country music. When they were packing to separate, he saw a brace of books she'd earmarked for the local opp. shop. Some were by Leon Uris and Morris West, but there was a pile by a Thomas Wolfe with swaggering titles and plenty of exclamation marks, and he took them. Marjorie sneered. A bit much for you, I would have thought, darling. Though thick enough, maybe.

He took them anyway and tonight he kept up his assault on *Look Homeward Angel*. As he read and ate he heard the girl snore in the next room.

> And when the bells broke through the drowning winds at night, his demon rushed into his heart, bursting all cords that held him on the earth, promising him isolation and dominance over sea and land, inhabitation of the dark . . .

Sounded fine to him. He read on until he sensed that the fire in the next room needed wood, and when he got up and went in he found it all but out. As he was rekindling it, he heard the girl's voice behind him.

'What? The. The. What the fuck is this?'

He turned and saw her sitting up, breasts exposed, until she realized and opened her mouth in surprise before clawing the quilt around her. She was wild and angry looking.

'Oh.' He straightened up, wiped his hands. 'You're awake.'

'Yes, I am. What the hell is this? What's happening here? What've you been doing?'

'Listen, I—'

'Where's my clothes?' Her nest of crumpled spiky hair made her look feisty and mean. Her face was smeared with mud and the warrior-look it gave her took him aback.

'I'll go get them.'

'What've you done to them?'

'Washed them.'

He went out into the black cold to the wash-house. It was quiet out there and he felt like staying, but he went across to the clothesline in the yard outside and unpegged her clothes. They were still wet.

'You'll have to dry them by the fire,' he said when he went back in.

She looked hard at him. He backed some chairs up to the fire and draped her clothes across them, avoiding till the very last the pair of plain white panties. Then he added a few split lengths of jarrah to the fire and sat in his rocker.

'Something to drink?'

'No.'

With its turned posts and mirrors, the mantel glowed like an altar in the light of the fire.

'Hungry?'

'No.'

'I can't believe that,' he said with a grin.

'I don't give a stuff what you believe.'

Jaccob shrugged. It stung all right. He left the room a moment and came back with a glass of wine for himself.

'How did I get here?'

'You're asking me?' He almost got up and stood over her, but he took a drink and tried to be calm. 'Are you sick? You were delirious as far as I could tell. Found you down there across the road from my place. Lucky you didn't go into the river.'

369

'Ah. No, I'm not sick. I remember.'

She seemed to soften a moment, as though it wasn't a good memory to have. And suddenly it was obvious to him.

'Listen, I don't know what you took, but it can't be much good for you if you've gotta ask where you've been.'

Drugs. He didn't know much about that business. It made him nervous, made him feel old.

'Pass me the clothes, will you?' She was abrupt. With one hand she pointed, with the other she held the quilt to herself.

'Wet, you mean?'

'Listen—'

'OK. Fine. Here.'

The wet jeans fell in a dollop on her head. The blouse and parka landed near by, and the panties fell well short.

'You gonna watch me dress as well?'

Jaccob left the room. He sat in the kitchen and bit a cold potato. Anger was slow in him these days, but he was beginning to simmer. Should have thrown her out the moment she opened her bloody mouth, he thought.

When he went back, she was shivering and lacing her newly polished boots. He put Marty Robbins back on the turntable and set the plough into the furrow. She looked up and wrinkled her nose at the first bars of 'White Sport Coat'.

He suddenly saw it. 'You're pregnant.'

'Bye.' She walked out. She was back in a moment. 'Where's the fucken door?'

Jaccob pointed. She went down the hall and was gone.

Ronnie walked out against that big slab of dark cold. The sky was starless and without a moon. Her feet were dead in the wet boots. She felt as though her bones were constricting in the chill. Her clothes moulded to her flesh. She couldn't even see her own house across the dark. She had no torch. She sensed a quavering, a faintness. She was hungry. Her teeth ached. Of course I'm bloody pregnant, she thought; what did you think it was, you dumb old prick, a pillow?

She thought of the way he'd handled her panties. No, he was safe enough, nothing had happened. Stoned, Ronnie, you were wrecked. You idiot! She started to shake. A hard cold rammed her cheek. The house behind sloped away at an angle and a blade of dewy grass ran across her nose. It took a moment to know she had fallen. Oh, shit, what a mess.

She got herself up and went back into the lighted house.

I left the .243 leaning against the wardrobe and got into bed. Ida's buttocks were cold against me. I knew I wouldn't sleep for a while; every nerve seemed alive and awake tonight. I was surprised to feel Ida turn and move to me. I felt her lips against my throat. She rose from beneath the fug of the blankets and her long breasts fell against me, and, strangely, I thought of our daughters, and their daughters. Women. Strangers. But soon my mind was swept clean of any thought but the grip we had on each other, the configuration we made in the dark, and I knew I was alive and my blood moved in me.

Jaccob watched her eat in silence. His old sweater was too big for her by half, and she felt like trash, scoffing and gulping the way she did. She wiped up congealed gravy with a potato, looked at him no more than a second.

'How old are you?' she asked.

'How pregnant are you?'

Their chins came up in unison.

Ronnie wondered about him. He had a look about him, like he was someone in need of kindness. That defeated air might have attracted her once. He was old and burnt; the sun-wrinkles in his face were like dry creekbeds. His mouth was small and set, and he had a permanent squint. Jeans fifteen years out of date, elastic-sided boots, flannel shirt, the whole thing. He looked like the sort of bloke who delivered your firewood in the city. But she liked the way he seemed perpetually embarrassed. He was always shifting his hands about.

'Sorry I hit you.'

She regarded him with surprise.

'You were going berserk down by the road.'

'How come you live here on your own?'

He smiled patiently and she squirmed. Yeah, he thought she was rubbish all right. She gulped some wine and spluttered. He laughed.

'I'll drive you home.'

She fisted up inside again. To hell with him.

In his small car she could smell him, and it made her think of her father. The smell of wood, linseed oil, some damn thing.

'Why are you driving me? It's only five hundred metres.'

'I'm being polite and neighbourly. It's cold and you're not well. Why, do you wanna get out?'

The headlights showed rising mist as they drove along the

river before heading uphill along her gravel drive. The place looked lonely tonight. In the hard lights of the car, the house was sad and rickety, just too pathetic for words.

'Where's your friend?' he said, pulling in and swinging the car round in the yard.

'S'pose you wanna come in now?'

'Gawd no. Just be careful, all right?'

'What?' She got out and glared at him, saw his face green in the dash lights. 'What do you mean?'

'The baby.'

She clapped the door shut and walked away.

Later that night Ida slept in the crook of my arm as I lay awake and waited for my pulse to ease off. Outside, something coughed. A cow? A starter motor? I felt full of blood, bursting with it as my heart kept at it. Pretty soon something from a long while ago came to me. Blood.

Blood comes hot out of a boy's face. Two brothers carry him across sloping pasture in the twilight, the crash of the shotgun still in their ears. Their pockets are stuffed with apples from the orchard and the crazy old woman is shouting from her place up the hill. She's framed in the doorway of the big white limestone house, waving her fists. The boy moans: can't see . . . can't see. The brothers lift him across the fence, hear the wire ping away in the gloom. Stars are coming out. They get him on to the kitchen table and in the lamplight see the blood in his eyes and the pieces of shot. Their father does not look surprised. He sees the bulges in their pockets. He pulls an apple out of one boy's pants and squeezes juice from the pock-holes. He sits down and looks into the fire. The boy weeps blood. It seems a long time before the father goes out to the truck . . .

History. Yes, that was when history started in on me. The day after the dog was taken, the day Jaccob found Ronnie half-crazed down by the river. If only we hadn't had so many things to hide, so many opportunities for fear to get us. You can keep it all firm and tidy in you for a time, but, Godalmighty, when the continents begin to shift in you, you can't tell tomorrow from yesterday, you run just like that herd of pigs, over the cliff and into the water.

As I stumbled into the light-shafted bathroom, I came upon Ida before the mirror with the make-up box on the basin and her face half painted. She had on her dark woollen suit, her pearls, and a pair of stockings. Her hair had that hard sprayed look I hated. Before I could even open my mouth, I saw her eyes in the mirror and I knew to shut up. She was going to church. She hadn't been to church since Christmas, and only then because Jennifer, the most pious of our daughters, was visiting to diminish the joy of the season.

I knew Ida believed in something – she was a convent girl after all – but church on a Sunday?

'There's a cup of tea on the stove,' she said.

'Can I've a shower?'

'You'll fog up the mirror.'

I slapped her on the arse and got a pained look. I went for my cup of tea.

The morning was cool and bright with the sky blue from one rim to the other. In the yard, the red circular blocks of jarrah I'd sawn yesterday lay steamy in the light. Hens, magpies, insects moved out there.

'You want to come?' Ida said, clacking in on her heels.

I shook my head.

'I'll have the car. What'll you do?'

'Oh, maybe go down the river.'

'Fishing?' She laughed.

'Well, you're going to church.' Somehow I couldn't meet her gaze as she kissed my brow and went out tinkling the car keys.

The Sink is the kind of place that's always failed to deliver. Soldiers came to this wet little valley thinking it might do good by them, all hidden away, but nothing came of their visions. Before the soldiers, before the wars, my father bought our side of the valley and he saw families come and go. In the end there were only three properties, though. Us, the Minchinburys, and the place across the valley where some hopeful always seemed to be setting up for a fall.

I've always lived here. When we married, Ida and me lived with the old man. My brother lived with us too, but he died a year after we married. He didn't have much to live for anyway. We used to string lines out in the yard for him to walk along. He was a strange sight, feeling his way along, him and his black eye-patches. He just died in his sleep one night as though he'd decided enough was enough. The old man stayed around a few years more. He wasn't hard to live with – he hardly even spoke any more. He moved out to the truck shed after Wally died. Then he was sick a long time and he died in the district hospital. I never knew my mother.

By the time the farm had become my own, my second brother was a big success in the wheat-belt, and he wasn't interested in this place. So I stayed. I had no other ideas. Ida was expecting a baby. We'd worked hard here. I didn't think to leave. Now I can't and poor Ida never will.

That Sunday morning I walked down the pastured slopes to the river. Paperbarks dunked their heads into the water all along the bank amid long grass and rooty tangles where insects hummed. I walked along to the bridge where I sat and watched the water roll slowly under. Caused a lot of trouble, that fancy little bridge. Old Doctor Minchinbury built it when I was a boy, and he wanted us to pay half, but we didn't have that sort of money. The rich think everybody's rich. That's their sin, forgetfulness. Oh, how I hated them, the Minchinburys, them and their fancy city talk, the cars and the parties, and the sight of the fruit dropping to rot on the ground up there by that big white house. By the time I was a teenager, there was only the daughter left. She always seemed old and terrifying, but she can't have been more than thirty, maybe forty. She was mad, at least we thought she was. Good God, maybe she had dreams too. I can't even think of it.

Sitting on that bridge, I had the feeling that I'd somehow missed my chance. Thirty years living like a hillbilly in your father's house. I got bitter thinking about it.

It was still only nine in the morning. Jaccob was back in his dream. He twisted and buckled beneath the blankets, and in the dream the cat springs up silent, settles in against the baby, that warm bundle to purr against. The little girl-child shifts. Pastoral scene, pretty moment for calendars. But now look. That little petal mouth against the fur as the cat snuggles closer. Ticklish. She breathes it deep, dark-thick, giggly a moment in slumber, then stifling. The family cat purrs. The only child smothers without even time to wake and cry. To wake and shriek. Wake up! Wake!

Jaccob heard the crash at the door and he came to. He knifed out of bed and stood in his room a moment, naked and hot with panic from the dream. He pulled some jeans on and went down.

He threw the door back and saw it was the girl, his neighbour. She looked sallow and sick. Yes, she was obviously an addict; he wished he'd never come across her. She could do what she bloody well liked. She could rant and bellow and he couldn't care less. He'd have nothing to do with her from this second onwards and he stepped back to close the door, but she seized him by the arm. He felt her fingers in his flesh. It was cool out here. He wrenched his arm away.

'Please?'

'What? Why'nt you just—'

'Listen to me. Everything's dead.'

'Yeah, I know, God is dead and so are Mum and Dad. The answer is blowing in the wind.' He laughed.

Then he saw the blood she'd left on his arms. It was on her hands, on her jeans.

The girl's yard was full of carcasses and they were stiff. White ducks and geese lay in drifts, like the remnants of an alpine thaw. Jaccob wandered amongst them, gingerly feeling their necks, finding some punctured, most broken. Many had open abdomens. Their shit and guts and gore all over. The girl took him behind the shed and showed him the disembowelled goat. It lay buckled and open eyed, as though still being pursued.

'It's eaten the guts out,' she said, but he saw it clearly enough. The animal was tethered.

He touched the wound. It was a fairly clean incision. He'd been expecting a mauling gash.

'There's a hole in its head,' she said. 'Two holes. Awgh. Horrible.'

'Teeth, you think?'

She shrugged.

'Been dead a while, I'd say. You hear anything?'

'No. I was asleep.'

'You're a sound sleeper.'

'I was tired. That's all. Oh, shit, look at this. Everything we had. It's scary. I mean, what would do it?'

It was his turn to shrug.

'I thought cockies knew everything about the bush.'

'Hell, I'm no farmer.' He thought of that silhouette in the orchard.

'It's wild dogs or something. Must be. Oh, God, it's my fault. One day alone and this happens. What do I do?'

'S'pose you ring someone at the shire office.'

'Haven't got a phone.'

Damn her, he'd have to do it himself. She was looking at him; what did she expect, middle-aged resolve?

'Don't s'pose you'll be able to bury this lot by yourself. You got a shovel, I imagine?'

As he dug in the gravelly earth with the sun on his back and the stink of blood and bowels rising from the awful pile with its weaving net of flies, Jaccob tasted red wine from the night before and he felt his faint headache get a hold, mounting with his anger and the exertion and the worm of worry in him. The girl looked on, biting the skin behind her fingernails in a way that made him sick. When he'd finished, an hour later, he threw the shovel down and went to his car without a word. He needed a shower. He saw her with her fists by her sides in the mirror as he swung away.

The shower took the dirt off him, but not the rest. He had to notify somebody, but it was Sunday. No use phoning the shire. In any case, over the phone he'd sound like a fool or a drunk – or both. Maybe he could go in and see somebody.

He made himself drive slowly on his way to town. He had no idea what to do or where to start. He wondered if perhaps he was overreacting. Someone'd lost some stock – it happened. He was just upset about losing privacy, that's all. And that dream; he could have done without that. His empty stomach churned.

Town was a cluster of shops and houses along the highway the Sink road eventually ran into. It was an apple town on the wane, a small, hopeless little place. Jaccob was a stranger here. Nothing was open on a Sunday except the churches, Protestant and Catholic with their smattering of parked cars. In the park beneath the Anzac memorial by the river, some families picnicked. They looked like weekenders passing through. He saw the ugly war statue and its message LEST WE FORGET.

He pulled up outside the Bridge & Beam pub. A fat old woman with silver hair piled back off her face was sweeping the veranda. Half-dressed people straddled windowsills on the second floor to get a bit of sun. Jaccob sat there in his car. He didn't know anyone here, which was how he'd always wanted it, but who could he talk to? He'd met the estate agent a few times, but it was pointless talking to him. What could he say, anyhow? He felt his mind bog down with it all. He felt a little faint. Things shimmered at the edge of his vision. He needed something in his stomach, that's all. He'd taken a hiding from that red wine – and the whiskies on top.

A car passed, covered in a homely patina of gravel dust. Local plates. Normal, regular. Nothing unusual, nothing out of kilter. The interior of Jaccob's car warmed in the sun. He got out for some air.

He stood awkwardly under the gaze of the hotel guests above and wiped the sweat off his face. He set out along the forlorn main street. In the windows of the shops were little notices written on cardboard from old Cornflakes packets. FARM HELP WANTED . . . PRAM FOR SALE – IN GOOD NICK . . . CLEAN METHODIST GIRL NEEDS ROOM AND FACULTIES . . . Faculties, he thought; I could do with faculties. Everything in the shop windows seemed faded and forgotten. Stale insect strips, old Coke and Bushells ads, curling paperbacks (*Love Nest*, *Truckin' Man*), the desiccated bodies of flies and silverfish. Jaccob walked. He couldn't sustain a proper thought. Some kids tore by on bikes. He felt bile at the back of his throat.

Ida Stubbs came upon her neighbour puking in the street. At first she thought he was a drunk from the pub, but when he finished his quick little retch and came up for air, she saw his sun-cured face and she recognized him.

'Are you all right?'

He nodded, looked up, seemed puzzled a moment.

'Oh. Mrs Stubbs.'

'Too early for a hair o' the dog on a Sunday.'

He tried to smile.

She got him back down the street to the milk bar and bought him a drink. She sat him at a Formica table by the window.

'Thanks. But . . . a spearmint milkshake?'

'They're out of strawberry and vanilla. They never have chocolate and the banana's well worth avoiding. Anyway, the milk'll put a lining on your stomach.'

'My mother used to say that.'

Ida smiled, but it stung a little. Coming out of the church with the smell of incense on her, she'd felt younger than she had for years. My mother, indeed.

'I didn't know you were a churchgoer, Mr Jaccob.'

'Oh.' He left off sucking the green milk. 'I'm not.'

Some blood had returned to his face. It wasn't a bad-looking face, really, all beaten and burnt. It made him look older than he was, though he was still young enough to be her son. Sons. She'd missed not having boys.

'I got married in a church,' he said, 'went to a funeral or two. But that's about all the church I've had lately.'

Ida laughed. 'I think you missed my point. That was a polite country way of asking what brings you to the metropolis.' She laughed again.

The man looked embarrassed. This was the most they had spoken since he'd moved here. Outside, kids weaved up and down on grotesquely modified bikes. She knew some of them – the banker's boy and the little pain those new teachers had brought with them. All townies.

'Listen, would you mind if I left this stuff and just had a soda water?'

Ida laughed. 'Course not. Give it here – I'll drink it.'

She got him another drink and watched him sip meekly.

'How do you get hold of someone from the shire council on a Sunday, do you think?' he asked. 'S'pose I should have come across and asked you and your husband before I drove in.'

Ida looked at him. He wasn't just embarrassed, the man was frightened. He looked crook. The council? She became careful.

'On a Sunday? I'd say it was a dead loss.' A lie so soon after confession, but she felt something out of whack here. 'I thought you'd be after a chemist, the way you look. Is it urgent?'

'I don't . . . really know.'

He seemed to be considering something, sizing her up.

'Actually, I don't know what it is at all.'

'Maybe you'd best tell me. After all these years I reckon I must know a thing or two.'

He tried a thin smile and looked into his drink. 'Well, the other night . . . It sounds stupid to a farmer's wife, I imagine . . .'

She shrugged.

'One; the other night I thought I saw something in the orchard. Only a shadow, it was too dark to see, but I sort of felt, knew, sensed that it didn't fit. Like it didn't belong. I had the idea it was long and bigger than, you know, native animals. I just thought I imagined it, you know, man alone, new to the area, city slicker. And then two; last night the couple across the valley, the young people, they lost ten big birds – those Muscovies they've got – and a goat.'

'Well, stock goes astray. Birds especially. You—'

'When I said lost I meant killed, mutilated. Disembowelled, I guess you'd say.'

Ida felt her chest tighten. 'Ah.'

He opened his hands in a gesture of uncertainty.

'I just thought we might be in for a dog problem in the valley. Wild dogs. Maybe the shire could lay baits for us or something.'

Ida got him up out of there before he knew what was happening, and on the street he looked flabbergasted.

'What I suspect,' he said, 'is that we've got trouble on our hands.'

'Keep your voice down, Mr Jaccob!'

A slight breeze lifted dust along the street. In summer this place was like a desert and Ida hated coming in here to buy anything at all. She walked him across to the river to give herself some time to think.

'What about the Agriculture Protection Board? Someone told me once—'

'Look, you don't want those twits out there.'

'I just—'

'You're not a farmer, are you, Mr Jaccob?' She found herself fiddling with the brassy little brooch on her lapel. Maurice had given it to her, the occasion slipped her mind.

'No. I'm not, but I don't see—'

'What you should be able to see is that it's a Sink matter. We'll sort it out ourselves like neighbours should.' Listen to you, Ida, she thought; like neighbours indeed! But she thought of that little dog and the bloody collar on the chain. Something was wrong all right, but Maurice wouldn't want anybody tramping about in uniform on his land. The sight of an officer of any species was enough to get him sweaty. His family was like that. Of course it's rubbed off on me too, she thought; I don't want busybodies poking around my home.

She just needed a moment to think. Her wool suit seemed tight and prickly all of a moment.

I was still sitting on the bridge mooning when Ida came thrash-arsing around the bend, and only the sorry slack flesh that passes for my backside kept me from going into the water. The ute wallopped across the bridge and skidded to the other side of the road. She backed it up with a tearing of gravel. She threw open the passenger door.

'Shit and corruption, woman, what're you doing? You been hearing the wrong gospel, or what?'

'Get in.'

She looked dead serious. I obeyed.

R onnie saw the car pull in and she picked up a scarf and
went out to meet him. As she got in she heard the mournful
country music and she could barely keep from grimacing.

'They said seven,' he murmured, as though to apologize for
being late. 'What's your name, anyway?'

'Ronnie.'

'Jaccob. Murray Jaccob.'

She didn't quite shrug. She felt all splintery and nervous and
her rounding belly felt suddenly obvious and awful. Going up
to the neighbours' place for dinner wasn't her idea, that's for
sure. But anyway, here she was, being dressed, fed, nursed, and
chauffeured by someone she didn't even know, who was taking
her to more old strangers, and it was clear he wasn't getting a
thrill out of it either.

'This whole thing is really weird.'

He didn't reply. She wished her mouth didn't run on ahead
of her so much. Her mouth was never any use to her when she
needed it. As they drove she thought about this old guy, Murray
Jaccob. She still hadn't thanked him for the other night. He had
done her a favour, after all. But, shit, everything was so
miserable right now she wondered if he might have done her a
bigger favour by not finding her down there and letting her
freeze to death. Oh, violins, Ronnie. But things were shitty, you
couldn't pretend otherwise. She felt the pull of the car twisting
up the gravel drive of the Stubbses' place where the house lights

spilled out on to the grass and the silhouette of a man stood in the doorway.

I was washed and dressed and nervous as a heifer. Their lights cut their way toward me. Jaccob's little Toyota turned in and when the engine shut off the only sound was the creeping up of the night. No yapping dog. Just the night. Jaccob got out first. The girl seemed to hesitate.

Inside in the light, I saw that Jaccob wore a sports jacket with a pair of dark trousers and suede shoes. It wasn't a bad outfit, though it made me self-conscious, not having dressed up. The girl had on a pair of jeans that looked as though they were made of PVC. She had a torn windcheater and oil in her hair. My daughters were prissy little misses when they were young, and in a way I hated their smart frocks and sensible shoes, but I guess I had more to be grateful for than I knew.

I brought Jaccob and the girl into the living-room with the fat grey sofa. Ida came in smeared with sauce of some kind, and with cords of hair hanging steamy over her face. She saw Jaccob's clothes and blushed.

'Anyone for a drink?' I asked.

'What do you have?' the girl asked.

'What would you like?' I cranked up a smile.

'Oh, sherry'll do.'

'That'll suit me too,' Jaccob added, and I knew he was lying, but nervous.

'Sherry.' Sherry!

I found some sherry in the cooking cupboard in the kitchen and as I pulled it out, Ida raised her eyebrows at me and I grinned. When I got back I noticed that the space between Jaccob and the girl on the sofa was enough to land a plane on. I wondered how the girl had gotten herself into those jeans. She was obviously pregnant. Where was the boyfriend? I looked at Jaccob. Surely not.

No one said much. We quaffed our sherry. La-de-da.

For dinner Ida served up potato pie, and we all managed to slum long enough to drink beer. I used to brew my own. It tasted good and it hit like a hammer. The girl, who I discovered was called Ronnie, had what people used to call an elfin face – kind of perky and well made. All through the meal I kept thinking about where the bloke was, where her parents came from, what she was doing at the Sink anyway? She didn't look like any farm girl to me. She ate like she was used to some higher life. It caught Ida's attention too, and our eyes met and Ida's brows went up again.

'So how are you finding your place, Mr Jaccob?' she asked, as if she didn't already know.

Jaccob looked caught. 'In general, you mean? It's a beautiful old house.'

'Yes,' Ida replied, as though it really hadn't occurred to her before. 'Yes, it's always been the grand place of the valley.'

'Yeah,' I said. 'It's a nice place to watch the fruit drop.' I could barely keep a grip on myself when I thought of that house – that great white thing. It was like an object that wouldn't let itself be destroyed.

Jaccob laughed uneasily.

I poured more beers. Everyone was drinking quickly out of discomfort.

'When I was a kid,' I said, 'it was full of cats.'

'Cats?' The girl moved her cutlery like she was performing a brain operation.

'Yeah. The woman who lived there was pretty keen on them. She had hundreds of 'em. She lived alone.'

'Funny,' Ida said, 'how lonely people often keep cats when they're such uncompanionable – is that the word – unfriendly sorts of animals. No loyalty. You wonder what comfort that can be.'

'Yeah.' The girl smiled. 'They are their own masters, aren't they?'

'Clean sort of animals, though,' Ida murmured. 'Still, they're not my cup of tea. You see those women on TV with Siamese cats on the backs of their chairs, and you'd swear the cats knew more than they let on. Untrustworthy. Not like a dog.' She seemed to darken in the face a little then and there was a silence. 'Apple pie?'

While Ida was out of the room getting the dessert, the girl said:

'Over at Bakers Bridge there's some weirdos who have this strange thing about cats.'

'Bakers Bridge is nothing but weirdos nowadays,' I said. 'They all come down with their dole money and sit on good farmland and let it go to waste. Bloody vermin.'

'Which weirdos are these?' Jaccob asked the girl. 'I mean which particular brand of weirdo are they?' He laughed. He seemed to be loosening up a little. 'There's orange ones and ones that think the world is gonna blow up just after the flying saucers lift them off. There's even the old hippies, still there going grey in—'

'These are serious types,' Ronnie said.

'They're serious about cats,' I said, trying to catch Jaccob's eye for a laugh. 'What do they do, turn 'em into handbags?'

She smiled a little.

'Close. They kill 'em. For blood. Sacrifices, you know. They're sort of witches.'

I laughed, but no one else seemed to think it was funny.

'Sick bastards,' I said.

Ida came in with the pie.

We ate and didn't talk much until the girl launched into it.

'Well, let's get to the point then.'

There was an awkward pause.

'Yes,' said Ida, 'why not.'

'Well?'

I ate my apple pie. Jaccob put his spoon down.

'I hear you lost some stock,' I said to the girl.

'Two geese, eight Muscovy ducks, and a goat.'

I kept on eating my apple pie. The log fire had begun to burn down a little.

'They had their guts torn out,' said Jaccob, 'even the goat.'

'You buried them?'

'Yeah,' she said.

'Pity. Would have been useful to have a look.'

'And leave fresh meat lying about when something's lurking around out there?' She looked at me with proper contempt. 'You must be kidding.'

'Was its throat cut?'

'No,' Jaccob said. 'Two holes in the head.'

'Bullet holes?'

'Looked like teeth marks to me.' He shrugged. It annoyed me, him doing that.

'What do you think it was?'

'A big dog? A few of them?' Again, he shrugged.

'Any tracks?'

He looked at the girl. She looked disgusted.

'We didn't think to look,' she said.

'If it'd been a dog,' I said, wiping cream from my lips, 'the birds would have been mauled and there'd be feathers every-where. The whole place would be covered in 'em. There'd be tracks and scuffs all over. You,' I said to the girl, 'couldn't have slept through it if you were dead. If it was dogs.'

The girl looked me straight in the eye. 'There was barely a feather out of place. Their necks were broken, some with punctures. I didn't hear a thing.'

Jaccob looked grey.

'Well,' I murmured.

'Maurice.' Ida's tone was disciplinary. I knew it was my time to speak.

'We had some trouble too. The other night.' I poured myself some beer. 'We had a dog torn off its chain. A small dog. There wasn't anything left except the head in the collar.'

'Fuck,' said the girl, and Ida flinched.

'There wasn't a sound. Except for the dog screaming.'

As I looked around the table, I knew something had begun to roll forward – I didn't know what – and it was big and quiet and definitely to be worried about.

'I got a print in a cast. I looked all morning for some trace.' I pulled it out of the sideboard drawer behind me and put it, sweet and honey-smelling, on the table before them. They both held it like it was made of glass. 'What we're looking at here is not dogs. Funny we should be talking about cats earlier on, because that's what we've got on our hands.'

'Maurice?'

'A what?'

'Some kind of cat.'

'That's ridiculous!' the girl yelled.

'What would you know?' I yelled. 'How long've you lived here?'

She drank off her glass of beer and glowered, mouth puckering as though she tasted something foul.

Ida got up and came back with more bottles of beer.

'Let's keep this civil, shall we?' she said. 'All neighbours here. What kind of cat, Maurice?'

'Something wild or outsized or maybe foreign. My guess is it's a feral breed of house cat.'

'Oh, bullshit,' the girl said. 'A house cat turned wild is still a house cat. This thing killed a goat, for God's sake. How could a house cat do that?'

'I'm not talking about a cat that used to belong to Mrs Bloggs that's decided to go walkabout and decides he likes the wild outdoor life. This is a cat whose ancestors were house cats maybe two hundred years ago. They grow bigger than you think, bigger than we know.'

Jacob seemed to stir at this. 'I had a friend once who had a skin, a pelt from a bush cat that covered the bonnet of his Datsun.'

I whistled. 'You ever see it?'

He shook his head. 'People exaggerate, I s'pose.'

'Now if that goat was killed by teeth in the skull, and we have to take this young lady's word for it—'

'Then the teeth'd have to be an inch long or more,' she said. 'Ever seen a cat like that?'

I shook my head. 'Not yet.'

'We're talking about tabby cats!'

'Any schoolkid knows that our house cats come originally from wild stocks from India and Europe. In the beginning, this is.'

'But that's ancient history.'

'There's no kind of native animal on this continent that can do anything like what we're talking about here. It has to be something foreign, something introduced.'

'Oh, but that leaves dogs, pigs, foxes—'

'You know damn well that this isn't a dog or a bloody pig. Look at this pawprint. That's a cat. A big cat. Two hundred years of breeding in the bush from strays. The big ones, the fast ones, the mean ones survive. The quiet ones. They slowly get bigger, faster, meaner, quieter. You know, it's what they teach at school these days. You know how many litters a cat has a year. Hell, the way we walk through the bush, the big ones'd be well warned, that's why we don't see 'em. God knows how big they get; they're lords of the bush.'

I fell back breathless. The whole thing seemed more plausible every word I said.

'Well, whatever it is,' the girl sighed, 'we should tell the authorities.'

'It won't help, and there's no point. We've got it out into the open amongst ourselves. We've had our losses and that's the end of it. Just to satisfy ourselves, Mr Jaccob and I will go out and take a look around tomorrow night. Agreed?'

Jaccob stared at me a moment, then nodded.

'Right then.'

'Is that all?' the girl demanded. 'Is that all you're going to do?'

I got up, barking the chair back on the boards.

'I'm going out for a bit.'

And I left them all there at the table, around the stand of brown bottles, and I went out hoisting my coat on. The fire was out. They all looked grim as mourners.

On a winter's night down this way, the cold darkness is like two black sheets of glass pressing you breathless. My throat burned. Stars peppered the sky. I hugged myself, not knowing where to go. I walked up the hill a little way, got to the first wire fence and heard it bulleting down the line in the dark as I pushed down the top strand. For a few moments I stood listening to that eerie sound in the dark and I was overcome by how vulnerable I was, here out in the night alone. And the sound of that wire fence took me a long way back in the past. Did they remember? The cats? Was that what this business was all about?

I stumbled back down the slope. Or was I just a bit pissed and ratty with nerves?

In the tractor shed I smelt the good regular smells of diesel and hessian. Rodents tinkered in the dark behind piles of junk. That business about the mob over at Bakers Bridge was a bit of a shock. Witches. I thought we didn't have that stuff any more. That girl . . . no she didn't look the type. But what is the type? What do they look like? I started to shiver.

Before long, the voices of Ida and Jaccob could be heard from the front of the house, and a few moments after, the car started. I saw a stray beam of light as they turned around. I could hear the little Jap motor winding across the valley and then come back our way and climb a little to stop at Jaccob's place.

Quiet. Cold. I heard the faint clunk of dishes from the house. I went back in, forcing myself not to trot like a child frightened of the dark.

*

With the father gone for the doctor in the truck, the two brothers leave the whimpering boy on the kitchen table, go out to the tractor shed, and take a can of petrol across the paddock to the fence. They wait in the orchard beside their neighbour's house. In the light of the windows, they see the cats poised on the sills, gently brushing aside the filmy curtains which used to be so white and grand billowing there on hot afternoons. In time, a black tom comes out to look at them. It pads across fallen leaves and fruit and it rubs itself greedily, arrogantly against their knees, then purrs in their arms. One boy takes off his shirt and pours petrol on it. His brother holds the cat while he strokes its back with the wet shirt. The cat squirms a little, begins to spit and scratch as they tie the petrol-soaked shirt to its tail. The match flares. The cat shrieks and then explodes.

When they pulled up outside Ronnie's house, she didn't get out. She hadn't left any lights on. The place was lonely looking. She felt jittery and weak with anger.

'Good grief, what an evening.'

Jaccob nodded in the green light of the dash. He looked preoccupied. For a moment she wondered what that shithead man of hers was doing tonight – probably playing in some hopeless joint with some hopeless bunch of characters who remembered him from the old days when everybody just had to recognize him. Probably be some hopeless-looking woman sitting beside the sound desk trying to look unmistakably connected to him and the band – oh, she knew all about that.

The engine was still running, Jaccob was waiting.

'Listen,' she murmured, 'I can't face this place tonight. I'm, you know, a bit spooked being on my own after all this business.'

He said nothing.

'Well, could I . . . stay at your place?'

Jaccob shrugged and turned the car around.

Ronnie woke at three in the morning and went down the cold wooden stairs to find Jaccob rocking in the dimness by the long glass doors through which she could see only the darkness of the valley. He turned a lamp on. He had a glass in his hand. She didn't know how to read the look on his face.

'You OK?'

He just rocked.

'I felt a bit strange then,' she said. 'I don't know. As though I was about to have a nightmare, as though I was about to slip into it. But I stopped myself. I woke up.'

'Lucky you.'

'What d'you mean?'

'Nothing. It's nice to be able to back out of a nightmare.'

She pulled the blanket tight around herself.

'That stuff about those people over at Bakers Bridge,' he murmured. 'Were you serious?'

'Yeah.'

'How do you know about them?'

'Oh. I met them once. It's only fifteen or twenty miles.'

'Did you see it happen? That stuff about the cats.'

'Cats! You don't think I'm one of them, do you?'

'What, a cat or a witch?'

'A friend saw it. She was kind of interested.'

'You don't think maybe they've got something to do with this, do you? I mean,' he tried to laugh a little, 'the goat and everything. All those birds with their bellies open.'

'You don't know much about it, do you?'

Jaccob smiled. 'I don't even know if it exists.'

'Black magic? Of course.'

'Black cats and everything, eh?'

393

She sank back against the sofa. 'Oh, cats again. Listen, what do you think is killing the animals?'

'Stubbs may be right, it could be a feral cat, or more than one. Jesus, for all I know it might be the Tasmanian tiger.'

She didn't laugh. 'Yeah, people talk about that still, don't they?'

'I s'pose it doesn't sound so stupid really, a marsupial cat, or is it a dog?'

Ronnie looked at him. He wasn't a happy man.

'I don't know you at all,' she said.

'Neither you should. We're strangers.'

He got up and went to bed and Ronnie sat there in that dim room with its mismatched furniture and bare walls.

I sat up in the dark, shivering with cold and memory.

Running, one boy sees over his shoulder the ball of light cometing around the yard, the cat afire and screaming like an evil spirit, cutting back across its own path.

The morning was cool and overcast and Ronnie spent the day with Jaccob. They helped each other in a stiff, self-conscious way with the chores, first at his place and then at hers, where the cow had to be disentangled from the fence it had demolished in mad pain from an engorged udder.

In the shed where she milked there was a big bench stacked with picture frames she'd half stripped of their ugly red varnish. Jaccob, who was watching her with a look that she took to be amusement, picked up a frame and ran his hand over it.

'Oak.'

Ronnie peered along the length of the cow.

'Found them in an old shop in Balingup. Promised myself I'd do them up one day.'

Hiss of milk. Far away, the petulant song of a crow. Ronnie put her cheek against the warm side of the animal and she began to hum as a strange sadness came upon her. She kind of liked this bloke. He was awkward but not stupid. She was the one who felt stupid.

The headache got bad so Ida put herself back to bed. It was the kind of headache she used to have at school, the night before a spelling test. The pain would be like a hand clamping down on her skull and she could almost feel fingers creeping in under her scalp going hot and cold in waves that made her too frightened to move her eyes. She was no squib when it came to pain. Oh, the kinds of pain she'd lived with. Years of periods (now mercifully gone), and childbirth (let no one tell you it didn't hurt), secret pains she kept until the last minute like the cartilage in her knee she hobbled around on, keeping the house running and the children and Maurice in their routine until the day she couldn't even walk to the toilet. Ah, those were just everyday pains; but the headaches, she hated the headaches. She pulled the blankets up to her chin and wedged her head between the pillows to keep it still. She lay with her eyes closed and the hot colours burst before her.

Now and then during the day the pain would slacken and she would have some respite for a while. She didn't get up for fear of bringing back the pain before schedule, so she had time to think, and what she thought about was Ronnie. She liked the girl in a way. Of course she was rude and disrespectful, but she was so alive and energetic, at least for a girl who looked so pale and badly fed. Reminded her of her younger days. She'd been cocky herself once, but girls in her day could barely even think the things that Ronnie was saying last night. Was she deserted? Did she have money? She was small; she'd take a hiding getting a baby out. She wondered what the dickens a girl with all the advantages was doing here. It seemed so wasteful that it made Ida angry and she felt the fingers tighten on her skull and then the colours cracking like fireworks.

Through the fizzing and spurting, a memory came to her. It just arrived, blurring and ghosting but now and then coming clear despite the pressure.

Rain hits the windscreen of the truck. A woman – that familiar young woman – drives with her eyes slitted in concentration. Two small girls sleep on the seat beside her, mouths black with liquorice. Windscreen wipers labour against the torrent. The road is pelted with leaves and twigs, furred with the impact of water. As she rounds a bend near a rail-crossing, she sees an overturned semi and its garishly painted trailer jack-knifed at the side of the road. Behind a spear of light, the vision fades a moment and she sees only the heat of pain, but quickly it's back again and she sees the zoo-like bars on the trailer, some twisted wide apart. Great sods have been turned up in the accident. Someone is backing a tractor up to the overturned truck, and another man is hauling up a chain. The woman pulls in beside him and winds the window down. Rain spatters in on the children.

'Everything all right?'

The tractor driver looks over. He seems sick. A man in overalls comes across, steps up to the window.

'No problem, lady.' He has a beard and an American accent. DENVER BROS CIRCUS is embroidered over the pocket of his overalls. She can almost feel his gaze, as though he sees she's only a farm wife from some lost valley. She brushes the skirt across her knees. 'Nothin's happened. Drive on.'

'But is anyone hurt?'

'No one's hurt. Look, this never even happened.'

She gives him her coldest look. The girls begin to stir. She winds the window up in his face and drives on . . . Lord, she'd forgotten all about . . . the reds and flamebreaks shot in from every corner. Ida lay dead still.

Jaccob stood by while Ronnie skimmed the cream from the turning milk. Bulbs of sweat hung on her brow. The afternoon sun rested on the windowsill and dust motes twisted about. It had been a long day with their curiosity and their caution; nevertheless it had been a good day's work for a retired man and a girl who looked as though a day's work'd kill her. It stopped him thinking about things. She seemed like maybe she was a decent sort after all, this girl, just frightened, that was all. He started to wonder how she was going to get on alone.

'What does your . . . boyfriend do?' The sun was warm on his back.

'Oh, he plays guitar. Used to be in the Clever Young Boys in Black.' She said the name with an upward intonation as though she expected him to be familiar with it.

'When's he coming back, you reckon?'

She shrugged. It was an obvious effort to be nonchalant. You had to admire her guts.

'It's tough luck about your birds. I like Muscovies.'

She smiled.

The sun began to die on its soft bed of trees. At the bottom of the valley the river went coppery and the swamp glittered. Smoke rose perpendicular from the Stubbses' chimney over on the west side. Sun caught their windows as in a mirror. The wind was already dead.

If you need a lift to the hospital any time, just let me know. I mean if your boyfriend isn't around.'

'Don't worry, you'll hear me screaming. Thanks. Anyway, he'll be around.'

He looked at her through the veil of steam.

'So. Tomorrow night you have to go a-hunting?'

He nodded.

'Men!'

He shrugged.

'Do you know anything about shooting?'

'No. Not really. I shot rabbits when I was a kid.'

'Why the hell are you going, then?'

'I don't know. Stubbs seems to think it's important. And,' he laughed, 'I didn't want him to despise me.'

'Boy. I don't understand men.'

You said it, love, he thought.

Jaccob and the girl came after dinner when it was dark and the paddocks were moony and still. He brought his .22 but he had no ammunition for it, so I went to the bedroom for a couple of boxes and left him with the women who chatted quietly. In the bedroom I found some bullets, pocketed them, and looked out the window, but all I could see was my own face, eyes narrowed like shutters. When I returned to the kitchen Ida was laughing with the girl over some joke I'd come in too late for and Jaccob was standing by the stove with a blank cast on his face. I put the box of longs in his hand and he looked at the women.

'No prizes for guessing who'll be enjoying tonight's proceedings.' He tried to smile. He was worried.

'Come on.'

He followed me out to the ute. The women didn't even say goodbye, and I felt like a fool for feeling miffed about it.

The air was hard and metallic.

'You should have worn some warmer clothes,' I said. I gave him the .243. 'I'll drive. You hold this.'

Jaccob juggled the two rifles a moment and settled them across his lap.

I drove slowly down towards the girl's place with the window open. The moon lit some patches of pasture well, but it also made the sort of shadows that cause you to wonder. A rabbit stared up into the headlights. I smelt the swamp and the night-wet stands of grass as I took us down by the river and slowly up the gravel drive to Ronnie's place.

In the yard beside that shoddy little joint, I got out and rigged up the spotlight on the roof of the cab.

'You know what to do?' I asked.

He got out.

'You just stand up here and move the light slowly. Sort of search the paddock, you know. If you see anything, just knock quietly on the roof and I'll stop.'

'Yeah. I did it when I was a kid.'

'Can you shoot?'

'I s'pose you mean can I hit anything.'

'It can be helpful.' I switched the light on. The motor idled.

Jaccob shrugged in the reflected light.

'Well, I'll shoot from the cab.'

I got down and he jumped up on to the tray. From inside the cab I could hear his elbows on the roof. I put the ute in gear. Jesus, I thought; here we are looking for something we don't know anything about. I knew something was out there, something that didn't belong, and I wanted to kill it and nail its pelt to a tree so all the hidden eyes could see it. I wanted things to feel right again.

We jolted up the rocky pastured slopes. The beam of the spotlight reached out like an arm to make a hot white oval that moved from stump to fence to rock, to climb the trunks of trees and send shadows spilling across the ground. It was cold. We ground along soft firebreaks and lit up meadows of spiders' eyes, and the sound of the motor in low gear grew stranger as the night went on. Out in the dark there was no definition, no assurance, nothing familiar, no sign, beyond that floating oval disk, that we hadn't stumbled off the edge of the world entirely. I couldn't be sure the world was anything but that oval disk. My eyes followed it. I drove automatically and the ute thumped and rattled tools as the wheel bucked in my hands.

Now and then a roo floated by like a ghost, or a fox hid arrogant behind the blaze of its eyes as it retreated deeper into the bush. The night was eyes, and I wondered if I'd recognize the right eyes when I saw them.

We lurched and jerked and tossed on the hard and slew and swayed in the soft. We lay weals upon the night, the way we always do in this country, making enough noise you'd think we were warning every secret and fearful thing to beware and flee.

As we came to the top of the property where a hoard of boulders rose from the side of the hill, each stone a sleeping beast in the light, there was a sudden thump on the roof from Jaccob and I flinched and stomped on the brake, ready to see some white shadow turning its flank to me, when all I saw was Jaccob as he rolled down over the windscreen to land with a crump on the hood. The motor idled. I stared. Jaccob lay before me with the light tilted full in his face, and I began to laugh.

'What the fuck?'

Laughter had a good hold of me and I put my head on the wheel, jerking silently, until my leg gave out on the clutch and the motor stalled and Jaccob was rolled off the hood and I could hear myself half choking in the still of night.

Jaccob got in beside me, rubbing his elbow.

'I wanted a break, not a fracture.'

I got a hold on myself, sighed, and sat back.

'It's bloody cold out there,' he said.

He mashed his fists to get some blood into them.

'What the hell are we looking for, anyway?'

'Eyes,' I said. 'You know what cats' eyes look like?'

'I know what a cat's eyes look like.'

'Well, that's what we're looking for.'

'Cats don't kill dogs and goats.' He said it out of anger. It was clear he wasn't so sure.

'You don't know anything about cats.'

Jaccob's teeth showed in his shadowy face. 'Oh, I know enough, old man.' It seemed to cost him something to not go wild. I realized I didn't know a damn thing about him.

'I'll spell you on the light,' I said.

Ida looked at Ronnie and Ronnie looked back. In the end they smiled again. They were enjoying themselves. They turned glasses in their hands.

'We're very different,' Ida said. 'I know what you're thinking.'

Ronnie grinned and put on an expression of mock outrage. 'I wasn't thinking that at all. I was wondering how you kept your age so well. Geez, you've done all right.'

'You don't even know how old I am,' Ida said with laugh. 'Why is it that women flatter each other and men ignore us?

Well, I'm sure they wouldn't mean it, either. Anyway, you're a fibber. You were thinking how different we are.'

Ronnie took a drink.

'S'pose you're right.'

'I'm from the farm and you're from the city. We may's well be from different planets.'

'You really reckon?'

Ida got up and went to the window, though all she could see was herself reflected. It was warm inside. This was her place, this was what she knew, and it wasn't so bad.

'You think we're getting a bit tipsy?'

Ronnie drained her glass. 'I'd say there'd be some truth in that.'

'Well, I'll tell you a joke and it'll explain the way we're different. Oh, maybe it's more about Maurice than me. You eat pork?'

'Yeah, I shouldn't, I guess.'

'Oh, fiddlesticks, of course you should. See?'

'No.'

'Good. That settles that then.'

'We *are* getting a bit wrecked here.'

'Wrecked. Now that's a young person's word. See, you're young and I'm old.'

'But you're not!'

'I am too, but that doesn't mean I'm not stronger than you. I could box your ears, girl.'

'Tell me the joke.'

'*Then* I'll box your ears.'

'Oops, sorry about the carpet.'

'Here, one for me, too.'

'Now the joke.'

'Oh yeah, the joke.'

Ida got herself back into the sofa and hyperventilated a little while Ronnie snorted into her glass. Their shoes were off and their eyes narrowed from resisting laughter.

'Right, the joke. Now there's this bloke, see, and he's driving along a country road and he goes past a piggery and sees all the normal signs of piggeries – which probably means he was looking with his nose – and then he sees this big porker leaning up against the fence with a cigarette in his mouth, looking kind of handsome and thoughtful, and *then* as the driver slows down, he has to take a second look, because, lo and behold, not only is the pig dragging on a Marlb'ro, but he's got a bloody wooden leg. Excuse me. Anyway, anyway, a wooden leg. This pig's got a wooden leg.

'Well, the passer-by, he's pretty amazed by all this, so he stops the car and goes up to the farmhouse and gets hold of the farmer and says does he realize that there's a pig in his yard with, with, with a prosthetic piece—'

Ida took a drink and disciplined herself a moment before going on. To Ronnie, it was a wonderful dream.

'Anyway, the farmer says, "Yairs, yairs, that's a beautiful pig that, a most flamin' amazin' pig. A pig like ya never met before. I could tell a few stories about that pig down there. That pig is my greatest companion, my loyal friend, and I owe that pig more than a man can repay."

'The visitor's fairly dumbfounded and he asks him, you know, to elaborate.

'"Oh," says the farmer, "one time my kids were asleep in the house and the wife was away shopping and I was down at the boundary putting in a few strainers and the house starts burnin' down. Course, I knew nothin' about it, but the pig was knockin' off the rosebushes in the front garden and he sniffs out a fire and quick as a wink he tears inside, drags the kids out of bed, gives them mouth-to-mouth on the front lawn and then gets the garden hose and singlehandedly puts out the fire before I've even woken up to the problem. I owe that pig my children, the fruit of me loyens.

'"But that's only one story. There's a dozen others. That pig carried me home one day from the back paddock when I broke me leg. Just carried me back and put me down beside the phone. That pig helped me shear five hundred head o' sheep last year. That pig worked me out of debt. That pig sorted out marriage troubles 'tween me an' the wife. It opens the car door for her when she gets home from town. That's a sensitive pig; clever, compassionate – geez, it's damn near human!"

'The passer-by is really touched by this, you see. And he comes back to the pig's wooden leg. "I s'pose," he says, "the wooden leg is a souvenir from one of those adventures then, sort of a wound in the battle of friendship?"

' "Oh, no," says the farmer, "nothing like that."

' "Oh," says the passer-by, "then how do you explain the wooden leg?"

' "Well," says the farmer, "a pig like that, it'd be a shame to eat it all at once." '

Ronnie sat a moment and felt herself fill with sick, shocked laughter. And then Ida exploded into shrieks and giggles and they both fell to the floor, writhing.

'That's it,' Ida said, with her head under the coffee table, 'that's the difference between us and you. We're farmers.'

'You ever been resuscitated by a pig?'

'Only by the smell of one, dear.'

'We can't be that different,' Ronnie said, still lying on the floral carpet.

'Well, maybe not that much for us. We're girls.'

'Are you scared?'

'Right now? No. See, I've remembered this other joke.'

'No, no,' Ronnie pleaded, 'I'll die laughing.'

'Well, then you'll owe me a favour, dear. Can we drink lying down, you think?'

Up on the back with the cold handle of the lamp in my fingers and the wind in my eyes and cutting through my clothes, the night and the darkness seemed closer and I felt less protected by the car. I braced against the back window of the cab and rested on the roof, pushing the light back and forth, sighting along the beam until I felt like I was in it, that it was my eye, that the light was me.

Stumps, fallen trunks with upsearching grey arms, the broken teeth of Jaccob's fences, the dam with its startled covey of wild duck, the fruit trees like a stood-down regiment of old soldiers – everything melted in and out of vision in a dreamy, dislocated way where things were created out of darkness, yielded themselves up to the oval disk, and ceased to be a moment later. I found myself sinking into a matrix of tiny lights, fine black holes, and there was no telling space from matter.

A blur settled into view. Big white blur. It brought stillness – there was no vibration.

Jaccob shook my leg. He stood on the ground and was tugging on my trouser leg.

'What's up? What's the matter with you?'

He snorted.

'Don't tell me you were asleep.'

I looked down at him and then up at his house.

'C'mon,' he said, 'let's get some coffee.'

'I drink tea.'

I ran an icy hand over my face.

'Think you better try coffee.'

The spotlight made an eye out of one of the house windows. I switched it off. As I got down I felt the blood move in my legs; my knees felt like someone had knocked two-inch nails through them.

I stood there looking at the old Minchinbury house, and though it might've been the cold, I knew I'd never quaked like I was quaking now. There it was, the place I hated with its bull-nosed veranda and long scroll-silled timber windows, the lime-stone blocks rendered and painted white at the front. Even rebuilt, it was the same thing I remembered. A big, beautiful, pointless, idle place. Walking up those timber steps, I made myself breathe and I did not obey the messages my legs sent me; I did not fall down.

I'd never been inside before. It was a mess. That comforted me, in a way. Furniture was haphazard and covered in dirty crockery and clothes. Smudged glasses and an overflow of ash stood on the hearth. So this was how the rich lived.

In the kitchen Jaccob put the kettle on a gas ring and looked fidgety.

'Got the feeling we're not going to find anything, you know.'

He was right, I knew, but I said nothing.

'Whatever we're looking for won't be stupid enough to blunder into our light. If it's not been seen before, it won't show itself now, tonight. How do you think it got so big?'

I felt myself getting angry. He was right, but this thing was meant for me, and I was going to get it myself, I knew it.

'Why don't we get a professional hunter down here,' he said. 'We don't know what we're doing.'

'I know what I'm doing.'

Jaccob was silent a moment. The kettle growled.

'We don't even know what it is,' he said.

'I've told you what it is.'

Jaccob shook his head. He was smiling as though I was a crazy bastard, and my skin prickled hot and I felt my mouth run away from me.

'And another thing. Take some advice from an old man. Don't get involved in that girl. There's no use in it. She's a loser.'

He had me against the kitchen wall before I could draw breath. Where he grabbed my jacket I felt his knuckles against my ribs.

'I reckon you should mind your business,' he said through his teeth.

'We're neighbours,' I said, fighting for air.

He let go of me and stood back.

'Jesus Christ, now I can see how feuds get going down this way.' He looked a little shaken himself.

'No,' I murmured. 'You don't know the first thing about it.' I went cold as well, saying that. My heart was hard with fright.

'Veteran feuder, are you, Stubbs?'

I could still see poor Wally on the table, tearing at his pulpy eyes, and the cat squealing off in flames. I'd started it all, this whole nightmare.

He looked straight at me where I was, still against the wall, and very slowly he broke into a thin smile.

'Reckon I'm not the warrior type, son,' I said.

He took the kettle off the gas ring after a moment and made coffee. With that bloodless grin on his face, he gave me a mug, and I realized that I liked him. Not because he could be tough and push an old man around, but because suddenly it was clear that he had things twisting darkly in him too. It wasn't what was out there that frightened him most, it was something more secret. He didn't look right in this house, as though he hadn't gotten it beat into place yet. I thought maybe, if one day we could swap stories, he might understand mine and me his. I was right, but a lot happened before I was to find out.

We went out again in the ute and saw nothing. After his place we gave up. When we pulled up outside my house, every light was burning and Slim Dusty played flat-out on the radio, pouring into the yard.

The women were in the kitchen, pissed as sticks.

I started shouting.

Jaccob picked up the girl like she was a kid and took her out.

I heard his car start, even over my own bellowing.

Ida sat with her eyes closed to me. I felt utterly without hope.

'What the bloody hell do you think you're—'

My voice gave out. I didn't have the strength or the words

to keep yelling. I followed Ida to the lounge-room. I looked at her. I held my fists like they were animals.

She rolled on to the sofa, lit a cigarette, which I hadn't seen her do for fifteen years, and said:

'Go to hell, Maurice.'

The night is full of stories. They float up like miasmas, as though the dead leave their dreams in the earth where you bury them, only to have them rise to meet you in sleep. Mostly the scenes are familiar, but sometimes everything is strange, the people unknown.

A boy sits in his father's lap out on the back veranda as the sun makes its way down among the trees. He smells tobacco and neatsfoot oil on his father and he listens to the creak in his chest. The carcass on the fence is stiff now. The boy strains, listening for the sound of a horse. The man from the paper is coming. Inside his mother is singing. She thinks they are going to be rich. But the sun rests in the jarrahs and no one comes.

This is not my memory. It comes to me now and then and I see it clear and sharp as though I am there, but it's before my time, things don't look right. These people ride horses. Their clothes aren't familiar, and yet when I dream it everything feels in its proper place, and sometimes I think this is one of my father's memories. I have no way of telling. It's terrifying to think you can remember things you shouldn't possibly be able to. It's like that childhood fear of having your soul slip from your body in your sleep. The darkness, those black sheets of glass sliding over you, upping the pressure, pushing you through the glacier of time and space and story.

After Jaccob went up to bed, Ronnie went out on to the veranda. It was cold and she hoped it would clear her head, but it just made her teeth ache. She stood at the rail and looked out into the darkness. They weren't kidding themselves — something was out there. She wished the memory of those people from Bakers Bridge hadn't come to mind, but it was all that talk about cats. She knew there was no point in telling Jaccob or the others what she'd really seen that night over at Bakers Bridge; they'd think she was one of the weirdos, they'd think she was sick and depraved for even being there, and sometimes she wondered if it wasn't true. But she hadn't known about it. It was all such a lark to Nick — that bastard. She liked old Mrs Stubbs, and she didn't want to frighten her off. The old girl had guts and she was pretty smart in her own way. Geez, hadn't they hit the piss tonight. Ronnie'd talked like a maniac and Ida was spilling secrets all over the place, about the days when her and Stubbs used to screw in a hollow log down in the paddock so his old man wouldn't hear them, about how they used to steal honey from the wild bees at the edge of the forest, and the days they used to row downriver out of the valley and haul an unsuspecting sheep off the bank at some distant neighbour's place and row it back up here laughing like larrikin kids, so they could butcher it and barbecue it for themselves. They went through all the beer in the house — even that vile homebrew — and then they'd knocked off the sherry. It was sad that Ida had never had the son she wanted. The daughters sounded awful. Ida showed her photos of them: greying, sensible mothers in running shoes and corduroys and styleless haircuts. They looked like they ran church youth groups; their smiles hadn't the least trace of fun in them. They looked like slaves to common sense and she felt sorry they were all Ida had.

Ronnie wished she'd known about Ida a long time ago. She couldn't help thinking she wouldn't be in such a bloody mess if they'd been able to talk last year when she first moved in. She looked out into the bitter cold night.

She wondered if you could be held responsible for something you saw but didn't take part in. Why had Nick taken her to that place? God, she hadn't even thought about it for six months and now she couldn't get it out of her mind.

Ronnie swayed in the dark.

Out there, something moved. She heard it step across leaf litter. The trees beside the shed; it had to be there. She looked around for something stout. Beside the back door was a furled umbrella, one of those yellow ones people give out at agricultural shows. She focused on it well for a moment, but it tended to reproduce itself a little. Ronnie, she thought, you're pisseder than you think. But bugger it. Some prick was out there scaring people and she was going out to give him a spanking.

As she felt her way down the steps in the reeling night she was barely able to suppress a giggle. Common sense and sensible shoes, that's what you need, Ronnie Melwater.

Ida felt the bed churning through space. She held the edge of the mattress and kept her eyes closed. The headache was coming back and she knew it'd be worse by morning, compounded by the worst hangover a body could anticipate, but all she could concentrate on now was the way the bed, the room, the house spun crazy through the dark. With her lids squeezed shut until moons burst into view behind her eyes, Ida Stubbs prayed that this spinning would take her away, out of this place for ever.

The thump was clear enough to wake him in a moment. Jaccob lay still and listened. There was another sound, a muffled rattle from out in the yard. He pulled on some jeans and went to the window. He could see nothing. The moon was cloud smothered. Opening the wardrobe he pulled out the .22. He turned no lights on as he went downstairs, and he slipped a bullet into the breach. The metal was cold against his hands.

At the back door he paused a moment to even out his breathing. As he pulled it open, he felt the jarring cold and slid the barrel out before him. Straightaway he heard the sound. It was a kind of hissing-scraping noise, quiet but distinct. Jaccob was suddenly full of breath again and for a few seconds he couldn't move. When he could make himself work, he cocked the gun and stepped out.

Hiss. Scrape. There it was.

Hiss. Scrape.

And panting. There was the faintest hint of something panting and it made his skin rise.

Jaccob eased himself on to the side veranda, and it took him some time to be able to distinguish the orchards and paddocks, the shadowy lines of fences and sheds in the dark. He heard the river and the swamp. He heard the blood in him. He heard the tiny click of the screen door as he let it come to.

He saw something light, but he'd barely registered it. He stepped out to the veranda rail. The wood was rough with cold.

Hiss. Scrape.

He looked down along the limestone foundations where the grass grew long against the house, and saw that light-coloured blob reeling across in an arc with the panting close now, and he brought the rifle to bear as it came.

He fired. The umbrella shook. The dull crack sounded up

411

and down the valley and Ronnie cried out like a wounded rabbit.

He lowered the rifle as a poisonous rush of fear billowed up in him.

Ronnie continued her shuffling dance with the yellow umbrella until she came to the wooden steps.

'There's nothing out there.'

Jaccob made a weak little noise and went inside.

I stumbled in the dark to the window. There were no lights on up at Jaccob's. It was his .22, I guessed. That typical flat smack they made. Ida snored mercilessly. I waited. A light came on. I shivered in my pyjamas. The light up there went out. I figured a kill or a disaster would cause more ruckus than that, so I went back to bed and spent the rest of the night failing to sleep.

'Let the dead bury their dead,' Ida mumbled some time before dawn.

I shoved her in the ribs.

'You won't be soundin' so bloody smug in the morning, my love.'

'And milk,' she said.

You can't argue with a sleeping drunk.

This is Ronnie's dream, though it might as well be mine nowadays, I have it so often. It's quite short, and like the others, always the same.

There is firelight. There are voices raised. They are hammering in the nails and the tree is soft and the cat is mad with pain as they dance. Blood is like tar in the flickering light and suddenly the cat tears itself down and comes at Ronnie, pawing her belly until her shirt is open and there is only laughter.

When I dream this, I get up and find Ida's old Bible and the stuff about demons and spirits and miracles will make sense to me for minutes on end until the fear wears off.

Jaccob heard her scream and he was awake again, sweaty and awry in his bed. She was sobbing now; he could hear her in the room down the hall. He sighed and pulled on his trousers. He listened to the sound of her retching as he dragged on a shirt and blundered his way downstairs, bruising his shins on furniture until he thought to turn a light on to help find her a bowl. But when he got to her, Ronnie was back on the pillow, finished, and the sour-sweet stink of her puke was in the blankets. She groaned at the sudden light.

'I'm crook,' she said.

'Don't say.' He wiped her face with the edge of a sheet.

'No one's takin' this baby . . .'

Then she was asleep again.

She looked so pitiful. He turned the light out and sat by her. She was just a kid. He didn't know anything much about her. She was as silly as a wheel, though you could tell she knew more than she let on, maybe more than she herself realized. Plenty wasn't being said. Shit, she didn't have a chance, this one.

He put a hand on her. A curve of her calf muscle had exposed itself, and he ran his hand down the smooth warmth of her skin. It was a woman's flesh, all right. She might be eighteen, twenty maybe. He knew he should take his hands off her, but he ran a palm up her thigh and across her cotton panties. Her little belly was round and hard as fruit, and Jaccob sat there aching with his hand on her till the first cautious bird broke into song, and the light showed the mist rising on the slopes and the sorry lump in his jeans. He saw the hopeful, childlike outline of her face, and he felt the kind of pity he'd always reserved for himself. Little by little, the sun came up on him.

Ida Stubbs held her head and closed her eyes against the light. Even her teeth ached. She could hear Maurice moving about in the kitchen, but there was no way she'd be getting up before noon. Oh, Lord, maybe she'd never move again. She thought about last night. She thought carefully and was ashamed. That poor girl Ronnie. I let her drink so much — and her with a baby coming, what was I thinking? Where was my brain? Right now her brain felt as though it'd been cooked and eaten, and Ida pulled the blankets to her chin and felt old and stupid and sad and pathetic and irresponsible, and, and everything.

She wondered about the men. For all she knew they might've killed whatever'd been causing the trouble. But she remembered how angry Maurice had been and how quiet Jaccob was, and she knew it couldn't be. She lay still and let her mind roll with the morning. The grip on her head was terrible. Sometimes she slept light and dreamless, but when she woke again it would still be the morning and Maurice could still be heard putting wood in the stove, and she'd continue thinking about the last few days.

She couldn't recall a time like this. There'd been bushfires and cockeyed-bobs, some floods and droughts and grasshoppers here before, but they were the kinds of things which announced themselves; terrifying because you knew what they could do — but this, this was worse. There was no knowing what might happen, what it was all about, and it seemed to Ida as though everything in the valley had stopped and nothing could go on until they knew what was out there.

There had to be something out there. Unless they were all

imagining it, unless they'd dreamed up all those ducks dead, and the goat. But she'd never seen those herself. Unless. Maybe Maurice was right – they'd been relying on the word of people they didn't know, people who weren't farmers. Though there was the dog. Poor Coco. God, how it hurt to have him gone. Ida turned on the pillow. No, they weren't imagining it, but . . . but it could be a trick. Come to think of it, she hadn't actually seen poor Coco's . . . remains. Maurice had hid it from her. Out of kindness. Or. No, she'd heard the scream. But still, she couldn't say she'd seen it with her own eyes.

The sherry taste in her mouth became sickly and unbearable. Ida reached across to the water jug by the bed. Beside the jug was the honey-smelling cast of the print. She picked it up and sniffed it. It made her shudder, it was so puke sweet. She turned it over in her hand. Now this was something definite. This was no imagination. Nor was it a wild pig or goat – nothing hoofed. Some memory, the edge of something in the past, floated at the back of her mind. Rain. A rainy day. On the road. A dream? Something. It was hard to keep a thought alive with a head like this.

Ida slipped her fingers into the depressions in the cast. Each was big enough to rest a full knuckle in, and if she bent her hand into a loose fist, the curves fitted snugly. For a moment it made her smile. If she had a bigger hand, like a man's hand . . . She pulled her knuckles out and then slipped them back in. My God. A man could do that. A big hand could make this footprint!

She sat up and winced at the pain.

Someone was trying to frighten them. She thought as clearly as she could. Now where was that music-playing boyfriend of Ronnie's? Where was he? He'd never been what you'd call well disposed. Sometimes when he deigned to wave as they passed in their cars, Ida had the feeling he was laughing at them, sending them up. Funny how he'd been gone only a few days and this business had begun to happen the same time. Or. Or that talk about witches at Bakers Bridge. What was Ronnie up to? Should she trust her? What kind of a baby was she having?

Ida's mind galloped and swayed on and her blood packed her flesh until it almost hurt and it became hard to get her breath.

The men. Could it be the men frightening the women? No, that was stupid. Maurice hated practical jokes as much as he hated impractical people. Now. Now. Now, was it something or someone?

She drank some water. Her head constricted and it cramped up the muscles in her eyes. Everything tightened. She looked at the penny-spots on the backs of her hands and began to weep. Back on the pillow she felt the tears running back into her hair, across skin that almost hummed. She heard the rain coming across the valley and it sounded ominous and unpleasant though a long way outside of her. She listened to the rumble of tears across her drum-flesh and tried to breathe.

I sat there all morning on the sofa where I'd slept. The bloody house was full of beer bottles and lipstick-smeared glasses, and I was damned to hell if I was about to clean everything up. My eyes were sore and my back ached, and I didn't have the willpower to do much more than sit and look down the slope to the black bend of the river as drizzle turned to rain and swallowed up the light so the valley blurred like the grey end of a dream.

Toward noon I saw Jaccob walking down in the rain to the road. He trudged in the softening pasture and when he got to the road he headed for the girl's place. He looked dark and small with all that land and sky and rain around him, and before long he disappeared into it, and there was just the valley and the distance to look at.

I wondered what he'd shot last night. If it was the girl,

he was certainly in no hurry to confess. Maybe, I laughed to myself, he's looking for a shovel. I shocked myself, thinking that way.

There were some scones left going stale on a tray near me and by noon I was hungry enough and lazy enough to eat them. Then I cleaned and oiled the .243 to keep my hands busy. Mostly I didn't think. I waited. Looking back, I suppose I'd been waiting for this half of my life. Something was going to happen.

The cat burns. The boy stops to watch a moment, and then he's running with a great and sudden light erupting behind him. Something has happened, and it can't be undone. He'll remember. It'll always be done. When he's an old man it'll still be happening: over and over and over and over.

J accob didn't know much about milking a cow, but he'd watched Ronnie do it yesterday and he remembered the general idea. He made a fair job of it, and the cow seemed pleased to be out of the rain and she left no doubt about what hurt and what didn't. She smelt like a farmhouse, that cow, and the milking soothed him.

Coming back he realized he should have covered the bucket. Rain dimpled the milk's surface as he sloshed along with it steaming in the grey noon light. The valley was quiet but for the sound of the rain and the occasional disgruntled cry of a bird he wouldn't know the name of.

Jacob saw no movement from the Stubbses' place and he figured that, like his own, it contained one snoring, sick woman in it, and that things would likely be that way all day. She was a good woman, Ida Stubbs. He thought perhaps she might be of help to Ronnie in the next few months. The girl was going to need a lot of it.

417

Jaccob walked and the ground squelched beneath him as the rain found its way into his eyes and down his collar.

Babies.

He felt that stony feeling in him again. The memory of that little box slipping into the hidden fire as the wailing relatives hugged one another and looked at him with pity and wonder. Strange, but it was only after the funeral that he felt anger. Marjorie was soggy with tranquillizers and dozing in the bedroom when he went out and gassed the cat. He could still feel it bucketing around in the bag. Jesus, it felt good making something pay. The yowl reached a pitch of fury as the monoxide and the motor and the heat filled the garage. Cot death, they reckoned. Kids die. It's a mystery syndrome. But he'd seen the cat leaving the nursery that night before Marjorie got up to check. Oh, it sauntered out casual as you please, and he thought nothing of it until he saw the fur on the pillow where the face of his daughter had been, warm as blood, not long before. But it was years now. Five? Six? Sometimes he wondered if he'd simply needed to think it was the cat that smothered his daughter, that a mystery, a syndrome just wasn't enough.

He stepped up on to his veranda and shook off some of the water. He looked at the milk and thought it must be rather diluted by now. He kicked his boots off and went in. The moment he was inside he felt he was back in a maze. That old feeling he'd come down here to escape.

The girl was up.

Ronnie got out of his rocker as soon as he came in. He had water in the wool of his sweater and the milk rolled in the bucket.

'Did the cow,' he said. 'How you feeling?'

'Shithouse.'

'You look it.'

Well bugger you, she thought.

The deep marks in his face stood out hard in the afternoon

light. He looked old and sad as hell. He went into the kitchen and she heard him pouring the milk down the sink.

'Thanks a heap!'

'It's full of water,' he called back.

He came in again and stood by the window.

'Anyway, I did it for the cow, not for the milk.'

'Not to be neighbourly, then?'

He looked at her a moment. 'You're a silly little bitch.'

'Well, fuck you too.'

'Tell me, why do you have a she-goat and a cow when you're never in a fit state to milk the poor bastards?'

'You seem to forget that I don't have a goat any more. Anyway, who are you to tell me how to run a farm? You don't know the first thing about it.'

'Run a farm? You couldn't run a bloody tap, girl.'

'You're a prick.'

'And you're a spoilt twat. You'll kill that baby, you know.'

Ronnie tried to rub the dried spew off her sleeve. She set her teeth hard as a rabbit trap, but it was no use. She was going to cry, shit on it, she was gonna melt in front of this old creep.

'You'll never know, mate. You'll never have to carry one. You're a fucking male and you wouldn't know what a baby was if it crept up and bit your balls off! You're a fucking bastard!'

She got down the stairs to the back door with him yelling behind.

'I nearly shot you last night, you little idiot!' she heard him call as she got into a run and felt the jarring in her spine. She didn't remember. She didn't know. She didn't know what she'd done. He'd probably raped her and abused her and everything and she didn't give a shit. She ran out in the rain and the weight in her jugged around and the ground spread and slimed and skidded beneath her and the rain was in her face.

*

The weather set in. The river bed fattened. A cold southerly burrowed through the lupins on the slope. I emptied a box of shells into my lap and felt the smooth, brassy jackets with my fingertips. The valley soaked up rain and light and all sense.

When a man dreams things from the past, you'd think he'd be able to rearrange them in new sequences to please himself. You'd think your unconscious mind would want to do it for you, to spare you the grief and shame. But no. In my dreams, it all happens as it happened, and I see it and be it again and again and the confusion never wears off.

After a shower and a fistful of aspirin, Ronnie lay in her bed as dusk came on and she scrutinized the cracks and crazes time had left in the plaster of the ceiling. They'd never gotten around to fixing it up – that or anything else – and to look at it was to remind herself of what a joke the whole business had been. She could see now how Nick'd just been marking time, letting her have her fantasies until it was time to shoot through. It was like some lousy film. He'd left her high and dry.

She felt like hell. Head, limbs, even her mouth ached. She saw it all again, her dancing across the paddocks like that, knowing all the time she was having herself on, getting fuel enough from the booze to kid herself that she knew what she was doing. She must have been out of her mind! And that snail-slug of a bullet slowly turning across the dark at her to smack a hole in the umbrella just near her head. Yes, she remembered now. The breeze it made. Oh God, Ronnie, you're hopeless. There's no one now. Only you and this poor deformed little bastard in you, soaking up the poison. You'll lose him, you know. Him too. A woman can feel it. Mother's instinct. She laughed. Oh, Mother dear. It was bitter between her teeth.

*

For a while late in the day, Ida was able to read a book, but mostly the headaches were too much for her. The light of the bedroom was melancholy. She tried to find an explanation for the way life had come to a halt, but instead she came up with old memories. Like those stories she'd heard about American subs surfacing off beaches near here to get rid of mascots that had grown too big to be kept? Cougars, mountain lions, that sort of thing. And those prints someone'd found in the caves at Margaret River. And everybody the last few years talking about the thylacine, the marsupial dog or cat or whatever it was, coming back from extinction. And what about that time she'd come across that circus truck in the rain? Yes, she remembered that now. She'd had the feeling something dangerous had escaped there. Oh, there were so many things. Those thickets that ran all the way to the coast, and the miles and miles of forest. There were places for hidden things to breed. If they flourished, wouldn't they widen their territory? For a moment she thought she could make some sense of things, but her head thrummed like the engine room of a ship and there was still that creeping feeling of a trick. She knew she was old and silly. Could it be a cruel game?

Now and then Ida thought she would suffocate just thinking of it.

In the end I couldn't bear to see the steel-dark rain breaking up the earth, beating everything down, and so I went in to see Ida.

I saw myself in the mirror. I looked insane, I guess, not right, and Ida looked suddenly terrified.

'Ida, you ever wonder why Wally was blind? I mean what the real story was?'

She gazed up. She looked pretty damn wild herself.

'Everything makes me wonder. That brother of yours. He used to take the patches off to scare me. I s'pose I secretly thought your father'd poked them out for him.'

That got me. It took a moment to recover from that. It wasn't the moment for defending the old man, poor bugger.

'I sort of wanted to tell you. The real reason.'

Her jowls were all jumpy. She sat up in bed.

'I don't want to speak to you.'

'I just wanted to tell you. It'll explain things a bit.'

'Don't speak to me until you're prepared to tell me what's going on here, Maurice!' She couldn't hear. She was too frightened to listen. 'What is it, what's going on here? Who are you kidding? What kind of sick game, what is it?'

She fairly reared up in bed and her breasts rolled about in her nightie as she reached for the wax cast and I felt it hit me in the belly as the shouting got louder and I fell back against the door jamb. Then she began to scream without any words at all and the sound of it hit me harder than anything she could throw. It sent me back out of the room, that high squeal putting ice in me, coldness from another place and another time, it was the crazy woman's scream pursuing me from the flames. I stood in the living-room and heard it refuse to stop and I went hot and cold and shimmery and saw the gun and reached for it and put a shell in it and went back to the sound. I went in there. I shot upwards in that melancholy space and saw her mouth go wide and silent as plaster sprinkled on to the bedclothes. I put the gun aside and lay on the bed.

'That was a bit strong, don't you think?'

Her eyes shone madly and then fogged over with weeping.

I lay there listening.

In a beautiful Guy Fawkes curve the burning cat finds the open door. The old woman shouts in surprise and the white house swallows up the cat. And the curtains, how quick the curtains take, spitting and crackling like fuse-coil, licking up the timbers, the panelling, the drapes. Now, listen to the awful keening noise, the cat sound of her burning. The Minchinbury house roars.

The sky drinks it up, the noise and light, the smells of cooking flesh and fur. It's the sound of hell, you know. She's burning and her cats are burning, and he's running, that farmboy, the silhouette, the flat shadow boy, he's running. There I am, here I am, with my chest fat with panic. A silhouette. Light and heat behind. This is the light to which the dreams come like moths. They come from everywhere, to beat themselves against the white heat inside my head.

There was still light in the sky when Jaccob drove across to Ronnie's with some soup and a lumpy little loaf he'd baked from a CWA cookbook. No lights were on. He stood on the veranda. The cow looked at him dolefully from across the fence. He'd made a friend there. He looked at the door a moment and decided to let himself in. It was a small place. Even in the twilight he found the bedroom quick enough. Ronnie was sitting up in bed. She must have heard the car. She looked afraid.

'Sorry,' he said. 'I didn't know if you'd be sleeping. I brought you some food.'

'I don't want anything.'

'You have to,' he said, trying to sound gentle. 'For the baby.'

'There's no baby any more, it's dead.'

Her voice was toneless. In a flurry, he put down the food and whipped back the blankets to reach for her. Ronnie squirmed away.

'Oh. I'm sorry.' He felt like a fool.

She looked amused. 'Nick'd never do that.'

'I'm sorry.' He looked at the bone-coloured wall. 'Can't you feel it kicking, or something?'

'Yeah. Yes, I can. I was being stupid. I think I'm going crazy.'

Jaccob got off the bed and went to the window to hide his face from her. She'd scared him. He didn't even know her, and the idea of her losing this baby made him panic. The room was almost without light now. Outside, the rain was hammering the ground into mud.

'Haven't you ever done anything bad?' she asked. 'When you knew you couldn't help yourself, wouldn't help yourself? That's what I do. Do you? Or are you always calm and smart and kind?'

He turned to face her. She sounded so young, but he'd heard that kind of sarcasm before. Was it sarcasm or innocence?

'I've done things.'

At this she smiled, and Jaccob turned his back to face the grey-blue evening light.

'No use looking out there,' she said. 'It's us.'

Then they heard the sound of the shot from down the hill. They saw each other in the gloom.

In the morning I woke to the water thunking on to the end of our bed. I'd made a nice old hole in the roof with that shot. The water made such a miserable sound that it drove me out into the day. Ida had slept nervously beside me as though I might cut her throat in the night. I could feel her relief as I got out into the morning chill.

Fowls hung grimly to their roosts, shaking themselves in the rain, and up on the pasture steers stood unmoving in the mud. The forest stood like a fortress behind. I got into my raincoat.

The lower pastures were miry, and I moved everything up to harder ground, leading them up with a few bales of feed on the back tray of the ute. It was cold and lonely moving around out there. I knew it'd be better out there with Ida. I loved that complaining chit-chat we could keep up in the cab when there were things to be done.

I drove slowly and let the stock follow and they snuffled and slapped tails and smacked mud and crud about. It was lonely, but peaceful enough.

Up at the northernmost reach of the property, in the stumpy pasture before the thicket country, I found twenty sheep with their bellies torn open and their skulls punctured.

It was a long day for Jaccob. Ronnie was determined to stay at her own place and he felt anxious for her in a way he couldn't explain to himself. He kept out of the rain, pacing, reading Thomas Wolfe, puzzling.

At dusk the rain stopped. Jaccob went out to split kindling for the fires. Under the lean-to by the machinery shed he got some pleasure for himself seeing the hard-grained jarrah stripped down to sticks.

He rested on his axe and smelled something burning. It smelt like carpet. Like wool. The wind was coming around from the west again. Now there was the smell of burning flesh. He bent and took an armful of wood in, and when he came out the light was gone. He sorted the kindling into another manageable load and smelt that whiff of barbecue. Lights were on down at the Stubbses'. He stood still and felt his skin prickle. Everything was hard to pick out in the dark. Jaccob made slits of his eyes and tried to pare the darkness into parts.

'Anybody there?'

What a rube he felt, saying that.

The drip of sagging gutters. No stars, no moon.

He must have known when to turn because he caught the movement out behind the shed, though it was less than he'd seen before.

He flinched. The phone was ringing inside the house. He hugged the wood to himself and ran.

For a moment I thought he wouldn't answer. Plenty of things rolled through my mind. But he answered. Breathless, sounding scared as hell. I stood there smelling of petrol and scorched meat. Those sheep had made a lousy fire. Ida looked at me as though she hadn't heard what I'd just told her.

'It's you, then,' Jaccob said.

'What's up? You sound a bit shaky.'

'I think I just saw something.'

'Jesus.'

'What?' He was getting his breath back. 'What's up with you, then?'

'Twenty sheep, that's what.'

He took a moment to let it register.

'Come over,' I said. 'Bring the girl.'

'Go to hell. You come here. I'd drive if I was you.'

It was raining and Ida noticed it. She could smell manure and upholstery and Maurice's shaving soap in the cab of the ute. The hot apple pie roasted her thighs through the tea towel. There was a strange electric taste in her mouth. It was what her old mum used to call a queer feeling.

'Here we are driving next door,' she said.

'Yeah, well. Under the circumstances . . .'

He looked normal enough. He had the gun behind the seat. She saw him put it in.

'Why didn't we have any sons, Maurice? Sons would have been nice.'

She saw the lights of the big white house through the scarecrow regiments of fruit trees. Maurice looked nervous now.

'Sons? We weren't given any, I s'pose.'

'You think they're given?'

'Gawd, woman, I don't know.'

'Because if they're given, then, you know, they're not given as well. Withheld, I mean.'

'That what they tell you in church once a year?'

She decided to let this pass. Her cheek rested on the cold window.

'You think we've done something?' she asked. 'Like "the sins of the fathers" and everything?'

He stopped the car. Right there. Right then.

'Ida, I've tried to tell you. The answer is yes.'

He drove on and she felt all breathless and confused and the serenity was gone and she knew she couldn't trust him.

That great looming white place looked at me as though it remembered. I could still feel that fourteen-year-old hysteria, thinking the fire would chase me down the hill right to the river itself. I thought: this night has been waiting for you all your life, Stubbs.

Ida noticed how dirty everything was. The big dining-room table was in need of a polish. The walls were bare and wanting paint or paper, she thought, and some nice things hanging, like a picture of a waterfall, or men on horses. It was the kind of place Ida imagined people took piano lessons in. Jaccob didn't look right in it, as though he wasn't quite master of the place. Maurice looked like something was about to bite him. And Ronnie. Ida had the urge to tidy her up a bit too. You could see the blue shadows of veins in her, she was so pale. She seemed grubby tonight, and cool. The coolness caught Ida unawares. It made her careful; it made her look closer at everybody.

'What are you grinning at?' Maurice murmured as they were shown into the living-room.

'Nothing, dear, what?'

'You were grinning like an idiot. What's funny?'

'Was I?' She felt a thrill of panic. The queerest feeling. She had no idea.

Jaccob and Ronnie came in behind them and everybody found chairs. This was a meeting. Ida felt away from it all.

'Why don't I fix us a cup of tea?' she asked, before anyone could speak. 'I brought an apple pie.'

Jaccob looked at her strangely. Perhaps I sounded too cheerful, she thought. They were all looking at her the way they really shouldn't be. Ronnie's eyes were narrowed. Maurice looked puzzled. She didn't like it. She got up and found the kitchen anyway and heard them talking tensely out there. The kitchen was a real bachelor's effort. Everything looked wrong, badly organized, unhygienic. She stood in the kitchen while the billy boiled and she could hear their voices coming and going. Now and then the pitch would be raised a little. Ronnie used some strong language; heard that plain enough. They prefer it this way, she thought; there's things they don't want me to hear. She planned to surprise them. When the tea was in the pot she found a tray and some spoons and plates and she ran the water and left it running as she crept back to the living-room.

'Well, let's get a dogger out here, straightaway,' Jaccob was saying. 'This has gone far enough. Someone's got to tell the authorities and get—'

'Authorities, authorities!' Maurice yelled. 'People suddenly want to be told what to do. This isn't the city, mate.'

'Oh, cut all the country bullshit. At least we could get someone out hear who knows what they're doing. This thing could go mad, it could kill people. We need someone from the shire or the government. This is serious.'

'They don't know what they're on about. They'll tell you it's a dog and they'll take some notes and set some baits and tramp over our land with their badges and uniforms, putting their noses where they're not wanted. They'll laugh at us, you fool. It's just bloody interference.'

'Let 'em laugh,' Jaccob said. 'What's a bit of pride, for Godsake? What've you got to lose?'

'Or hide?' asked Ronnie tonelessly.

The room got quiet. Ida stood in the doorway, holding the tray. Her arms were beginning to shake with the strain. Yes, she thought. What have you got to hide, Maurice? And then she looked at them all. Their faces were hard with fear and secrets, she could see it straightaway.

'Nothing,' Maurice said. 'Not a thing.'

He was lying. What he said in the car. He was lying.

'Come on,' Jaccob said, softening. 'You might as well tell us. Like you say, we're in this together.' His mouth twisted a little with irony. 'Neighbours, and everything.'

Ronnie smiled. 'He's growing dope in the forests.'

Jaccob looked startled.

'It's not true,' Maurice protested. 'You need your arse kicked, girl.'

'Face it,' she said with a laugh, 'you haven't got the legs for it.'

Ida felt herself harden up against Ronnie. No, it wasn't drugs. Maurice didn't know the first thing about them, not like this tart. Ida could see she looked the sort.

'Well, you must admit,' Jaccob said, 'that from where we stand you're sounding a bit paranoid. We've got something dangerous here and you don't want to do anything about it.'

Maurice was floundering now, she could sense it. He was holding his hands up against their innuendo like an old politician.

'It's only natural for us to think that we're not quite in the picture,' said Jaccob.

Natural! Ida thought. None of this is natural. Something is going on here. The whole land, the night, the valley is poisoned. What have these people been doing? What have they meddled with? What weird rites have they fiddled with? Why did you people come here? she thought.

Ronnie curled her lip in a sneer.

Then she saw their hands. They all had tumblers of whisky in their hands.

Maurice stood up and emptied his glass. He noticed Ida

then, saw her at the door, and he looked at the empty tumbler and then at the tray she was holding.

'I have done something about it,' he said. 'I set fire to those carcasses up on the hill. I thought it was time to bait them up. Tonight we'll cut some saplings to make a blind and we'll drive up to the back of my place, camouflage the ute, and wait until it shows. Or them. There's a lot of meat out there. Anything that comes will be startled a few seconds by the headlights, long enough to give us a good shot.'

'A good shot? You must be insane!'

'It's here!' Ronnie shouted. 'Jaccob saw it just now out the back and you've left all that meat out there? Ow. Ouch. Oh, shit.'

No one spoke. They looked at Ronnie. She'd gone way back in her chair with her hands on her thighs. She looked a long way away. Ida felt herself going away. This was all a trick. Leave here, a voice told her. Get on the bus, say the Our Father. She was slipping.

'Is that a contraction?' Jaccob asked after a while when all of them seemed to be going away down the wrong end of a telescope.

'How would I know what a fucking contraction is?' Ronnie shouted up the lens.

Ida shook. She looked at Maurice. She didn't know him. Not the way a wife should know a husband. There was a terrible cold rushing into her, a winter wind blowing right through. She was a stranger here, and they were impostors. There was just a hollowing wind and she was going.

Jaccob didn't move. He watched Ronnie who wore a ludicrous expression of rapture, as though she was the bleeding Virgin Mary herself. Ida Stubbs looked like she had heartburn, standing there with the tea tray, and for once the old man seemed to be out of his depth without pretending he wasn't. This should be a funny scene, he thought, but I'm as scared as shit. If we locked the doors, maybe if . . . now there's the cellar . . .

Ronnie felt the baby flexing his muscles. It was alive in there. It hurt, but she was keeping it alive on her own, with her blood and her water, with everything she had, and it worked. She was a mother. Nothing could stop her being a mother. She had the house, the land, she could grow things. There wasn't anything else.

I was seeing my shadow running down the hill with the flames behind, my guilty silhouette swallowed up in the night, my real form gone for ever while that firelight was behind me. I was always that shadow. With that burning house, that fact, I'd always be a silhouette.

The girl regarded her belly and I tried to get Jaccob's eye. I had to let him know I wasn't mad.

'You can't have that baby right now, you know,' I said. 'You'll have to wait for the authorities.'

Ronnie looked at me in great surprise.

Jaccob thundered with laughter. He would come around, I knew.

And when Ida dropped the tray and the tea and the pie and the whole business, and went barrelling through the house towards the door, no one moved.

The fire was out. The room was suddenly cold. I looked at the wash of broken crockery and food and liquid on Jaccob's jarrah boards, and I wondered what had brought me to this place, this still moment.

'Stubbs?'

I looked up at Jaccob. I liked him.

'Is she all right? God knows it's not safe out there.'

'Probably just needs some air,' I murmured. 'I'll get her. It's a bit unnerving for everyone, this whole business.'

Jaccob watched the old man leave the room. He poured himself another Scotch, a good one this time. He wanted to be calm.

'What a mess,' he said.

Ronnie looked up from contemplating herself.

The old man was out there shouting. 'Ida! IIIdaaaa!'

'Oh, Christ.'

In a single jerk, as though she'd abruptly returned to reality, Ronnie got to her feet and began to hiss.

'Get her in here, dammit, she'll die out there!'

Jaccob got up. Stubbs met him at the door.

'She's probably gone home,' Stubbs said. He had a gloss of sweat on his cheeks. 'I'll drive down and see that she's all right. Stay indoors.'

Jaccob watched him jog out to the ute. God, what a fiasco, he thought.

He went in and sat with Ronnie. He got up again and found the .22 and left it by the door. When he came back in Ronnie stood up and sat down again. She looked as though she was about to cry. He put his hands in his lap and looked at them. Maybe the old girl had the right idea – just climb back into bed with a hot toddy and goodbye. But something was out there and he began to believe it would kill them if they didn't kill it first. It's gonna come into our beds, there's no use going to bed over it.

He heard Stubbs's ute skidding back into the yard.

The old man came running in.

'She's buggered off.' He caught sight of Jaccob's rifle. 'Bring this.' Glancing at Ronnie, he waved a hand and said: 'Lock the house and stay here.'

'You're kidding! I'm not staying here on my own.'

The old man looked at Jaccob. 'Get her in the ute, then.'

R onnie sat wedged between the two men, buffeted by their shoulders as the ute thrashed up the paddock. She felt it sway and judder in the waterlogged pasture. They slid to miss stumps and hummocks. Wet grass glittered in the lights. Every time Stubbs changed gears on the column-shift he clipped her breast with his elbow and she barked at him. What she saw ahead was a crazy rushing dream.

'Slow down, dammit!' Jaccob yelled.

'Can't see her anywhere. Where the hell is she?'

'Look out, Stubbs! For pity's sake!'

Ronnie saw the grass sliding aawy to the side as they skidded in a great curve and fishtailed back on line.

'She can't have gone far.'

'This is bloody madness.'

Ronnie felt something capsize, like a juggernaut rolling in her. She had a baby in there. This shouldn't be happening.

Jaccob braced himself against the dash as the old man drove crazy and hard and the ute crunched and rattled with the cab filling with the stink of their sweat. Roos stood still out there. The eyes of birds, rabbits, spiders showed in the mad light. He knocked shoulders with Ronnie and felt her knee against his. It was all over. He might as well forget the place now. The new life was over.

They topped the crest and the north gate loomed much too quick. Posts, wire leaping into largeness. He should have warned . . . Stubbs was standing on the brakes, he could feel it, and he pressed his own feet to the floor as they drifted sideways in a skid. Clods of dirt hammered under them. Should have bought a set of bloody golf clubs and a flat in Cottesloe by the sea, like any other harmless retired bastard.

They were going to go right through the fence. Jaccob covered his face, hunched to protect himself, felt Ronnie sag against him, but there was no shock. It just became quiet. He looked out. They'd stopped broadside to the fence, a foot away. The engine was stalled. Jaccob heard three people breathing.

'Shit a brick, Stubbs! Take it easy.'

Jaccob got out. Wind hustled in the trees up in the distance. The forest. There were great trenches in the mud from their four-wheeled skid.

From higher ground he heard the throaty sound of a nightbird.

The old man slocked over in the mud. 'You hear that?'

'A cough. Or a growl. From up there.'

Stubbs pointed north-west along the other side of the fence.

'What do you think?'

'My wife's out here somewhere, boy, what'm I s'posed to think? Open the gate. I'll rock us out.'

*

Somewhere. She was somewhere. Cold. Mud. Bog. Break. Bend. Fence. She kept running. Get in there. See and not be frightened, right into the thickets up there and see for herself. She wouldn't be tricked and frightened. She didn't care what they all were or who they worshipped – she was gonna see for herself. Ida felt the thrill of sense in her as she rode over the ground, blowing fog out before her. It was high time she faced it. It was only bush, only soil, only sky. There was nothing to be afraid of.

Jaccob took the spray of mud in the chest as the ute's wheels spun in the firebreak. He pushed until lights burst behind his eyes. It rocked and whirred and the tyres bit firmer earth and the whole shaking mess floated up on to hard ground. The mud was cold and he gasped and tasted monoxide. The brake lights glowed. The old man stuck his head out the window.

'We're right now. Come on.'

Jaccob ran to catch up.

I gunned the ute through the gate and across the other firebreak into the stumpy ground of Jaccob's back paddock. Up there, at the far limit of the headlights, were the forest and the thickets and the places a man couldn't go. Don't be up there, Ida, I thought. Just don't be there.

I drove hard. No one spoke. I just kept it up towards where we thought we'd heard something. In a moment, the ground turned to slush. I was feeling strong as a boy, not even touching the earth. Dreamy with weightlessness. She knows, I thought. She's cunning, old Ida. She's leading us to it. We belong here. We are strong.

Then I heard Jaccob shout. The wheel was gone from between my fingers and the world turned and my head went flat and it put burn behind my eyes.

I was cold.
I saw the stars return. The whole sky.

Jaccob crawled out on to the muddy ground. The front tyre
was above him against the cloudy sky. There was wind and
he found he could get up. The ute was upside down. He saw,
across the exposed driveshaft and tangled exhaust, old Stubbs
on his back, muttering in the dirt. Out in front the headlights
made ragged white furrows in the earth.

And somewhere something else moved.

When it all stopped turning, Ronnie felt the pressure in her
neck. Somehow she could see her left nipple in the dark;
it was close enough to push into her eye. Her feet were
above. No, up and behind. No seatbelt. This was her clearest
moment before the world began to end, before the crushing heat
and dark came upon her, squeezing juice out through every
orifice and wrapping its rough tongue around her belly in a
welter of spasms that forced her ribs into her lungs into her
pelvis into her baby. There was no air for screaming. That
dark thing in the dream, that angry crucified thing was coming
at her for every bad thing. You could call it pain, something
told her.

Jaccob stood in the crooked dark and saw the old man move,
reaching into the upturned cab. For the girl? All he could see
was a foot against the windscreen. Why couldn't he just make
himself bend in and pull her out? Why couldn't he move? It was
the sound from out in the dark, that's why.

The old man had his rifle.

'Urgh.'

Here it came.

437

'Bloody thing.' Stubbs's voice was quaking. 'Bastard stinking mongrel sick of a thing.'

'Curgh.'

Jaccob heard him cock the rifle. It was moving steadily out there, coming at them.

The old man had the weapon up. Jaccob could see the shadow of him aiming. This was the moment. Jaccob's body was suddenly sore and shaking. He knew he should get the girl out but there was Stubbs pointing the gun into the dark where the low, throaty grunt was coming from. Yes, it was coming. Yes. Yes.

But a sniff? A weepy sniff? No. This had happened before to Jaccob. He knew this. No! Wrong!

Jaccob turned. He saw the silhouette rearing up and he realized that the car was between him and Stubbs.

I heard it breathe and I knew I had a moment to kill the past, to fight it and wipe it away. The gun was all buck and flash and I was still strong.

Crack! Ronnie heard a tendon snap. Crackack! Brain, soul, something. She was on her way.

Jaccob made it round and drove the old man down in a tackle as the third shot went off. The barrel ploughed mud and muzzle flash. Stubbs's head rang against the upturned fender. Jaccob hit him and thought nothing and heard the hollow gurgling from out there and he knew the sound belonged to death.

*

438

Up in the mud and the furrows of light, my Ida drowned. She felt the heat and the wind in her throat. Blood was her only voice. For perhaps a second she had hold of a thought, a memory.

Ah, but you, Darkness, you know all this. I tell you night after night. Nothing will shock you. Maybe I go on at you in the hope that there's something beyond you. Some nights I sit here and talk and sob and stare out into the blackness thinking that if I look hard enough I'll see the light behind. But I stay out until the break of day, waiting, hoping, and there's only the sunrise again. I suppose there's some comfort in the fact of the sunrise. People used to take it as a sign that everything was under control.

Nobody comes out here. There's been no blue lights, no detectives, no curious social workers. It's almost a year.

Some afternoons I go down to the river and drag out the old bondwood dinghy I keep on the bank, and I row myself around the bend a little where the sun comes through the paperbarks to light up the water so bright you can barely see. I'll just drift along from there, maybe put a line over for bream, or maybe even a marron, or perhaps I'll read a querulous and dutiful letter from one of the daughters asking why her mother doesn't write back any more. I say she's having her change of life when I write back, sitting there with the light and water all around, balancing the pad on my knee. It's only a matter of time before they find out. That's how I live now, knowing I'll only have this time for a little while. I should have known earlier to always live like that. There are small times of pleasure and I'm in no hurry to lose them before they're taken away by force.

I think about fear and panic a lot. I have quite a bit to do with them. You see I've known panic and I've been dead rational and I don't like either of them. Oh, maybe panic has a moral sense about it. When you're hysterical, you at least believe in what you're doing, however bloody stupid it is. But being rational is all about overriding what you believe in.

The moment I saw what I'd done that night, I became calm. I was suddenly sober. I measured things up. I planned. Surely this is possession! Jaccob was the same.

That night we stood by and watched the girl push out a dead baby. She didn't bleed much, though we worried. She didn't know who she was. We fed her pills and she slept. It happened very quickly. We buried Ida and the child in the forest. It was hard work but we dragged and dug without fuss. We discussed the options. We were at one purpose. We required certain things to be done. I do not have dreams about this. I barely recognize myself in my recollection.

It was two hours' drive in to the port town. Ronnie slept or was unconscious or in a coma. I know she was alive. Jaccob drove carefully. We rehearsed what we would do in our minds. We saw no other cars.

There was mist and we were grateful for it.

Just before five we coasted into the emergency admissions entry at the regional hospital with our lights out, motor idling. We took the trouble to wear some of Ida's pantyhose on our heads. Lights were on but no one was around. We hit the bell and left her at the door. Her head was on the thick rubber mat, her feet together in the blanket.

Jaccob drove smoothly and leisurely out of town through the mist and neither of us looked back. I was full of respect and terror. He wanted his time alone, he said. When everything caught up he'd go quietly, but he wasn't going to help anybody speed up the process. I knew what he meant.

At dawn we ran Jaccob's car into the river. Then we got drunk on Japanese whisky and told our stories. We made our vows of silence.

Now he drinks and I dream. It's killing the both of us.

My dreams are not symbols, they are history. Even the ones I don't understand, the ones I don't even know the characters in, they are all full of the most terrible truths. They settle on me, the guilty running silhouette. Yes, call me Legion for we are many.

I pay my bills. I buy my groceries and Jaccob's. I burn the letters that she sends him, those warped, crazy love notes. I go into the forest and look up to see if maybe some bough might fall my way. I learn things from books. Now and then I find a suspicious carcass or a pawprint, or I see a shadow between trees, but I go about my business.

The Americans have found bauxite in the forest. They'll be digging before long. That estate agent was across the valley the other day. I suppose that musician boyfriend could come around. It's a matter of time.

I can't redeem myself. That's why I confess to you, Darkness. You don't listen, you don't care, though sometimes I suspect you are more than you seem.

I live my life.

I am an old man.

Listen to me!